'That baby, how is he?'

'Baby?' asked the woman, now sounding as harassed and exhausted as Gerry felt.

'The one I gave you when you first got here this evening. He had a terribly cut face and was wrapped in old grey and brown cretonne.'

'Oh that baby. That one died.'

She could not wait for whatever Gerry might be going to say next and went off on her next grisly task of collecting damaged bodies for the mortuary. Gerry walked away, trying hard to stop the thoughts that had been edging near her conscious mind all night. For the first time since her own baby had been born dead she had held a child in her arms. There had been a moment, as she felt its heart beating against hers, when she had been seized with a powerful, tugging feeling of deprivation, fiercer even than the misery that had tormented her during her convalescence. And now that child, too, was dead.

THE PARROT CAGE

DAPHNE WRIGHT

SPHERE BOOKS LIMITED

A *Sphere* Book

First published in Great Britain by Michael Joseph Ltd 1990
Published by Sphere Books Limited 1991
Reprinted 1991 (three times)

Photoset in North Wales by
Derek Doyle & Associates, Mold, Clwyd
Printed and bound in Great Britain by
BPCC Hazell Books
Aylesbury, Bucks, England
Member of BPCC Ltd.

ISBN 0 7474 0559 X

Sphere Books Ltd
A Division of
Macdonald & Co (Publishers) Ltd
165 Great Dover Street
London SE1 4YA

A member of Maxwell Macmillan Publishing Corporation

For my sisters, Dione, Ianthe, and Oenone,
(none of whom are remotely like the
Alderbrook sisters)
and for Crispin

Author's Note

Apart from such obvious historical events as the Blitz and VE Day, everything that happens in this story is a product of the author's imagination, as are all the characters (who bear no relation to any real people, living or dead) and the organisation RE(1)R, for which some of them work.

Prologue

February, 1967

'And you worked for him, Mrs Suvarov, I understand,' said the pleasant young man in the shabby lovat tweed jacket. He was sitting in front of her on a low tapestry-covered stool before the fire, his spiral-bound notebook on his knee and a biro, which had leaked sticky red ink over his fingers, in his right hand. Deceptively humble, dangerously charming, he was interviewing her about her late husband's career for a Sunday newspaper.

'Yes, for a few years,' she answered, regretting the fact that she had agreed to the questions. The young journalist was nice enough and as yet had not probed too far, but even so, she wished he would go away.

'What was he like to work for?'

Mrs Suvarov thought back through twenty years of marriage to the time when she had hardly known Peter and tried to say something that was both truthful and uninteresting enough to stop the young man's questions.

'He was very demanding – wanted everyone to give

their best – but . . . ' She paused, telling herself that it was ridiculous for a middle-aged woman who had had seven months to get used to her widowhood to cry in front of a journalist like this. Then she took a deep breath to stop her voice from wobbling and said: 'He was the first man I had ever met who knew me and spoke to *me* – as opposed to the person he thought I was, if you see what I mean. It was one of his great gifts.'

'I understand,' he said, and for a moment she really thought that he did. 'All the people I have talked to have said he was the most remarkable man.'

Her deep violet-blue eyes softened and he realised how beautiful she must have been before she had grown so desperately thin. Her lips curved into the first smile of the morning and her voice was soft, and very confident, when she spoke.

'He was. We loved him, all of us.'

The young man thought that he had the opening for which he had waited so patiently.

'There were three of you, weren't there? Three sisters, all working for him until the end of the war. It's a wonderful story.'

'Oh, I see,' she said coldly and with the disappointment sounding unmistakably in her patrician voice. 'In fact there were four of us; but I thought you wanted to write about him.'

'I do, Mrs Suvarov. The article I've been commissioned to write is about your husband and his transformation from revolutionary Russian refugee to head of a secret wartime department that is still never talked about and appears in none of the books.'

'But ...?' she prompted, leaning back into the russet velvet wing-chair.

2

'But while I was doing the preliminary research, I learned about these sisters, all ravishing, they say, and all very brilliant, who worked for him. The only one I could find is you, Mrs Suvarov; I . . . I sort of hoped that you might put me on to the others.'

'It's such a long time ago, Jonathan,' she said very directly, 'and best forgotten.'

'But why? We won; you won. Why shouldn't people be allowed to read about how you did it? Wouldn't you like to tell it?'

'It may all sound glamorous now, but it really wasn't. We were simply a rather dull, small research group.' She ought to have stopped there, but something he had said or some expression on his ingenuous face had activated all the memories that she had tried to suppress, and so she told him: 'And there were some very bitter things done and said then.'

Because he admired her, and was coming to like her in these elliptical and difficult conversations they had been having at intervals for the last two weeks, he did not say, 'all the better', but that was what he thought. Several of his colleagues had been looking into the wartime conflicts between SIS, SOE and the Free French in London and the various missions they had sent into Occupied Europe; producing stories of tremendous courage, appalling danger and disaster, and catastrophic muddles and terrible hints of betrayal. Stumbling across hints of a still-undiscovered wartime secret in his research, he had decided to try to trump them all with revelations of his own.

He sat on the low stool, feeling the warmth of the fire at his back and smiled, brushing his long fair hair out of his eyes with his inky hand. Then, as gently as possible, because he could see that he had upset her, he said:

'Wouldn't you feel better if it were told?'

'Why should I need to feel better?' She knew how dangerous it was to let him tempt her into a dialogue; she should just have answered the questions he actually asked and not participated in the unspoken ones.

'It might get rid of some of the bitterness.'

'You'd have been a good interrogator,' she said irrelevantly.

'Would he have approved of that?'

'Peter? Yes, I suppose he would,' she answered slowly and turned her head away from him. It was a while before he noticed that she was looking at a silver-framed photograph on a table at her side. From where he was sitting, Jonathan could see that it was a grainy portrait of a dark-haired man; he looked about forty, with well-cut features and far-seeing, intelligent eyes set under strongly marked brows. Apart from the man's mouth, which looked gentle despite its firmness, the face seemed to express steely determination. But there was a hint of something else too, some indefinable but powerful attraction. Jonathan laughed at himself for reading into an old photograph all the things he wanted to find in the man he was trying to discover.

'And the others, your sisters?' asked Jonathan, getting back to the matter in hand.

'God knows. We never actually agreed to forget it – or bound each other to silence, or anything like that. No, don't say anything,' she said as he sat up, expectant as a puppy that sees the chance of a walk or a game. 'I shall think about it, and then I'll ring you up.'

'Then they are alive?'

She looked so sad, sitting there in the huge chair, that

he began to wish he had not pressed her. He had never left so good a story unfinished, but this time he stood up, stuffed his notebook into his sagging pocket, and stood over her to take her hand.

'I am sorry to have raked up those bitter memories.'

She smiled up at him, disarmed by his concern and by the warmth of his hand. No one had touched her since her husband had died.

The winter sun blazed into her white room, dimming the flames in the fireplace and outlining all the comfortable shabbiness of the beautiful furniture and the faded Aubusson rug that Peter had loved so much.

'I'll think about it,' she promised.

GERRY

1940

1

It was the first weekend of the twins' summer holidays, Felicity was home on a rare forty-eight hours' leave, and the ugly old house had taken on an unaccustomed gaiety. Mrs Alderbrook might be too exhausted to notice it, but her eldest daughter felt the lighter atmosphere as soon as she came down for breakfast. She poured herself a cup of coffee from the silver pot on the sideboard, listening to the twins' chatter.

'You sound very cheerful, Annie,' she said as she carried her coffee cup to the big table and sat down.

'Oh Gerry, who wouldn't be with eight whole weeks' freedom from school?' retorted her sister.

Gerry laughed and tried to remember the days when she, too, had felt that their home represented freedom.

'You must have some proper breakfast, Gerry,' said her mother from the head of the table. 'Remember Doctor Granard's advice.'

'I still feel so sick in the mornings, Mother. I'm sorry, but I just can't face scrambled egg at this time of day.'

'It's kedgeree this morning,' said Ming, who was always the peacemaker. 'Mother got up specially early to make it for us as a treat.'

Gerry looked across the polished mahogany at her youngest sister and saw the anxiety in her dark-blue eyes. Don't spoil it, she seemed to be saying. Don't start an argument. Give in for once. Gerry smiled in reassurance, and Ming got up at once.

'Shall I get you some, Gerry?'

'Well, thank you, Ming. Just a little.' A few minutes later Ming brought her a plate with a tactfully small mound of nauseating-looking yellow rice and haddock with the bones sticking out like half-submerged barbed wire.

'When did your new cook actually leave, Mother?' asked Annie brightly, apparently not having noticed any of the tensions that her twin had tried to defuse. As their mother answered, Gerry wondered for the umpteenth time how a pair of twins could be so different. It was not just that they were not identical; their entire characters were worlds apart. Annie took after their father, sandy of hair, forthright of voice and opinion and with the kind of self-confidence that never doubts. But Ming, who was as fair as Gerry and, like her, had inherited their mother's startling dark, violet-blue eyes, was timid, gentle and so aware of her doubts that Gerry sometimes wondered what would have happened to her if she had not had Annie to protect her and push her through life.

Gerry put a forkful of sticky rice into her mouth and almost gagged on it. But she forced herself to swallow it. She did not want to provoke her mother; not, like Ming, because she was afraid of the likely explosion of temper, but because she recognised that her mother had had a lot to put up with since the last of the maids had left three weeks earlier. When Gerry had masked the taste of the haddock with a mouthful of sweet, milky coffee she looked up and saw that Annie was staring at her intently.

'I thought people only felt sick *before* a baby was born,' she said, sounding interested. Mrs Alderbrook looked anxiously at her eldest daughter and then, as though she had not got the strength to intervene between them, got up and carried her plate out to the kitchen. Ming looked down at the table. Gerry took a deep breath to keep her voice steady and tried to answer calmly.

'Yes, in a way, Annie. What the doctors call "morning sickness" happens only at the beginning. This is different . . . '

'You mean because the baby was stillborn? I'm not meaning to be beastly.'

'Annie,' said Ming, for once loudly and with anger. 'Gerry, she doesn't understand. She just wants to know.'

'I know. It's all right, Ming. And it's months ago now anyway. I suppose that is why, Annie. Granard said that everything inside is rather messed about and that I can't expect to feel well for some time.'

'Annie, go upstairs, will you, and wake Felicity?' said Mrs Alderbrook, coming back into the dining-room. 'We can't leave breakfast lying about all morning for her.' When she had obeyed, her mother said quietly to Gerry: 'She doesn't understand. She's only fifteen and none of it is really real to her. It's not meant to be cruel.'

Gerry just nodded, concentrating on the view that she could see through the heavy red curtains that bordered the window. She thought that if she tried to speak again she might cry, and it had been her pride before her marriage that, of the four of them, she alone had never cried in front of their parents.

Ming refilled Gerry's coffee cup and then followed her

11

twin out of the room. Gerry took a sip and then said:

'I'm sorry, Mother. I don't seem able to brace up. This keeps happening.'

'I know. Don't worry about it. Granard says that you will gradually feel stronger and stronger, provided that you rest and eat and keep calm.'

'Calm! I'm far too calm. That's half the trouble. If only I had some job to do. Then at least I might have something else to think about.'

'You're not well enough yet, Gerry. And there's plenty to do here in the house as soon as you are,' Mrs Alderbrook added, her normally well-disciplined sense of grievance sounding in her voice for a second. Gerry heard it and, although her mind understood and sympathised with her mother, the sharpness in her voice was too much for Gerry's composure and the tears poured over her darkened eyelashes. She put the cup back into the saucer, spilling some coffee, and pushed her chair back from the table.

She almost bumped into her second sister, appearing casually late for breakfast, and pushed past her without a word.

'What's up with Gerry?' asked Felicity, shutting the door behind her.

'Oh, Annie was tactless about the baby.'

'Poor old Gerry. It really has rotted her up. She always used to be so tough and now I've never seen her so fragile. Has she told Andrew yet that she doesn't think she'll be able to have any more?'

'I don't think so. She sometimes shows me his letters, though never the ones she writes to him. She definitely didn't tell him in the first letter after the baby, because she let me read the one he wrote back then and he was talking about having more and forgetting about this one.'

'I don't suppose Gerry liked that much,' said Felicity, sitting down at the table and pinning up her shoulder-length fair hair at the same time.

She looked very like Gerry; in fact they had been taken for twins by strangers more often than Annie and Ming ever were. The elder sisters had oval faces with fine skin and classically good features that might have been a little dull had it not been for their splendidly coloured eyes and for the character that showed in their expressions. That morning Felicity's hair seemed more gold than her sister's and her skin clearer and more luminous than Gerry's, but that might have been simply because Gerry had still not recovered from her difficult pregnancy and the terrible, nineteen-hour labour that had ended in the birth of her dead son.

Felicity leaned forward to pick up the folded newspaper and spread it open on the table.

'Darling, must you?' said her mother. 'I need to clear the breakfast and if you start reading that you'll . . . '

'I'll deal with the crocks, Mother. You go and put your feet up or something. Please? I've only got forty-eight hours' leave and it's such a luxury to read *The Times* at breakfast in peace.'

Mrs Alderbrook shrugged and left the room for the depressing scullery to start preparing the vegetables for luncheon. She had never peeled a potato in her life until her cook departed to join the ATS, let alone cooked a whole meal, and she had never realised how difficult it all was and how dreadfully time-consuming.

As soon as she had gone, the dining-room door opened again and Gerry came in to drop into a chair beside her sister.

'Hello, old thing,' said Felicity, folding up the newspaper again. 'I thought you couldn't be far away.'

'No. Thank God you're here, Flixe. I can't talk to the others; I try sometimes, but it just makes it all worse. And as for Mother . . . '

' "Come on, darling, brace up"?'

'Not really. At least, yes. She never says any of it, but I can't help thinking all the time of what she's suppressing and all the things she's said in the past and what she might say in the future. It's vile of me, because she's been good to me; she really has. I couldn't have dealt with it on my own.' Gerry reached over to her old place to pick up her coffee cup. 'But now, we just get across each other all the time. I wish I could get away.'

'Well can't you? I thought the whole thing about being a married lady meant that you were no longer under their control.' There was a slightly acid note in Flixe's voice that made Gerry look sharply at her. Flixe smiled wryly. 'Well, that was why you married him, wasn't it?'

Gerry started to look outraged and then succumbed to a rueful laugh.

'I always did think you were brighter than you pretended, Flixe,' she said, taking a sip of the cool coffee. 'Brighter than me, actually.'

'Oh?'

'Yes. I didn't realise that was part of it until we were well and truly married.' Suddenly she felt hungry after all and started to butter a piece of cold, rubbery toast.

'Poor Andrew.'

'Oh, don't you start. Mother's always trying to put his point of view and telling me what I ought to do for him and the bloody regiment. I thought you at least would understand that I need to keep some part of myself free of him.'

14

'I understand all right, ducky,' said Flixe. 'I'm just surprised it's taken so long in coming. After all, it's over four years since you let him take you over.'

Gerry was silent, trying to remember the excited pleasure she had felt as the good-looking, charming, well-bred Captain Kyrle had started to pursue her. Smarting then from her father's refusal to let her go to university, she had wondered whether she would be stuck at home for ever in a life she had come to loathe. Andrew had appeared as a heaven-sent means of escape, a kind of young Lochinvar, who would carry her off on his white charger to a life in which she would be busy, fulfilled and happy. She laughed bitterly at herself for her stupidity in believing that she could ever be happy living someone else's life.

'It's not that bad, Gerry,' said Flixe gently. 'There's a lot about Andrew that's thoroughly admirable – and you must love him a bit. Sugar please.'

Gerry automatically pushed the Dresden bowl towards her sister.

'Yes, of course I love him. I really do. It's just all much more difficult than I had expected. When he sent me home from Palestine to . . . to have the baby I really missed him. Honestly I did. But he was determined that I should have "proper English" doctors, and it did seem sensible, I mean now that Mother is settled here for good. It was all planned. As soon as the baby was safely weaned, I'd take him back to Palestine. Even when the war started I meant to go back.'

'So what changed your mind?' asked Flixe, stirring sugar into her coffee.

Gerry chewed a mouthful of toast, swallowed and then fished a sheet of paper out of the pocket of her green tweed skirt.

15

'Sometimes when I get his letters, I feel as though I don't know him at all. Read this one – the PS.'

Flixe wiped her fingers on her napkin and took the letter, to read:

Darling, why on earth do you want to join the WRNS? It's a ridiculous idea. And you need to take care of yourself after all that horrid business. As soon as the Mediterranean is a bit more settled, you'll want to come out here again. Why complicate things for us by joining up?

'I didn't know you were thinking of joining up,' said Flixe, who had been a Fany since the war started.

'Oh yes. I've been thinking for ages that I must do something and then when France fell and everybody went over in their boats to get the men off at Dunkirk, the war seemed to be to do with us after all, and I felt so useless and thought that the WRNS would be the best. But they won't take married women unless they have their husbands' permission. So . . . I'm stuck.'

Flixe looked under her dark lashes at her sister and wondered what she ought to say, whether it would be better for Gerry if she simply accepted the explanation or tried to force her to face what Flixe was sure was the truth. In the end she decided that it was so unlike Gerry to hide from anything that she did push her.

'As was said in a rather different context, Gerry, patriotism is not enough. Why did you really decide not to go back?'

Gerry pushed away her plate with its load of toast crumbs and smeared marmalade as though it sickened her.

'Oh, Flixie, because with the baby dead and no hope of any others, my future as Andrew's wife suddenly seemed so bleak. My whole life would be ruled by the needs of the regiment and Andrew's job. What would I have of my own in all the years until he retires? It's not even as though I'd see all that much of him. You see, it's not that I don't want to live with him, honestly; I do care about him. It's just that I can't bear the deadening job that being his wife entails. If I thought I could be myself I shouldn't mind; but all I'm allowed to be is Mrs Andrew Kyrle.'

Flixe, who had her own views about her brother-in-law, thought again that Gerry was deceiving herself, but could not press any further. To Flixe, Andrew had always seemed infuriatingly possessive and unaware of all the things about Gerry that made her valuable. In Flixe's more charitable moments, she had wondered whether his determination that Gerry should have no friends or interests that he had not bestowed on her might not be based on fear that if she were a free agent then she might no longer love him. At other times, particularly when he had tried to break the tie that linked the two sisters, interrupting their increasingly rare meetings or forcing them to include him in conversations that had nothing to do with him, she thought him pompous, selfish and arrogant.

For the first two years of their married life Andrew had been posted in London, and Flixe had seen a certain amount of them, wincing often at what she saw as Andrew's attempts to belittle Gerry in public. At the time Flixe had said nothing to Gerry, who had always seemed to be unaware of what he was doing, but had watched her growing unhappier and less and less like herself. Once they had gone to Palestine, Gerry had written home regularly, and her letters to Flixe had been so full of her old self – caustic, funny, brimming with energy and intelligence – that Flixe had been reassured. Now it seemed that all her first prejudices had been justified.

'Well, it's all a bit academic at the moment anyway, since no civilians are going anywhere, except possibly America, for some time,' she said. 'There must be some kind of work you could do. Why not come and stay in the flat for a bit and see what you can find? I know there's only one bedroom, but I'm away a lot, driving these generals around, and even if we're both there together, one of us could have the sofa.'

'Flixe, you're a dear. But I don't think I can. If I could say to Mother, "Look, I've got this job and I'll have to go and live in London," that would be all right; but just to announce, "I can't bear living here with you" is a bit ungracious after all she's done for me. I think I'd better see what I can do by letter. And if you hear of anything, will you let me know so that I can apply?'

'Of course I will,' said Flixe warmly. She drained her coffee cup and got up. 'Now we'd better do the washing-up. Come on.'

2

Three weeks later Gerry was standing in the stable behind the house, heaving a shabby saddle on to the back of her long-suffering mare Buttercup and muttering to herself so angrily that the elderly hack shifted nervously away from her hands. Gerry automatically gentled her.

'I suppose I shouldn't take it out on you just because you're the only one who won't answer back,' she said remorsefully.

She leaned forward until her head was resting against Buttercup's neck. The gently-pulsing warmth under her skin, and the familiar exciting smell of straw and dung and horse sent Gerry straight back to the early, uncomplicated years of childhood, and for a moment she was soothed. Buttercup snorted and tossed her head, setting the bit clinking against the bridle. Gerry pulled herself together and patted the mare's neck. Then she led Buttercup out of the stable, mounted and rode off up the hill.

She had escaped from the house because she could feel her temper rising uncontrollably and knew that if she did not do something she would lose it and say something unforgivable to her mother or Annie. Ming's white face and trembling lips had shown Gerry just how threatening her voice was sounding and so she had made herself apologise. Then she had left all three of them and gone to her bedroom to change into her riding things.

Once she had ridden up onto the crest of the hill, Gerry stopped the mare so that she could look down at the old yellow-grey stone tiles of the house. It was ironic, she thought in cold depression, that the marriage which had promised eternal escape should be the one thing that had locked the prison gates of her home again. If she had not succumbed to the temptation of Andrew's proposal she would be free to be in on the war like everyone else; like Flixe, who seemed after all to have arranged her life so much better than Gerry had.

Buttercup stood patiently in the hot, hay-scented air, flicking the flies off her skin with little twitches and swishes of her tail, but at last she began to fret and sidle. Gerry woke to her responsibilities. She picked up the reins again and urged the mare into a gentle canter.

Gerry had not thought of a destination, only of getting away from the house for an hour or two, but when she caught a glimpse of the Adamsons' tall chimneys through the elms on her right, she realised how much she wanted Evelyn Adamson's undemanding sympathy and turned Buttercup down the lane that led towards the river. She rode slowly past fields of barley, studded now with scarlet poppies, thinking of Evelyn and hoping that they would be able to recapture the friendship they had established just before Gerry had married.

The fact that her mother disapproved of the Adamsons lent a tiny spice to Gerry's anticipation as she pushed open one of the iron gates that protected the drive up to the house. It had taken Gerry some time to understand all of her mother's antipathy, but part of the trouble was undoubtedly straightforward jealousy. To the wife of a serving officer with no money of her own, Evelyn Adamson seemed to live in grossly unfair luxury. Her house was large and beautiful, where Sudbrook House was cramped and an example of all the worst faults of Victorian builders, and Evelyn had the money to make whatever improvements and repairs she wanted instead of balancing the cost against all the other crushing expenses of life. But there was more to Mrs Alderbrook's dislike than simple envy. Unlike her own military ancestors, Evelyn's family had for generations been 'in trade' and even worse had intermarried with some mercantile Russians. Evelyn herself was wholly English as far as anyone knew, but she had first cousins who were full-blooded Russians. Even though there was no suggestion that any of them were Reds, to Mrs Alderbrook they represented something unsound if not downright dangerous.

Once Gerry had disentangled the various different strands of her mother's disapproval, she had learned to despise the mixture of snobbery and insularity that had created it. For her part, the hint of exotic foreignness in Evelyn's family was intriguing, and Gerry had to admit that there was a certain regrettable pleasure in flouting her mother's expressed disapproval of Evelyn Adamson.

Gerry rode up the drive, noticing that it was weedier than usual, which surprised her; but the glorious house itself looked just the same, basking in sun and generously open to all comers. Someone was before her that afternoon. A large black motor was parked in front of the stone lions that guarded the door, their backs warmed by the orange and green lichens that also patterned the long, low roof. Seeing the car, Gerry checked for a moment, but then shrugged. It was probably only someone of Bob's. Taking full advantage of the freedom Evelyn had given her in the year before her marriage, Gerry rode on round the back of the big house to the stables and made old Buttercup comfortable with a net of hay and a good bucket of water, before walking into the house through the garden-room door.

She was just scraping a small but obstinate lump of mud off one of her boots when she heard Evelyn's warm voice.

'Gerry, my dear girl, how lovely! We've been so worried about you. How are you now? Really all right again?'

Forgetting the mud, Gerry walked straight on to the gorgeous, if faded, silvery-green Persian rug and took her hostess's outstretched hands.

'I'm much better, thank you,' she said, sighing in relief to be back.

'Thank goodness. Now come into the morning-room. I've just made some coffee – I hope it's drinkable – and – '

'But what's happened to Ivy?'

'Gone off to the war, of course. We couldn't make her stay, even if we'd wanted to.' She pushed open a white, deep-panelled door and called out: 'Bob, here's Gerry. Introduce her while I go for another cup.'

'Gerry,' came the deep, drawling voice of Evelyn's American husband, 'come on in.' His wide smile was just the same, and so was his firm handclasp, but he looked older to Gerry. She reminded herself that the last year could not have been easy for anyone, even for people as

22

sensible and well-protected as the Adamsons. 'It's good to have you back again. Any news of Andrew?'

'Nothing much, Bob,' she answered, unable to tell this sensible, tolerant, practical man about her husband's refusal to let her join the WRNS. 'They're not allowed to say anything real so the letters that do come don't make much difference. If he'd been wounded or – anything – there'd be a telegram, so I know he's all right.'

Robert Adamson's shaggy eyebrows tightened across the bridge of his nose as he took in the listlessness of Gerry's voice. She had been such a live wire in the old days and always so full of ideas and plans that he was troubled to see her look beaten now. But it was not in his nature to ask questions about how she felt and so he tucked her hand in the crook of his elbow and drew her into the room.

She just had time to see that nothing had changed in its chaotically beautiful furnishings when she noticed a thin, dark man standing by the empty white fireplace. Presumably the owner of the motor, he took his pipe out of his mouth and waited to be introduced.

'Gerry, this is Evelyn's cousin, Peter Suvarov. Peter, this is Miss Gerry Alderbrook. Oh, no,' he caught himself up, 'it's Mrs Andrew Kyrle.'

'How do you do,' said the stranger, smiling slightly and offering her his hand. She took it, interested to meet one of the cousins at last and delighted with his deep voice, which had a faint, intriguing accent; but she wished that Bob had not corrected himself. It would have been so nice to be Gerry Alderbrook again in this particular house.

Evelyn came in at that moment with another cup and saucer. Limoges china, Gerry noticed and smiled to herself as she acknowledged that what her mother would

23

have kept as 'best' china, to be offered only to visitors she wanted to impress, was used every day – and allowed to be cracked and chipped – by the Adamsons. There was nothing in their house that was not beautiful, and there was nothing kept for show. It produced a feeling of the utmost pleasure and relaxation in Gerry and she let herself lean back against a huge, dark-green velvet cushion in the corner of the sofa. Bob brought her a cup and murmured:

'If it's really filthy we can always have sherry instead.'

Evelyn almost grinned and said, with no trace of self-consciousness or criticism:

'Oh, come on now, Bob, you must admit that I'm learning to do without the maids.'

'You haven't much to learn, Eve,' came that tantalising voice from the fireplace. 'Time was when you did the work of maids and gardeners and nurses . . . and heaven knows what besides.'

'One forgets so easily,' she said. 'And it's been a long time.'

'Twenty years,' he agreed and turned to Gerry. 'And so, Mrs Andrew Kyrle, tell me who you are.'

'Just that, it seems,' she said and even she could hear the bitterness in her voice. But she was too tired to apologise and in that house no one ever expected you to apologise for anything except deliberate malice.

'I can hear a story in that voice,' he said, strolling forward with his hands in his trouser pockets and his pipe between his teeth. Then he sat down at the opposite end of the sofa. 'Tell it to me.'

Surprised by his immediate and rather unlikely friendliness, Gerry looked up at him in silence; but he seemed to be genuinely interested. Wondering whether he always plunged into personal conversations with every chance-met acquaintance, or whether Evelyn and Bob could have been talking about her so that Evelyn's cousin already knew something about her, Gerry protested:

'I don't want to bore you.'

'If you do, we'll stop you, won't we, Bob?'

'Sure.'

Taking a gulp of the coffee, which was not surprisingly both excellent and strong, Gerry felt herself expanding a little and began.

'Well, I've been a bit ill and as soon as our old Doctor Granard told me I could stop being an invalid I went off to join the navy – to see the sea and all that. And they wouldn't have me. If I'd still been Gerry Alderbrook that would have been OK, but it seems that I belong to Andrew Kyrle now and without his permission I can't even do my bit for England.'

The deliberately flippant tone did not hide her indignation from any of her listeners.

'And won't he give it?' asked Suvarov. Gerry noticed that Evelyn was frowning at him, but since she had been longing to talk to someone who might sympathise ever since Flixe had left Gloucestershire, she started to tell them the whole story.

'No. Most of the other regular officers in Palestine have their wives with them and he thinks it's my duty to go out and sit around while he fights his war.'

'What's wrong with that?'

'Do you know how army wives have to live? I've watched it all my life. They're in a kind of glass box: watched by all the others to make sure they dress, behave and speak exactly like the rest and not allowed for one instant to complain about the limitations of army life or talk about anything except about three subjects, or . . . Sorry, don't let me get started on all that,' said Gerry, but her crossness got the better of her discretion and she produced a real indictment: 'They think the bloody regiment is the whole world – or at least the only part of it that matters – and that everyone and everything else is morally, materially, and spiritually inferior.'

'Whew!' he said and smiled. Bob took advantage of Suvarov's momentary speechlessness.

'Well, I can certainly understand why you don't want to live like that, but why do you want to join up?' he asked. 'Lots of people would be glad of the opportunity to stay in countryside like this and enjoy themselves.'

Gerry wondered whether to say something patriotic, but remembered that Bob and Evelyn knew her too well to be deceived.

'I'm so bored.'

Suvarov laughed, and his long dark eyes narrowed into sparkling slits in his lean face.

'So what can you do then, Gerry Alderbrook?'

The use of her own name seemed almost like a gift and she found herself smiling at him as though she had known him for years.

'Well, I read and write French quite well although I can't really speak it; I mean, no one would ever believe I was completely French. I have no degree, although I did once have a place at Cambridge. I can ride, run a house . . . Oh, dear, none of it sounds much use in a war, but there must be something I could do.'

Her voice began to wobble a bit and Evelyn quietly intervened.

'Peter, don't cross-examine Gerry like that. She's been rather ill for a long time, and is still convalescent, whatever

Granard says. More coffee, Gerry?'

'Thanks,' she answered shortly, holding out the blue and yellow cup. When the two men had gone out into the garden, she blew her nose and said:

'Evelyn, I am sorry about that. I suppose you're right. Aren't convalescents supposed to be over-emotional?'

'Gerry, what is all this? There's more than just not being able to join the WRNS. I know that what you have been through must have pulled you down horribly, but it's nearly seven months now.'

'I know. I can't think what the matter is. I keep bursting into tears for no reason at all. I'm foul to Mother – though she's pretty vile to me too. I've just got to get away, but without a job, what can I do? I really loathe the thought of Palestine and army life. I don't think I could bear it, but I can't just go and live in London on my own with nothing to do.' Her voice stopped, but Evelyn said nothing. 'It's partly wondering if I'll ever be able to have one, I suppose.'

'Well, what does Granard say?'

'That there's been a bit of damage to me and that it's not a good idea to think about having more,' said Gerry sadly. Then she added with a little more spirit: 'He says it's not my fault.'

'Gerry, of course it's not your fault. Why should it be?'

'God knows,' she answered drearily. 'It just seems to be. That's why I have to get away. I can't bear sitting around and watching the twins being happy, with nothing to do but think about the baby and listen to Mother retelling all the arguments we've ever had – and she's ever had about us all with Daddy; I mean, even down to my name. I've heard the whole stupid saga all over again.'

Too relieved to have got the girl talking to pursue her normal policy of refusing to listen to animadversions on Brigadier and Mrs Alderbrook, Evelyn poured each of them another cup of coffee and said:

'What about your name?'

'It's too ridiculous but it sums up the whole business really. My father's mother was called Marjorie and so when I was born he wanted to call me after her, but my mother thought it was the most frightfully low-class name. In the end – I suppose she must still have cared about him then – she agreed, but stipulated that it should be spelled in the proper old English way with a "g" and an "e".'

'Hence Gerry. I see, I always thought you must be Geraldine,' said Evelyn, avoiding the tricky issue of the Alderbrooks' relations with each other. 'Oh, help, it's nearly twelve. We won't get any luncheon unless I start now. Will you come and give me a hand, Gerry?'

'Of course. Evelyn, it's so good of you to let me come and moan all over you.'

'Don't be an ass,' came the reassuring answer as Evelyn led the way down the stone-flagged passage to the kitchen.

Later, as they were companionably peeling carrots and potatoes from the kitchen garden, she said:

'Gerry, obviously I can't invite you to stay here – I think your mother would call in the police and tell them you'd been kidnapped – but why not go and stay with Felicity for a week or two?'

'I can't,' said Gerry, dropping a neatly peeled carrot into the bowl of clean water and picking up another from the gardener's trug. 'She did ask me, but you know she's with the Fanys and having a terrific time driving generals around all over the place. I don't want to cramp her style by moping around her flat. And I don't suppose it would be any better. Everyone I knew in London is bound to be working or else gone away.'

'I see. Give me those. I'll put them on the Aga and then we'll go and lay the table.'

Gerry did as she was told and made a determined effort to drop her depression and enjoy the little lunch party. In Evelyn's uncritical friendship that was not hard, and by the time they started on the austere and creamless trifle, Gerry had regained some of her sparkle. Bob was relieved to see it and was moved to go to the sideboard and get out a celebratory half-bottle of Sauternes. There was enough for a good glassful each and it seemed necessary to mark the occasion with a toast. Gerry had been assuming that it would be 'Absent friends', as it usually was in the bleak days after France had collapsed, but instead Suvarov raised his glass and said, looking directly across the oval mahogany table at Gerry:

'Here's to work and freedom.' They all drank and, as he put his glass down, he went on, smiling that smile again: 'There's always plenty of both when you know where to look.'

'Will you help me?' demanded Gerry, hardly even remembering that he was not an old friend.

'Yes, I think I probably will.'

3

Gerry clung to Suvarov's half-promise for as long as she could and did her best to behave decently to her mother. But both undertakings were difficult and she began to feel as though she were being wound up like a cello string to snapping point. The war news got worse and worse as German fighters battled with the Spitfires daily over the south-east of England. Tempers at Sudbrook House seemed to get shorter every day, although the twins provided a certain buffer between their mother and Gerry: Annie by her imperviousness to tension and Ming by stopping them all from saying the worst of the things that hovered in their minds.

There were times, too, when Gerry enjoyed her sisters' company for its own sake, although she would have traded weeks of it for a couple of hours with Flixe, who at least understood and could talk about Gerry's real difficulties. The twins rode with Gerry and entertained her with tales of their school life, but, although she was fond of them, she had very little in common with them.

Then Flixe came home for another weekend's leave. She took one look at Gerry.

'What's the matter, old thing?' she said. 'You look even more washed out than last time I was here.'

'Oh, this and that. Look, why don't we go for a walk?'

'I'd better say my piece to Mother; then I'll come.'

'I'll wait in the stables,' said Gerry shortly, unable to bear the prospect of listening to her mother's veiled criticisms as she welcomed her second daughter. Gerry trudged off to the stables, telling herself for the twentieth time that it was absurdly childish to feel jealous of Flixe's uniform. It was only a very few years since she had been able to feel delightfully superior when Flixe was still cursed with their old school's navy coat and skirt and ugly hat while Gerry could show off her newly acquired civilian elegance. And the Fany's khaki was no more becoming than that old despised navy blue. Gerry kicked at the muddy puddles with her riding boot and cursed to herself as she felt water seeping in through some tiny crack in the leather. It seemed the last straw.

Felicity emerged at last, pulling off her uniform cap and unpinning her opulent fair hair, casually sticking the hairpins in the breast pocket of her tunic. Gerry pushed her own hair back behind her ears, deciding that it was lank and stringy, and almost hated her sister for the sensuous and luxurious way she ran her fingers through that thick mass of hair, startlingly gold against the brilliance of the blue sky.

'Gerry, why do you stay here like this? It must be driving you barmy. I'm sure Mother wouldn't mind if you left for a bit – she'd probably welcome the freedom too.'

There was nothing but concern in Felicity's voice and affection in her deep-blue eyes. The hair-tossing performance must have been quite unintentional, thought Gerry, as she leaned towards Felicity's encircling arm.

'Oh, Flixe, I don't know – except that I'm still so pathetic. I've applied for all those jobs you suggested and a couple that Bob put me on to, but there's been nothing so far.'

'Aha, well I don't think it'll be all that long now, old thing.'

'What d'you mean?'

'They've been asking questions about you. I oughtn't to tell you – careless talk costs lives and all that – but someone wants you.'

'Who?' demanded Gerry, hardly daring to hope.

'God knows. It's never the ultimate lot who do the vetting.'

Felicity was relieved to see some light sliding into her sister's dulled blue eyes and a faint curve rounding the lips that used to smile – or mock – all the time, and felt that her slight indiscretion was justified. It had shocked her profoundly to see the once-elegant, sparkling Gerry reduced to this tired, bleak, pale woman, who clung so uncharacteristically to any offered hand. Felicity hugged her and then withdrew.

'But, look here, if they do call you for an interview, Gerry, I think you ought to be a bit more lively. Couldn't you . . . well . . . '

'Brace up?' supplied her sister with some of the old mockery in her voice.

'Just so,' answered Flixe, grinning to hear it. 'You know, do something about your hair – and put on a bit of lipstick. I mean, you do look like a washed-out dishrag.'

'Thanks.'

'*Je t'en prie*,' said Felicity, holding the bridge of her nose to achieve a precise imitation of their most detested French governess, and they both roared with laughter.

'Oh, Flixie, it's good to see you again. I've really missed you. Now tell me about all these generals.'

'The generals are all quite dull – but most of them have ADCs, which is nice.'

'Anyone in particular?' asked Gerry, relaxing into the warm gaiety with which Flixie seemed to surround herself.

'Not really, though Johnny Blenkarne turns out to be much less wet than we always thought him.'

'No! How astonishing. But don't you remember that time in the blackberry bush when ...?'

'Come on, Gerry, he was only thirteen then – and he was jolly frightened of you. We all were.'

'Frightened! You, Flixe? Don't be dotty,' she began, but then in a quite different voice added: 'Oh, God, look – there's Mother waving.'

'Can't we pretend we haven't seen her?'

'You can. I'll have to hear all about it for the next six weeks if I do. Come on, support me.'

They walked with lagging steps towards the back door of the house, where Mrs Alderbrook was standing holding something yellow in her right hand.

'Heads together, giggling as usual. No one would think you two had grown up at all. Even Ming and Annie are more sensible.'

Felicity could have hit her mother at that moment as she watched the liveliness fade out of Gerry's face, and she spoke with a biting sharpness that neither of the others had ever heard her use before.

'What do you want, Mother?'

'Really, Felicity? What a way to speak. There's a telegram for Gerry.'

Felicity automatically reached out and put an arm

around her sister and urged her to sit down on the mossy stone mounting block beside the stable door. Then she took the yellow envelope from their mother and slit it open. Taking out the single sheet without reading it, she handed it to her sister and put a hand on her shoulder.

Gerry unfolded it and tried to focus on the few words. At first she could read nothing; then the sense seemed to leap out at her and she leaned back against the damp wall and smiled and smiled.

'Is dear Andrew coming on leave then?' asked her mother.

Gerry looked up at her and said lazily, almost as though she knew that it would annoy her mother:

'No, nothing so dull: they want to interview me in Storey's Gate.'

'The War Office,' said Flixe. 'Good for you, old thing.'

'No, it doesn't sound like them. But it must be official. Thank goodness.'

Mrs Alderbrook had no difficulty in interpreting the look of relief on her eldest daughter's face and drew in her breath sharply. She had done her very best for poor Gerry after the baby, and it was just too bad of her to be so ungrateful. Mrs Alderbrook turned to get back to the pots and pans, which seemed to have a life of their own and a determination to get the better of her.

In her new happiness, Gerry could see what her mother was suffering and called out:

'Don't go back to the kitchen. Why don't you stay and talk to Flixe while I make luncheon today? I'm sure I can, you know.'

'Don't look so astonished, Mother,' said Felicity gaily. 'Just accept the offer and come and show me what's been going on in the garden since I was last here.'

After lunch, which even Fanny Alderbrook said would have been all right if Gerry had not undercooked the sprouts, Flixe said she wanted to ride. Ming looked as though she wanted to join her sister, but Annie had other plans for them both and explained them loudly. Ming subsided, and so Flixe and Gerry went off to the stable alone.

'Do you want Buttercup?' asked Gerry. 'I'm lighter than you so perhaps I'd better ride one of the twins' ponies. I used to exercise them while the twins were at school anyway.'

'Yes, thanks. Who'll do that once they're back at school and you've gone to London?'

'I don't know – or care that much. Mother won't be able to keep any of them much longer. It's not as though this was a farm or anything – they're a luxury.'

'But she'd never get rid of the twins' ponies. I mean, what passport would they have then into the right world?'

'Perhaps even Mother will acknowledge that all that's a bit out of date now.'

'Don't you believe it. Remember what Grandfather always said.'

They chanted in unison:

' "Any girl ought to be able to ride like a gentlewoman, carry on a respectable conversation in French and run a proper household." ' Then Flixe asked musingly:

'Do you suppose that was why he married a Frenchwoman – so that any daughters he might have would be able to speak it from the cradle?'

'I don't think so. Mother once told me in a very weak

moment that it was a fantastically romantic story – almost like Natasha Rostova and Prince André in *War and Peace*. And then when she died he was inconsolable, but made sure that Mother grew up with all his own sentimental devotion to France and the French.'

'Hence all those bloody governesses. Do you imagine he was really as awful as she thinks?'

'But she doesn't. Oh, I know what you mean. Heaven knows, but I've begun to think that it must have been more the life they led than anything he actually taught her. I mean anyone who was made to be hostess in "Government House" at what was it – sixteen? – would develop a certain *folie de grandeur*. And presumably that was why Daddy married her – you ought to be careful, Flixe, of all those ADCs. Mother found that the glamour was illusory.'

'It's a salutary tale, isn't it? But don't worry about me, Gerry. Those ADCs of mine are just fun – nothing like what Father must have been to her. Mine are no threat: chaps to dance with, that's all.'

'All the more reason to be careful. I look forward to meeting some of them.'

'Oh, no, Gerry darling, you're a respectable married woman; you can't move in naughty circles like mine.' It was supposed to be only a joke and Flixe winced at the expression she saw in her sister's face. She thought for a while and then said carefully:

'Gerry, London's changed a lot in the time you've been away. It's going to be quite a shock to get back to.'

'I'm oversensitive, am I?'

'I didn't really mean that,' said Felicity, although she had. 'But look at all this.' She pointed down towards the valley where the river flashed its brilliant reflection through the deep green of the huge leaves that hung stilly on the old trees. 'It's all so peaceful and glorious here: butterflies, bees buzzing, country smells, lavender in the gardens. London's dirty and smelly, and we're all waiting for it to be smashed to bits when the bombs come. People are frightened, and bored, and bad-tempered, and grabbing every last bit of enjoyment they can. It isn't a time to be fragile, Gerry.'

'It sounds wonderful. Flixe, the green and butterflies and what-have-you may seem marvellous in contrast, but I feel as though I'm drowning in them. The only times I feel alive now are talking to you or being at the Adamsons'. The rest of the time I'm desperate.'

'I know, ducky. And I'll help if I can.'

'Flixe, do you really not know what they want me for?'

'No, honestly. I imagine it's something rather secret; the main recruiting places are well enough known and I've never heard of wherever-it-is in Storey's Gate.'

'I'd rather like to work there – it's just off Parliament Square, isn't it?'

'Yes, but you wouldn't be there. They never interview for those sorts of jobs in their own offices – that would give away far too much.'

'Oh,' was all Gerry said, feeling remarkably foolish and unsophisticated. 'When are you going back? Can I come up with you?'

'Tomorrow evening. Of course. Will you stay with me?'

'No; it's sweet of you, but there's so little room. And Aunt Anna will have me in Eaton Gate, I'm sure. I'll ring her up tonight. Oh, Flixe, I hope they take me. I couldn't bear to come back here now.'

'They must be fairly sure of you or they wouldn't even

get you in. But forget about it now. Shall we take a cup of tea off Evelyn?'

'She may have people. I don't think we'd better,' answered Gerry, not wanting to risk meeting Evelyn's Russian cousin again until she had got through her interview. If it were indeed he who had fixed it up, it would be very embarrassing for both of them, and if it were nothing to do with him, well, then she would be embarrassed.

'You haven't quarrelled with Evelyn, have you?"

'Certainly not. But I don't think we ought to go bursting in if she's got a house full of guests.'

'So likely,' said Flixe, gently sarcastic. 'Well, I haven't seen her for ages and I'm not afraid of her guests. I'm going. See you later.'

Gerry watched her turn Buttercup towards the Adamsons' and then urged her little sister's pony back the way they had come. There was no one like Flixe, of course, but there were times when her insouciance was just a bit thick.

Nevertheless Gerry was glad of her sister's company on the journey back to London on Sunday evening. Their train was unheated, vilely crowded and seemed to stop for ages at every minute station. Once they limped to within fifty miles of London the lights went out and Gerry gave up even trying to read the Penguin she had stuffed in her handbag on Flixe's advice.

She felt so tired – and dirty – by the time they got into Paddington that she turned back to Flixe to say:

'Shall we go a bust and share a taxi?'

'If we can get one. But it's more unlikely. No, look over there: it's just not worth joining a queue like that. It'll have to be the Underground. Thank God we're both on the same line.'

Plunging down the stairs towards the Inner Circle platform, Gerry was buffeted and felt her toes crushed beneath the boot of a passing private in battledress. She bit back a furious reproof and hobbled on.

Felicity got off the tube at High Street Kensington, with a cheerful promise to telephone Eaton Gate in the next day or so. Gerry watched her go with regret, but Sloane Square was soon reached and she made her way off the train and up into the fresh air.

It was usually only a five-minute walk round to Eaton Gate, but that had been in the days when she could see where she was going. Now all the street lights were blacked out; no passing car's headlights flashed across the pavements as they turned. There was nothing to help her find her way.

A slowly moving figure ahead of her held something in its hand that flashed down at the pavement every few seconds. Gerry hurried towards it.

'Do forgive me, but I can't see a thing in this murk. Are you by any chance going anywhere near Eaton Gate?'

'That's a new one on me,' came the cheery reply, the words slurred. 'But it'd be a jolly good approach if I had a bean to spare – or if I wanted a woman tonight, which I don't.'

Standing blushing furiously in the dark on the edge of the square, Gerry could have wept from her frustration and exhaustion. She transferred her bag to her right hand and put out her left towards the railings, so that she could creep along the edge of the pavement. Then a memory hit her: no railings. At last she began to feel the comforting warmth of anger and with it the defiance that set her walking more firmly in the direction of Eaton Gate. She tripped often on uneven paving stones and misjudged the depth of the gutter as she stepped off the pavement to cross the road, jarring her ankle badly. But at last she turned the corner into the right street.

It was impossible to see the numbers of any of the tall, narrow houses, but she counted from the end and rang the bell of the one she thought must be right. Footsteps reassured her that at least she would be able to ask which it was and a moment later she heard the click of a switch and then the door opening.

'Gerry,' came the voice of her mother's oldest friend. 'Is that you, darling?'

'Yes, Aunt Anna, it's me. Thank God I've got here.'

'Come in, come in,' she said as she pushed the door to behind Gerry and switched on the lights.

Coming in out of the darkness, Gerry felt almost as though she were waking out of a nightmare. Everything from the polished golden parquet floor to the warmly flamboyant Chinese wallpaper that covered the hall walls gleamed with colour in the sudden light. Gerry dropped the shabby green canvas bag on the floor.

'Heaven, Aunt Anna.'

'My dear child, you look like death,' she answered, leaning forward to kiss Gerry.

Anna Kingsley was a tall woman, slender and elegant. Her discreetly tailored Paris dress was unadorned except for a pair of magnificent diamond clips at the neck. The smooth blackness of the fine barathea set off her pale, distinguished-looking face to admiration, and the delicate silvering at her temples seemed almost like wings against the upswept dark hair.

'Goodness, you smell delicious,' said Gerry before she

could stop herself. But Anna Kingsley only laughed.

'It's called *Ombres du Paradis*,' she said. 'Very expensive. But never mind that now. Come on upstairs quickly. There's a fire and supper's waiting. Trays, I'm afraid. You don't mind, do you?'

'Of course not. It's so good of you to have me.'

'Pure pleasure, Gerry. How's Fanny?'

'All right, I suppose. I mean, quite healthy and all that, but a bit . . . She must be miserable, I think, but she won't ever admit it.'

'She always was reserved – but she's a good friend in bad times.'

'Yes, I know. She's very fond of you; she always says so.'

'And I of her. Now, enough of this. You must be ravenous.'

They sat down on the huge, soft armchairs that were covered in the most impractical possible pale-yellow silk and Gerry stretched out her good flat brown shoes towards the small fire. Then she turned to the black-and-gold lacquer tray table beside her chair and felt hunger suddenly bite at her.

'Smoked salmon, Aunt Anna! What a treat.'

'It's the easiest thing for a picnic supper and now that I haven't a cook any more, it's really the only thing I can manage.'

'I wish you were *my* godmother,' said Gerry, too tired to think before she spoke. As soon as the sense of it reached her she blushed and tried to cover the discourtesy, but Anna Kingsley laughed again.

'Don't be silly – it's a compliment. And if I didn't already have those twins of yours I'd volunteer. Now, hurry up with that and get to bed. You won't get any kind of job looking as you do tonight.'

4

But she did get the job, after a series of interviews with different men, some in battledress, others in civilian suits. One of the sessions was conducted in French, in which Gerry felt she acquitted herself reasonably well, but she was puzzled that none of the questions she was asked seemed particularly relevant to the war. She had spent hours trying to work out sensible answers to questions about what she thought had gone wrong with the French defences and what Hitler's intentions were towards Britain and what ought to be done when the invasion happened: but it was all for nothing. The cold-eyed interviewers seemed more interested in her life at school and with Andrew's regiment, and even in the skills her grandfather had considered so important.

Months later she realised that what they had been trying to find out was what she was like and not what she knew. At that stage she laughed at her younger self for assuming that anyone would be interested in what a twenty-three-year-old married woman thought about Hitler's possible invasion or strategy and tactics.

It was not until the last interview at the beginning of

September that she was given any clue as to what job she might be hired to do. Then she was ushered into yet another empty, dusty room, by a Wren almost as immaculately turned out and beautiful as the one who had first explained the position of married women trying to join up. This time the man behind the bare table was Peter Suvarov, wearing the uniform of a major of an artillery regiment.

He smiled at her in the way she had remembered as he shook her hand.

'Sorry to mess you about like this. All the mystery is thought to be necessary, but it's over now. You've come through all the trick questions and games with flying colours – just as I expected. I only hope what I have to say now won't seem a shocking come-down.'

'I'm sure it won't,' she said, having been brought up to be polite.

'I run a new, very small, semi-autonomous department concerned with an aspect of security, both internal and external. The department consists of a group of analysts – academics mainly – and me. At first that was adequate, but recent developments mean that I have to spend a great deal of time politicking – for more money, for our continued existence, for a sight of material from overseas, all that sort of thing – and we need someone to coordinate activities in the office.'

Gerry began to look interested and to feel that she might enjoy such a job. She smiled across the table as Suvarov concluded his explanation.

'It's an exceedingly sensitive job, requiring absolute, undeviating discretion and loyalty. And, of course, intelligence. There's no glamour attached to it; salary is on the lowest official scale; you won't get a uniform; our

43

very existence is under constant threat – and if the man who had us set up in the first place loses his influence we won't survive unless we can demonstrate our value for money. The army (or the bits of it that know anything about us) hates us; the other intelligence departments despise us. Any questions?'

'Yes: who's the man you spoke of? Why are you despised? And what are you actually doing?'

He laughed. 'I told them you had the sort of bluntness that would get straight to the heart of any problem. But I can't answer any of them. You'll get to know all about it if you take the job.'

'I don't seem to have much option, sir. I'll take it,' said Gerry, without a moment's thought.

'Good girl. Start next Monday.' He handed her a piece of paper. 'Report to this house in Queen Anne's Gate at eight-thirty, destroy the address and telephone number as soon as you have memorised them and never under any circumstances whatever tell anyone that that is where you are working.'

'Yes, sir.'

'Oh, and by the way, Gerry, one of our eccentricities is that we don't call anyone sir. Christian names only.'

She could not understand why that should make her blush as she shook his hand and turned to go, but she put it down to another late effect of her long-term weakness.

Gerry's next problem was to find somewhere to live. Although Anna Kingsley's house was a paradise of warmth, elegance and comfort and Anna herself insisted that there was plenty of room for them both, Gerry wanted to regain some independence. She looked at innumerable sets of rooms that she would be able to afford to rent on her meagre salary and hated them all. For some reason it seemed to her to be important not to use any of Andrew's money for such a purpose. He paid her a generous allowance, and had made arrangements with his solicitor to provide money for emergencies, but her pride insisted that she support herself while she did work of which he might disapprove.

After ten days' disheartening search she found a pair of rooms in a reasonable house at Chiswick. She thought she could bear to live in them, but she asked Anna Kingsley to inspect them before making up her mind. Anna gave Gerry a lift to Chiswick in her Riley and even before they reached the mall, she said:

'Gerry, are you sure about this? It's going to take you hours to get in to Whitehall every day. And Edwin – at the War Office, you know – tells me that one of the first casualties of the bombing is going to be the buses, so you might even find yourself walking in.'

'I hadn't thought of that,' said Gerry in a tired voice. She took off her gloves and smoothed them in her lap. 'But anything any nearer is just so horribly expensive.'

'Well, let me – ' Anna was beginning as she wound down her window to signal a left turn.

'No, really, Anna. It's terribly sweet of you to offer, but I wouldn't dream of letting you.'

An almost mischievous smile twitched Anna's delicate mouth as she explained.

'I wasn't going to offer you money. If you won't let me put you up in Eaton Gate, I didn't expect you to swallow that. No, I have a friend who has rooms at the top of a house in Dover Street. Last time we met he said something about most of the other tenants having fled to the country.'

Gerry's tense face relaxed as she contemplated the possibility of swapping Chiswick Mall for Dover Street.

'You might well be able to take over one of their leases for a bit. Let me ask him to dine, and we'll see what can be done.'

'You're an angel, Anna,' said Gerry with feeling. 'Now we've come this far, I think we'd probably better look at the rooms, don't you?'

'Why not?' said Anna easily. But when she had inspected them, she turned very courteously to the landlady and explained that after all they were not really suitable. Gerry smiled at the woman apologetically and privately hoped that she was not going to regret turning them down so soon.

But Anna's friend, duly summoned to dinner, proved to be very helpful. He confirmed that he was the only tenant left in the house and undertook to find out whether any of the absent ones could be persuaded to sublet to Gerry for a sum that she could afford to pay. Too worried about where she was going to live to think about much else, Gerry took in very little about the man except that his name was Jeremy Oldridge, that he looked about thirty-five, behaved pleasantly and seemed to be on very good terms with Anna Kingsley.

Three days after the dinner, he telephoned to say that only the basement tenant had replied to the agent's enquiry, but that if Gerry were prepared to live there, it was hers for the asking.

'Mr Oldridge, thank you,' she said. 'I don't think I mind about it's being a basement. May I bring Anna round to have a look at it?'

'Yes of course. I'm afraid that I cannot leave the office just now, but the agent will give you a key if you call at

46

his office.' He gave her the address and half an hour later she and Anna were unlocking the door to the flat.

It consisted of a sitting room, a bedroom with a lumpy-looking four-foot-six bed, a very small and squalid bathroom and an even smaller kitchenette. Instead of sneering at the flat's lack of amenities or referring to the grime that smeared the heavily barred windows or the depressing smell of ancient dust and mildew, Anna simply pointed out that from Dover Street Gerry would be able to walk through Green Park, across the Mall and down through St James's Park and be in Whitehall within a quarter of an hour of leaving her front door. Gerry, obediently refraining from correcting Anna's assumption that she would be working in Whitehall, agreed that the position alone made the gloominess of the rooms worth putting up with, and added bracingly that she would hardly ever be at home during daylight hours and so she probably would not even notice it.

Anna smiled at her valiance and produced what comfort she could.

'It really won't be too bad, Gerry, once you've cleaned the place and let some fresh air in, and if I lend you some lamps and rugs and things it'll become habitable quite quickly.'

'Anna, you don't have to do that. I shall probably spend hardly any time here and you mustn't feel responsible for me. I have no claims on you.'

'No one has any claims on me, Gerry. I have never subscribed to the philosophy that to be human you have to give other people rights to your time, money, sympathy and what-have-you. I think it's vital for sanity that you're free to give them where you want and stop giving them when you want.'

Gerry, smarting still from the slap Andrew had dealt her when he refused to let her join up, envied the older woman's freedom as a prisoner envies the people he can see through the bars of his cell. Before she could find anything to say, Anna went on:

'But I have endless spare bits and pieces which I very much want to give to you so that you can brighten up this basement.'

'Thank you, Anna. That's terribly kind of you.'

'Good. Come on, let's go back to Eaton Gate and raid the attics. I think you should build on that rusty colour of the tiles in the fireplace. You'll never make this place look light, so why not have it warm and cosy?'

'Whatever you say, Anna.'

'Good. Come on.'

Later that afternoon, Gerry found a taxi and loaded it with all the things Anna had provided and then spent a happy evening pottering about arranging her loot. There was a vividly embroidered shawl in old rose and gold to spread over the dingy sofa; there were two lamps converted from *famille rose* porcelain jars, and a shabby but pretty old French needlework rug in tones of the same subdued browny pink. With a few books and a picture or two the room would be quite bearable, almost attractive. The minute slip of a bathroom would need serious scrubbing to make it usable, but she could tackle that the next day.

Soothed by the whole business of being able to create her own surroundings, not in the least lonely, she washed in cold water at the sink in the small kitchen, and got into bed. She was just deciding that the book Anna had lent her was rather dull when the telephone rang.

'Gerry? Is that you? It's — '

'Flixe!' she cried, not waiting. 'How lovely of you to ring. Are you in London?'

'No. But I probably will be next week. Aunt Anna's just been on the telephone and she gave me your number. I thought I'd welcome you back to the land of the living – and congratulate you on getting the job.'

'So you got my letter? Good. You're a duck to ring.'

'How are you feeling, old thing? Better?'

'So much better, Flixie,' Gerry answered, smiling down into the black Bakelite receiver as though her sister could see her expression down the wires. 'You can't imagine.'

'Not nervous about the work?'

'I don't think so . . . I mean, a little, but not seriously. Sorry I can't tell you anything about it.'

'Don't be a clot. I can't either. And anyway, we've nearly had three minutes. Best of luck. I'll see you next week.'

'Yes. We might have lunch. Will you telephone when you get back?'

'Of course. Well, good luck. Keep your pecker up.'

'I will. 'Bye, Flixe. Sleep well.'

Gerry put the receiver back on its cradle and slid further down the bed, thinking what fun she and Flixe could have well away from home and – her mind flinched at the disloyalty of her thoughts, but she made herself acknowledge them – without Andrew to become restive as they talked to each other or wanting to be placated for every minute of enjoyment she won away from him. There was a wonderful sense of freedom to this life that seemed to be opening out for her.

She slept well and woke in good time the next morning with a vigour that she had not felt for ages. It did not seem worth taking down the blackout curtains since she

49

would only need to put them up again when she got back from work and so she washed, dressed and ate an exiguous breakfast by artificial light, before opening the area door and catching a glimpse of blazingly blue sky. Happily taking the fine weather to be a good omen, she locked the door behind her and climbed up the broken iron steps to the pavement.

Walking down Dover Street towards Piccadilly, she found herself smiling at complete strangers, and she did not mind that some of them grinned back at her in obvious amusement. It was a heavenly day and as she swung round the gate into Green Park to walk down the broad path towards the Mall and saw the first turning leaves fluttering down past the houses that backed on to the park, she wondered how Felicity could have thought that Gloucestershire was any more attractive than this. Even the air seemed to hold a kind of promise as its new coolness stung her face. One of the phrases Flixe had used on the telephone the previous evening came back to Gerry and she realised that she did indeed feel reborn.

She found Queen Anne's Gate with no trouble at all and thought it looked very pretty with its elegant, old houses of rosy brick and white paint, most of them with elaborately moulded white stucco canopies over their front doors. She was frivolously sad that her office had no canopy, but felt quickly sobered as she was coldly scrutinised by a young man who seemed to be standing guard just inside the front door.

'Margery Kyrle,' she said when he asked her name. The cold frown was replaced by an immensely charming smile.

'Alias Gerry Alderbrook, Peter says. You're expected, Mrs Kyrle: third floor, fourth door on the left.'

'Thank you so much,' said Gerry, puzzled by the combination of suspicion and a friendlier charm than she had met with for years. She set off up the stairs, wishing that she were a little fitter and trying hard not to pant as she reached her destination. The door stood open and, bearing in mind her mother's animadversions on the ill-trained maids who had knocked at any other than bedroom doors, she walked straight in. Before she had a chance to say anything, her new employer stood up with an open briefcase in his hand.

'You're five minutes late,' he said without a trace of the smile with which she had expected to be greeted.

'The parks were so lovely, I suppose I just loitered a bit,' she said in casual apology.

'We're far too busy here to carry anyone who does not do her fair share. Make sure you're not late again.'

'Yes, I beg your pardon,' she said, hurriedly revising her opinion of him and wondering whether she was going to be sacked before she had even had a chance to show what she could do.

'I had hoped to be able to show you around myself, but I'm due at the Chiefs of Staff and can't stop. Look, I've asked Antoine Eynsham to introduce you to the analysts and then I'd like you to read through the files I've put on your desk – over there – so that you get a proper idea of what we're doing. God knows when I'll be back, but whenever it is, we'll sort out the best way of working.'

'Yes, s—' she began, but remembered in time that he was not to be addressed as sir. Not quite being able to call a man so strange and angry as he was that morning by his Christian name, she left it at that and he hurried out. She was beginning to wonder how she was going to find the Mr Eynsham who was to introduce her to her

51

fellow-workers when Suvarov came hurriedly back, a piece of paper in his hand.

'You'd better sign that, Gerry, before Antoine gets here – I always forget these formalities, but it has to be done.'

She took the paper from him and he was gone before she could ask any questions. A little cheered to have heard him call her Gerry, she took the paper to the desk he had indicated, ignored for the moment the daunting piles of buff folders that were heaped on it, and read what he had given her.

A tall man in his late forties wearing grey flannels and a tweed jacket came into the room just as she was signing her name to an undertaking not to reveal, orally or in writing, anything that took place in Queen Anne's Gate.

'Mrs Kyrle?' he said in a gentle New England accent.

'Yes, you must be Mr Eynsham,' she answered, surprised to find an American working for Suvarov, but rather pleased. The only other American she knew was Bob Adamson, and his quietly amused friendliness had prejudiced her in favour of his compatriots.

'Antoine – or Tony,' answered Mr Eynsham, taking off his round tortoiseshell spectacles to reveal short-sighted brown eyes.

'Thank you. And I'm Gerry. Er, Peter said that you'd show me around.'

'That's right. I'm his senior analyst and he wants me to introduce you to the rest. We don't live up here in the rarified air of seniority – we pig it down on the floor below.'

Gerry followed him to the door and said a little breathlessly:

'At my last interview with him he said he would explain exactly what we're doing once I got here, but he had to

52

rush out this morning . . . Can you tell me?'

'Simple really, Gerry – in here – we're supposed to monitor the effect of what's being done in Occupied France both by the Germans and by us, and assess public and private opinions about it all here and there and watch for any anti-Allied conspiracies.'

'Are we doing anything in France?'

'We'll soon have to,' he said, opening the door for her. 'If we're to save them – and us – from Hitler.'

Gerry smiled vaguely as she preceded him through the door, looking curiously at the scene that confronted her. The smoke-filled room ran the whole width of the house, and seemed hardly to have been altered since the days when it must have been the principal bedroom. The elaborate plasterwork of the ceiling, the carved white-marble chimney-piece and the delicate *eau-de-nil* colour of the panelling were untouched. But the curtains had been replaced with thick blackout material and between each of the three long windows were pairs of sturdy wooden filing cabinets.

The centre of the room was taken up with four massive, ugly desks that were piled with loose papers, manila folders, wire baskets and assortments of pens, ink bottles and apparently chewed india rubbers. Two young men who, Gerry thought, looked very foreign were leaning over a file that lay open on the desk nearest the fireplace, and a middle-aged, red-haired man with a limp was walking away from them, still saying something to them in French, which Gerry could not quite catch.

The fourth occupant of the room, a blond-haired man in RNVR uniform, with wavy gold rings round the cuffs of his dark-blue tunic, was reading a sheet of flimsy paper as he idly turned his swivel chair first one way and then the other.

'This is Peter's new assistant – Gerry Kyrle,' announced Mr Eynsham. 'Gerry, we'll sort out ranks and services later, but from the left: Sandy Macpherson, Mike Endlesham, Michel "Dubois", and Philippe "Cluny"; together with me the brains that keep RE(1)R on the go.'

'Tony, where's Peter?' demanded the RNVR officer, paying no attention to Gerry. 'I need him to sort out this wretched business with Baker Street – I simply cannot get them to answer the simplest question.'

'Don't ask me, Mike; he'd already gone to the Chiefs when I got up there. Gerry'd be your best bet. I'll leave her with you while I get back to my cubby-hole.'

The young man stood up lazily and strolled towards Gerry as though to shake hands. She could not help staring at him as she noticed how the dark blue and gold of his uniform served to accentuate the smooth fairness of his short hair and the perfection of his handsome face. His eyes were a cold grey-blue, and they seemed to examine her with a patronising criticism she found surprising. Having looked her up and down, the officer held out his hand and, when she took it, he said with a gleaming, if slightly malicious, smile:

'Well, Gerry, it'll be marvellous to have the ear of our gallant leader all the time. What I want is—'

'I'm afraid you'll have to wait a bit,' she put in hastily. 'You see, I really haven't a clue as to what's going on yet and he said . . . he told me to read a whole lot of files.'

'We'll let you get back to them as soon as you've received our most pressing demands. Now, to give you the clue you so badly need if you're going to be of any earthly use to us. . . . ' he was beginning. Gerry felt her mouth opening in surprise. She had never been addressed

54

in such a fashion by a stranger in her entire life. Straightening her shoulders, she shut her mouth with a snap and was irritated to see that he had noticed her surprise and was amused.

'This department,' he said so slowly and distinctly that his tone was an insult in itself, 'which exists only by the grace of God and an unnamed politician, depends for its life blood – that is, direct intelligence – on underground newspapers, illicit posters, gossip and intelligence reports from France. Peter was promised by the Chiefs of Staff that we would get copies of whatever came in from whatever source, direct, but of course they let us see only the bits that they don't want, or that are so innocuous that they're no good to us.' He paused for breath and Gerry took advantage of it to interrupt.

'And what do you expect me to do?' she asked coldly.

'Make Peter get us the real stuff, of course,' he answered patiently, like a tired adult answering some silly, self-evident question from an importunate child.

'Steady on, old boy,' came a protest in a slow, lilting voice from the red-haired man on the other side of the room. 'Gerry, he's teasing you. Run off upstairs and read your files. The boss'll be back sooner or later and you can pass on Mike's message then. Don't fash yourself.'

Feeling that there were all kinds of unspoken messages whizzing about the room, Gerry smiled politely at the Scot.

'Right. Of course. Yes, well, I'll see you all later, I expect. Thank you. Yes, goodbye.'

She closed the door behind her, but it was not thick enough to shut out the burst of laughter and the sound of the naval officer's voice.

'Old man Peter won't put up with that for long. What

he needs is a super-efficient machine, not a county girl, all pearls and "what Daddy thinks".'

'Now, that's not fair,' said the Scot, whoever he was, 'it's her first day and you've no call to make assumptions. Suvarov's no fool – if he chose her, there'll be a reason.'

'If he did. But didn't someone say her father's a Brig? She's probably been wished on us by some army spy.'

'Well, we shouldn't have any trouble pulling the wool over those pretty eyes if that's so – she seemed dumb as a coot.'

Gerry felt rooted to the spot in embarrassment and fury. Why should those wretched men judge her so quickly? Not wanting to give them the satisfaction of knowing that she had heard their comments, she forced herself to walk as quietly as possible up the creaking, drugget-covered stairs to the sanctuary of the third floor. There she sat down at her table and tried to work out why the handsome young officer should have been so contemptuous. The American civilian had seemed pleasant, she thought to herself; perhaps he would be able to tell her what she had done to deserve it. Trying to ignore her anger, she started conscientiously to read the files put out for her.

By the time Antoine Eynsham came back, two and a half hours later, she had rehearsed the questions she wanted to ask him at least six times. Before she could begin to speak, he forestalled her.

'I'm sorry to interrupt you, Gerry, but some of us are going out for a spot of lunch now – there's quite a decent place round the corner – and Mike and I wondered if you'd like to join us.'

Irritatingly aware that she was blushing, and finding herself unable to ask her questions after all, Gerry answered as coolly as possible.

'Thank you, but I'm not hungry – I don't often eat at lunch time.'

'As you like,' said Eynsham, shrugging, and turned to go. Afterwards, as she listened to his feet on the stairs, Gerry realised how ungracious she must have sounded, and, in fact, that she was very hungry. If only he had not mentioned Lieutenant Endlesham, she might have been able to be more sensible, but she could not have faced him again before she had had a chance to straighten things out with Suvarov. She turned back to her files, reading, re-reading and cross-checking the reports analysing popular opinion in various countries, assessing possibilities of resistance to the Germans, and detailing various groups of people unsympathetic to the Allies until she felt that she had the whole pattern in her head and would be able to answer any questions he was likely to put to her on their contents.

When at last he came back, the thin exciting September sun had gone, and the window showed the dull grey of a typical London twilight. Gerry had finished her files and was sitting wondering how she was going to last without fainting until she could leave and have some dinner. A cup of tea had been brought into her office at four o'clock and she had wolfed down the two misleadingly named 'Rich Tea' biscuits that had been offered with it, but she still felt tired and empty.

'Well,' he said, the old smile back in his eyes and sounding in his voice, 'I gather that you decided not to lunch with the boys.'

'It was kind of them, only . . . I mean . . . Damn,' she said, the old Gerry Alderbrook resurfacing just in time, 'I decided I could not go out with them until I knew a bit more about where I stand in relation to them, and what I

57

am supposed to be doing, and what you expect of me. Don't laugh.'

'Good for you,' he said, disobeying her final instruction, as he flung his briefcase on his desk. 'I gather they gave you rather a rough time.'

'It wasn't so bad,' she said, suddenly realising what an ass she had been to take them seriously; after all they must have known that she would have been able to hear their parting comments after she had left their room. 'But I did make rather a fool of myself.'

'Not really – and it may have worked better than the way I'd planned; but I wouldn't have thrown you to the lions like that deliberately. Now, what do you want to ask?'

'Well, it's primarily about this report that Analyst 5 has filed about the South American consortium. Oh, but no. I'm sorry. Don't worry about it now.'

He had come to stand by her desk and the light of her green-shaded lamp lit up the tiredness of his thin face, accentuating the lines that ran from his straight nose to the finely shaped lips and deepening the dark crescents under his eyes.

'What's the trouble?'

'I had realised how tired you must be. Please don't mind me. I can go on reading.'

'No. The files were just a way of keeping you out of mischief till I could get time to attend to you – they're all either vague background reports, suspicions that have been dropped or cases that were invented for training purposes. Didn't you notice the dates?'

'No. Was that a test too? I was working so hard on the contents.'

'Poor Gerry. What a frustrating day for you – nearly as

bad as mine. Never mind, let's have a biscuit. Would you like one?'

'Oh, yes, please,' she said with such feeling that he looked rather surprised. 'Only not Rich Tea, if there's a choice.'

At that he laughed again, and suddenly he looked much younger.

'You must be hungry. No, I asked if you'd like a whisky.'

'Sorry; well, why not? Thank you.'

He poured generous measures into three glasses and looked up as he was recorking the bottle:

'Tony, good. Now we can get down to initiating Gerry properly in RE(1)R.'

For a moment Gerry could not think what he was talking about, and turned to look behind her. It was a shock to see the tall American standing quietly in the doorway, watching them both. He smiled at her and then walked forward on his silent, rubber-soled shoes.

'Are you sure, Peter? Wouldn't tomorrow do as well – you look dead.'

'Not quite; just whacked; but tomorrow'll be no better. You start – explain how the analysts work and how their stuff is processed.' He went to the leather-seated swivel chair behind his desk and swung it round so that he could look out of the window. He might almost not have been there and Gerry tried not to look at the back of his head as she worked to concentrate on what Tony Eynsham was explaining to her in his soft, unemphatic voice.

5

As the weeks passed, Gerry began to understand more of the job she had undertaken to do and even to enjoy doing it, but when the German bombers started to come night after night to flatten and burn London, she wished that her task could have had more direct relevance to the war. Despite the apparently enormous pressures on her chief, everyone else's workload at RE(1)R seemed so light as to be unpatriotic. Day after day she had to walk past bomb craters and blackened buildings, and read reports in *The Times* of the horror that was being wreaked on the East End and the Docks, before sitting down to process dull reports on how France was being divided between the Germans and Pétain's Vichy government. At a time when England's very survival seemed to be in doubt such work seemed to be irrelevant.

It was all the more difficult to cope with because she was so tired. Even when she learned how to sleep through the sound of distant explosions, the yelling of fire-engine bells and the stuttering cracks of ack-ack guns could wake her from the deepest sleep. Flixe, whose work still seemed to be keeping her out of London, sent Gerry a box of earplugs with a little note that made her laugh.

> My dear Gerry [it read], If all the reports I hear
> are true, you must be in serious need of sleep. These
> disgusting-looking pink things were recommended
> to me by the wife of one of my generals. She says
> that his snores are loud enough to rattle the
> silver-topped bottles on her dressing table – and it is
> a good ten feet away from their beds. Bombs could
> hardly be worse, she thinks. Let me know if the
> earplugs help. Mrs General will be so pleased if they
> do. Love, Flixe.

Gerry tried to use them; but lying in blocked silence,
with no idea of how the raid was progressing, proved to
be so terrifying that she decided that she preferred the
noise.

Throughout the first nights of the Blitz she used to lie in
her bed, rigid with a mixture of resentment and fear: not
so much of death in the bombing, but of what would
happen later. Everyone knew that as soon as Herr Hitler
had battered London into extinction, he would invade,
and it was hard to see how he could be stopped. Churchill
might say that the Battle of Britain had been won, but
could even the heroic survivors of that struggle beat off
an entire invasion once the heart of the country had been
ripped out? But gradually resentment superseded fear,
and anger gave Gerry a strength she had not known she
had.

She soon gave up even trying to sleep during the raids
and that helped too. One evening when the bombing was
at its worst, her front door bell rang. When she opened it,
expecting an ARP warden or some other official

complaining about an infraction of their rules or checking on her stirrup pump and gas mask, she found Jeremy Oldridge, the tenant of the top two floors. Immaculately if informally dressed in thick flannel pyjamas under a flamboyant silk dressing-gown, he stood on her front-door step.

'Good evening, Mrs Kyrle,' he said demurely. 'I thought I might take advantage of our short acquaintance and invite you to a chess match. Do you play?'

'Well, yes,' she answered, a little surprised.

'Excellent. I can't sleep in all this racket and it would be a work of charity if you'd play. If I'm not disturbing you, that is,' he finished.

'Goodness no,' answered Gerry. 'And in any case, I owe you far too much for finding me these rooms to refuse. Come in, please.' She stood aside and he walked past her towards the little fireplace. 'Would you like a drink?'

'That's very civil of you. A little whisky would be nice.'

Gerry laughed, not at all displeased to have such a distraction from the raid.

'Whisky I have, but I'm afraid no chess set.'

'Never mind,' he replied, putting his right hand into the pocket of his wonderful dressing-gown. 'I have this.' He held out a miniature travelling set made of ebony and ivory.

'How pretty,' exclaimed Gerry. 'It looks Indian.'

'Yes, I think it must be. I picked it up in an *antiquère* in Paris last time I was over there. Ah, Paris. Isn't it desperate?'

'Ghastly,' she agreed, pouring his whisky and fetching herself a glass of wine. 'Did you know it well?'

'Well, I really know Bordeaux better. Anyone in my

62

part of the wine trade would. But I've often thought of Paris as my spiritual home. And the thought of those wretched Germans trampling over the Tuileries, browbeating the waiters in all my favourite restaurants . . . It's all too frightful.'

Gerry felt that there were far worse aspects to the invasion of Paris and the fall of France, but decided that Mr Oldridge was merely trying to entertain her and distract her from the noise outside, and so she smiled and pulled up a small table. He laid out his chess set.

'I challenge you, Mrs Kyrle.'

'I accept your challenge, Mr Oldridge. And may the best man win.'

They played five games over the next three hours and Gerry won all except the last.

'I expect I've worn you out,' he said as she eventually conceded defeat. Gerry smiled across the miniature board.

'Well that is a work of charity in itself. I'm so tired that I can hardly hear the racket any more. I may even sleep.'

'I hope you do,' he said politely as he folded the board up and put it in his dressing-gown pocket. 'It's been delightful. Thank you very much.'

'It was fun,' she agreed. 'We must do it again. Good night.'

She locked the door behind him and got into bed, to fall asleep almost at once. She was woken soon after six the following morning as the all-clear shrieked through the dawn, and smiled to herself before turning over to bury her face in the pillow and sleep again until her alarm shrilled in her left ear.

She walked into Queen Anne's Gate that morning in a far more relaxed state than usual, thinking that if she could rely on the six hours' sleep she had achieved the night before, she might be able to cope with all the other tiresome effects of the bombing: the rarity of being able to have a bath or cook a meal because of the number of gas mains that were put out of action every night; the fear; the foul smells that hung like an evil miasma around every bombed building; even the bad temper and irritability of the analysts.

Climbing the stairs to the third floor, she acknowledged to herself that dealing with them was the part of her job that she liked the least; and yet it was probably precisely for that purpose that Suvarov had recruited her in the first place. Any of the typists already employed at RE(1)R could have done all the paperwork she had been given so far, and apart from that her job appeared to consist of nagging the analysts for their reports and trying to insulate Suvarov from their moods and petty quarrels.

He was already at his desk when she walked in, undoing the buttons of her overcoat. As usual he looked pale.

'Are you all right, Peter?' Gerry asked.

'What? Yes, of course. Harassed and sleepless. That's all.'

'My sister sent me a box of earplugs as a defence against the noise of the raids. I've only used a pair. Would you like the rest? They really do keep out the noise – if you've strong enough nerves to put up with the terrifying silence.'

He looked up and his face softened so much that she found herself smiling gaily back at him. Then he shook his dark head.

'No, but thank you – and your sister. Look, could you go and chase up Philippe? His report on the Communists is overdue. He promised it for Tuesday.'

'Yes, of course,' she answered and, as soon as she had

hung her hat and gas mask on the coat rack by the door, went downstairs again.

There she was presented with a familiar sight. Philippe and Michel standing about two feet from each other near one of the filing cabinets, yelling French insults at each other. Gerry sighed. She had learned to read French easily as a child, and could understand most of what the two men said to each other, but she was not happy speaking it.

'Look here,' she said loudly in her own language. 'Will you two stop it? The chief is upstairs trying to work and with you two bellowing like a pair . . . of rutting stags, he can't hear himself think. And he looks as though he's been awake all night.'

'Haven't we all?' asked Mike Endlesham, shaking with silent laughter at Gerry's simile. She glanced at him for a moment, recognised that he was laughing at her yet again and turned back to the two Frenchmen, wondering whether to ask about their quarrel or try to distract them with questions about recent French history. She had used the technique once or twice before and had listened patiently to lectures about the divisions in French society since the Great War; about the Dreyfus case; about Marshal Pétain; and about Michel's great hero, General de Gaulle, who was about to save France's honour virtually single-handed.

Just as she put her question about how Marshal Pétain could have struck such a chord with the majority of French people that he had been allowed to sign an armistice with their worst enemy, Madge pushed open the door of the analysts' room with her tea trolley. The clatter of cups and Madge's breezy Cockney voice were punctuated by a burst of sardonic laughter from behind her and she turned to face Michael Endlesham.

'Well, Mike? How have I blundered now?' she asked with a defensiveness that his often bitter teasing had taught her.

'My dear child,' he answered in the patronising tone that always infuriated her, 'how can you be so blind? Haven't you noticed from our reports yet? Perhaps you don't even read them. It is we who are France's principal enemy, and always have been.'

'Is that true?' Gerry asked Philippe, as she accepted a slopped cup of tea from Madge and two Rich Tea biscuits. 'I mean I know we were during the Hundred Years War and all that, but since the last war, at least, surely we've been allies?'

'Ostensibly,' answered Mike before Philippe could get a word in. Gerry turned back to face him. 'But when a member of the Vichy government can announce that it would be better for France if Germany won the war than us because then France would be able to take advantage of German weaknesses and rule all Europe . . .'

'Can you blame him?' demanded Michel, 'after Mers-el-Kebir?'

Gerry had no need to ask for explanations about that. The newspaper reports after the action in July had been quite illuminating enough and still appalled her whenever she thought of them. After Pétain's armistice with Hitler, something had had to be done to ensure that the French fleet was not used against the British. The French naval commanders had been given several options: to join the fight against Hitler, to be towed to some far-away neutral port for the duration, to scuttle themselves, or to be sunk. At Mers-el-Kebir in North Africa, they had refused to cooperate and had indeed been sunk. Thirteen hundred French sailors were killed.

'And Dunkirk,' added Michel in a voice of deliberate provocation, 'when you British ran away and left us at the Germans' mercy.'

'You bloody swine,' shouted Mike, his face almost the same colour as the dirty *eau-de-nil* wall behind him. Gerry, who had never seen him so upset, wondered what on earth could be the matter. Remembering her errand, she gulped the remains of her sweet tea and asked Philippe for his overdue report.

'It is nearly finished, Gerry,' he said in a wheedling tone of voice. She laughed.

'Nearly is not enough, Philippe. The chief said I must not leave this room without it. How long will you take?'

'Ten minutes. No more. I promise.'

'All right; I'll wait. And Mike can explain about our national enmities.'

She looked at him out of the corner of her eyes and was relieved to see that his face had resumed its normal colour. He shrugged.

'Well, if you're really interested . . .' She assured him that she was and he fished in one of his wire baskets for printed evidence of the way the British were hated in France. He produced underground newspapers and Communist posters that had been smuggled out of France and eventually reached the offices of RE(1)R. From them she learned that Britain was pursuing an imperialist war and that France must resist it if she was to remain free; if not she would become nothing more than a British dominion.

Having been brought up to think of Communists as close relations of Satan, Gerry was able to dismiss most of their propaganda, but one poster made her so angry that she could not stick to her normal policy of not interrupting Suvarov's work, and when she handed him Philippe's report half an hour later, she let him see some of what she was feeling.

He listened patiently, but he did not answer, and so she tried again:

'I suppose it's not surprising that people who believe the sort of thing that Communists believe should—'

At that Peter interrupted:

'Do you know what Communists believe, Gerry?'

Brought up short by his quiet question, she answered honestly after a moment's thought.

'No, not really. Just that they hate us and want a revolution and want us in Russia's power, which I suppose is really the same as Hitler's now that Russia's made that shameful treaty with him.'

'One day, when there's more time, I'll tell you what real Communists want and then you'll understand a bit more.'

'You don't approve of them, do you, Peter?' The horrified tone of her voice made him laugh, but he answered seriously enough.

'No. But one of the saddest things in my life was discovering that an ideal like that, which has so much in it designed to help humanity, should in operation have turned out to be so inhumane.'

'I'm sorry. I suppose I wasn't thinking about what I said, and it's true that I really don't know anything about it. I didn't mean to annoy you.'

'You didn't. And if I hadn't an appointment in ten minutes' time I'd have started your education right now. Never mind; there'll be another time,' said Suvarov, picking up the file he had been reading.

That episode marked the beginning of a change in their

relationship. Because he had shown her something he really minded about as he talked to her, Gerry felt that she was beginning to get to know Peter as someone more accessible than the occasionally frightening senior officer she had been employed to assist. She began to allow herself to talk more openly over their whisky each evening, even expressing her doubts about what they were supposed to be doing and asking whether the internal government of France would ever really be the business of the British.

Peter Suvarov seemed pleased that she was interested enough in the politics of France and its occupation to ask questions, and he answered them with growing ease. One evening about four weeks after she had started work, he reached for the whisky bottle at about six o'clock as usual. It had been a bitterly cold day, and Gerry had had to replenish the small coke fire every hour or so since she had arrived that morning. By six, the room had at last warmed up. The last coals were glowing red in the black grate, the green-shaded reading lights on each desk threw circles of light on to the polished wood. There were no sounds except the gentle hiss of the fire and the clink of glass on glass as Suvarov poured the whisky. The room seemed miles away from anywhere else, small .and intimate, and Gerry was glad that Eynsham had chosen that evening to work later than usual. She smiled at her chief and asked him how he had come to work for the department.

Peter handed her a glass and went to sit back in his chair, with his feet stretched forward on to his desk, and began to explain to her why he had been anxious to have a part in RE(1)R and why it was such an important place to work. He told her that he could see little point in fighting only to defeat the enemy if the post-war world were to remain as it had been before.

Gerry was a little puzzled and asked Peter what kind of world he wanted. He rubbed his thin hands across his face and smiled at her.

'It would take a long time to explain it all, but we ought to be fighting for a better, safer world; one in sympathy with basic democratic ideals. The only way even to begin to work for such a world is to ensure that countries liberated from the Germans are eventually put into the hands of people who want the same things as we do.'

'I see,' said Gerry, watching him more carefully. 'But there's more than just that, isn't there? Tell me about the world you want, Peter. What would it be like?' He laughed again.

'Oh, it's simple things I want, Gerry: in my world, everyone has enough to eat, free access to the best medical care and the best education; everyone has the right to a say in how their country is governed; no one need fear arbitrary imprisonment or forced labour. There is no censorship. There is no death penalty. And so on.' Gerry listened, but protested.

'But we haven't got all of those things here.'

'No, my dear, of course we haven't. But we are nearer to achieving some of them than the occupied countries can be,' he said.

'Well, even so,' said Gerry, curious to see how earnest he had become, 'it does sometimes seem a bit premature. I mean, until there is the faintest possibility that we might win and be in a position to do anything at all about the occupied countries.' Peter laughed once again, his eyes narrowing, as he answered.

'We'll win. I'm sure of it.' She smiled back, warmed by his certainty.

'I wish I could sound so sure when I try to calm the boys down when they get bolshie.'

'It's only a knack. I'm sure you'll learn. But I'm glad you're trying. Most of them have good reasons to be depressed even without the war news.'

'Oh?' she said, hoping for more. 'Tell me about them.' Suvarov took his feet off the desk and explained with uncharacteristic stiffness that he did not intend to pass on personal details about any member of his staff to one of the others. Gerry blushed and changed the subject, but she filed the hint away in her mind and found it comforting to think that perhaps Michael Endlesham's antagonism might have its roots in his own troubles rather than in her failings.

The personal business of his staff was the only subject that Suvarov considered to be taboo; on every other topic he was happy to talk and seemed more open and approachable than usual. Gerry found herself hoping that Eynsham would not appear at all. She rather liked him, and he had occasionally defended her against the more vicious of Endlesham's outbursts, but on that particular evening she wanted her chief to herself. When they eventually put the guard in front of the fire, switched off the lamps and left the building, it dawned on her that they got on rather well together.

After that evening she began to watch him, and the more she watched the more concerned she became for him: he seemed to be fighting on about five fronts simultaneously and only to her and to Eynsham did he ever allow himself to seem discouraged. It was no wonder that he usually looked ill. Like the rest of them, he could not be getting much sleep. Gerry increased her efforts to see that the information from downstairs was properly presented, accessible, as accurate as possible, and filed in a way that made it quick and easy to find again so that he would not have any friction in the office that she could prevent.

For some reason her concern for Suvarov made it easier to deal with the analysts, and as she ceased to expect them to beat her in their games of one-upmanship, she found that they ceased to play them. Even the sarcastic and bitter Mike Endlesham showed her a more human side, and began to let her see some of the real despair behind his mocking exterior.

One evening after she had had to talk Mike down from a nearly hysterical outburst about the absurdity of the work they were all trying to do when they would have been more use on an assembly line in.an armaments factory, Suvarov came back into the office looking more angry than she had ever seen him. He put his briefcase down on the desk in the window and started to walk round to the chair. Then she saw him stop, shrug and turn back to face her.

'Gerry, I can't do any more tonight. Will you dine with me?'

Feeling very glad that her close acquaintance with the second-floor had been teaching her not to blush, she smiled at him.

'That would be very nice. Now?'

'Why not? Get your hat and we'll walk over to the Ritz. I can't stand this place any more tonight.'

He stood waiting by the door as she pulled on her old and far from elegant felt hat and picked up her gas mask.

'Gerry,' he said, watching her from under his bruised eyelids, 'did I ever tell you how much you help here?'

'No. I'm glad. Though I often feel that I hardly do anything. You work so hard and all I do is calm the boys down and process their information.'

'It's quite a big all; before we had you it got increasingly difficult – they need someone to comfort them and I can't do that; partly because I have to be tough with them and partly because . . . I just don't have anything left for that side of things. And,' his voice changed and became lighter, more teasing, 'now that you rewrite their reports I can read them in no time at all. It's wonderful; they used to be so turgid it would take minutes to work out what they had meant to write in each sentence.'

'I hadn't realised it was so obvious. I'll try to vary the style sometimes.'

'No, don't do that. You write clearly and with such conciseness that . . . I knew as soon as I talked to you at Evelyn's that weekend that you would never waste time and that's nearly the most precious commodity at the moment.'

'You'll make me blush in a minute,' she said as they crossed the bridge over the little lake in St James's Park. 'Look at the way the moon's reflected on the swans down there – don't they look extraordinary, all silver like that on the black water?' They stopped for a moment, leaning on the elegant iron railing of the bridge, shoulder to shoulder, looking down towards Whitehall and watching the stately birds paddle gracefully along the lake that had been so carefully planned to lead the eye towards the fairy-tale roofs behind the Horse Guards. The strange night light slid off the willows that curtained the edges of the water and lit odd parts of the whole scene, making it look somehow artificial. There was a sudden stiffening in

Suvarov's shoulders, which Gerry felt and wondered at, but all he said was:

'God, it's good to stop for a moment.' Then he stood up. 'Come on or we won't get any dinner.'

'Peter,' she said suddenly. 'Do you specially want to go to the Ritz?'

'Not particularly, no. It's just convenient – and the food's better there than in most places. Why, is there somewhere you'd rather go?'

'No, it's just . . . ' She stopped, shy all over again, but the memory of his exhaustion and the way he had relaxed against the bridge made her go on. 'It's just that I've some lovely steaks from Harrods and my flat's very close. We could talk there, without anyone overhearing . . . I mean, if you wanted to.'

'That's generous of you. I'd like it. Lead the way, Miss Alderbrook.'

'It's only a tiny flat – one room, really; though it's possible that if the ground-floor tenant decides to stay in Wales as they think she may, then I could get that. My sisters' godmother helped me furnish it, but it is quite shabby, really.' Gerry knew that she was babbling, but could not stop. He touched her elbow lightly with his cupped hand.

'Gerry, it's all right. Don't go social on me or I'll have to take you off to the Ritz. OK?'

'OK, Peter. Sorry.' They walked on in silence, up St James's Street and across Piccadilly and into Dover Street. She stopped when they reached the house and put one hand on the temporary wooden gate to the basement steps.

'Down here; servants' quarters.' He laughed, held the gate open for her and waited for her to precede him down the steps. She opened the door under the steps and as soon as he had followed her in, she switched on the lights.

'Come on in. What would you like to drink? There's some whisky left or wine.'

'What kind of wine?'

'Not bad. My sisters' godmother, who is the most generous person alive, gave me a case of more than respectable claret when I moved in, and I've only had one bottle so far.'

'Then wine, please.'

She made him sit down in the one comfortable chair that stood by the empty grate and brought him the bottle, a corkscrew and a glass.

'What about you?'

'I'll be in the kitchen. I'll have some later. It won't be long.'

She left him then and set about cooking the steaks, using the last of her butter and a precious bottle of tomatoes from Sudbrook House that she had been hoarding against some special need. When she had put the dish in the oven, which for once lit at the first attempt, she washed up the tools she had used, dried her hands on her apron and peered into the looking glass she kept by the door. Her face looked back at her, oddly alive and healthy-looking. So often her skin looked thick and dully grey, but – perhaps it was the oven's heat – that evening it looked rosy and almost as though it had just been treated by some expert with expensive cosmetics. She smiled sheepishly at herself, and quietly shut the kitchen door behind her.

Suvarov was sitting where she had left him, the corkscrew in one hand, the claret bottle on the floor and the glass she had given him balanced precariously against

75

his waistcoat. He was fast asleep. Moving with extreme delicacy, she removed the glass and corkscrew and carried the bottle away to the kitchen so that he would not be awakened by the sucking pop of the cork. Then she came back and curled up on the lumpy sofa, sipping her wine and watching him. The sight of him lying back in such abandon of sleep in her chair made her think of her husband, and she began to realise how much she had been missing his physical presence over the months since she had come back to London. For so long her mind and emotions had been caught up with the death of their child and her struggles to find some kind of life for herself that she had not understood how much she was being affected by the simple fact of Andrew's absence. It was strange, she thought to herself as she sipped her claret, that something you took for granted, that often irritated you, could in fact be something you relied on for ordinary contentment. Belatedly, and with a kind of shock, Gerry realised that she was lonely.

Peter's eyes opened, very wide, just before she had decided to wake him and, without saying anything, he smiled at her. She had never seen his face so naked. Then he seemed to collect himself together. The smile resumed its familiar lineaments and he said, rather thickly:

'Did you say something about claret, Gerry?'

She unfurled herself, stood up and brought him his glass, wanting to let her fingers touch his as she handed it to him and therefore taking enormous care to avoid them.

'The steaks should be just about cooked,' she said and was glad to hear no hint of breathlessness or confusion in her voice.

'Something smells jolly good anyway.'

Gerry was glad that she had plenty of practical things

76

to do so that she could control the absurdities that were dancing through her mind and when at last they were sitting at the round cherry-wood table, she could think of nothing to say. He helped her out.

'So, Gerry, tell me about your sisters. One's in the Fanys isn't she?'

'Yes, did I tell you that?'

He shook his dark head and she saw the thin white strands in it.

'No, I think I met her somewhere. Very like you, no?'

'Sometimes you sound awfully foreign, did you know?' He smiled, but did not comment and so she nodded. 'Yes, Felicity – she's prettier though, and great fun, too. I miss her.'

'She's not stationed in London, then?'

'No, all over the place, it seems. She's got enormously discreet since the war – she used to tell me everything, but now she's very cagey. I don't quite know what she's up to.'

'Everyone is supposed to be cagey. Why are you surprised?'

'I didn't really mean about the war; when we were last at home – when she was telling me to brace up and tidy myself up or you'd never give me a job – she hinted that she was living in a rather, er, racy kind of a way, which is unlike her. She was always pursued, of course, she has that kind of energetic fragility that seems to draw men to her – of course it's entirely illusory: Flixe is made of tempered steel and toughened glass . . . '

'You sound almost bitter, Gerry, and most unlike yourself. Don't you get on with her?'

Gerry was so surprised that he should have put such a construction on her words that she got up to fetch the

77

wine bottle, which was still standing on the hearth where they had left it. She handed it to him and as he was refilling both their glasses she tried to answer him.

'I hadn't realised what I sounded like and I don't want you to think that I don't care for Flixe. She's probably more important to me than anyone else. And I miss her terribly; I'd thought that when I came to London again I'd see much more of her . . . that it would be like the time before I was married.' She paused and thought about how to explain to him the complete importance of the bond between them, how to explain that even if she sounded as though she were criticising her sister, she would defend her against criticism from anyone else in the world, including their family; how they could be so angry with each other that it felt like hate; how they were often foully jealous of each other; but how the existence of the other was the most important thing in life.

'When we meet after being apart for any length of time neither of us can stop talking – I feel as though I have to tell her everything that's been happening to me – but after that first rush of enthusiasm, I suppose we do get cross with each other. We live such different lives; perhaps it's that.' Finding it so difficult to explain, Gerry wanted to change the subject by asking Suvarov about his family, but since he had never spoken a word about anything personal she felt she could not. Instead she said:

'Things are rather different with the twins. I don't know them nearly so well. They're six years younger than Flixe – eight than me. Do you know . . .? I'd never thought of how lucky they'll be, to be leaving school in the war. I mean it'll be quite obvious what they should do and there'll be none of the hideous arguments I had.'

'With your parents?'

'Yes, well, primarily with my father, I suppose. Mother says worse things, but he's the one who thinks that education damages women for life and ... and all that sort of thing. Look, let's talk about something different: he's away in the desert and there's no point thinking about him if one doesn't have to.'

'Of course. There's one thing I want to know ... ' His voice seemed very serious and Gerry braced herself for some difficult question. She watched his dark eyes and could see no glimmer of light in them. 'Where did you learn to cook? That was the best beef I've ever eaten.'

In the spurt of releasing tension, Gerry burst out laughing.

'I just follow the recipe. But if you're serious I'm glad – at least you won't have missed the Ritz too much.'

'Not at all. But I ought to get going soon, Gerry.'

'Must you?' she said before she could stop herself and then hurried to cover it up. 'It's a good idea though, before tonight's raid starts.'

'Yes. You seem quite secure in this nice basement – I shouldn't move up to the ground floor even if you do get the chance.'

'Well, I could always keep my bedroom down here, but it would be convenient to have more space – especially when the top-floor tenant comes down as he usually does on bad nights.'

'Does he indeed?'

'You need not look like an outraged maiden aunt – we play chess, actually, until the all-clear.'

'It's not conventions that perturb me. No, Gerry, this is serious. Do you know who he is? Come on, how old is he – and what's his name?'

'I suppose in his thirties. He's called Jeremy Oldridge;

he's some kind of businessman. Wine, I think. Peter, what is the matter?'

'Gerry, you are involved with extremely secret work; as you well know, part of our task is internal security: anyone is suspect until we know exactly who and what they are. I don't like your sharing night-time air raids with some civilian.'

'Well, I can't exactly refuse to let him take refuge in the safest part of the house. I mean that would look very suspicious. And he's thoroughly respectable – an old friend of the twins' godmother.'

'Is he though? Well, be careful, won't you? Does he ever ask about your work?'

'Only when we first met – as anyone might. It's all right: I just said that I had a dreary filing job at the War Office. Look, Peter, why should you be suspicious of him?'

'No particular reason; except that I'm suspicious of any man of fighting age who is not in the services – and some who are. Just promise to be discreet and very careful of yourself.'

'Yes, of course I will. I signed that wretched piece of paper, didn't I? I'm not likely to talk to anyone. Don't look like that; there's no Gestapo in London.'

'No, but there are some highly unsavoury characters. It oughtn't to touch you, though, if you keep quiet.'

'Of course,' she said as soothingly as she used to speak to Ming when she was upset by family quarrels. Then another thought hit her with the force of a sandbag. 'Peter, you're not facing that sort of thing are you?'

He shook his head, but those dark eyes were watchful.

'I seem to have been very stupid,' she said. 'I assumed that all those days you spent out of the office you were with the Chiefs or the War Office or in Baker Street or something. What is it you're actually up to?'

'Nothing that need concern you, Gerry. Now, good night, my child. Sleep well, and work out your moves carefully.'

'I always do – and I usually win, at least with Mr Oldridge.'

'We must play one day. Thank you for my nice dinner.'

'It was a pleasure.' She stood in front of him, almost barring the way out of her flat. 'You will be careful, won't you?'

'Now who's behaving like a maiden aunt?' he said, putting both hands on her shoulders and gently turning her aside.

After he had left her, she washed up their plates and glasses, cursing mildly that the hot water had failed again, thinking round and round what had happened. Until that evening she had thought of Suvarov as her chief, nothing more; the very idea of being frightened of him would have seemed absurd. But now he had eaten her food, she had watched him fall asleep in her chair, she had felt . . . In the privacy of her own room, Gerry blushed and tried to ignore the things that he had made her feel.

But she could not sleep and even welcomed the air-raid sirens when they came, and the two knocks at her door as Jeremy Oldridge came for chess and sanctuary. As always he was wearing thick flannel pyjamas that looked as though they had been freshly pressed, an extravagant dressing gown, this time with a pattern of peacocks woven into the thick, dark-red silk, and a cravat at the neck to hide any glimpse of his skin. Gerry almost laughed at the idea that there could be anything improper in their decorous sharing of the bombing. They shook

81

hands and she got out her new full-sized chess board. He waited until she had seated herself ceremoniously in the chair and then he bent his long legs and sat on a cushion on the floor on the other side of the table.

'Will you give me a pawn, Mrs Kyrle, tonight?'

'Certainly, Mr Oldridge,' she answered and then, driven by some emotion she did not want to recognise, added: 'if you feel you ought to accept concessions from a woman.'

'Now, now, there's no need to be waspish. You're a better player than I, and I only want to make the game worth your while.' Neither spoke as an enormous thump seemed to buffet the atmosphere. 'That one was close,' he said coolly. 'Your move, Mrs Kyrle.'

6

Gerry was almost too embarrassed to look at Suvarov the following morning when she arrived at Queen Anne's Gate, but he greeted her with a cheery:

'Well, did you win, then?' She smiled ruefully.

'Actually, no, not last night. I gave him a pawn and something seemed to go wrong with my concentration.' She would not say any more, could not tell Peter that every time she tried to think out her next sequence of moves his tired face seemed to slide between her eyes and her brain, and the strange but delectable sinking inside her that she had first felt when he took the wine glass from her absorbed all her faculties.

'Well never mind. Look, there's been no post this morning. See to it, will you?'

'Yes, certainly,' she answered, pleased to be able to go and do something easy and away from him.

When she had tracked down the usual large stacks of post and opened, dated and distributed it, she could concentrate on the twenty or so letters addressed to herself. All but one were written to her in her official capacity, and she dealt with them first, looking up now and again at her chief. Once he caught her eye and smiled faintly, almost as though he knew what she was thinking. She quickly went back to the letter in her hand.

'Oh! Can they do that?'

'What?'

'Some new regulation that says we all have to do a stint of firewatching if we work less than fifty-five hours a week . . .'

'I should think you do more than that most weeks, Gerry.'

'Yes, I know; it's just that I'd never thought of that and I suppose one should do some anyway. It would be more use than playing chess. Perhaps I should do Sundays at least. Never mind. Oh, that reminds me, Peter.'

'Yes?'

'My mother has written asking whether I can go home over Christmas. What should I tell her?'

He looked up from his papers and smiled quite kindly as he said:

'I don't see why you shouldn't go if you want. There's not so much you have to do at the moment, and I don't suppose many of the analysts will want leave then. Yes, all right.'

'Thank you. It's not exactly that I want to go, but since she's asked — and the twins will be home, and perhaps Flixe.'

When he did not comment, Gerry shut herself up and got down to work, feeling rather a fool. He went out about half an hour later and she found it much easier to concentrate when she had the room to herself and there was no temptation to look up and perhaps catch his eye. She told herself sternly that she was a married woman and that however irritated Andrew had sometimes made her, and however much she was missing him, she had no reason to behave like the girls at school who had dealt with boredom and homesickness by fantasising about the art master or the chaplain. She hoped that Flixe really would be able to get leave for Christmas so that they could laugh away the whole silly business.

That evening she got back to the flat just as the telephone started to ring. Hoping that it was Flixe, she ran across the room to get to the telephone before it stopped ringing, barked her shin on one of the chairs and then dropped the receiver as she tried to pick it up, but there was still a voice at the other end when she got it on to her shoulder at last.

'Gerry, is that you?' came Anna Kingsley's voice, rather faint. Gerry stopped massaging her shin.

'Yes, Anna, has something happened?'

'Oh, Gerry, it's too stupid; I tripped over some sandbags in the blackout and fell down somebody's area. They say I've broken my ankle; it's not serious, but they can't set it yet for some reason and I can't get to the ARP post. I promised the WVS I'd go tonight because they're short-handed and I hate to let them down, Gerry. I know it's a lot to ask, but could you . . . I mean, if you're not busy this evening?'

Remembering all the things Anna Kingsley had done for her, Gerry quickly said:

'Anna, of course I shall. I'd be glad to and . . . oh, hell, nearly three minutes. Quick, tell me, where do I go?'

'You're an angel. It's the post at Holborn – on the corner of Warwick Lane and Newgate Street. Ask for Ben Calbourne and tell him—'

'OK Anna, don't talk. I'll see to it. Where are you?'

'St George's.'

'I'll look in when I can. It's all right; I never sleep during a raid anyway. Good night.'

Changing quickly into a pair of trousers and a thick jersey, Gerry scribbled a note for Jeremy Oldridge and pinned it on the front door to explain where she was and then set off towards Holborn. She had hoped for a taxi or at least a bus, but it seemed that her luck had run out and she had almost reached her destination before a taxi passed her with his flag up. But there seemed no point in hailing him at that stage in her journey and so she plodded on.

The first siren howled before she reached the ARP post and she hurried the last few hundred yards, looking anxiously up at the sky every so often. But she reached the corner of Newgate Street before anything happened. The ARP post was housed in a temporary-looking hut that had been erected on the site of a flattened building. Gerry pushed open the door to the shriek of cheap hinges and looked in.

There was a row of shabby tables opposite the door, and several canvas-seated chairs of the kind that furnished village halls all over the country. Sitting at one, in front of a row of telephones, was a tired-looking woman dressed in a navy-blue siren suit with an ARP armband around her right arm. Behind her, chalking something up on a dusty blackboard, was a large, bald man wearing serge overalls. Gerry advanced toward him.

'I say, are you Ben Calbourne?' He turned, the chalk in one hand and a greying yellow duster in the other.

'I am, and who might you be, miss?' came the answer in the richest Cockney that Gerry had ever heard.

She explained and was curious to see that the large man seemed genuinely distressed when she told him what had

86

happened to Anna.

'Poor old Annie. That's too bad. She's a regular old trooper, you know. Keeps us all going on the bad nights.'

'Yes, she would,' said Gerry, rather faintly, wondering how that immaculately elegant woman managed to fit into this dingy hut and how she took to being addressed as 'Old Annie' instead of 'Miss Kingsley'. Gerry was upset to recognise in herself a reaction that her mother might have had and did her best to smile properly at Calbourne, who was pouring some liquid from a brown enamel jug into three thick white mugs. He gave one to the woman sub-warden and one to Gerry. She sipped gingerly and discovered that the liquid was hot, sweet, kitchen tea.

'This 'ere is Miss Atkins,' announced Calbourne, nodding towards the sub-warden. 'You'll meet the other sub-wardens as they come in off their patrols.'

'Good evening,' said Gerry, politely, just as the roar of heavy aircraft sounded above them.

''Ere they come. Got your tin hat, miss?'

'No, I'm sorry. I haven't.'

'Tut, tut. Never mind. I think we've a spare – old Chummy's.'

Gerry did not ask who old Chummy was and whether something had happened to him, for she was suddenly engulfed in sound. During the nights of chess games, she had learned not to wince at the thundering explosions of the bombs or shiver as the sharp, rusty cackling of the ack-ack guns smacked into the night air, but now, that tiny bit nearer the main target, she began to realise something of the reality.

'But shouldn't we go out and do something?' she asked, breathless but determined to do her bit.

'Not till we're called, miss. The others are all out there now and we can't just go charging off into the blue like. What if there was a real humdinger and none of us was 'ere to see to it?'

'I see. But it's hard to wait, isn't it?'

'There's a lot of things is harder than that . . . ' he was beginning as the telephone rang. The woman picked it up, listened, spoke shortly and then said: 'OK, Ben, now's your chance. Smithfield sector. Not a bad incident.'

Gerry followed Calbourne as he led the way at a half-run out of the hut, across the main road and up towards what remained of Smithfield Market. Gerry followed him, no longer afraid of the noise or even the risk of being bombed now that there was something to do, but worried about how she would live up to Anna's standards. When they reached their destination, the police had already arrived and were setting up yellow diversion signs. One, a young constable, hailed them:

'Ben, good. There's a gas mains gone. No fire yet, but God knows when – see to it will you?'

Calbourne just nodded, then yelled to Gerry:

'Stand there, make sure no clot lights a match and don't let anyone by who isn't meant to be 'ere.'

Gerry stood, shivering, where she had been left and looked around her. When the constable had done whatever it was he had to do, he came over to her:

'You're new, aren't you, miss?'

'Yes, Constable. I'm just standing in for a friend in the WVS. Shouldn't we go and do something?'

'No, the Heavy Rescue boys'll be here in a tick. Your job is to stand here like old Ben said and mine is to make sure there's no disturbance. Can't go doing other people's jobs.' Seeing that she was about to protest he said soothingly: 'It's too dangerous, miss. Each to his own skill.'

'Look, what about the people? I mean, shouldn't we at least make sure no one's hurt?'

'No one here at the moment. It was only a tiddler and all they got was a bit of the market. We'd not have sent for Ben if it hadn't been for the gas. Look, there he is.'

'Come on, miss. We done all we need to 'ere. Back to the post.'

'Well, goodbye, Constable. Thank you,' said Gerry putting out her hand. With the amusement licking around his face, the young policeman took her hand. Then Gerry turned and ran after Calbourne, feeling rather let down.

As they crossed Newgate Street, she was transfixed by the sight of St Paul's between the tall narrow buildings on either side of the street. Wren's great dome, which had always seemed to her to be the most beautiful of London's buildings, was astonishingly silhouetted against a sky of fire, every colour from deepest madder to bright orange, highlighted here and there by the blindingly white light of flares and the little hock-bottle-shaped incendiary bombs. If one could only forget, she thought, the reason for the flame and smoke and flares, one could almost revel in the tremendous weird beauty of the sight.

The fat ARP man, hearing her stop, looked back and watched the expressions fighting each other in her face, itself lit only by the glow of the burning East End.

'Poor blighters down there,' he said with feeling.

Together they trudged back to the post, where Miss Atkins welcomed them with an offer of more tea from the brown enamel pot. To Gerry's surprise, she learned that the pot had been filled hours earlier with a mixture of tea, milk and sugar and was kept warm on a low gas ring. The resulting brew was now thick and treacly and so full of tannin that it almost took the roof off her mouth. Even so, she accepted a mugful of it and found its strength oddly comforting.

The two wardens then set themselves to entertain her until the next call with descriptions of some of the really bad nights they had seen. Gerry heard in horrified silence what it had been like on such-and-such a night when the local water mains was bombed and so there was no water for the fire engines' pumps, and what the old woman and her canary had looked like when they had eventually been dug out from under her house after seventy-three hours, and the kinds of things people said and did when you got to them, and how even the most brave and cheerful might be found a few hours later shaking so badly they couldn't even hold a mug of tea.

She listened and admired them – and Anna Kingsley – for doing this particular duty night after night, risking themselves, losing sleep, and having to see and deal with such terrible things, and hoped that she would not let them down if they were all called out again.

There were four more calls before the German bombers headed for home and the all-clear wailed through the icy grey dawn. By the time she and Calbourne had returned from the fourth incident, Gerry had learned enough to be quite useful. When a messenger boy came running with the fifth call, Gerry reached almost nonchalantly for her tin hat and gas mask and followed Ben Calbourne out of the post quite cheerfully.

When they reached the incident her naïve self-assurance quickly evaporated. A row of mean-looking houses had been hit and the middle of it had collapsed. There was no fire yet, but even from where she stood,

Gerry could hear the screams of people trapped in the mess of bricks and timbers. The air was full of grit and plaster dust and she began choking as she tried to speak. Calbourne gave her a buffet on the back and said:

'Round up them survivors, tell them to get to the Rest Centre – where I showed you at the beginning – and find out if there's any WVS housewives as can produce hot drinks. Got that?'

'Yes,' answered Gerry and walked towards the nearest group of people, who looked pathetic as they stood in the street dressed in their bedraggled pyjamas and dressing-gowns, their hair full of dust, and most of their faces showing long, still-bleeding cuts. When she had told them all where to go, she went back to find Calbourne, trying to ignore the myriad smells that made the air harshly acrid and horrible to breathe.

'What does that to their faces?' she asked. Without turning from whatever it was he was doing, he said:

'Glass splinters from the windows. Any WVS arrived yet?'

'Not yet. The policeman said the ambulances would be here soon, though.'

'Well, you take this one then and do what you can; there's a toddler too, they say, not far below where we got this one.'

He turned at last and put into her reluctant arms a small bloody bundle wrapped in what looked like half an old curtain. With trembling fingers, Gerry parted it. Even to her inexperienced eye the child was obviously less than a year old; it was breathing with difficulty and the tiny gasping sobs it made were infinitely more frightening than full-blooded howling would have been. But worst of all, the small grey face had been slashed and cut all round

91

the eyes and mouth.

Irrational tears poured down Gerry's face, turning the gritty dust that smothered her skin into a kind of muddy clay. She hugged the baby, looking helplessly around for someone to tell her what to do. Other wardens and sub-wardens from Calbourne's ARP post had arrived to help, but all of them were already fully occupied with their appointed tasks. The police were busily directing people and vehicles, the Heavy Rescue men were dragging timbers and boulders away from the heaps of rubble that buried no one knew how many more wounded. At last she took out her handkerchief so that at least she could wipe away some of the blood from the small face, but just as she realised that there might still be glass in the cuts so that wiping them might make the wounds worse, she heard an ambulance bell and turned in relief.

When the powerful grey vehicle pulled up about fifty yards away, Gerry ran towards it, as carefully but as fast as she could. The double doors at the back of the van opened and she almost thrust her burden at the woman who clambered down.

'Can you take it? I don't know what to do and it's obviously in horrible pain. Will you help?'

'Of course. Keep calm,' came the steady voice of a professional nurse. 'Is he yours?'

'No. I'm here helping out for a friend who's broken her ankle, and I'm so useless. I don't know where anything is or what—'

'Never mind now. I've got him. Find out from whoever gave him to you or any neighbours where he came from and whether his mother's there and alive. Go along now.' There was severity in the voice then and Gerry,

92

chastened, hurried to obey.

She spent the rest of the raid running errands for anyone who hailed her and trying to comfort the bewildered and injured victims of the explosion. By the time the grey dawn broke, helping the rescue workers at least to see what they were trying to do, Gerry was worn out. Ben Calbourne saw her sitting at last on an upturned dustbin, her head in her hands, and called over with rough kindness:

'There's nothing more you can do 'ere now, miss. You go on off home. And when you see old Annie, give her my best.'

'All right, if you're sure. Sorry I wasn't more use.'

'You were good enough, miss, for a first night. See you again then.'

She turned away and began to walk towards the West End. Passing the end of the street, she recognised the nurse from the first ambulance and hurried over to touch her elbow and ask:

'That baby, how is he?'

'Baby?' asked the woman, now sounding as harassed and exhausted as Gerry felt.

'The one I gave you when you first got here this evening. He had a terribly cut face and was wrapped in old grey and brown cretonne.'

'Oh that baby. That one died.'

She could not wait for whatever Gerry might be going to say next and went off on her next grisly task of collecting damaged bodies for the mortuary. Gerry walked away, trying hard to stop the thoughts that had been edging near her conscious mind all night. For the first time since her own baby had been born dead she had held a child in her arms. There had been a moment, as she felt its heart beating against hers, when she had been seized with a powerful, tugging feeling of deprivation, fiercer even than the misery that had tormented her during her convalescence. And now that child, too, was dead.

A taxi passed her as she was walking up Holborn and she flagged him down gratefully. He took her a most circuitous route, to avoid the craters and smashed sewers and water mains, he explained, and looked over his shoulder when she did not answer. She obviously had not even heard him, but some blankness in her eyes stopped him repeating himself and he said no more.

Gerry sat stiffly upright on the leather seat, her eyes open but seeing nothing, her mind reliving the moment when she had held the warm, still-breathing body of the child against her breast. Her own child had never breathed, and they had never allowed her to hold him. But now, at last, she knew what it would have felt like; what it felt like to have a child's heart thudding against your own, its hands grasping your fingers, its heavy head lying against your arm. She shuddered as though she were very cold.

The taxi deposited her outside her door at seven-thirty, and it was a moment before she realised that she was home. She paid and tipped him and then let herself into the flat, realising that she could not fling herself on her bed and sleep her exhaustion away. If she were to be at the office promptly she would just about have time to wash and change.

When she opened the office door three-quarters of an hour later and said good morning to Suvarov, he took one look at her and demanded:

'What on earth have you been doing to yourself? You

look absolutely terrible.'

'Oh, I'm sorry,' she said automatically. 'I stood in for a friend last night at an ARP post. Got back an hour ago. I'm just tired. I'm very sorry, but I'll be all right if you tell me what you want me to do.'

'Look, you're not fit to work. Go home now and get some sleep. Come back this afternoon.'

'But . . .'

'Do as you're told.'

'All right,' she said, buttoning up her coat again. 'Thank you, Peter; I'll come in on Sunday if you want.'

'Oh, no you won't, Gerry. Wake up. It's Christmas. You're going home.'

7

Christmas came and went and Gerry half wished that Suvarov had made her stay in London and work. There was nothing much to do at Sudbrook House; Mrs Alderbrook was even more tired and irritable than when Gerry had last been at home; Flixe had not been able to get leave, and the twins, affectionate though they were, were no substitute for her. The one undoubted benefit of Gerry's two days and three nights in Gloucestershire was that she slept voraciously. Not only was her old bed infinitely more comfortable than the lumpy one she had in Dover Street, but there was no noise all night, no fear, no feeling that she ought to be out at some ARP post helping the wardens and WVS.

After more sleep than she normally had in ten days or so, Gerry returned to London much less tired than usual, but feeling low, and glad only at the prospect of getting back to work. But nothing much was happening in the office either, and Gerry plodded through her dreary days, listening to the BBC when she got back to the flat each evening, writing letters to Flixe and Andrew and even her mother, and trying to alter a batch of old clothes she had brought up to London with her so that they would be wearable again. Everyone said that it could be only a matter of weeks before clothes rationing was brought in, and Gerry had been determined to salvage what she could from the wardrobes at her mother's house.

One morning, five days after her return to London, she stormed into the office with an open letter in her hand. Suvarov looked up, mildly surprised at the noise she was making.

'My mother is sending my twin sisters to stay with their godmother for three days before term begins. Can you believe it? They need clothes or something. It's mad at this juncture, but I can't stop it now. According to this, they're arriving this afternoon. Oh, why couldn't she have telephoned? Then I could have explained,' she said as she hung up her gas mask and started to unbutton her thick camel coat.

'She probably tried. Come on, Gerry, you know as well as I that most of the telephone lines were put out of action on the twenty-ninth.'

'Yes, I suppose so. But you'd have thought that reports of the fire storm might have shown her that London's not the place for a couple of schoolgirls who don't have to be there.'

Gerry sat at her desk and began ripping open the envelopes of the day's post, wishing that she had not started the discussion and knowing that her reactions to her mother could never be rational. Striving for a calmer voice, she went on: 'Never mind. I can't do anything to stop it now. Mother wants me to meet them at the station and take them somewhere for a treat this evening while their godmother does her ARP stint.'

She looked across the room at him and smiled

placatingly. 'It would mean leaving here about two-thirty. I wouldn't ask if there was a flap on, or anything.'

'No, that's OK. I should just be able to manage on my own for one Friday afternoon,' answered Suvarov with a smile.

'Thanks.'

By the afternoon she was quite glad to be leaving early even though she was still furious at what she saw as her mother's criminal carelessness in sending the twins into the middle of a city that was still being bombarded if not nightly at least several times each week. Gerry was also irritated at the prospect of the usual frustration of waiting for a train that did not appear on time and finding no one able to say what had happened or when it might come.

But for a miracle the twins' train reached Paddington only about twenty minutes after its advertised time. When they came to the barrier both of them looked expectantly around, each one carrying a small overnight case in her left hand. Annie was wearing her navy uniform overcoat and, with her sandy hair and freckles, looked the very picture of a healthy, hockey-playing schoolgirl. But Ming, looking tired and pallid, was dressed in a pale tweed coat and skirt that had once belonged to Gerry and suited her as little as it suited Ming.

'Twins!' shouted Gerry, waving. 'Here I am. How was the journey? It can't have been too bad since you're here so early.'

'No, not bad at all, Gerry,' answered Annie, who was always the spokesman for the pair of them. 'But Ming felt a bit sick.'

'Are you all right now, though? You do look rather pale.'

'No, I'm all right, Gerry,' said Ming, her voice so much fainter than Annie's that Gerry wondered yet again whether Annie had somehow stolen all the vitality that had been available and left her twin with none.

'Good,' she said bracingly. 'Now, Aunt Anna suggested that we go to the cinema this afternoon, but since the train was so early there's plenty of time to go back to her house to change and leave your bags. She's lent me a key. Shall we go?'

'Yes, please,' answered Annie, picking up her suitcase. 'How is Aunt Anna?'

'Well, I haven't seen much of her – we're all so busy these days – but she sounded very perky on the telephone when I rang her up this morning after I'd heard you were coming. She's firewatching tonight, though. Did she tell you?'

'Mummy did. What does she have to do?'

'Well, in amongst all these beastly bombs Jerry drops things called IBs – incendiary bombs – and if they're spotted in time they can easily be put out, so people like Aunt Anna patrol their key buildings to stop any bad fires from starting.'

Ming shivered and Gerry quickly turned to see if she were all right.

'Don't worry, Ming. Are you afraid? You mustn't be. It's not what we call a bomber's moon tonight; there'll be hardly any moon at all and they don't like that. Sometimes they don't come at all on black nights. And Eaton Gate isn't in the bit of London where the bombs are dropping – it's mostly in the East End, you know. Ah, here we are. Annie, here's half a crown, will you get the tickets? Three to Sloane Square, please.'

Gerry and Ming waited with the luggage, while Annie

queued for the tickets, and then all three of them walked down to the Inner Circle platform, where Annie looked around her.

'But where are the shelterers, Gerry?' she asked in a voice of great disappointment.

'They're further down – on the Bakerloo platform. The Circle is hardly underground at all – it wouldn't protect you from anything.'

'Can we go down and see? Please, Gerry,' wheedled Annie.

Ming turned to her twin sister with a look of such cold disapproval on her face that Gerry was quite startled.

'Really, Annie, how can you?' Ming said. 'How voyeuristic.'

Annie tossed her reddish-fair hair back from her face and shrugged.

'Oh, you've just been listening to that ghastly bolshie you're so fond of.'

'Bolshie?' Gerry repeated, fascinated to see that Ming was beginning to fight back against Annie at last and apparently develop her own character and opinions.

'Oh, Ming has a pash on a wretched woman called Roseheath who's come to teach history. I can't bear her, but she and Ming have a real thing going – it's something chemical between them, I think. Come on, Gerry, whatever Ming thinks, I do want to go and see the shelters.'

'Well all right,' answered Gerry. 'I don't really see why you shouldn't. Do you want to come, Mingie, or will you wait here with the luggage?'

'I'll wait. I don't want to stare at other people's misery,' announced Ming, turning away from both her sisters.

'All right. Don't talk to any strange men,' said Gerry.

She and Annie took the lift down to the Bakerloo platform, where they stood while Annie examined the sheltering families, who were already pitching their camps along the curved wall. A strip of clear platform had been left at the edge so that people could use the tube trains, but the rest was already full of bedding rolls, shopping baskets, picnic food, chatting adults and playing children at half-past three in the afternoon.

'I thought it would smell worse,' said Annie, staring interestedly around at everything there was to see.

'I gather it did at the beginning,' answered Gerry, amused, 'but there are better arrangements for lavs and washing and things now. Someone comes along with carbolic in the mornings when all the families have to clear out.'

'Well, I can't think what Ming was being so sanctimonious about: these people aren't miserable – look at those men playing cards over there under the cocoa advertisement. They all seem quite happy to me.'

'Even so she's quite right, you know, Annie. I mean, think of having to leave your house and not know if it'll still be standing when you get back in the morning, and having to come so early to bag a place, and really give up all normal life.'

'Yes, I suppose so. We'd better get back or Mingie will be thinking we've fallen under a train or got arrested or something. She always expects dreadful disasters to happen.'

'Don't you?' Gerry asked, seeing for the first time that the twins were not as easy to read as she had always imagined; she had seen Ming as Annie's shadow, always doing as she was told; now Gerry began to suspect that Ming was not quite the cipher she had always seemed.

Perhaps in her own way she too exercised a certain power. Gerry decided to try to get to know the twins better – as people, not simply as little sisters to be bossed or protected.

They found Ming safe and unmolested beside the two small suitcases when they got back to the Circle platform, and were soon on a tube train heading for Sloane Square. The twins spent the twenty-minute journey reading the advertisements, most of which were new since their last pre-war London visit: there were the few old faithfuls like the Stephens ink blot and the Amami shampoo advertisement, but there were also 'Careless talk costs lives' posters and Ministry of Food exhortations to eat plenty of potatoes, and pictures of the 'Squander Bug' tempting feckless housewives into extravagance or waste. Gerry sat back listening to her two sisters commenting, arguing and laughing at each other.

When they all got off the train at Sloane Square, Gerry led the way out of the station and round to Eaton Gate. In the hall she found a note addressed to herself and put it in her bag while she took the twins up to their bedrooms. As soon as they had unpacked their overnight cases and Annie had announced that she would be having first bath, Gerry took the envelope into the drawing room.

Dear Gerry [she read], So sorry I can't be with you all this evening, but you'll find everything for supper in the Frigidaire. Please help yourself to a drink – and give one to the twins if they've reached that stage. Here are three tickets to the five o'clock performance of *Gone with the Wind*. You may have seen it, but it looks the most suitable thing for the twins. Take them and I'll be back as soon as I can. Anna.

Smiling at the effortless efficiency, Gerry stuffed the note into her bag and went to pour herself a glass of Anna's always excellent sherry. It was rather early for a drink, but she felt that she deserved one. She took the glass over to one of the yellow chairs, picked up the latest *Spectator* and sat down with it until the twins came back, when she put down the journal and said:

'Look, Aunt Anna said there was food in the fridge. Are you hungry now, or will you wait till we come back from the cinema?'

'We're always hungry. Is there time to have something now? What are we going to see?'

'*Gone with the Wind*, Annie. And yes, there's about half an hour before we need to leave.'

'All right, you sit there and we'll forage and bring you something too.'

Gerry sat back, thinking that it was really very nice to be waited on for once. When the twins came back with a tray loaded with an eccentric mixture of delicacies, they seemed to have forgotten their disagreement about the war and the shelterers, and they began to entertain her with a lot of new jokes and apparently slanderous descriptions of school, the mistresses and their fellow pupils.

'Will you be sad to leave?' she asked at one moment in the taxi on the way to the cinema.

'In a way,' answered Annie, as usual speaking for both of them. 'We take school cert. in the summer, just after our birthday, and then we'll leave.'

'Aren't you going to take Higher?'

'No. We thought we'd get in on the war and then do all that sort of thing later, didn't we, Ming?'

Ming nodded her silvery-blond head and then said:

'I'll miss Rosie, though. She's so sensible. But she thinks it isn't fair on poorer girls to stick it out at school while they're in factories and things.'

'Goodness, this Roseheath of yours sounds very radical.'

'Oh, no, Gerry. And despite Annie's insults, she's not a bolshie. But she has got very sensible ideas, *I* think.'

'That sounded almost like a snort, Annie. Don't you agree?'

'No, I think she's silly. I nearly told Father some of the things she's trying to teach Ming. I know he'd take us away, but it's a bit difficult in letters. I hoped he'd be back this year, but Mother says no.'

'I thought you two always thought the same about everything. Look, here we are. Golly, look at that queue! Isn't Aunt Anna brilliant to have got us tickets?' said Gerry, beginning to think that despite the oddly unattractive sanctimoniousness she had instilled in Ming, this new teacher of hers was doing a lot of good in helping Ming to emerge from Annie's shadow.

Absorbed in her ruminations, Gerry hardly noticed the beginning of the film, but gradually it caught her attention and she laughed and cried as much as her younger sisters. The scenes of Clark Gable's masterful behaviour made her think sentimentally about Andrew, and she began to compose a letter in her mind to make him laugh about it. When the final determined scene faded from the screen and they had stood for the National Anthem, they sat down again in the stalls and waited until the rush was over. Then they made their way out into the street, where, to Gerry's complete astonishment, a taxi with its flag up passed them and she hailed it at once.

'Well, what luck that was,' she said as they sat back all together on the main seat. 'Now, did you enjoy it?'

'Yes; much better than staying at home in spite of the bombs. When do they start, Gerry?'

'Usually about half-past eight, but one can never be quite sure. Anna said she'd try to be back when you get in, but if she isn't you must promise that if the raid starts you will go straight away to the basement. You know, where I showed you.'

'But I thought you said they don't bomb Eaton Gate.'

'It's all right, really, Ming. They never have yet, but it's so much better to be safe than sorry.'

'Yes, of course. Here we are. Good night, Gerry.'

'Good night, twins,' she said, blowing a kiss through the taxi window. 'If you'd just wait until they're safely in and then take me to Dover Street,' she said to the cabby.

She got back to the flat just as the horrible rising and falling wail of the siren started. Paying off the taxi, she ran down the steps to her front door and quickly let herself in, checked the blackout by feel and then switched on the lights. Wondering whether she ought not to have stayed with the twins at least until Anna got home, she took off her coat and hat and changed her shoes.

The evening and night passed as usual with chess and noise and finally sleep, which was broken by the alarm clock at seven o'clock. Gerry dressed, breakfasting as she did so on a slice of bread and cup of tea. Just as she was about to leave the flat, she looked at her watch. There would be time for a quick telephone call to Eaton Gate, she decided, just to double-check that everything was all right with the twins. Telling herself that she was being needlessly anxious, she dialled the number, to be answered by the thin, high humming of a damaged line.

Something's probably happened to the telephone exchange or the wires. They're always going in raids she said to herself in a deliberately calm voice, but three minutes later she was out of the flat and running down past Green Park and Hyde Park Corner, across Belgrave Square and through the tall, white streets to Eaton Gate.

By the time she reached the turning, breathing was agony and she had a dreadful stitch in her side, but she could not let herself stop. Rounding the corner she saw the smoking ruin at once, and saying under her laboured breath, 'No, no. It isn't. Can't be,' she reached the yellow police signs and hailed a young-looking officer.

'What happened? Have you got them out?'

'Look, miss,' he said without even looking at her, 'we've had a major incident here. We can't be doing with sightseers. Please move along.'

'I'm not,' she said in a furious gasp. 'My twin sisters were in that middle house last night. Have you got them out?'

Without producing any apology, he gave her his full attention at last.

'How many people?'

'Just the two of them. They're fifteen. They were alone.'

'The neighbours say the house is owned by a Miss A. Kingsley, who was thought to be out at the time of the incident.'

'Was she? Well thank God she's all right. Where is she?' asked Gerry, but before the officer could reply, she went on again: 'But my sisters were definitely there. Oh, what's happening?'

'Steady on, miss,' he said, putting a heavy hand on her shoulder. 'If they're there, we'll get 'em. Strong houses these, not like down near the Docks.'

'I know,' she began when she heard a cry:

'Gerry, Gerry!' She turned away from the policeman to see Anna Kingsley hobbling across the road, her hair flying out of its pins.

'Anna, thank God,' said Gerry, holding out both her hands. 'Look what's happened. They haven't found anything yet, nor heard. Where were you?'

Anna's hand gripped her waist hard and stopped the incipient hysteria before it even began.

'At the post. It was a bad raid: I've only just got off duty.' She squinted across the road at all that was left of her house and, with quivering lips, but in a voice of enormous detachment, said: 'Direct hit, I see. Well, I expect they are safe in the basement.'

'I'd told them to go straight down when the sirens sounded. Oh, God, I wish I'd stayed with them.'

'Why? So that you could be down there, too? Don't be silly. Listen, Gerry. I'm here now so that when they're brought out I can take care of them. Hadn't you better go to work?'

'Work! Now? Anna, how can I?'

'Gerry, you can't do any good here, and you have responsibilities.'

'No, I can't go. Pe— the people I work for will understand. But I suppose I ought to telephone at least.' She looked around helplessly, as though expecting to see a telephone box.

'There's a kiosk at the corner, there,' said Anna, pointing towards Sloane Square. 'Off you go.'

Gerry obeyed, looking back towards the house every few yards, finding it hard to leave even for a few minutes. When she got to the red telephone box on the corner, she found herself absurdly incompetent, first dialling the number before she had put in any money and then pressing button 'B' instead of 'A'. But she got through to Suvarov in the end and tried to tell him what had happened, but she was stuttering so much that he could not understand her.

'Gerry,' he said with a note of command in his voice.

'Yes,' she said, staring out of the sticky windows of the kiosk.

'What's happened?'

Something in his voice made her able to pull herself together and at last she spoke quite calmly.

'My sisters' godmother's house was hit last night,' she said. 'The twins were there, and though there's still no sign of them the rescuers think it's possible that they could be alive.'

'Gerry, there isn't anything to say except . . . I'm sorry,' said his voice with such warmth that she felt a shred of comfort in her mind. 'Do you want to stay there now?'

'Would you mind?' she asked dismally, her eyes closing. In her fear she longed for her husband with a passion she had not felt since she had said goodbye to him in Palestine.

'Of course not, Gerry,' said Peter. 'You stay there until they've got them out.'

'Thank you, Peter. I'll get back as soon as I can.'

She put down the receiver and left the booth to walk back to Anna's side. Although Gerry recognised that there was nothing she could do to help in the rescue, she could not have left while her sisters were still buried. Four men were digging in the rubble of Anna's house and two to the right of it, and spectators were kept several yards away, helpless behind the yellow barriers.

'Is there . . . do they think there's any hope?' she said to Anna by way of greeting.

'Yes,' answered Anna carefully. 'It seems that it was the

108

Farringdons' house that took the full force and pushed mine down from the side, if you see what I mean. They are probably quite all right, somewhere in there, protected by beams or something.'

'And what about you? Will you be all right standing here? I mean, with your ankle. Shouldn't I try to find you a chair or something?'

'No. I'm all right.'

After another hour, Gerry managed to persuade Anna to sit on the steps of a house opposite her own to take the weight off her plastered ankle, and together they waited, hating the smell of smashed brickwork and drains that hung all round in the heavy, dust-laden air. They watched the rescuers digging long, thin shafts and carrying the debris away in soft baskets. Every so often the leader would yell for silence and everyone would strain forward even though only the people down in the trench would have been able to hear anything. The light started to fade soon after four and Gerry was desperate at the idea that the men might have to knock off so soon. The only torches they were allowed to use were quite inadequate.

She peered forward into the gloom. From the debris that the men were throwing out of their way – Anna's delicate porcelain vases and the remains of some of her rugs and pictures – it seemed that they had reached where the ground floor had been. It could not be much longer. She looked up, cursing the short winter days and the blackout and the Germans, and her mother for allowing the twins to come to London. Gerry must have spoken aloud, for she felt Anna's thin hand on her wrist.

'Don't, Gerry. They had to get some clothes. And we all thought this part was safe – and God knows when it's all going to end. You can't just shut off your life because of the Germans. That makes them the winners.' Her hand tightened convulsively. 'Look, they've found something.' Breathless, Gerry watched as two of the men appeared climbing over the rubble with a limp, grey bundle between them. The waiting First Aid people sprang forward as the body was laid gently on to a waiting stretcher.

'They must let us through now,' said Gerry and went forward. No one stopped her and as she stood over the stretcher, one of the nurses said:

'Can you identify her?'

For a horrible moment, Gerry thought she might not be able to. The body was so covered with dust and scratches that it could have been either of the twins. Then the pale girl opened her dark-blue eyes and Gerry saw that it was Ming. She knelt down on the road beside the stretcher and took Ming's scraped and filthy hand in hers.

'Ming, dearest, you're out now.'

'Gerry, where's Annie?'

'They're getting her out now. Was she near you, sweetie?'

'Yes, but I think she'd fainted. She wasn't talking at the end. I couldn't see her, but at the beginning she talked to me.' Ming began to cough, desperately, as though something was tearing inside her chest. The nurse pushed Gerry out of the way, murmuring to her:

'It's the dust. You can't do anything now. We'll take her to St George's. Call round first thing tomorrow and they'll let you know how she's getting on.'

Gerry moved back and called to the men in blue dungarees who were back at their task.

'She says our sister was quite near her, but she couldn't see her.'

'OK, miss. We're trying.'

110

Don't stop, don't stop, whispered Gerry to herself.

They did not, but it was almost completely dark when one of them called:

'We've got her.'

'Thank God,' said Gerry, but Anna said:

'Wait, Gerry. It doesn't look too good.' Together they walked towards the ring of men who were now standing looking down at the body at their feet, barely illuminated by their dimmed torches. Gerry joined them, and did not need anyone to tell her that her sister was dead. There was a great, gaping wound in Annie's skull, but the blood had dried a long time ago; and the skin of her face was waxy and somehow shrunk against the bones of her cheeks and eye sockets.

Gerry turned away and Anna Kingsley was there, opening her arms and calling gently:

'Gerry, come here, child.' Gerry went and let herself lean against Anna's shoulder. Just before Anna's hands closed about her head, she heard one of the Heavy Rescue men say to his mate:

'They should 'a' stayed in bed. Look at them beds: 'ardly touched, they isn't. They'd 'a' been all right if they'd 'a' stayed in bed.'

Later, when she could think and speak without shaking, Gerry looked at Anna, trying for the moment to shut out what had happened and to suppress her pathetic desire for Andrew suddenly and miraculously to appear and take charge.

'Anna, what about getting you a hotel room?' Gerry asked, trying to do the things that Andrew would have done if he had been there. 'I'm sure you shouldn't stand about on that ankle any more. Or do you want to come back to Dover Street? Presumably Jeremy Oldridge has a

111

spare bed.'

'Yes he has, but I'd rather go to the Hyde Park. Don't fret about me, Gerry. You go on home and have something hot to eat. Would you like me to try to get Fanny on the telephone and tell her?'

'Would you, Anna? I've been dreading it. I should have done it before, but couldn't bear to worry her before we knew . . . ' Gerry's voice wobbled, and she turned away for a moment to regain control of herself. 'I'll talk to her as soon as I can, of course I will, but if you tell her first . . . And I'll have to try to get Flixe. I wish to God I knew where she was.'

'Don't think about any of it now. Go home, do yourself a hot bottle and have something to eat and go to bed. Go on, Gerry, I'll ring you up tomorrow, and we'll go and see Ming. The ambulancewoman said we wouldn't be allowed to see her today.'

Gerry obeyed, almost too tired to protest, and walked with painful slowness back to Dover Street. She had not had time to go shopping recently to queue for food and all she had in the flat was a bit of hard cheese and two eggs. She was not at all hungry, but recognised the sense of Anna's instructions and was thinking about turning the eggs into an omelette when there was a knock at the door.

It seemed rather early for Jeremy Oldridge, but she shrugged and went to open it. There stood Suvarov in his uniform.

'May I come in, Gerry?'

'Of course.'

'Is there any news?'

'They've got them out now. One, Mary, is in hospital.'

'And Annie?'

Gerry just shook her head.

112

'I am very sorry. How is Ming?'

Gerry had forgotten the evening when she had told him all about her family and was surprised that he knew the nickname. But she felt too tired and mangled to say anything about it.

'Coughing desperately when I last saw her and very anxious for Annie. They took her off to St George's. I don't know what'll happen when she hears that Annie is dead. They're twins, you know . . . were twins, I mean.'

'I know. You told me. Gerry, don't you think you – we – should go to the hospital now and tell her, before some well-meaning voluntary worker does?'

It was not the moment to protest that she was tired, but she could hardly stop the instinctive groan that rose to her lips. She had had about four hours' sleep the night before and had spent most of the day on her feet in torturing anxiety. But he was right. Without speaking, she put the eggs and cheese back under the little meat safe and picked up her coat.

'Gas mask, Gerry.'

'Oh, they're not going to drop gas. They don't need to, do they? IBs and HEs do plenty – what'd gas do that they don't?' He just looked at her and picked up the khaki canvas bag himself, slung it over his shoulder with his own and took her elbow.

He did not speak as they walked down Piccadilly towards Hyde Park Corner and Gerry was grateful for his silence. When they reached the big, dirty-white building that housed the hospital, Peter Suvarov led the way up the shallow steps into the pedimented entrance, turning to ask:

'Which ward, Gerry?'

'I don't know. I last saw her in the road – on a stretcher. I

115

should have asked . . . '

'Don't worry. Sister!'

A harassed, thin, dark-haired nurse took two steps towards them.

'Yes, what is it?'

'Female casualties from Eaton Gate?'

'Nightingale Ward, second on the left, third floor.'

'Thank you.'

Surprised by his efficiency, but a little repelled by it, too, Gerry walked up the steep stone stairs in his wake. When they reached the ward he pushed open one of the swing doors and gestured for her to precede him. She went in and walked slowly down the long rows of white-sheeted patients, searching for her sister. But it was Suvarov who found her and who pulled up two chairs.

Ming was lying there so pale that it was hard to believe that she was not dead too. Suvarov took one of her limp, scratched hands, between his and said:

'Mary, here is Gerry with something to tell you.'

He nodded furiously to Gerry as she fumbled with the words and she made herself speak very simply to tell Ming that her twin was dead. Then Gerry sat down on the second chair and watched her chief stroke the hand he held and once lay one of his hands on Ming's forehead and then wipe away the tears that seeped out from under her closed eyelids. He said nothing for at least five minutes and then very gently began to talk. Gerry had never heard his voice sound so warm; it was as though the sounds carried their own consolation quite divorced from the sense of the words he spoke.

As she listened she began to learn for the first time something of his life. He, too, had had a twin, it seemed, and lost him when they were only a few years older than

114

Ming herself. No one who had not had a twin could understand what it felt like to be the one left behind, anguished by the thoughts of how you should have saved your twin, knowing that whatever happened in the years to come, whoever came to love you or be loved by you, you would always be lonely, hurting in the place where your twin should have been joined to you.

At first Gerry listened in horror, wondering what he could be doing to thrust his own sadness on to poor little Ming, who had so much of her own to deal with. But gradually Gerry understood that he was trying to bring her sister back into the daylight where fears and feelings could be spoken about and to reassure her that she was not alone, that other people had felt what she was feeling and survived. Moved nearly to tears both by his care for her sister and by the thought of the unassuageable loneliness he described, Gerry watched Ming listen, a faint colour coming back into her pearl-pale cheeks. Then she began to talk in her turn.

After a little Gerry could not bear to listen and, murmuring something about finding some water for Ming who was still coughing between each sentence, got up and moved out of earshot. Her respect for Peter Suvarov had always been firm, but that he could sit and listen to all that raw pain without saying anything to try to quieten it made her think of him with awe. He did not even try to say anything to soothe Ming as she struggled with the dust in her lungs and throat; he just sat, his hand on hers, taking into himself all the terrible things she wanted to say.

8

Ming was to be released five days later, by which time her sister would have been buried. Gerry was just beginning to panic about how she was going to organise a funeral when Anna Kingsley told her that she would make all the arrangements, as well as telling Fanny Alderbrook what had happened. It was clearly impossible to take the body down to Gloucestershire and so the burial was arranged for three days after the incident in one of the huge London cemeteries. Gerry, trying desperately to track down Felicity, assumed that their mother would come up for it, but Anna told her that too would be impossible. For a time it seemed as though there would be only the two of them at Annie's graveside.

But after several abortive and frustrating telephone calls, Gerry managed to get hold of Felicity and told her about the bomb and what it had done to the twins. After the first shocked silence, Flixe promised to be at the cemetery in good time and then said:

'But how's Ming? Is she very bad?'

'Not too awful, Flixe. The hospital say that she can come out the day after tomorrow. They've assured me that there's nothing physically wrong with Ming, but the shock of the explosion, let alone being buried for all those hours and hearing her twin die just out of reach, has weakened her badly. She's coughing a lot, but that'll soon cure itself, apparently, as all the wood and brick dust she swallowed is spat out of her lungs.'

'Poor little creature. And is she desperate about Annie? It's hard to think of them separated . . . '

'I know, and yes, she is. Oh, Flixe . . . No, we can't talk now. And I ought to ring Mother to tell her about Ming. See you tomorrow.'

'Yes. 'Bye.'

As soon as she had put down the receiver, Gerry asked for her mother's number to pass on the hospital's verdict. It was impossible to tell how Fanny Alderbrook was taking the news of Annie's death for it was not in her code either to weep or to say anything revealing in her daughter's hearing. When Gerry said that she and Flixe would encourage Ming to go home as soon as she was released from the hospital, her mother said:

'No, Gerry, please do keep her with you until she really is strong enough. My three evacuees have arrived here and quite apart from their turning the place into something like a madhouse, they probably have all kinds of infections, as well as nits. Poor little Ming ought not to be exposed to them until she is really fit.'

'Evacuees, Mother? You?'

'Don't sound so surprised, Gerry. You're not the only one who wanted to do her bit, you know. I couldn't possibly have accepted any at the beginning of the war when you were so ill, but now that my time – and the house – is my own . . . I'd arranged their arrival so carefully for when the twins . . . ' Her voice threatened to

117

break, but she rallied. 'For when the twins' term had begun.'

'But how do you manage? Aren't they the most fearful nuisance?'

Gerry thought she could almost hear a smile in her mother's voice when she answered:

'Noisy, of course, and very rumbustious, but I think once they've got over their homesickness we'll get on quite well.'

'Where did they come from?' asked her daughter, wondering whether her mother had hit on one of the few middle-class families who had agreed to evacuate their children.

'Stepney. Oh, Gerry, I must go. It's three minutes. Thank you for telling me about Ming. Give her my love. Goodbye.'

Gerry was left to stare at the black Bakelite receiver in her hand and wonder how her mother really was. Her voice had been strained and there had been that one moment when she sounded distressed, but Gerry wished that her mother might have managed to say something about Annie. Gerry rubbed the back of her hand across her eyes, which suddenly felt hot and tight, and blessed Anna Kingsley for being there, for doing and being all the things an ideal mother would have done and been. She had made all the arrangements for the funeral and had promised to house Ming when she was let out of the hospital.

Anna had left the Hyde Park Hotel within two days of the bomb and moved into the ground and first-floor flat in Dover Street. When she was not sitting at Ming's bedside or talking to the undertakers, she spent her time buying furniture and searching the ruins of Eaton Gate for anything she could salvage from the wreckage of her home before the looters picked it clean. It slowly dawned on Gerry how much the loss of her house must have added to Anna's unhappiness at her god-daughter's death. Not only had the Eaton Gate house been a refuge for Anna, but she had filled it with the furniture, paintings and books she had collected over nearly thirty years. There must have been memories locked up within its walls that now seemed fragile and fugitive. As Gerry thought about how Anna must be feeling, for the first time she began to wonder about her as a person rather than simply as an old friend of the family and a substitute mother.

Anna Kingsley's apparently perfect life began to look less perfect as Gerry examined it more closely. Anna had buckets of money, of course, and a host of friends and acquaintances, but no family that Gerry was aware of; and the only real friend, as opposed to the people she dined with, seemed to be Jeremy Oldridge, at least twenty years her junior. It was all very well for Anna to explain to Gerry that she allowed no one to have any claims on her so that she could be free to give wherever she wanted, but might that not leave her a bit like the Miller of Dee? If Gerry had not come to live in London, who would Anna have been able to ask to stand in for her at the ARP post that night before Christmas?

Gerry knew that this horrible time was not a suitable moment to explore the conundrum Anna presented, but as they sat side by side, waiting for the unknown vicar to begin his funeral service, Gerry did find that thinking about it helped her to deal with the frightening abysses of her own feelings. Someone pushed into the pew beside her and she looked round to see Felicity, wearing her best black hat. They smiled sadly at each other and then stood up as they saw the vicar coming towards them.

Apart from the wonderful, sonorous words, the service was bleak, and it seemed to Gerry to be somehow absurd that the three of them should be trying to mourn her lively and forthright sister alone in that dusty, echoing church. Together with Anna and Flixe, Gerry stood and knelt in the appropriate places, murmured the correct responses, and tried not to look across the aisle at Annie's plain, sad coffin.

When it was all over, there was not really anything to be said and the three of them stood oddly embarrassed in the ugly Victorian church as the busy vicar shook their hands and murmured consolatory phrases that seemed to have no meaning. When he had left them alone, Flixe announced that she had come to the cemetery in a small truck borrowed from her chief and offered them both a lift back into the middle of London. Anna Kingsley declined without giving any reason and walked quickly away, leaving the two sisters to look at each other in puzzlement. After a minute or two, Flixe said:

'Gerry, you look pretty awful. What's up?'

'Besides Annie and poor Ming? Nothing in comparison. But I sometimes think that if only I weren't so bloody tired, I'd be able to cope better.'

'Yes,' answered Flixe with unwonted seriousness, 'the lack of sleep does make it hard to keep a sense of proportion about one's difficulties and decisions.'

Gerry was surprised to hear that Flixe, who had always seemed to take life so lightly, should have any difficulties, but she said nothing as they settled themselves in the canvas bucket seats of Flixe's small dark-green truck. A little later, when they were some way from the miserably depressing graveyard, Flixe broke the silence.

'Isn't it ironic? Both you and I are involved in this war and around London every night.' She stopped and then qualified her words: 'At least you are and I quite often am, and we're OK, but two schoolgirls who come here for three nights have to cop it like that. People like Andrew and Father, regular soldiers, actually fighting at the moment, are all right; but Annie's killed. Where's the justice in that?'

'God knows. It's so unfair that she never had a chance – a few years at school and that's all – never fell in love; never discovered what she was like; never tasted . . . ' Gerry found that she could not go on and turned her head away from Felicity. Then, in a choked voice, she said: 'Look, Flixe, the pigs have got St James's – that lovely church.'

Felicity did not even look.

'I know. I went round it this morning with my new chief. The worst was standing beside the hole where the Rectory was; it's still smoking, black and smelly, and then you lift your eyes and see that perfect gilded ceiling half smashed, all the windows blown out and the whole lovely thing ripped open to the filth and the rain and all the looters who care to pick their way over the wreckage.'

Gerry hardly listened; she was curious that the insouciant Felicity should mind about something so impersonal as the architecture of a London church, but even more to know about her new job.

'You mean you've left the Fanys?'

'Yes, I wasn't getting anywhere – or helping the war. Anyone could have driven those generals . . . they could have driven themselves for that matter. Endless wasted time. I wanted to do something I could get my teeth into.'

'Architecture,' commented Gerry. There was no discernible expression in her voice, but Flixe knew her well enough to understand.

'Yes, you're right of course, old thing,' she said in a far more generous admission of her own inconsistency than Gerry could ever have made. 'But even though it's not helping the war effort, at least it's going to help to make post-war England more . . . well, better anyway. And it uses my brains, which chauffeuring never did.'

'So what do you actually do with the buildings?' Not only was Gerry relieved to be able to think and talk about something other than their dead sister, but she was curious about this new side to Flixe, who had always seemed quite happy with the horses, clothes, young men and dances that had made up her life before the war.

'We get them properly surveyed so that the committee can decide what immediate structural repairs to do: we organise the removal of things like special painted ceilings, carvings, stained glass and so on, to safe places so they don't get even more damaged by the weather, vandals and looters, and generally keep proper records of what's going on where and how much it's going to cost to put right.'

'None of that sounds like you, Flixe. You're not pulling a fast one are you?'

'Gerry! Your language is getting as sloppy as mine. I suppose it's all those boys you work with.'

'Yes, probably. But come on, Flixe, give.'

The blond head shook, but Gerry thought that there was a gleam of the old mischief in her sister's deep-amethyst eyes. She was about to press further when it dawned on her that if Flixe was being so evasive then there must be a good, official reason, in which case it ill behoved Gerry of all people to push her into indiscretion.

'I promised to get back to my office and it might be quicker to walk from here,' she said instead.

Flixe took a quick look at her sister out of the corner of her eye and grinned.

'You mean you're not supposed to let me know where you work. Don't worry, old thing. I'll drop you somewhere discreet. Where would you like?'

'Thanks, Flixe. The other side of St James's would be marvellous.'

'OK; then I'm going to see Mingie at St George's.'

'Oh, good. I say, Flixe, does your job ever take you into the country?'

'No. We're only concerned with London. Why?'

'They're going to let her out tomorrow, and Anna's going to have her to stay for a bit, but I do think she ought to get home as soon as possible. Yet she's hardly fit to tackle a train journey yet. She ought to get out of London, not least because it might happen again. She won't be going back to school for a bit, of course, but I thought you might be able to drive her home.'

'Not a chance, I'm afraid. But I'll ask around in case anyone else is going.'

'Thanks. If you're based here now, I'll see more of you. Good,' said Gerry, thinking that if they had some time she might be able to talk to Flixe about her muddled mind and clear it a bit.

'Here we are. Hop out. See you soon, old thing.'

Felicity waved cheerfully and drove off. Only then did it dawn on Gerry that her sister was no longer in uniform. More and more she wondered what Flixe was up to. When she reached the office she shared with Suvarov, he said:

'How's your sister?'

'Rather perky . . . apart from missing Annie, I mean. She says she's got a job with an architect or something.'

'I mean Ming,' he said drily and Gerry felt herself blushing.

'Very weepy, as you'd expect, and dreadfully quiet. She really ought to get out of London, but can't face the thought of the journey on her own. I thought Anna Kingsley might have offered to take her down to Gloucestershire, but she hasn't and I can't demand it when she's done so much for all of us . . . and anyway she herself must be in a bad state about losing her house.'

'I've got to go and see some people of Bob's next weekend. Shall I take her in the official car?' Gerry turned round from the coat rack where she was hanging her hat, her face alight with grateful eagerness.

'Peter, would you? I can't think of anything better. You were angelic to her that day in the hospital and I know she trusts you absolutely.' For a moment he was silent, staring at Gerry with an expression she could not understand. She wondered if she had revolted him with her enthusiasm; but surely in a matter like this one did not have to pretend that one did not care? It wasn't as though she had been gushing about something that did not matter. He carefully aligned the pencils that were ranged in front of whatever it was he was working on, and said in a distant voice:

'That's settled then. I'll ring her up if you'll give me the number sometime and fix it with her.'

'Thank you, Peter,' answered Gerry, trying to sound as subdued as he did. Then she wrote the number on a corner of scrap paper and gave it to him.

'Thanks. Gerry, this report here about the trade links with Vichy. I know you rewrote it, but did you add anything?'

Searching her conscience, Gerry at last shook her head.

'No, I'm sure that all the facts and inferences were Mike's. I just put it in that order and straightened out some of the sentences. But I suppose it's possible that I've misinterpreted something he'd written. What's the problem?'

'It's these anti-Gaullist businessmen over here.'

'Yes, they did sound sinister, didn't they? But there's not much they can do to the Free French. I mean, it seemed from Mike's report that they're only writing and saying bitchy things about de Gaulle's people; they haven't any power to do anything to them.'

'No,' he said, drawing out the long vowel. 'But didn't you notice that the English people they've latched on to are already on our books, so to speak? Don't blush – you've had your own problems to deal with and you're not expected to be an analyst. Look, get Mike up here, would you? In about fifteen minutes.'

'Of course, Peter. I'm sorry.'

'Off with you.'

Gerry was quite glad to have an excuse to escape downstairs. She found it quite exhausting to be worrying all the time about what Suvarov was feeling and thinking. It had been bad enough in the days when she was just desperately anxious to get through the work in time and not annoy him by sloppiness or misunderstanding an order. But now, when she searched his dark eyes for signs of unhappiness, dissatisfaction, anger, or boredom, and worried about the mornings when his face looked as though all the colour had been washed out of it, she felt as though her every word or expression mattered and might be wrong. And she was ashamed of herself for feeling so.

The analysts greeted her with less than their usual ribaldry and she relaxed into their unspoken sympathy. They had none of them said much to her about what had happened to her sisters, but all of them had found ways to make it clear that they sympathised with her. Like Gerry, all of them had left the office every night since the Blitz began with the thought somewhere in their minds that they might arrive the next morning to find one of their friends or colleagues dead or injured.

Eynsham touched her shoulder when she walked past him as he was standing by Sandy's desk.

'All right, Gerry?' he said kindly.

She smiled and nodded. 'Well enough, thanks, Tony.' Then she turned to Mike. She was relieved to see that he was looking quite peaceful and healthy for once and thought that she might escape the effects of his ill-temper when she passed on Suvarov's request.

'Mike, the Chief wants to see you in about quarter of an hour.'

'Aha, Mike, how 'ave you overstepped the boundaries this time?' called one of the two French boys who sat together between the long windows.

'Shut up, Philippe, there's a good chap,' said Mike easily enough. 'Gerry, what's up? Have I transgressed?'

'No,' she began and was interrupted by the Scot.

'What is it about us all that we skirt round the Chief like a bunch of schoolgirls?'

'It's all right for you, Sandy. You're a phlegmatic Scot. But he's a damn frightening fellow – comes of being a foreigner, I suppose. All that storming the Winter Palace in 1917 or whatever it was he did when he was eighteen.'

'But, Mike, you don't mean that he's a Communist, do you?' asked Gerry, genuinely horrified at the prospect,

126

but remembering for the first time how Peter had hinted at Communist sympathies the afternoon when he had said that he was too busy to explain it all to her. They all laughed at her, but for once the laughter had a kindly sound to it. Sandy produced the answer for them all.

'D'you really think that the various governments of this island would have employed him for the past twenty years or so if he had been? He was a Bolshevik, we understand, in the dark days of the revolution, but once he got here he saw the error of his ways, we believe. It's all been kept rather dark, but somehow he must have persuaded the interested parties that he could be useful to them.'

'And perhaps he bought his way in with information,' suggested Mike. 'I don't know anyone who admits to having the whole story, but I have heard suggestions that Suvarov was pretty close to a lot of the top chaps in 1917. If it's true, he could have been pretty valuable to the FO.'

Gerry, finding it hard to come to terms with the idea that Suvarov, idealised and admired as he was, could have been something that she had been brought up to loathe and fear, thought that she had better change the subject.

'I see. Look, you lot, will someone explain to me what's really happening in France at the moment? I don't think I've grasped it properly yet.'

'Why do you want to know?' asked Michel, his thin, white face hardening.

'Just because when I translate your reports into the kind of English that Suvarov and the Chiefs of Staff can understand, I may be making ghastly mistakes simply because I don't know enough of the background to make sense of some of the points you make.'

'That's fair enough, Michel,' said Sandy. 'You'd better start.'

'OK, Gerry,' he began, but stopped as soon as he saw the door opening. Madge came in rattling the tea trolley and handed slopped cups to all the British. When she had gone, he started again: 'How you can all drink that filthy stuff I can't imagine.'

'Never mind, Michel. Start the lesson in International Relations and the Fall of France.'

'Well, Gerry, you know that after the British had evacuated their army from Dunkirk . . .'

'And a hell of a lot of yours,' chipped in Mike, his voice sounding bitter as aloes once more. 'And there'd have been even more if your government had not stopped us taking your people off earlier. Churchill said that it was to be equal numbers. If you're planning to lighten the Stygian darkness of poor Gerry's abysmal ignorance, you might at least be accurate.'

Even though she had had plenty of time to become accustomed to Mike's attitude to her, Gerry still could not absorb remarks like that without hurt. Silently, she turned to go, knowing from experience that it was better to ignore Mike than try to explain herself. Before she reached the door, she heard Eynsham's gentle voice.

'Gerry, have you a minute? I've a paper in my office I need to redraft.'

'Oh, certainly, Tony,' she said, keeping her back to them all. 'Now?'

'If you can manage it,' he said, catching up with her. He opened the door and ushered her out into the passage. When they reached his little room, he made her sit down and gave her a cigarette.

'You mustn't take old Mike too seriously, you know,' he

said gently.

'Oh, I know it's silly of me,' she answered. 'But it just gets on top of me when day after day he goes on about how ignorant I am, and stupid, and useless.'

'I'd begun to think he was hurting you, Gerry, so I'm going to break one of Suvarov's most stringent rules. You need to know about Mike. He's very unhappy.'

'Aren't we all in one way or another? I don't see why that should excuse the sort of treatment he hands out,' Gerry said, thinking of Annie lying dead in the wreckage of Eaton Gate and of Andrew so far away from her.

'No need to be waspish, Gerry. Mike was blown up at Dunkirk and quite apart from the fact that I think he's often in considerable physical pain, there's desperate anxiety – and guilt, too.'

Gerry had been about to make some conventional and meaningless comment of sympathy, but something in Eynsham's soft brown eyes stopped her.

'Why guilt?'

'Because he was rescued from the wreck of the ship he'd served on, he saw the men who had to be left on the beaches.' Gerry opened her mouth, but Eynsham forestalled her. 'One of them was his brother, Gerry; his younger brother. The boy seemed to have been wounded; he was crying; and he screamed for Mike to come and get him. The men who had rescued Mike had to hold him down on the deck to stop him jumping back into the sea.'

'Oh, dear God.'

'Yes, I imagine Mike hears those screams rather often.'

With her own feelings of responsibility for Annie churning through the grief in her mind, Gerry felt that she could really understand what Mike Endlesham must have been going through.

'Poor man,' she said with real compassion. 'How ghastly. Do they know where the boy is now?'

'Yes. One of the Oflags. The wound was not particularly severe, and he's thought to be fine now . . . '

'But over there. No wonder Mike gets so upset when Michel goes on and on about Dunkirk. Why hasn't he been told? I know he's French, but surely he wouldn't tease Mike if he knew.'

'Being French hasn't much to do with it,' said Eynsham with a smile. When he saw that Gerry was not laughing, he went on quickly: 'No, I know that's not what you meant. I agree with you, but Suvarov believes in every man's inalienable right to keep his private miseries to himself. He also believes that Mike's quite capable of telling Michel if he wants him to know. The last thing Suvarov would ever do would be to deny to his subordinates something he guards so jealously for himself.'

'I suppose so,' said Gerry slowly, stubbing her half-smoked cigarette out in the ashtray. 'And I quite see that you'd never go behind his back . . . So why have you told me?'

Eynsham smiled kindly at her through a cloud of smoke.

'Because Mike's behaviour was hurting you. Because I think he needs the kind of help a girl like you could give him. Because I trust your discretion. I think that about wraps it up.'

'Thank you, Antoine. My discretion sometimes gets a little threadbare, but I'll stick to it . . .'

'Yes, do. Peter can be . . . unpleasant when he's angry.'

So you love him, too, thought Gerry as she looked at the homely face and gentle brown eyes of the American academic. Eynsham wondered why she suddenly blushed.

9

On Thursday evening as Gerry was getting ready to leave the office Suvarov looked up from his papers.

'Don't forget to bring your bag in tomorrow morning — as it's an official car we oughtn't to make a detour to pick it up, and I don't suppose Ming could carry hers as well as yours.'

'You mean . . . you want me to come as well?' said Gerry as though in a daze.

His lined face seemed somehow smoothed as his mouth twisted into a kind of smile and his long dark eyes narrowed at the corners.

'I can't do without my assistant, Gerry. I know it means working on Sunday, but it's important. Bob's my only contact with the Americans, and we need to know what they're up to with Vichy.'

'But they're not part of the war,' said Gerry, forgetting for a welcome moment all the tricky tangle of feelings and constraints that seemed to absorb so much of her energy in those days.

'Not yet, but it can't be long now. But Gerry, would you mind staying at Evelyn's? It's going to be hard work

131

and I shall need you where I can get at you quickly. You don't mind not staying with your mother?'

At that she laughed.

'If you knew how much of my girlhood I spent wishing that I lived with the Adamsons! It's such a gorgeous house; and it's so easy to be there, no fuss.'

'Yes, it's strange how Bob has taught Evelyn to mellow.' It was so unlike Suvarov to gossip that Gerry could not think how to answer him and so she just waited. 'She used to be so – so tense and spiky.' Another pause followed, which Gerry eventually felt she had to break.

'Was that in Russia?' Suvarov came to with a bump.

'That's right, but I mustn't waste any more time. Off with you.'

She stood by the door looking back at him, his silvered dark head outlined by the small circle of light from his small brass reading lamp. She pulled at her courage.

'Peter, I've some more steak in the flat. Would you like to dine later?'

'Gerry, that is kind, but I mustn't. There is just too much to be done. Good night.'

It was dismissal. She obeyed, feeling stupid and wishing that she had never invited him. Obviously the friendly warmth of the one evening they had spent, when he had been relaxed enough to fall asleep in her chair, was to be ignored, forgotten. Acknowledging Andrew's legitimate claims on her, she told herself that that was just as well as she put her head round the analysts' door to wave to the few who were still working. But it would have been easier to keep her husband at the front of her mind if he were not so far away. And it would be easier to think of him with more of the old love if she could only straighten out with him the real reasons for his refusal to let her join the WRNS. Her work in RE(1)R was much more congenial to her than what she had heard of life in the lower echelons of the women's services, but that was not the point, and try as she might she could not get rid of a nasty taste in her mouth whenever she thought of Andrew's apparent selfishness, in spite of the fact that she missed him more and more each week.

When she reached her flat she ignored the steaks in favour of looking through her clothes to decide what would be most suitable for the weekend. Trying to choose between the practicality of trousers, which she knew that Evelyn did not mind, and a more conventional country coat and skirt she had had made before the war from pale greenish-blue tweed, it occurred to her that she had not spent so much time on such things for months. Perhaps it was when her mother had been buying her trousseau that she had last cared about clothes as anything more than providers of warmth and comfort. Andrew's lack of interest in any aspect of her appearance except tidiness and convention had started to kill off her own pleasure in the things she wore and then the miscarriage and long, dismal convalescence had completed the process.

She tried on the trousers but, deciding that they really were not very becoming, put on the tweed skirt instead. Its pre-war pleats hung well and swung luxuriously as she turned in front of the long looking-glass Anna Kingsley had lent her. But if she wore the jacket, most of the effect would be lost. Rummaging in her bottom drawer, she came up with a soft cashmere jersey in an unusual petrol colour. She pulled it on over her ecru crêpe-de-chine petticoat and smoothed it over her waist and slim hips. That was much better. That would do.

133

Getting back into the clothes she had worn all day in the office, she went up to see Ming, who was staying with Anna Kingsley in the empty flat on the first floor, which Jeremy Oldridge had persuaded her to rent until she decided what she was going to do about a new house.

Suvarov wanted to leave London by three the following afternoon, in order to get most of the way to Gloucestershire before dark, and the journey was the usual mixture of frustration and boredom. At one moment Ming said in her quiet voice, which seemed to have become even thinner and gentler since the bomb:

'I thought people weren't supposed to go on journeys if they didn't have to, but this is just as bad as pre-war Fridays.'

'You're quite right, Ming,' answered Suvarov seriously, 'but nothing will stop them while they have the petrol. Once it's rationed all this will be over.'

'Are they going to ration it?' asked Gerry.

'Think, Gerry,' he said in a voice quite different from the one he used to speak to Ming, 'they'll have to; and more categories of food and clothes and everything else. I don't know how many tons of shipping have been lost so far, but it must run into tens – even hundreds – of thousands. It is just not going to be possible to supply this population with all its imported luxuries at the pre-war levels.'

'You sound quite abrasive, Peter. Do you have something against "this population"?' Gerry could hear a certain acerbity in her own voice, but could not suppress it as she thought of the analysts' discussion of his political preferences.

'No, of course not, but a lot of people do not seem to understand that there's a war on.'

134

'I think everyone in London must,' said Ming and the other two were silent.

After nearly three and a half hours the blunt-nosed black car turned into the short drive of the Alderbrooks' house. Gerry opened the car door as though to get out, but Suvarov put a hand on her arm.

'It's all right, Gerry, I'll take Ming in. You just stay here.'

She sank back against the worn leather of the seat, wondering how he had known just how much she dreaded going into the house, and grateful that he should bother about her feelings, particularly after their small, mainly unspoken disagreement. Even she had not expected the tightening lurch of dismay as she saw the house lit up by the car's half-shuttered headlights; the ugliness of its proportions, the atmosphere of disapproval and striving she felt she could almost touch made her shudder. She lay back against the seat and closed her eyes, waiting for Suvarov to come back and take her to that other house, where everything was simple and where the atmosphere was of luxurious untidiness and un-threatened tolerance.

He spent nearly a quarter of an hour with her mother, but when he came back into the car all he said was:

'Well that's that. I think Ming was pleased to be back. She hugged your mother, anyway.'

'Isn't it odd? The younger two never seemed to have quite the problems Flixe and I had. They don't mind going back.'

'Did you at their age?'

'I can't really remember. I thought I did, but perhaps my memory's faulty. Now, tell me who it is we're meeting this weekend?'

He shook his head and looked at the strong back of the official chauffeur. Gerry winced at her indiscretion and tried to cover it, speaking in a chatty, social tone:

'Evelyn always has such interesting guests.'

'Yes, doesn't she? I'll never forget that day when you arrived in your breeches and muddy boots,' he contributed. 'I had never seen anyone so tense melt as you did that day. I asked Bob all about you, you know.'

'Did you, Peter? And what did he tell you?'

'Oh, lots of things, but the one that interested me most was when he said that you were the brightest thing he'd met in England and the most wasted.'

'He did? Golly, I wonder where he got that idea,' said Gerry, embarrassed as she had never yet been in his company. 'I hope you haven't been too dreadfully disappointed.' She felt Suvarov's thin hand on her wrist, just above her brown leather glove.

'Gerry, you have never disappointed me.'

The car turned into the drive of the Adamsons' house then, and Gerry concentrated on the way the stone lions lit up in the swinging swathe of light, hoping that that might curb her confusion. But she could feel that she was still blushing as she preceded Peter into the hall. There was no one there and from behind her he called out:

'Evelyn, *duschinka*, we're here.'

'Oh, Piotr,' called her voice from upstairs. Then Gerry saw her at the top of the broad, shallow stairs. She came running down to fling her arms around Suvarov's neck. ' "*Duschinka*"! I haven't heard you say that for years. How are you?'

'Fine. Tired, though. We both are.' Evelyn stepped back and held out her hands to Gerry.

'I'm sure you are. Come on up, Gerry; dinner's not for

an hour so you'll have a chance to rest a while. Peter, what about your driver?'

'Don't worry, Eve. He's going on to Stroud. He'll pick us up again on Sunday afternoon. I'll see you later, Gerry.'

She turned from the second stair to smile at him and did not see Evelyn's shrewd brown eyes narrowing as she looked at them both. She did not comment but insisted on carrying Gerry's small suitcase upstairs.

'Gerry, I hope you don't mind, but I've had to put you right upstairs. Since you know the house and all the others don't it seemed more sensible.'

'Yes of course – anyway I love those rooms with their windows in the roof. Please don't worry. Evelyn . . . ' Then she stopped.

'Yes. Is something bothering you? I mean something apart from Annie? Gerry, I was so sorry when I heard the news.' Gerry turned impulsively and Evelyn noticed how the girl had recovered most of the prettiness she had lost during her illness, despite the recent tragedy.

'Heavens no. It's just that: Annie, and what the dreadful business has done to Ming. And missing Andrew; being a bit lonely in London. It's so wonderful to be here. There's so much I want to ask you, when we have time I mean, and it is such bliss not to have to . . . I mean to be able to be here without worrying about what my parents think.'

'Get along with you,' said her hostess comfortably. 'Now, here you are.'

'Lovely. Thank you so much, Evelyn.'

'Dinner at eight. We're not dressing, but I'll probably change into a short frock.'

'Right. I'll be down.'

As the white-painted door clicked behind Evelyn, Gerry began to unpack her few clothes and hang up the skirts and frocks in the wardrobe. Something had happened, she was not sure what it was – or what it meant – but for the moment she had been released from her sadness about Annie. It was not that she no longer mourned her sister, or that she could forget what had happened, but that she had been able to put it into a different compartment of her mind. The sense of release brought a smile to her lips, and a kind of luxurious laziness to her movements. She realised that she could not rest and decided to take up some of the hour before dinner by having a bath.

The bathroom, which had been shared by the maids in the days when the Adamsons still had maids, was plain and rather bleak, but the hot tap let out a gush of nearly boiling water and Gerry could ignore the chipped enamel of the bath and the plain yellowed walls in the face of such glorious abundance. For the past months she had had to make do with shallow, tepid baths in her basement flat, and so she let herself fill the bath tub unpatriotically full and then lay in the hot water luxuriating in the sense of ease it brought her – and the comfort.

Suddenly she stretched her arms out above her head and rubbed her hot cheek against the wetness of her shoulder. All her muscles seemed to have been unlocked and she felt freed of something she had not known existed, as though she had been at the end of a chain, not knowing that if she could only uncouple it she would be free to move outside the circle of which it was the radius. Her head tipped back against the hard enamel rim of the bath and she felt the water lapping at the back of her hair. It would damage the set, but she could not care.

Gerry lay there in the bath until the skin of her hands and toes began to ripple and pucker, and the water felt cold when she moved. It took huge resolution to make herself stand up and feel the blast of cold air on her newly sensitive skin, but she did it and quickly huddled in one of the thick, soft towels Evelyn had provided. Then she rubbed herself until the friction made her skin glow all over again before she put on her underclothes. Feeling the silk of her petticoat falling down round her body was an extraordinary sensation and she shivered suddenly and hurried back to her bedroom to dress.

She had brought only one informal dress and quickly pulled it over her head and zipped it up before rolling on her stockings and shoving her feet into a pair of plain court shoes. Then she stood in front of the room's only mirror to deal with her face and hair. The violet colour of the wool frock made her eyes seem a much darker blue than usual, and accentuated the fairness of her hair. She began to regret that she had allowed the back of it to get wet as she tried to brush it into shape, not seeing how much more becoming the slight waywardness was than its usual sleek lines. But there was nothing to be done and, seeing how late it was, she flung the brush on to the bed and went downstairs.

Evelyn was standing in front of the hall fire, a glass of sherry in her hand, talking to a tall, dark-suited man, while Suvarov and Bob Adamson were standing with another stranger by the table with the drinks tray. For a moment no one turned as Gerry started down the last flight of stairs and she wondered what she should say, or whether she should just slide as quietly as possible to Evelyn's side. Then Suvarov turned, while she was still four or five steps from the bottom. He stood there just

139

looking at her and then very deliberately smiled and raised his glass as though in a toast. Gerry smiled back and walked down the last few stairs and crossed the hall to his side.

'Gerry, it is good to see you. And looking so well.' It was Robert Adamson's voice that broke whatever spell was holding them silent and she turned to him from Suvarov.

'Thank you, Bob. It is wonderful to be here.'

'London's a bit rough, I imagine.'

She nodded, and to her shame felt tears swimming into her eyes at the memory of Annie's body, filthy, tumbled on the wet black road in front of the ruins of her godmother's house. Bob gripped her hand and in a quite ordinary voice said:

'Gerry, you must let me introduce you to an old friend of mine from Washington, George Hillier. George, this is Mrs Gerry Kyrle.'

He was a youngish man, dressed in a dark suit of such extreme smoothness that Gerry was surprised. Neither Bob Adamson nor Tony Eynsham ever wore such elegantly cut clothes and she had unconsciously assumed that their comfortable informality was shared by all Americans. This unknown denizen of Washington's political circles was quite different. His mouse-coloured hair was cut very short and lay in impeccable order against his well-shaped head. Only his lively dark eyes betrayed the fact that hidden behind the elegant façade was a man of individual character – and perhaps humour.

'How do you do?' said Gerry, politely, holding out her hand. The young American took it firmly in a warm, dry clasp.

'Fine. It's good to be over here again.'

'You've visited England before the war, then?'

'Oh, yes, I've spent some time in Cambridge.'

'Really? When was that? I was due to go up in '35.'

'Yes, I was there then, off and on. What happened to stop you going there?'

'Oh, this and that ... My father disapproved of women's education,' Gerry said.

'That's tough,' he said. 'You ought to meet Bill; he had a tyrannical parent too. Hey, Bill, come and meet Mrs Kyrle.'

The other stranger, who was both older and far more ordinary looking, obediently deserted his hostess and strolled over to be introduced as Bill Ramsden. The three of them chatted easily together until Evelyn interrupted them.

'I think we ought to go in now if the rabbit is not to spoil.'

It was exactly like Evelyn, Gerry thought, to announce that she was feeding these clearly rather distinguished visitors on the humble, despised animal instead of bringing it in disguised as chicken as Mrs Alderbrook would have done.

'Evelyn, would you like me to help bring things?' Gerry asked.

'That's all right, Gerry, I'd rather you took the others in. You and me at the ends and the men between. You take Bob and Peter; I'll have the other two.' She did not miss Gerry's sudden pleasure and as she went to the kitchen began to rehearse, a little grimly, what she might be able to say to her.

Gerry, quite unaware how she had betrayed the self of which she was still only dimly aware, obeyed and led the way into the dining-room that led off the hall opposite the morning room. While Bob lit the tall candles that marched down the polished table in Evelyn's beautiful Georgian silver sticks, Gerry directed the other men to their places and waited by her chair until Evelyn arrived carrying a heavy tray. Then together they distributed the hot plates and handed round the dishes of casseroled rabbit and vegetables.

When she was sitting in what was usually Bob's chair at the foot of the table, Gerry thought that she had never seen the dining-room looking more attractive. Bob had turned off all the electric lights and the candle flames gleamed against the dark linenfold panelling and glinted off the carving of the beautiful old stone fireplace. She turned to say something of the sort to Bob, but he was deep in conversation with Bill Ramsden.

'Gerry.'

'Yes, Peter,' she said, turning her head towards him.

'Gerry, you're looking very lovely tonight,' he said in a voice so quiet that none of the others seemed to hear it. Whatever mood it was that held her in its grip prevented Gerry's usual embarrassed protest and she only smiled back at him and said:

'I'm glad.'

'Don't let Evelyn's good rabbit get cold,' said Bob on her other side and she picked up her knife and fork.

Despite Peter's having said that he would need his assistant for his meetings with the Americans, Gerry was excluded from their discussions throughout Saturday, and so she spent the time helping Evelyn around the house and garden. As they were in the kitchen washing up the breakfast dishes on Saturday morning, Evelyn said:

'Peter's looking much better.' Then she put another blue and white willow-pattern cup on the draining board

142

for Gerry to dry and went on: 'I think you must be very good for him.'

Gerry had an immensely clear picture of her left hand, the wedding ring and hoop of big emeralds and diamonds catching the light, as she picked up the cup and methodically wiped it with the drying-up cloth in her right. She carried the cup to the old oak dresser and came back to pick up the next one before she said anything. Then, without looking at Evelyn, she said:

'What makes you think it's me?'

'The way he depends on you, turns to you all the time, waits for you, looks out for you, and is so very much at ease in your presence. He's usually awfully restless, but last night he sat beside you on the sofa and hardly moved for simply ages.'

'Oh,' said Gerry inadequately, going back to the dresser, as though walking could help her through her own thoughts and Evelyn's. Gerry was still there, carefully hanging the cup on its brass hook, with her back to the room when Evelyn said:

'I'm glad you're married, Gerry.'

'Are you. Why?' The shock of that comment, spoken in Evelyn's usual, gentle, calm voice was enough to make Gerry's voice rough and very cold.

'Because he can be very fascinating, and because it must be difficult for you to work so closely with a man like that and keep your head. That's blunt, I know, but I think you're sensible enough to know what I mean and why I'm saying it.'

'Evelyn?' Gerry's voice was more normal and she came back to the sink.

'Yes, Gerry?'

'I do understand all that, but what would be so danger-

143

ous, if I were not married, say?'

She did not see Evelyn turn her head and look very carefully at the younger woman's face. After a moment or two, Evelyn spoke in a careful neutral tone.

'A lot of girls have fallen for him, Gerry, and have been very unhappy. Although it's always made me cross to watch him with them, I've sometimes thought that it's only partly to do with him. At the beginning I used to think it must be something to do with his Russianness – it seems to fascinate English women – and I persuaded him to call himself Peter rather than Piotr, which they all found so romantic. But in the last few years it seemed to be stopping; as though something in him had changed and did not call out to them all as it used.'

'Are you telling me that he seduced them? "All" of them?'

Evelyn dropped the bundle of teaspoons back into the sudsy water and turned to face Gerry.

'That sounded very cold, Gerry. I don't want to annoy you – still less to hurt you. I told you, I think you are doing a great deal for him and he obviously cares for you a lot. I just don't want to see you fall in love with him. It's not safe. And you have a husband.'

'Yes, I have.' At the tone of Gerry's voice, the other woman winced inside herself and took a while to work out what to say next. Then she decided that it was too difficult and so she said nothing. They finished that bout of washing-up in silence.

But before the weekend was done, Evelyn tried once more to tell Gerry some of what she wanted her to know. They were out in the vegetable garden, cutting late cabbages from the hard-frozen earth.

'Have you heard from Andrew lately?' asked Evelyn.

Gerry stood up and stretched her cramped back muscles, noticing the way the stark black trees were silhouetted against the silver fields, where the frost had not yet even begun to melt. Then she squatted down again and got on with her task, saying casually:

'No, not really: a few dull letters. It's strange that it's possible to miss him badly and yet not want to go back to the way we lived before. I find it hard to remember what he's really like, because the letters are so empty. But I sometimes think that he's not in fact quite like the man I thought he was.' Then she added with apparent irrelevance: 'You know Mother's always liked him a lot.'

'Yes, I know. She spent a whole afternoon once at the village bring-and-buy telling me all about his virtues.'

There was silence as Gerry bent down to pile the cabbages into her basket and pick up the knife she had been using. Then as she straightened up, scraping her wellingtons against each other, she said drily:

'That really ought to have warned me, I suppose. Just as Flixe's hostility should have.'

Evelyn put her arm around Gerry's shoulders for an instant.

'Oh, Gerry. Please be careful of yourself.'

That was all. She said not another word on the subject, even when they were alone together, and Gerry was left to think round and round what they had said and what they might have said.

10

Sitting in the back of the official car with Peter Suvarov on Sunday afternoon, Gerry had innumerable questions she wanted to ask him about the two Americans and the discussions he had had with them. Although she had not been allowed to sit in on many of the talks, she had been asked to type various minutes and memoranda. They all seemed innocuous, and could have been dictated to any of the typists in RE(1)R when Suvarov got back there on Monday. Gerry was curious to know why it had been so important for her to be there; but she could not ask that, or any of the other questions, with the uniformed driver sitting so close to them.

Every so often she glanced sideways at Suvarov's face, until the growing darkness hid everything except the gleam of his eyes, but his expression was too bleak to allow her to break into his silence. At last she just leaned back against the seat and yet again went over all the things that Evelyn had said to her.

The car jerked to a sudden stop at an unmarked road junction, and an enormous lorry lumbered across just in front of them. Gerry looked at Suvarov again and he must have seen the movement in the murk for he came out of his reverie and looked straight at her. The clouds that had obscured the moon drifted apart at that moment and she saw his face, drained of colour by the cool light. There was no comforting smile, just a long, long moment with his dark eyes looking at her with no expression that she could see. Then he looked away, but she felt his hand on hers and the warmth of that reached through both their gloves.

She, too, looked away, out of the car window at the thin-looking landscape of bare trees and flat, silver-grey earth. When his hand left hers she heard Evelyn's voice again:

'A lot of girls have fallen for him, Gerry, and have been very unhappy.'

It is not that I have some schoolgirl passion for him, she protested in vehement silence to herself. Really it isn't. He's just . . . so much the most interesting man I've ever met. And he makes me interested in so many things – and so much more interesting myself.

She told herself to stop making something out of nothing and ordered herself to think of some more suitable subject; but with Suvarov himself so near to her in the close darkness of the car it was impossible to stop thinking about him and the background to Evelyn's warnings. Despite her determination not to succumb to a childish crush, it was horribly easy to understand why all those girls had fallen for him. It was not so much because of his interesting face with the long-tailed black eyes and perfectly modelled lips, she decided, as the mixture of his powerful intelligence and the shadows in his eyes which touched some deep protectiveness within Gerry whenever he let her see them.

147

Evelyn had told her that Peter had changed since Gerry had gone to work for him, that he was happier, that he relied on her: could it be true? The possibility drove a strange shiver through her.

'Cold, Gerry?' came his voice, almost as gentle as though he were talking to Ming.

'No; but thank you, Peter. It was just a thought. I'm sorry I disturbed you.'

'You didn't. Look, the first edges of London. Won't be long now. Gerry, must you get back to Dover Street at once?'

'No, no; there's nothing I have to do,' she answered immediately, hoping that he was going to ask her to dine with him.

'Could you bear to come to the office then? Just for an hour or two? I ought to get all this weekend's business on to paper as soon as I can. I know it's unfair to ask you to give up yet more of your free day, but . . . '

'Don't worry,' she said, mastering her disappointment. 'Of course I don't mind.'

He leaned forward and said:

'Would you drop us at Queen Anne's Gate then, Rogers?'

'Certainly, sir. Shall I wait?'

'No, I'm not sure quite how long we'll be and both Mrs Kyrle and I are within walking distance of the office.'

'Very good, sir.'

Within less than half an hour the car drew up outside the white-painted door of the house in Queen Anne's Gate and Suvarov was getting out of the car on to the pavement. Gerry followed him, briefcase in hand, and waited for him to unlock the front door. He spoke briefly to the duty watchman in his cubby-hole by the inside

148

doors and led the way up to the third floor. Then he unpacked his notes and started to dictate to Gerry lists of all the points discussed during the weekend, decisions made and still awaited, and a mass of details he needed to assimilate.

She found it hard to focus her mind on the consequence of what she heard. The words were easy to follow and she scribbled them down with no trouble, but when he got to the end and she had covered nearly half a notebook with hieroglyphics, she could not have given a clear account of any of it. He put down his sheaves of notes at last and said:

'Thanks, Gerry. If you'd put it into shape tomorrow and get one of the confidential typists to type it by the end of the day we'll have done all we can. Now—' The air-raid sirens burst into banshee wails before he could finish and he just said: 'Bastards to come in on a Sunday evening. We'd better go downstairs and shelter.'

Gerry shook her head. 'Not after what . . . Annie. I don't think I could ever shelter again. But don't worry about me; I'll go back to the flat. I'll go across the park. They don't bomb parks.'

'No, Gerry. It's not safe. Come downstairs with me.'

'I daren't, Peter. Don't be angry, Please.'

She saw him walk towards her and in an instant she knew what was going to happen. There was nothing she could do or say. Part of her protested silently, but when she felt his arms around her and his cheek on her hair every protest was deadened.

'I can't let you go. I can't bear to risk you, Gerry. You're too valuable to me. I need you.' Then he lifted his head and she felt his hands slide from her back up to her neck and to her face. He held it so that she had to look at him. Just before he kissed her, he said:

149

'Without you it would all be such a struggle.'

His lips moved over hers and his hands held her, gently but inexorably. She moved closer towards him and put her arms on his, her hands on his neck. As he felt her move, he held her more tightly and lifted his head just a little.

'Gerry, I don't know how I have waited to hold you like this.'

'You too?'

'Oh, dear one, don't you remember that evening – just last Thursday, wasn't it?'

'I didn't know that that was it. I thought it was just me being stupid and . . . wicked.'

He laughed at her words, kissed her again and, saying, 'Come here with me,' he urged her to the side of the room where there was a huge, soft sofa.

'Peter, I can't,' she meant to say, but the words would not come. Instead she obeyed him and, with his arm still around her shoulders, sat back on the soft, feather-filled cushions. He kissed her again and began to touch her.

'Peter . . . ' At once he was still.

'Gerry, I couldn't force myself on you. Tell me to stop if you want me to.'

'It's . . . No, don't stop. Just love me.'

'You don't have to ask that. Of course I love you – who could fail to love you?' After that even the silent arguments of her mind and conscience were banished by his nearness, the immensity of what he made her feel and her longing to give him anything and everything she had to give.

Much later he said, looking tenderly down at her face, more beautiful than ever in its drowsy peace:

'Sleep now, Gerry.' Then he got up and came back a moment later with the rough grey wool blanket that was part of the emergency stores. He wrapped it round her, but she put out a hand to grasp his. From her sleepiness she murmured:

'What about you, Peter? Where will you sleep?'

'Hush, little one. There's no room for both of us there. Don't worry about me. I'll be all right. Trust me, and love me.'

'Always,' she said as her eyes closed.

It was hours before she woke, into a kind of golden blaze of early sunlight and inexpressible happiness. She turned her head languorously on the cushion, looking for him. When she saw him sitting at his desk, his dark head resting on his clasped hands, she was filled with compunction. She had been so comfortable and he must have sat like that all night. Without thinking, she slid off the sofa, wrapping the scratchy blanket around her body like a toga, and walked quietly across the room. There was a clock on his desk and she saw that it was nearly six. With a gentle hand she touched his head, saying quietly:

'Peter, wake up.' He lifted his head and what she saw in his face froze all the happy golden warmth out of her mind. She could not speak. The lines between his mouth and chin were more pronounced than she had ever seen them and his eyes had a self-hatred that almost stopped her breath. 'Peter, you look awful. You shouldn't have let me have the sofa. Lie down for a bit and go to sleep again.'

'I wasn't asleep, Gerry,' he said turning away from her. Then in a voice that had no life in it, he said: 'Gerry, I shouldn't have done it. God knows I ought to know better by now. And with you of all people. Gerry, go home now.'

151

She stood clutching her grey blanket around herself, unable to believe what he had said.

'What did I do?' she whispered. He winced, but in the same dead voice, he said:

'Nothing. It was my fault. I can't tell you how sorry I am.'

'No, Peter,' she said, walking round behind his chair so that she could see his face again. Then she knelt on the floor by his chair and, forgetting the blanket in the unhappiness she read in his eyes, put her hands on either side of his face. The blanket fell around her knees and he shut his eyes.

'Gerry, cover yourself up; you'll . . . you'll catch cold.'

'No, Peter. Tell me. What we just shared was more than this. You can't send me away like this now. You must have meant what you said. You couldn't have been pretending. I'll never believe it.'

She looked up into his face, trying to understand what was going on in his mind. If it had not been for the unmistakable misery in his dark eyes, she might have brought herself to ask for more than reassurance. But it seemed that he could not give her any. Putting his hands on her bare arms, he said:

'Gerry, nothing I said was a lie, then or now. But I shouldn't have done it. I was mad to touch you. You must go now, before they come in to work.' But there was something missing, although his eyes had actually focused on her and his hands were warm and gentle again.

'Don't you care at all for me?'

His head dropped forward until his forehead rested against hers.

'Yes, my dear, I care. Now go before I hurt you any more.'

152

Without speaking, she picked up her blanket and walked back to the sofa to collect her scattered clothes and put them on. There was something almost unbelievably squalid about the process and she felt filthy. How could something as radiantly wonderful – and sweet – have turned into this hell? How could he care for her if he was turning her out like some . . .? Even her mind could not bring that word to the surface after what they had said to each other the night before.

Just before she left him she turned in the doorway and said with only the slightest tremor in her voice:

'I expect it is the wrong thing to say, but I love you, Peter. And last night you made me feel more loved than I have ever been. I can't believe that it was just clever technique. You asked me to trust you, and I do, but I hope that you will bring yourself to be able to trust me enough to tell me what has happened to make you do this to us both.' She stopped, took a deep breath and then went on in a more distant voice: 'I'll come back later to see to all those reports. I expect you'll have meetings for most of the day.'

He said nothing and after a while she left him alone in the chaos of their office.

As she walked back across the park there was a metallic taste in her mouth that seemed vilely familiar. She had reached the bridge before she tracked down the memory. Years before, she must have been about five years old, she had rifled her mother's purse and taken a florin, an enormous amount of money it had seemed, she remembered. Just before she had been able to scamper out of the room she had heard the unmistakable sharp tapping tread of her detested French governess and had stuffed the heavy coin into her mouth to hide it. The taste that now filled her mouth was just the same. It seemed to be the very taste of shame itself.

She stopped on the bridge for a minute or two to try to collect herself. But, looking down at the water, Gerry felt as though the perfection of the dawn mocked her. The view down the lake towards the roofs of Whitehall that she had always loved so much was untouched and looking even more glorious than usual with the sun gilding the bare tips of the willow branches that dabbled in the steel-grey water. She could not resist leaning forward on the bridge and remembering the days when her feelings for Suvarov were innocent. From her present position it was hard to remember how they had troubled her then. Now the idea that any such basic affection could be wrong seemed absurd. She thought of Andrew, too, for the first time since Peter had kissed her. What she had just done was a betrayal not only of the vows she had made in the small grey stone church near her home on her wedding day, but also of the love that Andrew had tried to give her, and even of the battles she had fought to find her own love for him. Gerry turned her face back towards Queen Anne's Gate for a moment. Suvarov's tenderness and the feelings he had awakened in her body had shown her at last how poverty-stricken she and Andrew had been in their physical relations. For the knowledge Peter had given her she would always be richer. She tried to believe that he had taken nothing from Andrew except her ignorance and clumsiness.

As she looked up towards the black pinnacles of Whitehall's grey towers, she thought of the unhappiness in Peter's face and once more could not believe that he was the conscienceless seducer of Evelyn's veiled warnings. Besides, she thought that it was simply not possible for her to suffer such strength of feeling for a man who did not care.

A kind of resilience started to press the self-disgust out of her mind. Her hands, which had been gripping the rusty iron rail of the bridge, relaxed. She straightened up, looked once more down the lake and, almost as though her mind were speaking directly to some entity represented by the contrived beauty of the lakescape, promised: 'Very well, I shall not give way to feeling filthy and miserable. I care. He cares. There will be a way out.' Then she nodded decisively at the willow and, ignoring the highly surprised stare of another early pedestrian, walked off towards Green Park and Dover Street.

Towards the end of the next excruciating fortnight, during which Suvarov spoke to her as little as possible and she never looked directly at him, he said one evening:

'Gerry, I have to go down to Etchingham this weekend. Would you come with me?'

'Etchingham? Oh, the coding school those Americans are going to help with. Of course, if you need me.'

As usual she could not bring herself to look into his face and she saw his fingers tighten so hard on the pencil he was holding that it snapped in two jagged pieces. But when he spoke his voice was without passion of any kind.

'Yes, I have to go to see the coders. But it's my home, too. At least my wife's home.' Her eyes lifted in the sudden shock to look directly at him. I see, she said to herself, but why does he want to take me? And why the hell couldn't Evelyn have told me that? It would have saved a lot of trouble, and my ideas about poor Andrew wouldn't be in such chaos. Aloud she said:

'Of course I'll come.'

'Thanks. It's not an order, so if you change your mind tell me.'

She nodded and went back to her overloaded desk to process the increasingly dramatic reports of the analysts downstairs. But her heart was beginning to sing again. If he were married that might explain the dismissal; if he wanted to take her, Gerry, as protection against his wife then there was obviously something terribly wrong with their marriage and . . . Gerry even began to preen herself a little.

She began to paint ever more fantastic pictures of this mysterious wife, who had never been spoken about and who clearly cared nothing for her husband. By the time Peter opened the door of his own car for Gerry on the following evening she had worked herself back into a frame of mind in which she could smile at him.

He did not speak, except to ask if she was cold, during the entire journey in his uncomfortable little dark-green Morgan, but she did not mind. She felt as though they were back in tune with each other and supplied in her head all the conversations they might have had as they drove down towards the coast. It took nearly three hours to pick their way through South London and out into the Sussex countryside, past horrific bomb damage and around enormous craters that had still not been filled in. But they got there at last, sweeping down a long drive past a large square red-brick house with many windows that reflected the cloudy moonlight.

'That's the school. My wife and her sister moved out into the Dower House at the beginning of the war and offered the house to the government long before any requisitioning came in.'

'Oh,' said Gerry inadequately, thinking how rich his wife must be and how selfish to live in such splendour with her sister while her husband had to make do with rooms in London. Perhaps she was afraid of the bombing, thought Gerry disdainfully, almost ready to blame the unknown Mrs Suvarov for Annie's death. Only she was probably not Mrs Suvarov but the Lady Something Suvarov if she lived in a place like this.

The drive seemed to wind on like some dream-extended road that would end only in high cliffs above a nightmare sea. They passed a lake and enormous trees whose species Gerry could only guess at in the inadequate light until at last the car turned through some high open gates, whose wrought-iron curlicues spelled centuries-old extravagance, to draw up outside a neat little box of a Georgian house built of grey stone.

Suvarov took the key out of the ignition.

'Well, here we are. All right, Gerry?'

There was concern in his voice and she dared to touch his gloved hand. She could feel him still, hardly even breathing, and she withdrew.

'Yes, Peter. Of course I'm all right.' She opened the car door and got out, hearing and feeling the gravel crunch beneath her feet. He swung his long legs out of the driver's seat and came round to the boot to take out their bags. Then he led the way up the steps and opened the front door. Once they were inside, in sudden stuffy darkness, he shut the door behind them and then pushed aside a thick blackout curtain, standing back to let Gerry go first into the warm, brightly lit hall.

A tall thin woman with immaculately arranged dark hair was stooping to add new logs to a fire that burned below the white marble mantelpiece and warmed the black and white squares of the marble floor. Portraits of severe-faced men and over-decorated women lined the walls, hung from a rail on long, vertical, black chains. A cocker spaniel skittered across the hard, shiny floor towards Suvarov, its tail thrashing like a flail and its tongue hanging out. Gerry was surprised and rather touched that he should have aroused such evident affection in an animal. He had never struck her as the kind of man to spend time on something so ordinary as playing with a puppy or training it.

She watched him bend down and take the animal by the ears and receive its exuberant homage. Then he straightened up and walked across the black and white checks to kiss the thin, elegant woman on each pale cheek, before putting an arm around her shoulders and bringing her to where Gerry stood just inside the blackout curtain beside the baggage.

'Connie, this is Mrs Kyrle, my invaluable assistant. Gerry, this is my sister-in-law, Constance Wroughton.'

'How do you do, Mrs Kyrle?' she said, holding out a shapely hand. Gerry looked surreptitiously at the other hand but there was no wedding ring. Constance turned to Suvarov. 'Diana's in her drawing room.'

'Thanks, Connie. We'll go in. See you later.'

'Dinner in half an hour.' He waved in acknowledgement and led the way to the back of the hall where a panelled door stood closed. He opened it and ushered Gerry in ahead of him.

Even in the middle of her confusion and sickeningly muddled feelings, Gerry noticed that it was a beautiful room, rather under-furnished but with an atmosphere of complete calm. The panelling had been painted a warm oyster grey and instead of the family portraits that

158

decorated the hall, this room was hung with a collection of charming drawings of sunny, domestic scenes: a child playing, a cat on the windowsill beside a potted geranium, a woman dressing. Most of the furniture was made from some golden wood, satinwood perhaps or kingwood, and to Gerry's inexpert eye it looked as though it dated from the eighteenth century. There were flowers here and there in pretty porcelain bowls, and a sweet-scented fire of apple logs burned in the white fireplace.

Gerry stood still in the doorway. Peter gave her a little push, and when she moved out of the way he walked past her towards the fire where a woman was sitting with a soft, misty-rose rug on her knees. Gerry watched as he stood in front of her, almost as though in homage, and then leaned forward to take her hands and kiss her forehead. Gerry heard his voice as soft and gentle as when he spoke to Ming:

'How is it, Diana?'

Boiling with indignation on his behalf that this rich wife of his should sit to receive his greeting, Gerry watched her put one of her astonishingly thin hands up to his face and hold it there for a moment. Then in a voice that had a beautiful tone, slightly cracked, like a bell with a flaw in it, she said:

'I'm well enough. But you, my dear, you look very worn.' He shook his head and stood up to beckon to Gerry. Obediently as always, she walked forward, feeling clumsy and very puzzled.

'Diana, this is my assistant, Mrs Kyrle; Gerry Alderbrook to her friends.'

'How do you do, Gerry?' came that voice again and Gerry walked forward to stand in front of her. 'Forgive

159

my not getting up, my dear. This wretched thing keeps me chained to my chair.'

A steely cold vice gripped at Gerry's insides as she let her glance follow Peter's wife's fluttering hand and she saw the implacable wheels of the chair. The significance of the pretty rug, Peter's gentle concern, and Mrs Suvarov's regal reception of him all became instantly clear to Gerry, and so did her place in their tragedy and theirs in hers. This, then, was Suvarov's private misery at which Tony Eynsham had once hinted. Gerry's eyelids dropped over her eyes and she made a supreme effort to speak normally.

'Please don't think about it, Mrs Suvarov. It is so good of you to have me to stay like this.' The fluttering hand with the big sapphires on the third finger touched her own.

'Sit here beside me, Gerry, while Peter finds us something to drink.' Gerry, moving as though still in the nightmare, pulled forward a brocade-covered elbow chair and sat down. 'I am so glad he's brought you this weekend, so that I can tell you how grateful I am that you're being such a help to him. His life is so bleak alone in London and I know how much it has done for him to have your intelligent, sensitive help in his work.' Gerry could not answer; it was all she could do not to let the tears out of her mind into her eyes. She just tried to smile.

As though to protect her, Suvarov found things for Gerry to do at the coding school for the whole of the Saturday while he presumably sat with his wife and told her whatever it was that he had come to tell. Lying in bed that night, tired to a point where sleep seemed to be an impossible longed-for paradise, Gerry decided that of all

160

the hurts that were digging into her liked barbed needle points, the worst was the knowledge of the gentle, loving, tolerant peace between Suvarov and his wife, which was the absolute antithesis of the tensions Gerry felt about her own marriage. Well, now she knew what marriage should be about; she and Andrew had had their health until her miscarriage, which was as nothing compared to whatever it was that had wasted Diana Suvarov's limbs. They had thought they loved each other, they had married. Only recently had Gerry wondered whether each had invented the person they thought they loved. Now she was certain.

She must have slept in the end, for when she turned over restlessly for what felt like the thousandth time, she saw that there was light edging round the curtains. Relieved, she got quickly out of bed, wincing at the cold, and flung back the thick old yellow brocade curtains and looked out.

The Dower House had a perfect view of the lake and the carefully placed trees that led the way towards the main house; the stands of ancient oaks, the one massively stepped cedar of Lebanon and the three or four immense copper beeches whose last few leaves seemed to deepen the colour of the graceful redbrick house. Peter's wife seemed to have everything that Gerry had ever wanted – except her health, and without that what use was all the rest? But just at that moment Gerry thought that the bargain might have been worth while.

She looked at her watch and, seeing the time, rushed to wash and dress for breakfast. As she got her tweed coat and skirt out of the walnut wardrobe, she felt suddenly ashamed that she had selected the clothes with a view to showing Peter's wife just how well she dressed. As though anyone as young as Gerry, as lacking in character and knowledge, could rival someone like Diana Suvarov, whose beauty had survived despite the ravages of illness and who obviously had wells of fortitude and affection on which to draw. And, thought Gerry, determined to face the completeness of her inadequacy, who obviously loved her husband and was most greatly loved by him.

Biting the inside of her lower lip, she pulled up her stockings and snapped the suspenders through them. Then she found the correct shoes, put them on and went downstairs to the morning room, where she found Constance Wroughton laying the walnut table.

Constance looked round at the sound of the door's opening and smiled gently.

'Good morning, Gerry. I hope you slept well? I'm afraid Diana had rather a bad night and so she's not getting up this morning. She asked me to apologise to you.'

'Heavens, she shouldn't have done that,' said Gerry instinctively, and then motivated perhaps by memories of her muddled relations with her own sisters, went on more carefully: 'Do you always get on so well?'

Constance leaned across the table to put the last French flowered porcelain cup on its saucer and then turned back to look at Gerry.

'Why do you ask?'

'I've just been thinking about my dealings with my own sisters and wondering how any of us would measure up to what you and Diana have achieved and, well, doubting that we'd be able to.'

'It doesn't come all of a rush. We've both had to fight to get where we are now.'

'Fight each other?' asked Gerry doubtfully. Constance smiled ruefully and poured coffee for them both.

'Even that sometimes, but mainly ourselves. It helped, of course, that we were left the house together, and that it's so big, which meant that it was a job in itself. But of course it is very difficult for any two people to live together, particularly when one is trapped as Diana is . . .'

'And the other therefore has to do more of the Martha-ing,' supplied Gerry.

'Peter's right,' said Constance with apparent irrelevance, and Gerry seized on the introduction of his name to ask:

'Has Diana always lived here, I mean when they were first married?'

'No, they were in London for a few years – during the week; they always came down here at weekends. But once she got ill, she found London a terrible burden and I think it frightened her at a time when she needed absolutely every bit of resolution and courage to cope with her disease. Peter saw that and brought her back to me despite her protests.' She sipped her coffee and Gerry sat looking down at her plate, trying to concentrate on the pretty mixture of blue and yellow flowers painted under the glaze. Then Constance said: 'He has done everything he could for her, you know. I used to . . . Things used to be difficult between him and me, but I think we've come to recognise what each other does and respect it. I can see now what marrying Diana's cost him one way and another.'

'Cost him?' repeated Gerry in a small, high voice.

'No children; no real marriage, physical marriage, if you see what I mean; a weight to be carried all the time and wondering, always wondering, if he's doing enough for her, doing the right things. He is a good man, Gerry.'

'Yes, I know. May I help myself to some more coffee?' Gerry asked, unable to bear the conversation any longer.

'Of course. Oh, by the way, the local parson comes to the chapel every Sunday for morning service. I always take Diana. Would you like to come with us?'

'Chapel?'

'Yes, in the house. It's pure delight – tiny and quite perfect. You ought to see it while you're here, but you can always pop up this afternoon if you'd rather.'

'No, no. I'll come with you. But will your sister be well enough?'

'I expect so. By the way, Peter never comes. The C of E is not really his sort of thing.'

'No, I don't suppose it is.'

And so Gerry Alderbrook, after what felt like the worst shock of her life, spent a Sunday of complete English conventionality with morning service, then lunch back at the Dower House with the vicar and the commanding officer of the coding school, and then a bracing walk around the park afterwards, while Suvarov sat with his wife and talked by the fire in her drawing room. Then at the end of the day he packed Gerry and her luggage back into his little dark-green car and drove her back to London.

She sat quietly with her hands in her lap waiting for him to speak. They had reached Dorking before he started.

'Gerry, Diana's illness is not something I can ever talk about to anyone, and after . . . You had a right to know, but I did not know how to tell you. Any explanation I could find words for sounded as though I was trying to make an excuse and there isn't one. I had to show you.'

Gathering her courage to support her, Gerry answered him:

'I'm glad you did, for I understand now. And although I still hurt, it's bearable because I understand.'

'Does it help to know that I hurt too?'

'No. I knew you did all along. Oh, hell! Yes it does and I'm ashamed of that. It's all so bloody unfair.' He looked sideways at her and then drove off the road on to the wide grass verge. He switched off the ignition and turned to take both Gerry's hands in his own.

'Gerry, I've told you that I should never have done it—'

'I didn't mean that you were unfair, Peter,' she interrupted in a rush. 'Only life. I mean so unfair on Diana and on you and only at the end on me. Honestly.'

'Hush, Gerry; I wasn't going to say that. I was going to say that although I should never have done it and I am bitterly sorry for what I've done to you, I can't help but be glad of what we shared.'

'Oh, Peter.'

He dropped her hands, released the brake and drove carefully on to the road again. After a mile or so, he said:

'Gerry, I think I probably ought to organise a transfer for you. Would you prefer to work for someone else?'

The thought that she might be exiled from his company as punishment for her lapse into emotion made Gerry's insides knot themselves into an angry lump. When she could trust her voice, she said almost in a parody of the young women with stiff upper lips in the recent crop of patriotic films:

'Oh, I think I can take it, Peter.'

11

Gerry was immensely surprised to find a note from Felicity waiting on her doormat when Suvarov dropped her in Dover Street. They had had no communication since Annie's funeral. Gerry unfolded the single sheet of paper, hoping that nothing had happened to Flixe. She did not think she could bear to hear of any more trouble until she had had a chance to recover. But all the note said was:

> Dropped in to see you, but no you. Have nipped up for tea with Anna K. Perhaps I'll meet the mysterious Mr Oldridge. Do pop up when you get back. We might have supper together and catch up. Flixe.

Grinning absurdly to herself, Gerry flung off her hat and gloves and pulled the door of the flat shut behind her. It would be wonderful to spend the evening with Flixe and joke and chat all the misery and melodrama away. Perhaps she would be able to bury the memory of Diana Suvarov's beautiful face and wasted limbs if she and Flixe could talk for long enough and laugh.

As she took off her sapphire-coloured corduroy jacket and changed her shoes, Gerry tried to tell herself that it was a really *good* thing that Suvarov should have nipped their love affair in the bud; she should never have allowed it to come so close to flowering. Andrew was fighting thousands of miles away from home and she was his wife. However much she had hated his assumption of ownership when she was trying to join the WRNS she could not pretend that she had not betrayed him. It was a horrible thought. Looking back to that night when she had tasted the best and the worst of herself, she could not imagine how she could ever have let herself forget her husband and the things she had promised him.

She began to think that she must have been mad. Perhaps the perpetual, nagging tiredness, the skinning of her nerves by the nightly bombardment that had culminated for her in Annie's death . . . Gerry stopped herself. It would always be possible to find excuses for what she had done and there was no point. Her feelings for Suvarov had no future. It had to be forgotten. She was married to someone else and ought to concentrate on him even if she could not accept that she owed him unquestioning obedience.

Locking the door of her flat, she walked up the steps through the main front door of the house and knocked on the door of Anna Kingsley's flat. It was opened almost immediately by Felicity, ravishing as always in a sea-green jersey and speckled tweed skirt, her pearls reflecting the silky glow of her face. Gerry leaned forward to kiss her and wondered why Flixe hugged her so warmly, but the comfort was so welcome that she said nothing.

'Come on, Gerry, Anna's in the kitchen whipping up

the most delectable kind of supper and she needs help.'
Gerry followed her glowing sister into the small kitchen,
where Anna stood at the cooker gently stirring some
savoury mixture in a wide, shallow copper pan.

There was something incongruous in the sight of the
elegant Anna, wrapped in a voluminous white apron and
standing surrounded by pots and pans and all the debris
of a cooking session. But she seemed thoroughly in
control and displayed none of the panic or ill-temper with
which Fanny Alderbrook attacked her own kitchen.
Gerry breathed in the wonderful scents of gently frying
butter and shellfish and some kind of alcohol.

'Anna,' she said, sighing luxuriously, 'it's good to be
here. Thank you. That smells wonderful.' Anna lifted her
wooden spoon out of the mixture in the copper pan and
inclined a cheek towards Gerry, who kissed her, noticing
as she did so that Anna was wearing some of her
spectacular diamond earrings.

'I thought we'd better have one last beano before real
rationing starts,' she said as she straightened up again.

'They're grasping the nettle at last are they?' Gerry
said, watching Flixe scraping at one of the lobster shells
on the table.

'So Edwin tells me, and he usually knows.'

'You know a lot of awfully influential people, Anna.
What . . . '

'Never mind that now, Flixe. I'm going to need that
cream any minute. Can you hurry up with the shells?'

'What can I do, Anna?' asked Gerry, who was feeling
rather out of things as the other two laboured at their
tasks.

'Help Flixe, if you will, Gerry. She's scraping all the fat
out of the lobster shells and beating it into the cream and

she's being slower than an arthritic tortoise.' Flixe laughed, but before she could protest, Gerry could not resist saying:

'Lobster! Is it quite decent to eat something like that with so little food about and rationing about to start?'

'There'll be much more once rationing's here and everyone gets fair shares, according to Anna's War Office Edwin. And anyway nobody ever minds your eating expensive food – it's hoarding sausages that's the sin, isn't that right, Anna?' said Flixe with such determined gaiety that Gerry began to wonder just what her sister was doing.

Later, as they were eating the perfect lobster and drinking some superb white burgundy Anna had produced from her fridge, Flixe started to tease Anna about her culinary skills and beg to be told where they had been acquired. Anna smiled across the table at her, as though amused at her eagerness.

'No,' she said at one moment. 'There was no one at my parents' home who could have taught me dishes like this.'

'I can imagine, if their cook was anything like all of ours,' said Flixe warmly. 'So where was it?'

'France. There were times when I was so homesick while I was there that only cooking helped. The physical sensations of good, French cookery are so all-conquering that they give terrific solace.'

'And do you still cook for solace, Anna?' Gerry asked, interested. 'Will you teach me? I'd love to know how to do that.' Before Anna could do more than nod at Gerry, Flixe intervened.

'I think I remember Mother telling us once that you had spent several years in France. It was after she was married, wasn't it?'

169

'Yes. What else did she tell you?' Catching the slight edge in Anna's voice, Gerry assumed that Flixe was going to change the subject and so she did not intervene. But she had reckoned without Flixe's perennial interest in other people.

Flixe smiled apologetically at Anna and raised her glass, as though in a toast.

'I'm sorry, Anna. It sounds as though those years could not have been happy ones. I'd never have asked you about them if I'd known.' Anna raised her own glass in acknowledgement of the apology, drank some burgundy and then shrugged as she put the glass back on the table.

'There's no reason not to tell you. Fanny knows, but she disapproves so much that she'd never have passed it on to you. For most of the time I was there I was so happy – in seventh heaven as the Americans say. I was living just outside Paris with a man to whom I was not married.'

'You, Anna?' said Gerry, sounding shocked and quite forgetting her disapproval of Flixe's curiosity in her astonishment.

'That was jolly brave, Anna,' said Flixe, trying to remove the sting from Gerry's tone of voice.

Anna turned back towards Flixe, her fine-featured face colouring slightly. 'Yes, I suppose it was brave, although it did not seem so at the time. Then it was the only thing I felt I could have done. I loved him so much. And he could not have married me: he was already married and his church does not allow divorce.'

'And it ended badly,' suggested Flixe. Anna's dark-green eyes seemed to swim for a moment with tears that did not fall. Appalled at having shaken the self-control that had always seemed absolute, Flixe quickly stood up and collected the empty lobster plates to

170

take out to the kitchen. Gerry soon followed her with the dishes. When she had shut the kitchen door behind them, she whispered to her sister:

'Flixe, did you know anything about that before? How could we have known Anna so well and not known?' Flixe shrugged and turned to the sink to run the sticky plates under the hot tap.

'It's not really a matter for general conversation. Poor Anna. Look, we can't stay here talking about her. There's a soufflé in the fridge. Get it out, will you, and I'll find some pudding plates.'

A little surprised by Flixe's peremptory voice, Gerry did as she was told and preceded her sister back into the dining room. Anna appeared to have regained all her usual control and she smiled kindly at Gerry's anxious expression.

'Did you have a pleasant weekend, Gerry?' Anna asked. Gerry put the soufflé in front of her and then sat down at the table again.

'Not altogether,' she said moderately. 'Sometime I'd like to tell you about it, but not . . . not quite yet.'

'It's all right, Gerry. I understand. And I'm the last person to try to force your confidence.' They smiled at each other, even more in sympathy than usual. Then Flixe reappeared with the plates and they talked of other things.

When she had swallowed her first mouthful, Flixe looked at Anna with an expression of awed admiration on her face.

'Anna, this is ambrosial. What on earth is in it? I've never tasted anything so heavenly in the whole of my life.' Her trick of giving so trivial a matter such a weight of words broke the slight tension that remained and Anna answered in her usual easy voice.

171

'Just cream, marrons glacés, maraschino, crystallised violets, and a little gelatine. It's just an ordinary cold soufflé, Flixe.'

'Well, it's the very best I've ever tasted. And I suppose it'll be the last until after the war. We should take it seriously. *Au revoir, soufflé*, she said, licking the last of it out of her silver teaspoon.

'I'm glad you enjoyed it, Flixe, dear,' said Anna. 'Gerry, some more wine?'

'No, thank you, Anna. It was marvellous, but if I have any more I think I'll collapse on to the table in a stupor.'

'It can't be as bad as that. You don't look flushed and your speech is still perfectly discreet.'

'Unlike mine,' said Flixe cheerfully. 'Still, I can't regret going overboard about cooking like yours. Now, we'd better help you with the washing up and then I'll have to push off.'

'Wash up, indeed! Certainly not. Gerry is exhausted and ought to be in bed.'

'I must say I am rather longing for my pillow. Thank you, Anna. It's been lovely.' Gerry stood up, leaned over to kiss Anna, and tried to express all the sympathy she felt for her but was too shy to put into words.

When she and Flixe had left the flat and were standing on the pavement outside Gerry's iron steps, she said:

'Flixe, how is it that people always tell you things? I thought I knew Anna better even than Mother, and yet I had no idea about any of that.'

'I don't know. I don't always set out to make people tell me things, although I always want to know. And I suppose they respond to that. Didn't you get the feeling that she's been rather longing to talk about it? I've often thought she must be so lonely.'

'Lonely? Anna?' Gerry said, surprised that her extrovert sister should have divined the essential unhappiness of their mother's old friend.

'Oh, I know she has hosts of friends,' answered Flixe, too accustomed to being corrected by Gerry to take her remark as anything but dissent. 'But not all that close. It's almost as though she deliberately keeps her distance. I don't know. And we won't solve any mysteries tonight. Good night, Gerry old thing. Look after yourself.' Felicity leaned forward to kiss her sister's cheek.

Gerry watched her go, wondering whether Flixe had always got on to the important things about people so quickly, and whether her intuition would have saved her from the mess in which Gerry had found herself. But the memory of that mess was too painful, and she herself was too tired, to let her mind think much. She was turning to climb down the steps when Flixe reappeared, a quite different expression on her face. Gerry waited to hear what she had to say, and it surprised her.

'Listen, old thing, you will tell me if you need me . . . '

'Why should I need you, Flixe?'

'You've had a rough deal so far, Gerry, and since I haven't, I just want to . . . to . . . '

'Hand over a bit of your luck?' Gerry suggested.

Felicity laughed at that and said much more naturally:

'I suppose that was what I meant. Dearest Gerry, don't take things too tragically, will you.'

What do you know? Gerry asked silently. And who told you?

Gerry went to the office the following morning with much less reluctance than she had felt since Suvarov had propelled her, and himself, into their emotional swamp.

Although there could be no rescue from it, Gerry no longer had to feel humiliated to find herself there and that in itself made it far easier to look her chief in the eye, even smile at him.

If only there could be a decent bit of war news, she sometimes thought, then she might almost feel content again. But there was no reassuring news from any part of the world. Although the Americans had agreed to supply arms and ammunition to the Allies under their lend-lease terms, there was no sign of their actually joining in the fight against Nazi Germany, and Britain seemed to be making no headway. The U-boat attacks were increasing in intensity and in success, and thousands of tons of Allied shipping were sent to the bottom of the Atlantic every month. The British had to retreat from Greece in April, leaving a bloody mess behind and only hanging on in Crete by the skin of their teeth. Then at the end of May Crete fell.

Britain had lost control of the Aegean, and it began to look increasingly as though she would lose the Middle East as well. Gerry began to worry about Andrew's safety. Earlier in the month, Admiral Darlan, now virtually in control of Vichy France under Pétain, had allowed the Germans to use the air fields in French Syria in order to send supplies to Rommel in North Africa. For the first time since the real war had started, Gerry felt she had reason to be afraid for her husband – and father. Brigadier Alderbrook was facing Rommel in the desert and Andrew was somewhere in Palestine, horribly near those now-German air fields.

From the various reports and memoranda that had crossed her desk, she knew that General de Gaulle had been pressing the British to help the Free French move against Vichy in at least one of the French colonies, but with no success. There had been a badly botched attempt to take Dakar in West Africa the previous September, just after Gerry joined RE(1)R, and since then there had been no joint actions. But now with the new danger looming in Syria all that had changed, and an operation was planned.

The expedition began on 8 June and fourteen days later Damascus had fallen to a determined and brave commando raid. It was said that Pétain wanted to surrender, but that Darlan would not let him. The end came on 8 July, by which time thousands of men had died on each side, many of them Frenchmen killed by other Frenchmen.

Gerry listened to the heated arguments in the analysts' room as bits of news came in and wondered whether Andrew had been anywhere near the fighting. She heard stories of great heroism and gallantry and wondered how many were true.

'But what was it all for?' she asked at one point. 'Was it really all about the air fields?'

'Partly,' answered Mike, looking coldly at Michel, who had taken little part in the discussion. 'But surely it was mainly to recruit more members of the Free French. It was thought, was it not, Michel, that if there was something that could be seen as a Free French victory, then all the Vichyists in the Levant would flock to de Gaulle?' He was about to continue when Michel said quietly from the window:

'If that will help to get the Germans out of France it is justified, whatever it costs, however many are killed. You could not understand that, Mike, because your country is not under occupation. You English may be fighting this war, too, but you have no idea what it is really about.'

Gerry watched Mike's fair skin colour in a painful blush

at the sincerity in Michel's voice and thought it was time for her to retreat herself. As she carefully closed the door between herself and the two men who seemed to have got over their compulsion to hurt each other in vicious arguments, she wondered when Michel would go off and join his hero in Carlton Gardens. At least if he were gone, there would be fewer people to remind poor Mike Endlesham what had happened at Dunkirk, and presumably Philippe would stay with RE(1)R to explain the myriad French points of view when the British analysts needed any interpretation. It seemed sad – and wasteful – that the analysts' room should have been divided so often by the quarrels between Mike and Michel, but Gerry knew that they were merely a microcosm of the often bitter divisions between the French in London and their reluctant hosts.

She went back upstairs and settled down at her desk to sort out a bundle of reports from the analysts so that she could rewrite them for Suvarov. They were more complicated even than usual, and it was not until well after eight o'clock that she finished the last one. Then she clipped them together, put them in the locked tray for one of the typists, cleared her desk and left the building.

Walking slowly across the park, she wondered whether it would be too late to persuade Anna Kingsley to go out to dine somewhere with her, or whether she ought to stay in the flat and do what she could with the tin of sardines and packet of powdered egg that were the remains of her last shopping expedition. When she reached Dover Street she rang Anna's bell, but there was no answer. Reluctantly she turned and went down to her basement, thinking sentimentally of Andrew. However annoying he could be, at least when they had been living together she

176

had always had company. Eating alone, she decided, was not something that human beings should have to do.

On the doormat, she found a telegram. She bent down to pick up the sinister yellow envelope, remembering the day that Flixe had opened Suvarov's telegraphed summons for her. Trying to reason away her dread, Gerry thrust two shaking fingers under the gummed flap and ripped open the envelope.

Deeply regret to inform you Andrew Kyrle seriously wounded. Repatriation as soon as possible post-operation. Islip.

Wounded, not dead, thought Gerry. But wounded how? What kind of wound could send you home? What on earth should she do? Why couldn't Islip, whoever he was, have told her more?

It must have been Syria, she thought a little more calmly, unless Andrew had been sent to Iraq. But wherever it had been, he could not be in too bad a way if they were able to send him home. Yet it must be serious, or they would have put him in hospital in Cairo or somewhere nearer and taken him back into the regiment when he was healed. He must be in pain and was probably afraid, too. For the first time since she had joined in the war Gerry wished that she had managed to get herself sent back to the Middle East. At least if she had been in Palestine she might have been able to help Andrew bear whatever it was that had happened, and make the journey home less awful for him. Oh, poor Andrew: the army was his life; what on earth would he find to replace it? She put her head in her hands.

Into her mind came another, more selfish, worry: how

would Andrew's repatriation affect her and the life she had built for herself? Despite her sister's death, the miseries of the Blitz, her difficulties with the analysts at work and her frustrated love for Suvarov, she had been happier in London than at almost any time she could remember. She had discovered that she could use her brains to some effect after all and she had learned an immense amount since she had started working for Suvarov, not only about the war, its causes and its probable development, but also about herself and other people. It was true that she had missed Andrew increasingly, but now that he was on his way back to her, she began cussedly to remember the difficulties rather than the consolations of his presence.

Sitting there, with the telegram crumpled in her left hand, she tried to list for herself the things she had learned, as though to stop herself from listing all the things that she dreaded about Andrew's return. In the end she decided that the only one that really mattered was that she had learned how to know other people. In the old days, whenever she had thought about the men or women she met it had always been in relation to herself: what would they think of her? Were they more or less intelligent than she? How could she impress them? Or depress their pretentions? Now at last she had learned to look at them as they were in their own universe, and to be interested in them and want to know more. It was as though living on her own for the first time in her life she had been able to see the world and its inhabitants for what they really were. And she had been free. Now that freedom was threatened.

Gerry was ashamed of her self-absorption at a time when Andrew must be in beastly pain in some military hospital, but she could not help it. The war had taken her away from the battle she had fought for so long to believe that she was the kind of woman her father and Andrew wanted her to be, and she could not bear the thought of going back to it.

After nearly twenty minutes of fruitless speculation and growing anxiety, Gerry tried to pull herself together and make herself eat something. She could not face the struggle to turn the powdered egg into anything edible and so she simply opened the tin of sardines and ate the lot with a teaspoon. Then she washed the spoon, threw the oily tin into the rubbish bin and had a bath.

Rather to her surprise she managed to get to sleep and, undisturbed by either bomb or ack-ack gun, achieved a solid eight-hour night. It allowed her to reach a kind of rationality. There was nothing she could do for Andrew until he returned and no amount of retrospective anxiety could lessen his wounds. Until he returned the possible difficulties of being both his wife and the independent working woman she had become were irrelevant.

She had no more news of him until the end of August, when she found a brief note in her evening post from some unknown captain informing her that Andrew had had his right foot amputated in hospital in Cairo, had been fitted with an artificial limb, and would be reaching England the following day. Deeply thankful that the injury and its cure had not been worse, she took the note into the office the following morning and asked Suvarov for time off work to go to meet her husband. Gerry was reluctant to ask for extra time, but Andrew obviously had to be met off the boat train at Victoria, and there was no one else to do it; and although there was a lot going on in the analysts' room, the actual quantity of work coming her way was not enough to make her feel that she was scrimshanking.

Waiting for Andrew at Victoria Station, she wondered how they would meet each other; what on earth she would be able to say to him; how he would greet her; whether they could somehow get back to the time before the war, before her pregnancy even, when it was still easy to believe that they loved each other. Before she had left her flat, she had examined her face in the glass with exaggerated care, half believing that her faithlessness must be visible to anyone who looked, but seeing no physical change in her face except for the marks of tiredness that all Londoners wore.

As she stood amid the grime of the crowded platforms, with dusty pigeons flashing irritatingly past her head, and anxious, tired-faced men and women brushing past her, Gerry admitted to herself for the first time exactly what her mind had meant by that word 'faithlessness'. It was not, she acknowledged, the short, physical act itself that worried her – that could not hurt her husband unless she told him of it. No, the real betrayal was what she had felt in Suvarov's arms as he had touched her and talked to her, shown her what 'making love' actually meant to people who knew about it. He had taught her, without knowing what he was doing, just how clumsy, unfeeling, selfish and tyrannical her husband was in bed, and it was realising that she could never unlearn the lesson that was beginning to trouble her so much. She felt like Eve after eating the apple: never could she go back to the state of unknowing; but what she had come to know might threaten to destroy any chance she had to be happy with her husband or to make him happy.

Perhaps, she began to think just as the train appeared at the end of the long, curving grey platform, there are things we can do about it; perhaps now that I know I . . . But no – how could she talk to Andrew about anything like that? The rain-splattered train came rushing down the track towards her. She stood by the barrier, with both hands resting on the curved handle of her umbrella, waiting.

The train doors were flung back with a syncopated rattling crash and people started to edge down from the high steps: tired women with whining children; apparently happy, grinning servicemen with kitbags on their shoulders; a pompous, official-looking man followed by a tittupping, hurrying assistant in an ill-fitting suit. Then she saw a stick, carefully positioned below the step, a khaki-trousered leg following it. She was so sure that its owner must be Andrew that she started to walk forward, having to push her legs ahead one after the other as though she were wading through the stickiness of a bog. She reached the door just as he manoeuvred his other leg onto the platform and was turning, a little breathless, to someone behind him, who slung down his old leather grip.

'Thanks, old boy. Damn good of you,' he said. His voice seemed much more familiar than his face, half-hidden as it was by his formal, badged cap, and Gerry started. The movement caught his eye and he turned to face her. With an extravagant movement of his free hand he pulled off his cap and with it dangling from his outstretched hand, he said:

'Gerry! Darling, how wonderful!'

His face was alight, his dark, greeny-brown eyes narrowing in the intensity of his smile. In the split second

181

before she went to embrace him, Gerry remembered for the first time since their dead baby had been taken from her how it had felt to love him. Her own face seemed to loosen its bonds and she was able to smile back at him as she went towards him.

The hugeness of the relief she felt made her hug him tightly, feeling the brass buttons of his tunic right through the thickness of her gaberdine mackintosh. She let her head rest, just for a moment, against his cold cheek, but she could not speak. After a minute or two, he said gently:

'Gerry, I'm not very good at standing yet.'

'Oh, I'm sorry, Andy,' she said, pulling back at once. 'Does it hurt . . . much?'

'Off and on, but I'm getting used to it, and I can walk pretty well again.'

'I am sorry; but there's one thing to be thankful for, you won't have to go back and face it all again. Have they found a job for you yet? I've waited and waited for letters.'

'Yes, I'm sorry. But all the things I wanted to tell you were secret and so I didn't write at all. Islip said he'd telegraphed you when it happened.'

'Yes, darling, he did,' said Gerry soothingly, thinking that this was not the moment to tell him how little Islip had seen fit to tell her. 'But a job?'

'Yes. I gather it's something in the War Office. I don't quite know what yet, but I'm to start as soon as possible. How do we get to your flat?'

'Taxi I think. I mean, I think it's better waiting than fighting our way on the Underground.'

'All right. How is it? I think you said that Kingsley woman found it for you.'

'It's been fine, but it may be a bit small for the two of us. I think we'll probably have to get something bigger. But it's most frightfully convenient because I can walk to work – and you'll be able to get to the War Office. So much better than having to wait hours for buses that never come.'

'Yes, tell me about this job of yours,' he said, bending to pick up the bag at his side.

'Oh, don't, darling. I'll carry that,' she said, not averse to putting off any discussion of her work just for a while.

'So, what exactly is it?'

'This sounds silly, Andrew, but I can't tell you.'

'Don't be ridiculous. I'm your husband; if you can't trust me, who can you trust?'

This was worse than she had expected. Choosing her words with some care as they walked towards the barrier and Andrew handed over his travel warrant, she said quietly:

'It isn't that. It's like you and the letters you wanted to write. We're not supposed to tell anyone anything about it at all – of course it's not that I don't trust you. But what if someone else managed to hear what I said? That sort of thing. You know.'

'Told your sister?' he asked, so casually that for a moment Gerry missed the danger signs.

'Flixe? No, of course not. She wouldn't let me anyway. She's got pathologically discreet since all this started.'

'Not that it matters now, of course,' he went on, transferring his stick to his other hand in order to hold Gerry's elbow.

Why not? she wanted to ask, but so dreaded his reply that she said nothing about it.

'Mother will be so pleased to know you're back,' she

said instead. 'All the time I was there last summer, she was always talking about you and she asks about you every time I ring up.'

'We'll go for a weekend as soon as I've got things sorted out. I missed her a lot, wanted to have a week or so down there before I started this new job; but they didn't think there was time.'

'I don't suppose it's very comfortable at the moment; she's got three evacuees – six-year-olds, I think. The odd thing is that she seems to have got jolly fond of them. Perhaps it's because they're boys.'

'I'd have thought Fanny would find slum boys particularly difficult, or are they our sort?'

'No. From the East End, she said. But she's never really liked girls. D'you know, I hadn't thought until just now, but perhaps that's why she was always so dissatisfied with Flixe and me. Just dreadfully disappointed that we were girls. Thank God, that one's ours.'

They walked towards the cab together and he held open the door for her and waited until she was seated before trying to lever himself up off the pavement. She thought how charming and how absurd of him to follow the old conventions when it would have been so much simpler for her to stand behind him and help him in. He took her hand when he was at last sitting beside her and, leaning forward to close the sliding partition between them and the driver, said softly:

'Gerry, it's . . . Thank God I'm back. I couldn't bear it out there without you. I don't sleep properly when I'm not with you. And I just don't feel happy any more when we're apart. When you wrote to say you weren't coming, I was nearly desperate.' He raised her hand and kissed her wrist. The warm moistness of his lips made her remember

184

why that old love had never been quite enough. Her instinctive withdrawal made her ashamed of herself. But he misinterpreted her movement and said as he started to kiss her neck:

'Don't worry, darling. Cabbies' mirrors are specially angled so that they can't see what goes on in the back seat. Kiss me, Gerry.'

'Andy, not here. There's something, so . . . so shabby about kissing in taxis.'

'All right,' he said, as though humouring an invalid. 'After all, it's not going to be very long before I can kiss any bit of you I like.'

This time, slightly better prepared, she managed not to shudder. Telling herself that any husband coming back from a war, after well over a year's absence, would talk like that, would want to renew his marriage in the way Andrew obviously wanted, she gripped his hand and tried to look pleased.

In spite of her resolve it was almost all she could do not to sigh out her dissatisfaction forty minutes later as he lay on top of her jerking his way to his own release. Despite the violent physical joining of which she was part she felt that there was no real connection between them; he could have been with any woman – or on his own; he was completely oblivious to her as she lay quite still, her teeth clenched to prevent any of the words in her mind spilling out and hurting him.

When at last it was over and he rolled off her to relapse immediately into a kind of semi-comatose sleep, she wondered how he could do such things without a word to her, without even acknowledging that she was there. Did he not know that lovemaking was something that happened between two people, not something imposed by one for his pleasure on another? Obviously he did not.

She did not feel that she could get straight out of bed and get ready for work as she longed to do, for in that tiny flat he would be bound to wake, and so she lay beside him until he started to snore. Then she did slide out from under the blankets and, moving as quietly as she possibly could, got ready to leave for the office. Just before she went out of the door, she scribbled a note for him, saying simply: 'Have gone to work, darling. I'll be back at about seven and perhaps we could go out to dinner to celebrate. G.'

She hurried across the park, not even stopping on the bridge to see how the dreary grey weather of that dismal August day was affecting her view down the lake, and nearly ran up the stairs to her office. To her astonishment Suvarov was there, the first time in months that he had not been out at half-past two, and she stood in the doorway, still and blushing.

He looked up at her and she could see from the understanding in his eyes that he knew exactly what had just happened to her. Pushing down as far as she could the knowledge that Andrew would never have seen what Suvarov could so easily see, she just said:

'I'm sorry, Peter,' and turned to her own desk. He got up to come and stand in front of her and she hoped very much that he would not touch her. He did not, just stood there looking at her and speaking in his deep, slightly accented voice:

'Gerry, I am several kinds of brute to have done to you what I did, but I am not the kind of dog in the manger who would do it and then criticise you for going back to your husband.'

186

Without thinking anything except that she was with a friend who understood everything, Gerry said:

' "Going back" makes it all sound so very voluntary.'

'I am sorry.' There was a pause and then he said with a tentativeness that was new to Gerry: 'He didn't . . . hurt you?'

She shook her head. 'Nothing like that; it was all so unconscious. I might not have been there at all.' She made a sound like a laugh, but there was no mirth in her expression. 'God knows why I'm telling you of all people things like this.'

'Who better, Gerry? I care for you so much, and we both know that we can't be anything except friends. But listen, he is a young man – I don't want to put this in a way that might hurt you, Gerry, but it is worth saying – and the techniques of it all are quite tricky to learn. You have to be taught and perhaps he has not had the luck to . . . to love anyone who can teach him.'

Gerry was silent for a long time, but when she spoke she surprised him.

'That makes such sense that I don't know why I never thought of it. Will you tell me something else, since we're able to be honest with each other?'

'If I can.'

'Do you mind?'

'That you are sleeping with Andrew? Yes, with part of me I mind very much – so much that I can't talk about it in a proper spirit of detachment.' She looked up at that and saw that his face was taut and his mouth thinned to a single bitter line.

'I'm sorry.'

'There's no point in that. We are both sorry, and so would they be if they knew.'

187

'Diana might, but I doubt if Andrew would be anything except furious.'

It did not occur to Gerry until much later how odd it was that she and Suvarov should talk with such freedom about their spouses and the situation they had created between them. But as she walked slowly back to her husband that evening, she began to understand and to feel as though somehow Peter had withdrawn the pain and the shame of what had happened. He was so good to her, so careful of her feelings despite his manifold worries, that it seemed ungrateful and almost cussed to regret what had brought them so close. She could not have him as her lover, but he had shown himself to be very much her friend.

The bridge over the lake looked inviting once again and she mooned over her view for nearly half an hour, before turning for home with a smile lifting the corners of her lips once again.

12

'What did he say?' said Andrew in greeting as Gerry
eventually pushed open the door of what had once been
her private flat. Her mind was so full of Suvarov and the
way he had taken the fuses out of the UXBs of their
feelings that she almost reproduced his precise words.
Just in time the sight of Andrew sitting on the edge of
their bed putting a sock on to his artificial foot brought
her up short, and she asked:

'What about?'

'When you gave in your notice, of course.'

Gerry remembered how she had ignored the one
comment he had already made about her job and wished
that she could do the same again. But it had to be faced
and she could not pretend to have misunderstood
anything as direct as that. Feeling more nervous than she
had for ages and with a strange cold sweatiness breaking
out behind her knees and in her elbows, she said:

'But Andrew, it's war work. I can't just give it up. It
matters.'

His reddish face, which had once seemed so handsome

to her, was set in an expression of complete incomprehension. She could see no anger in it, but the blankness in his brown eyes began to arouse the sleeping rage in her own mind. She tried to calm it, understanding from somewhere that she could only strengthen his anger by showing her own.

'But I'm home, Gerry. You don't want to go on working now.'

'Was that a question?' she asked, trying to stop her voice shaking and giving him every chance.

'No, of course not.' The crispness that he used when speaking to his men began to edge into his voice.

'Then how do you know what I want?' The epithets she would have liked to throw at him were so real, so near the surface, that she wondered if he could sense them. His face began to redden in a way she had only seen once or twice before, and his lips started to quiver, not like those of a child who is trying not to cry, but with the effort of trying to hold down his anger.

'Gerry, what is all this? You're my wife. I can understand that you didn't want to come out to Palestine after you'd been so ill and with the Mediterranean so dangerous once the bloody French had surrendered, but—'

'Not all the French have surrendered,' she interrupted, suddenly furious that someone like him should so dismiss people like Philippe and Michel and all the other, more shadowy figures about whom she had only heard, who were risking frightful things to carry the war back into France.

'I always forget you're a quarter French. But never mind that now; it's not the point. You always did run away from important things into irrelevances. No, don't answer that. Gerry, don't let's get angry with each other. Your place is with me now. Why do you think that married women aren't being called up, even though the law allows it?'

'For the same reason that married women need their husbands' permission to join the WRNS,' she said coldly. But he did not understand and even smiled at her like a proprietory teacher applauding a stupid pupil's eventual success.

'Exactly. Women who have husbands have obligations and should not have to struggle out there as well. Now, come and have a drink and then you can change and we'll go out for dinner.'

'No, please don't try to bury this by being kind to me. I don't want kindness, Andrew, or to be told what I must do. I want to be myself, with all the inadequacies that may entail. I can't bear pretending to be just a female equivalent of you . . . in other words, you without the job, the power or the money. I am different, Andy, a different kind of person. I have a job to do and I want to go on doing it. It matters. I am reasonably good at it. And,' she went on, her voice rising into antagonism at last, 'what do you expect me to do while you're at the War Office? Sit around a little flat like this, just waiting for my lord and master?'

She was distressed to see an expression that looked like pain on his face. It was horrible to think that she was hurting him, but her future and her very self seemed to be at stake and if he were insisting on having it out now, she could not pretend again even if that would have saved him from being hurt. He rubbed his hands over his face and looked up at her. Trying not to remember the old battles she had had with her father and which, through love and weakness, she had eventually allowed him to win, trying to look back at her husband without shiftiness, she concentrated on the radiating green lines that marked the brown irises of his eyes.

'Gerry,' he said at last, his voice grating on her in its deliberate softness, 'don't you think that after all I've been through I deserve to have a wife who is a wife? I don't think you can quite understand what it is like to be a soldier fighting a war, to see one's friends die, to have to look at blood and brains and smashed bones, to listen to the guns and the explosives and to know that one may be next. To come back from that, wounded, I'd have thought one deserved the comfort of one's wife.'

Gerry turned away from him and walked into the tiny kitchen to fetch herself a glass of water. When she came back ready to speak, he forestalled her:

'Don't look at me like that, please, Gerry.'

'Andrew, I am trying to remind myself very strenuously that you must, indeed, be in a bad way after the things that have happened to you. But please try to have a little imagination. In London last year we were bombed for more than seventy nights on end. Do you think that we have not sat waiting for the explosion or the fire that is going to kill us? Do you think I have not seen blood and smashed limbs and cried over them? You might remember that my sisters were buried for fourteen hours after a direct hit and that one of them was killed. We had a war here that has killed far more people than yours' – her voice rose, alarming him – 'and you come and lecture me on my duties to the returning warrior. No, don't say anything until I've got it all out. There's one more thing.'

Andrew sat silent on the bed, looking truculent but ridiculous in his short dressing-gown and socks. Gerry then said in a voice so quiet that its coldness was the more remarkable:

'Did you think for one second that my illness after the baby died might mean that you should come back from your war?' That was easy to answer and he said in surprise and complete honesty:

'Of course not. Gerry, you don't seem to understand. I am a serving officer, under orders.'

'So am I. I don't have a uniform or a regiment or crested buttons. But I am fighting this war, too, and I can't give up because you've lost a foot. You said that we shouldn't be angry with each other and I agree. There's no point in screaming out insults. But this is too important for me to pretend about. I'm going to have a bath and then perhaps we should go and eat somewhere and talk about something else.'

She left him, surprised to find herself shaking all over as she undressed and got into the obligatorily shallow bath.

They did not revert to the quarrel, but by everything either of them did and said in the next few horrible days, they spelled out their positions in the unwinnable war that had been declared between them. Gerry found it unbearable to recognise that Andrew was as unhappy as she and that there was nothing to be done about it. There was no compromise possible: theirs was a battle which one would have to win and the other lose.

She hated to think what losing would do to Andrew, but the prospect of his winning was not bearable. With that knowledge in her mind, Gerry found it next to impossible to pretend that everything was all right between them and that she enjoyed his company, playing the part of the sort of wife he wanted. She drove herself to work harder than ever, and took up firewatching on two nights each week so that she had a reasonable excuse for being away from the flat. Andrew, she knew, took refuge with old friends and new acquaintances in his club. It was curious, she noted with a new detachment about a fortnight after his return, how he had always really preferred the company of his brother officers to that of his wife and yet had always managed to persuade himself that he needed her and pined for her and loved her.

When she had decided to volunteer for firewatching duties, she had been tempted to go back to Newgate Street and work for old Ben Calbourne, but the journey there was difficult and the distance too far to walk on any regular basis. She volunteered instead for an ARP post just south of Oxford Street in a road of discreet flats and houses.

There had been no bombing raids over London since the terrible night in May when over two thousand fires had been started in the city, nearly fifteen hundred people killed and many more severely wounded. The Thames had been low that night, and once the water mains had been smashed the heroic, struggling fire-engine crews ran out of water at fire after fire. It was probably the worst night of the entire Blitz. But it seemed to have been the last.

Along with all the other Londoners who had witnessed it, Gerry could not believe that it would not be repeated, and never once felt that her firewatching stints were time wasted even when there was no sight or sound of a German bomber. One evening at the beginning of October she had been on duty for two and a half hours with nothing much to do and had spent her shift tidying up the post and spring-cleaning it. She was just organising the paperwork for her relief when she noticed a large, shiny black motor draw up a little way down the road. Mildly curious to know who would be disgorged from such opulent luxury, Gerry stood at the doorway of her post, a bundle of requisitions and memos in her hands, and watched.

A smartly uniformed civilian chauffeur got out to hold open the passenger door and a young woman dressed in some filmy, sparkly white stuff emerged. She stood on the pavement with her back to the ARP post and Gerry decided in half-ashamed envy that the glamorous frock was rather vulgar in the way it clung to the girl's excellent figure, but even in her disapproval she could not deny its allure. Then a dark-haired man in khaki followed the girl.

Gerry mocked herself for her nonsensical idea that he was Peter Suvarov. True, there was a slight resemblance at that distance, but she must be very far gone in her schoolgirl feelings for him if she were going to see him in every dark-haired officer she saw around London. Whoever he was, he bent down as though to say something to someone still in the car, then he put his hand under the girl's elbow and they turned to walk towards the post.

As they walked, the man slid his hand around the girl's waist and she allowed her fair head to rest against his khaki shoulder. They walked together, not just in step, but as though they were somehow matched, connected. Gerry forgot the vulgarity of the girl's clothes and stood spellbound by the confident closeness of them both and longed to be able to feel like that herself. Something about the way they moved suggested that they trusted each other absolutely, and she felt that they were the very archetype of lovers. Tears formed unbidden in her eyes,

195

as they sometimes did at weddings, and she envied that girl with an emotion she had never known before.

It was not until the couple were starting up the shallow steps of one of the luxurious blocks of flats that she saw their faces in the light of the moon. Then she turned back into the post, her teeth locked over her lower lip and her hands crumpling the thin sheets of official paper she held. Oddly enough the first thought that gave itself words in her mind was: how could Flixe go round London dressed like that, showing herself off as though she were a streetwalker? Only when the pain in her lip brought Gerry back to her senses did she start to think of what might be the background to the picture she had just seen, of what there must be between her sister and the man she herself loved so much and could not have. How did Peter Suvarov know Flixe so well, and what could they be doing, embraced like that and walking into a flat that was miles away from where either of them lived? What the hell was going on?

'So sorry I'm late, Mrs Kyrle, I just couldn't get a bus. I say, are you all right?'

Gerry turned to face her relief, a cheerful woman from Kensington.

'Yes, I'm all right. Why?'

'You look ghastly – as though you were about to faint. Look, sit down and I'll make you a cup of tea.'

'No; no, thank you, Mrs Pickett. I must be off, or I'll be even more dotty at work tomorrow. I must get some sleep.' It was hard to keep her voice calm, but through all the turmoil in her mind, she knew that she must get away, be alone.

It was not until she had left the tiresomely concerned woman behind that she realised that she would be alone only until she got back to the flat. Then there would be Andrew to face. She ignored the bus stops in Oxford Street and set off to walk through Mayfair towards Dover Street, cherishing the short time she would have to herself. A cruising taxi idled by and the driver wound down his window to call:

'Taxi, miss?'

She turned her white face towards him and just shook her head. He shrugged and sped away. Gerry watched him go, half regretful. She had not realised how tired she was until that moment; her feet seemed to burn through the thin soles of her shoes at each step, and her eyes and throat ached. She wanted to ignore the implications of what she had seen, but she also wanted to know exactly what it had signified. As she crossed Charles Street, she thought of the evening at Anna Kingsley's the previous winter, when Flixe had been so determinedly kind. Had Suvarov told Flixe of Gerry's idiotic passion for him and how he had had to show her that she had no chance? Had they discussed poor Gerry and her greensickness, and both of them decided to be as gentle and kind as they could? Now it was not only her feet that burned. The whole of her body seemed on fire, a kind of beacon of angry shame.

When she reached the flat, she was in such a state of tiredness and muddled misery that she did not take her usual deep breath before going in to tackle Andrew. She just put her key in the door, turned it, and went in. He looked up from the newspaper with his now familiar expression of half-defensive anger and said:

'How did it go?' Then before she could answer, she saw him fling the paper down on the floor and get out of his chair. He still could not walk without his stick and it had fallen on the floor, and so he just stood there, his arms opening, and said:

'Gerry, dearest, you look terrible. Come here, my love.'

The kindness in his voice was too much for her shaky self-command and she burst into tears.

'Come here,' he said again and she walked into his embrace. His arms hugged her and his voice was gentle. She let her aching head lie against his jacket and rested for a moment. His hands took off her hat, without letting her go, and then started to stroke her hair. His lips brushed her forehead, and his voice murmured endearments. She hardly listened, just taking the comfort he offered, until he said:

'Darling, Gerry, you've come back to me.' She was too tired to contradict him, and not selfish enough to take what he offered and then deliberately hurt him, and so she just pressed closer and let him touch her as he would.

Much later, as they lay side by side in bed, he as usual asleep at once, Gerry wondered what she had made such a fuss about. What difference did it make if he wanted some pleasure from her and thought nothing of hers? It was something she could give him without trouble and if it would keep him happy and quiet, why should she deny it to him? There was no answer to such a question. She did not even try to think about it, just lay silent and sleepless, feeling quite alone and utterly without worth.

Sleep must have come in the end, though, for when her alarm clock went she was surprised to hear it. The room was completely dark, because of the efficient blackout curtains Anna Kingsley had arranged when Gerry took the flat, but she could not stay in bed, however tired she might feel. She was beginning to ease herself out from under the blankets when Andrew reached for her, his arms warm and heavy.

'Andrew, I must get up, or I'll be late – and so will you. The War Office doesn't like its officers to be idle.'

'No, I know, but I want to celebrate our remarriage, Gerry. Come here for just a minute, I want to cuddle you.'

'Andy . . . ' She was trying to frame a protest that would not hurt him, but she could not find words. 'Just for a minute then,' she finished drearily. He seemed not to notice her lack of enthusiasm and hugged her close, winding his legs around hers and fiddling with the satin ribbons at the neck of her nightdress.

'This is one of your trousseau nighties, isn't it?'

'Yes,' she said, surprised that he should have noticed and remembered.

'You wore it that first night in Paris.'

'You sound amused, Andy.'

'I was just remembering how frightened I was,' he said, stroking the soft skin of her neck.

'You? Frightened? But why?'

'I hadn't understood then how easy it was – or how much you would enjoy it.' He started to kiss her neck and did not see the expression on her face as she grasped the full force of his misunderstanding.

'Andrew, I must get up. Stop it now.'

'All right, Madam Headmistress. But only till tonight.' His voice was full of amusement and a kind of patronising tolerance.

How was it possible, Gerry asked herself as she escaped from the flat and set off towards her office, that two people so intimately joined physically should have so little understanding of each other's minds? She had had no idea on that first night that he had been frightened. But even so it was hard to believe that he could really feel nothing of her revulsion. In the early days she had always assumed that the reality of love was an instant and unbreakable understanding of the kind that she had found with Peter Suvarov.

Even before she reached the end of that thought, she had already realised its absurdity: there could never have been any love between Suvarov and herself. She had been merely wallowing in self-indulgent fantasy, and he had understood her only because he knew women so well, just as Evelyn Adamson had hinted. He had recognised Gerry's state of mind because it was all too familiar to him, and he had probably laughed about it with her sister.

Suddenly she felt a hot tide of hate pouring through her, whether for Flixe or for Peter she was not quite sure. But she felt humiliated and bitterly jealous of them both. How could they have deceived her like that? Flixe was hers, her belonging and her responsibility. How could Suvarov have seduced her? And how could Flixe, knowing that Gerry was working for him ... Gerry broke off the thought. Of course, Flixe did not know, unless Suvarov had told her. Gerry herself had never told Flixe where or for whom she was working, and Flixe had never been indiscreet enough to ask. So, she said to herself, it's him. He knows all about both of us, and he could do that to us. Bastard!

As she walked reluctantly to the office, she wondered whether it would be easy to get a transfer to some other organisation or department. But how could she ask him for it? When he had offered, way back in February, she had cheerfully said that she could deal with her feelings about him and wanted to stay in his office. And how could she justify to Andrew or herself her determination to continue working if she were prepared to leave RE(1)R just because the man she had so greatly loved was having an affair with her sister?

He was already at his desk when Gerry walked into the office and she could not forbear to look at him, searching the face she thought she had loved for signs of what he had been doing. His first smile was the same as usual, warm and warming, but it began to fade as Gerry did not answer it. With a sigh, so light that she half doubted that she had heard it, he put down the paper he was reading.

'Tell me, Gerry.'

'Oh, I can't bore you with my troubles day after day. Pay no attention. I'm just a bit tired. My relief was late, you know, last night at the ARP post and so I didn't get to bed for ages,' she said, surprised to hear no sound of the boiling emotions in her voice.

Before Suvarov could speak, the door of the office opened and Tony Eynsham came in, saying:

'Gerry, could you come? Mike's in a state and I think you're the only person who could reach him.'

'Of course I'll come. What happened?'

'He and Michel were quarrelling again and Michel said something about the British running away at Dunkirk.'

'Doesn't that bloody man understand yet how Mike feels having left his brother there?' demanded Gerry as they reached the door. She went in, aware that Eynsham had not followed her, to see Mike sitting at his table, very pale and shivering. Everyone else was apparently working, even the French boy whose quarrel had brought Mike to this pitch. Gerry touched him gently on the shoulder. He started violently.

201

'Don't, Mike; it's only me, Gerry,' she said.

At that he turned to her, but he did not speak. Gerry tried again.

'Mike, don't do this to yourself. Simon's all right; you told me so. He's in the camp and your mother's sending him good food parcels. He's a lot safer there than all those men in the Arctic convoys or the ones fighting Rommel in the desert.' She knew that he was not really listening, but she knew also that the sound of a kind voice occasionally helped to soothe his private miseries. But not this time. She glared over his head at the others and one by one they left the analysts' room. Then, as gently as she could, she laid a hand on his head.

'Mike, dear Mike, what is it?'

'He's dead. He was shot trying to escape.' He sobbed, once, but there were no tears in his eyes. She thought how much easier it would be for him if he had been able to cry. She pulled his head forward and cradled it against her shoulder, wishing that of all the things she might have said to reassure him she had chosen others. He let his head lie against her for a while and she hoped that her slowly growing affection for him would help just a little to ease his distress. At last he pulled away from her and said in a choked voice:

'Gerry, I must get out of here. Will you come for a walk?'

Mike's distress wrenched Gerry away from her own selfish preoccupations. He gave her, too, another reason to stay working for Suvarov, and for resisting Andrew's orders to relinquish her job: while she was apparently the only person who could calm Mike, her determination to remain could be justified. She went back to the flat that evening ready to resist any blandishment or order from her husband.

When she got back one look at his face made her heart shrink and her smile and voice were hard when she greeted him. He did not return either the smile or the words. Gerry shrugged and went into the bedroom to change her shoes.

'Who was that naval officer?' Andrew demanded. Gerry spun round and came back to the sitting-room, one shoe in her hand.

'What naval officer? Andrew, what on earth is the matter?'

'The one you were walking round St James's Park with, arm in arm, this afternoon. He was crying so I suppose you'd been telling him that you'd had enough of him, too, poor brute.'

That arrow was so wide of the mark that Gerry even laughed a little.

'No, Andy dear. That was poor Mike from the office.' Her laughter stopped abruptly as she thought of Mike. 'He's had the most frightful luck. He was blown up and half-drowned at Dunkirk and as they carried him on board the last ship, with the Stukas dive-bombing all the ships and the beaches, he saw his brother – his younger brother – left behind with all those other poor men. The boy was picked up and had been in prison camp since then.'

'Had?' repeated Andrew, sobered and ashamed of himself.

'Yes, poor Mike's just heard that he was part of an escape attempt that failed. He was shot just outside the wire.'

Andrew Kyrle laid his face in his hands and muttered:

'I'm sorry, Gerry. I'm sorry.' There was a pause while she tried to feel something for him. Then, when she said nothing, he went on: 'Gerry, promise you'll never let any other man . . . I couldn't bear it.' When she still did not speak he lifted his head and looked at her. Burying the memory of the short moment when she had believed that Suvarov loved her, she said quite gently:

'I'm your wife, Andrew. Yours.' And she believed that it was true in a way that it had not been until she had seen her sister in Suvarov's embrace.

But despite the shock she had felt when she saw them together, despite the determination she had felt then to burn away all her affection for Peter Suvarov, after a week or two Gerry had found herself just as deeply entangled as ever. There were even times when the knowledge that Flixe found him attractive and admirable enough to love gave strength to Gerry's feelings for him. Flixe had always been so choosy, and had always had the pick of any men around her. If she were so deeply involved with Peter, he must really be worth something.

Then there were other times when Gerry's anger and resentment almost threatened to boil over. It was a shock to discover just how jealous she could be – and how the jealousy could operate in two opposite directions at the same time. She forced herself to admit that she was furious with both of them. But at least the power of what they had made her feel helped to distract her from her battles with Andrew.

By the beginning of November she had not so much yielded to him as detached herself from the battlefield. Her physical self was at his disposal, but the real core of her identity was separate. There were times when she

204

almost felt as though she were sitting apart watching herself playing the role of his wife.

She was increasingly busy in the office, which also helped. The three principal sources of intelligence from France seemed to be overcoming their suspicions of RE(1)R and were at last forwarding streams of reports to Queen Anne's Gate. Gerry was certain that the intelligence they got was censored and doctored, but at least it was beginning to give a relatively clear picture of conditions in occupied France.

The reports that crossed her desk for rewriting or filing were not concerned with the victimisation, torture and killing of individuals by the Nazis, for which she was supremely grateful. It was bad enough to have to read of the effects of the occupation itself on the mass of French people: the curfews and restrictions, the starvation rations they were allotted while vast amounts of French produce were channelled away to Germany; the petty measures that were aimed at controlling the occupied, removing their self-respect, humbling them, turning them into chattels of their conquerors. Gerry had felt contempt and rage for Marshal Pétain ever since he had signed the armistice with Germany and put Britain at such risk of invasion, but just occasionally her emotions were tempered with a kind of sadness that the old man should have thought that by treating with Hitler he would be able to save France and the French from the terrible carnage and destruction he had seen at first hand between 1914 and 1918.

In spite of the amount of material she had to read and process, she had not yet been able to find any thread that linked anything that was happening in France to any of the groups or individuals who were under surveillance in

205

London. But she knew that she did not see everything. One late afternoon when the raw chill of fog was seeping through the edges of the ill-fitting window behind his desk, she ventured to ask Suvarov whether he had found anything. He was standing in front of their small coal fire at the time and she watched his face in its dim orange glow as he started to answer.

'Gerry, don't ask things like that.'

'Don't you trust me?' she asked, too surprised to feel a renewal of the hurt he and Flixe had dealt her.

'That's not the point. The less you know, the less dangerous you are to us all.'

'I see.' She was suddenly visited with so clear a memory of the scene in Mayfair that she actually felt faint. She leaned her forehead on her clenched fist and after a little while said as carefully as she could: 'It gives one a most unpleasant feeling – sinister almost – to know that people one . . . likes and trusts, are keeping things from you.'

'Gerry, it's not only you,' he said, sounding bored or tired to death. 'Part of the difficulty of this job is trying to keep the different parts of it separate and the people in each part unknown to each other.'

'But we're all here, anyway. You don't keep the analysts separate.'

'There are others, but I don't want to talk about them, Gerry. The clearer I can keep the divisions the less chance that anyone may think that they can get to information through you. Do you see?'

'Yes, I see. I'm sorry.' She just could not make herself say to him any of the other things she wanted to say or ask the questions that might soothe the beastly jealousy that sometimes made her even more ashamed than her love for him had done.

FLIXE

1941

13

Flixe was pouring a jug of cold water over her newly washed hair. She winced as the icy cold lashed her scalp but told herself bracingly that at least cold water rinsed the shampoo out quicker than hot. Two more jugs did the trick and, shivering, she wrapped an old pink towel turbanwise around her head and reached for her dressing-gown.

It was curious, she thought as she walked into her bedroom and sat at the dressing-table to cope with her eyebrows, how much she used to enjoy titivating herself before the war. But perhaps every pleasure could be turned into drudgery when it became part of the duty you owed to other people. Or perhaps she was simply cussed and as soon as she was told to do one thing would instantly want to do the other. All she wanted now, after almost eighteen months of her peculiar job, was to spend an evening dressed in her oldest, baggiest trousers and a tatty jersey, curled up on the sofa with a good book. How Gerry the studious would laugh if only Flixe were able to tell her. She herself laughed a little at the picture. And how her father would crow, she thought, not laughing at all as she remembered the innumerable occasions when he had castigated her for vanity or for flirting with his junior officers. Flixe tried to stamp on the memories and to concentrate on her task.

Her eyebrows reduced once more to smooth, perfect arcs above her deep-blue eyes, she took off the towel and started running her fingers through her wet hair to untease the knots before winding in the curlers. But she could not keep her father out of her thoughts, and she admitted to herself a little shamefacedly that her untapped resentment had played a large part in her almost instant acceptance of Peter Suvarov's extraordinary proposition.

If her father had once said simply, 'You look nice, Felicity,' would she have felt it so important to drag every guest's attention and admiration to herself and away from him . . . and from Gerry? It really was not, she silently assured her reflection, that she had wanted to take anything away from Gerry; but the number of times when they had been dressed almost identically and Gerry had been admired or kissed and Flixe criticised had made it impossible for her not to try to outshine her elder sister. How those criticisms had hurt! 'Your socks are wrinkled; anyone would think you were a slum child,' had given way as the years passed to, 'Must you have more pudding? Your spots are bad enough already,' and 'That frock is cut far too low for someone with your figure,' . . . 'You've far too much lipstick on; please remember that your appearance reflects on me,' and 'Felicity, do you think that at this year's Hunt Ball you could confine your peculiar instincts and avoid flirting too grossly?'

Gerry had had spots at fourteen, too, but they had never been the subject of luncheon conversation; she had worn her frocks as low and her lipstick as bright as Flixe, but Gerry could do no wrong (except on the subject of education). Even when she had been caught kissing someone in the bushes when she was about sixteen, she had been dealt with gently. Despite the gentleness, though, Flixe had never been able to forget the repellent expression her father had used in his rebuke: 'You see, Gerry darling, the sort of men you'll meet when you're a little older simply won't have anything to do with sucked oranges. You must keep yourself to yourself until a good chap falls in love with you and marries you.'

Oh, he was the most ridiculous man! Flixe mentally chastised herself for allowing his idiocies (no doubt rooted in some inadequacy of his own) to have any effect on her at all; but the constant harping on the theme of her untidiness, sluttishness, flirtatiousness and exhibitionism had bred within her an anger that had found no expression until the war had presented her with such a superb opportunity to get her own back.

The telephone bell shrilled through the small, cluttered room, and Flixe lounged over to a table by the window and picked up the receiver, listened for a moment and then said:

'Yes? Darling, of course . . . What? Oh, well, just a kimono at the moment. Oh, good. Yes, so do I. What time will you come? . . . I can't wait. A *bientôt*, then. . . . Yes, indeed.'

When she was ready, she stood examining herself to make certain that the dress looked as it should. Clingingly cut on the bias from pale amethyst satin, it outlined her figure as she stood still and yet the skirt swung seductively around her as she moved. Without vanity, she recognised how well the frock suited her, and she suddenly wished that it was Suvarov whom she was expecting. Inevitably came the memory of the one evening when she had had to act the part of his mistress.

They had walked embraced for about fifty yards to the entrance of the building. Once the doors had shut behind them, Suvarov had taken his arms from around her waist and then led the way to the lift and up to the office's flat on the third floor. He had let them both in and poured her a glass of hock from the well-stocked fridge. As he handed it to her their fingers touched and she had looked up into his lined face.

She remembered how he had smiled, as though he had understood all the half-formed thoughts in her mind.

'You're an exceedingly beautiful woman, Felicity,' he had said in that irresistible voice of his, which always made something within her shiver with pleasure. 'And it would be all too easy to fall under your spell. But it would do neither of us any good, and it might do you considerable harm. I've learned my lesson in a hard and painful way, and I know that I mustn't.'

Aware that she was blushing, Flixe had shaken her head and gone to sit in one of the uncomfortable chairs, sipping her wine.

'In any case,' she had said when she had been sure that her voice would have all the careless gaiety to carry off what she had to say, 'one should never mix business with pleasure.'

He had taken her cue and they had talked their way out of the dangerous moment. But she had not forgotten it and smiled to herself as she remembered what it had felt like to stand within his embrace and feel his lips on her hair. That surely was more than he had had to do for the pantomime. Suddenly irritated by her fantasies, she tartly

212

reminded herself that it was not he who she was supposed to be thinking about, and she had enough to do if she was to keep Jean-Pierre West-Grandison happy without succumbing to him completely. He was by far the most dangerous of the men in whom Suvarov was interested and the most dangerous to her peace of mind.

One of her straps was inching out at the shoulder of her dress and she was just pinning it in when the doorbell rang. Arranging her lips into a teasingly knowing smile that she found rather disagreeable whenever she caught sight of it in a glass, she went to open the door.

'Jean-Pierre! How lovely to see you.'

'Félicitée, so beautiful always. Here, these are for you.'

'Orchids! You shouldn't. I don't need flowers. Look, I'll just fix them in my dress and then we can go.'

'Let me help you. Have you a pin?'

She found one, and stood patiently while he expertly pinned the absurdly expensive and rather ugly flowers at her corsage, only letting his fingers stray a little way. Then he bent his undeniably handsome face and kissed her breast just above the flowers.

He took her as usual to one of the astonishingly expensive nightclubs near Piccadilly and was greeted with all the deference due to a rich, high-tipping *habitué*. Flixe relinquished her cloak in the ladies' room and returned to the hall to take Jean-Pierre's arm as they were shown to a prominent table. Champagne was quickly brought with all the paraphernalia of silver ice-bucket and thick white napkins. As soon as the waiters had left them, Jean-Pierre raised his glass.

'Félicitée, to your beautiful eyes.'

Flixe raised her own glass in response, smiled at him over the rim of the glass, and sipped the prickly dry wine.

213

'My dear,' she said softly as she put her glass down, 'you are far too generous. Champagne, the orchids, and all those presents you keep sending me. You spoil me.'

'Don't you like being spoiled?' he asked. It might have sounded trite or leering, but it was said with such self-derision and such a twinkle in his black-brown eyes that she could not help laughing.

'Of course I do,' she said far more naturally. 'But in the middle of a war?'

'What has the war to do with us, my darling?' he said, laying one of his firm hands over hers. 'I'm over-age for this ridiculous conscription and you're far too beautiful to bury yourself in khaki serge knickers and those appalling skirts. Thank goodness for your architect.'

'Yes, indeed. I'm learning a lot, too. It's extraordinary how one can have been visiting London all one's life and hardly noticed the churches and parks and statues,' answered Flixe, hoping to divert him from the subject of knickers.

'I wish I could take you to Paris, Félicitée. But I shall. When it's all over.'

'Do you miss it so much?' she asked, struck by the change in his voice and expression.

'Of course. I've always thought of France as my real home – and hated my father for exiling me at school here.'

'So why did you stay once you were grown up?'

He turned away for a moment to summon the waiter to refill their glasses.

'The demands of his empire. Enjoying its fruits as I do, I could hardly throw it all away once it became mine. But enough of my history, Félicitée. Shall we dance?'

She rose obediently and walked with him to the small

floor. As she turned to 'melt into his embrace' as she sardonically put it to herself, she found herself looking over his shoulder straight into the disapproving face of Johnny Blenkarne, one of the friends of her childhood. His hazel eyes were outraged as they stared at her and her companion. She dropped her painted eyelids and tried to pretend that she had not recognised him.

'My dear, what is it?' asked Jean-Pierre caressingly.

'What do you mean?' she said, pulling away from him far enough to look into his dark handsome face.

'You suddenly tensed, as though you were afraid. *Chérie*, you cannot be afraid of me, can you?'

Flixe smiled at him, leaned forward again and whispered into his ear.

'But of course, Jean-Pierre. What woman would not be afraid of a man as devastating and famously dangerous as you?'

He laughed and tightened his clasp of her waist.

'Good,' he said, and then: 'My darling, I'm glad you are wearing the *Ombres du Paradis*. I knew it would suit you. There's something about the way its first simple fragrance yields after a moment to a richer spiciness that reminds me of you.'

Golly, thought Flixe to herself, how long am I going to be able to hold him at bay? He was a far more sophisticated man than any of the others Suvarov had asked her to charm and she was afraid that he was going to demand his pound of flesh far more insistently than any of the others.

But she managed to keep the conversation relatively impersonal until the early hours of the next morning. They finished the first bottle of champagne and ordered another; they danced again; they ate the most expensive

215

dishes on the menu; and she managed by deft changes of subject and the odd deliberate misunderstanding to prevent him from moving their relationship on to the next stage. And all through the evening she was aware of the brooding presence of Johnny Blenkarne.

Once he passed near their table and Flixe was afraid that he was going to accost her. To control whatever damage he might do, she leaned forward to whisper to Jean-Pierre:

'There's a boy over there I used to know at home. He looks horribly tight. I hope he's not going to make a scene.'

Jean-Pierre turned deliberately to look at the young man.

'The RAF officer? Strange that he should have chosen a place like this to ease his Benzedrine hangover.'

'I beg your pardon?' said Flixe, genuinely puzzled.

'That's all that's the matter with him. They take it, you know, to cope with the hours they have to fly – and the terror. Then when they come off duty they have to come down from the high it gives them. They become desperately suspicious and often end up in tears. Poor children.'

Despite the apparent sympathy of his last comment, his voice was full of disdain.

'You sound a little contemptuous,' said Flixe, giving him a teasing smile to take the sting out of her comment.

'Not for the children. No, I feel sorry for them. But for the way the war is managed? Yes, I have plenty of contempt.'

At last, thought Flixe silently, here we go. But he brushed aside the subject of the war and talked again about her eyes and worse, and she was forced to suggest that they dance again to break up his increasingly intimate compliments.

*

216

She got to bed, alone, at half-past one and she was far too tired to think through all the things he had said and the moments when she might have pushed him further towards the subjects about which Suvarov needed to know. But she woke seven hours later and lay running through it all then.

Jean-Pierre was far more astute than she had thought when they first met, as well as infinitely more appealing. The fact that she was coming actually to like him made the evenings she had to spend in his company almost enjoyable, and yet it added to her difficulties. The whole point of the operation was for her to make him love her – or desire her at least – so that she could demand – or cheat – information out of him. So far she was not doing very well with the information and appeared to be in danger of falling into her own trap.

The flap of the letter box and thump of the mail on to the doormat got her out of bed ten minutes later. She pulled her kimono over her nightdress and thrust her feet into a pair of sloppy sheepskin slippers before going out into the dark little hall to fetch her letters. Then she made herself a cup of ersatz coffee and took it and the post back to bed. There was to be a meeting of the architecture committee at ten-thirty, but she did not have to report to her office before then.

Most of the envelopes contained bills, but there was a sad note from Ming, back at boarding school and struggling, she wrote, to get enough information into her thick skull to pass her Higher School Certificate. Without Annie, Ming had decided that she did not want to leave school at the first opportunity and had yielded to her headmistress's persuasions that she should take Higher so that if she wanted to try for university after the war she would be qualified to do so.

She wrote that her beloved Miss Roseheath seemed to have forgiven her for her decision, and that the new French master, a refugee called Monsieur Julien, was pleased with her progress in French. But so much of her depression came through the deliberate cheerfulness and schoolgirlish slang that Flixe reached for her own writing things so that she could send a reply straight away. That done, she turned to the last envelope and with a sinking heart saw that it had been delivered by hand and was addressed to her in Johnny Blenkarne's handwriting. She tore open the thin blue envelope and read:

Dearest, darling Flixe, tell me you didn't chuck me for that blasted middle-aged dago. You couldn't have. But if not, why were you dancing with him? Come to the Berkeley with me tonight, Flixe, please. I know you said it wasn't any good and I promised not to bother you, but I've only got twenty-four hours more before I go back on ops. Please, Flixe. Love Johnny.

Poor Johnny, she thought in detached sadness. But there was nothing she could do for him anymore and so she picked up her writing-paper again and tried to be kind.

Dear Johnny [she wrote slowly], Of course I didn't. I didn't know 'that blasted dago' then (in fact he's only forty, a half-French British citizen: satisfied?). I told you when we met the last time that I'd only make you unhappy. I've always liked you, but I can't love you. I'm sorry. I'd like to have been able to. You're kind and sweet and gentle and an old, old friend. Can't we leave it at that and stop hurting each other?

I'm sorry about the Berkeley, but I can't see my way to it. Good luck on your next tour. Flixe.

It wasn't really kind enough, but she had to keep him out of her hair some way or other, and it would only prolong his agony if she went out dancing with him. Shrugging, she put the note in an envelope and stuck down the flap, before getting out of bed to dress in a dark-blue coat and skirt for the meeting.

That evening when she got back to the flat she found Gerry waiting, her face porridge-coloured and tense.

'Gerry, you look awful. Come on in and tell me all about it,' said Flixe, unlocking the door and holding it wide open.

'Sorry, Flixe,' answered her sister in an oddly brittle tone. 'I didn't mean to lie in wait for you and pounce when you must be tired.'

Flixe laughed obediently at her elder sister's deliberately melodramatic apology.

'Never mind, ducky. My fatigue is not half as important as the way you're looking. Come on in and tell me.' She led the way back into her bedroom and pulled forward the low green nursing chair that stood under the window. 'Sit in that while I get out of these clothes. It's ghastly but despite the rationing I seem to be putting on weight and all my waistbands are getting tight.'

Flixe began to strip off her office clothes, every now and then looking at Gerry through her hair. When she

219

said nothing, Flixe tried to imagine what trouble could have brought her to the flat at such an hour.

'Are you ill, Gerry?' she asked at last.

'What?' said Gerry angrily. 'No, of course I'm not ill.'

'Then what is it? Something's obviously upset you badly. Please tell me. I'm sure I can help – or if not, then perhaps find someone who can. I've discovered that I'm quite capable after all.'

Gerry got up from the chair as though impelled by some force outside herself, and stared out of the window. Flixe looked a bit surprised and turned to face her wardrobe to pull out a pair of trousers.

'All right,' said Gerry eventually, looking out over Kensington High Street. 'There doesn't seem to be a polite way of asking this. So here goes: are you having an affair with Peter Suvarov?'

A lot of things became clear to Flixe at that moment and some of them meant that her voice came out harsh and stinging.

'Who told you that?' she asked.

'So it's true.' Gerry looked down at her dark-brown shoes, noticing in a detached way that the lace on the right-hand shoe was frayed and would not last much longer. It would be difficult to get another pair; laces were one of the exasperating items that kept disappearing from the shops. She was trying to develop that thought in order not to have to look back at her sister or notice the faint but insistent smell of her exotic scent, when she felt Flixe's hand digging into her shoulder.

'Gerry, this is important, who told you?' repeated Flixe, this time in a much gentler voice. Gerry turned away from the window to face her sister.

'Don't worry, Flixe. I just wanted to know, and now I do

know, I'll go. It's all right, I won't tell Diana.'

'Gerry, shut up and sit down,' said Flixe, worried both by the expression on Gerry's face and by the thought of Peter's security.

'So you know about Diana, do you?' Gerry's comment seemed so irrelevant to all the things seething in Flixe's brain that she missed the point of it and said briskly:

'Yes, of course I do. He told me ages ago. But listen, Gerry, that's not important now. You must tell me who told you. There's much more to this than you're supposed to know . . . '

'I've gathered that much. Both of you have made it very clear that I'm excluded from your . . . friendship. But I do think one of you might have told me. You must have suspected at least that I was working for him. That alone ought to have given me some right to know what you and he were up to.' She was silent for a moment, dealing with the massive surge of resentment. But hate it though she did, she could not eradicate it. 'And what are you thinking of? If he's told you all about Diana, you know he's married. How could you, Flixe?'

'Stop it, or I'll have to slap you,' came the answer, hard and quick as a whiplash. 'You're getting hysterical. Listen to me: it is very important that you say where you learned that we were having an affair. If you don't want to tell me, I can ring him up and you can tell him. It is crucial that we know.'

The urgency of it all made Flixe unnaturally earnest, but the issues were too important to bury behind her usual façade of light-heartedness. She saw that something was beginning to filter through Gerry's hysteria.

'No one told me,' said Gerry, slowly. 'But you see, I saw you. I was on duty at the ARP post by Charles Street

221

one night last month, and I saw you two getting out of a car and being very loverly on the pavement outside some flats.'

Flixe's deep sigh might have been misread if she had not added a quick explanation.

'Well if we convinced you, who must know how unlikely it would be, then with luck we really did persuade the man at whom the pantomime was directed.'

'Pantomime,' repeated Gerry stupidly. 'You mean it was an act?' Her voice sharpened into its normal incisiveness. 'Flixe, what on earth are you doing?'

Flixe went to her dressing table, dropped on to the stool and started to brush her hair as she thought about the security aspects of this new development. At last she made up her mind and turned on the stool to face Gerry.

'I'm not supposed to tell, but even Suvarov would agree, I think, that you could do more damage now from not knowing. Gerry, swear you won't pass any of this on?'

'Of course,' she said, and Flixe remembered with regret the old days, when she and Gerry had been able to tell each other everything as a matter of course. Despite their very different characters and occasional jealousies, they had formed an offensive and defensive alliance against governesses, grandparents, parents and the whole adult world. Now Suvarov had put up a great fence between them. Just for a second she felt a violent resentment against him. But it was quickly gone as she remembered everything else.

'I work for him,' she said gently.

'For Peter? You?' demanded Gerry in a voice that told Flixe exactly what her elder sister thought of her capabilities.

'Yes; don't sound so astonished: it's rather insulting,' she said in the old voice of half-defensive teasing.

'Sorry. I didn't mean to. I was just so surprised. How long?'

'Have I worked for him?' Flixe began to pin her hair back in a long roll. 'From the beginning of RE(1)R – it was I who recommended you. But never mind that now. What you saw was part of an operation.' Flixe raised her eyes from her own to Gerry's reflection in the dressing-table looking-glass and the expression of half-frightened hope told her a lot about Gerry's feelings for their chief.

'Recently,' she went on as calmly as she could, 'it's been important for me to get pretty close to a group of men, very rich men, who have close contacts with France – Vichy France, and so presumably with the Jerries. The easiest, or at least the quickest, way was to make one or more of them fall for me and . . . well, you know.'

'You can't mean what I think you mean,' protested Gerry, beginning to look a little angry again.

'I'm afraid so. In principle at least. Never mind, it's not important. I had to be introduced to them as a, well . . . somebody's girlfriend and it was easiest and safest for it to be as Peter's. That's all.' She pinned in the last of the roll of hair, and turned on her stool to face her sister again.

'I don't know what to say,' announced Gerry.

'Then don't say it.' There was a note of warning in Felicity's voice that made Gerry look at her very surprised. Flixe might have taken her to task about her appearance once or twice, but she had never spoken in such a tone of cold authority before.

'No, nothing like that,' said Gerry quickly. 'Lord, I haven't any right to approve or disapprove. But, Flixe, I hadn't realised. Was that why I hardly ever saw you – for nearly a year?'

'Partly. Peter wanted to keep us separate and,

223

besides . . . ' Flixe looked at her elder sister's serious face and decided that she was just not going to confess to all the other feelings that had kept her away. 'Tell me something, though, Gerry.'

'If I can,' she said carefully.

'You've fallen for Suvarov, haven't you?'

Gerry stiffened immediately and Flixe began to regret her question.

'I don't know what you mean. Do you mean that he talks about me? To you?'

'Not much, but enough for me to have realised that he cares a lot about you. You look as though you were about to be sick.'

'Not really – it's just rather humiliating.'

'I don't see why. He's one of the most fascinating men either of us is ever likely to meet, ravishingly handsome, brilliantly clever – and dotty about you; there you are, unhappily married for five years to a pompous, stupid man: how could you not fall for him?'

'Andrew's not stupid,' said Gerry, seizing on something they could talk about that did not bring Suvarov's name into the conversation. 'The rest I give you, but not that. That's what most of the problem was. He was intelligent; he had been to Cambridge; he seemed quite different from all those others that Mother produced for us.'

'You know, Gerry,' said Flixe, walking over to Gerry's chair to pat her shoulder, 'this is the first time you've really explained why you married him.' Gerry looked up at her sister, smiling for the first time that evening.

'Well the recent events have made discretion seem a little redundant.'

'Yes, I suppose so. Are you dreadfully shocked by my activities?' Flixe was irritated to hear a familiar note in her voice; it was the old sound of supplication. She reminded herself that she no longer needed Gerry's approval; it was years since she had decided that she was not simply a second-rate version of her elder sister, but a quite different creature, just as a cat is different from a kestrel. Neither was better than the other; merely different. Why should she suddenly want Gerry to tell her that she was doing the right thing?

'Well, I was for the moment, but that was before I understood. My only . . . well, negative feeling is that it must be so horrid for you.'

Flixe laughed shortly and with no mirth in the sound.

'I can bear that. Heavens! Compared to what some of the women working for Baker Street and so on are risking and putting up with, this is quite literally nothing,' she said, looking at her watch. Then she turned back to Gerry:

'I'm going to have to throw you out now, ducky. The man in the car may be coming here later and there are things I must do first.'

'Can't I meet him?'

'Certainly not. He'd take one look at you and realise that I'm not what I seem at all. And why should you want to meet him? Peter would strangle me if I involved his Gerry Alderbrook in this kind of thing.' Flixe winced inwardly as she heard the waspishness of her voice and hurried to cover it. 'No, don't say anything more. Get going. We'll meet soon.'

'Yes, but when, Flixe? There are things I need to ask you – not about the man in the car or anything like that. Things I need to know about . . . me, really.'

'OK. Tomorrow; why not lunch – at the Charing Cross Corner House. Now, hop it.'

She hustled Gerry out of the door and shut it behind her with relief. While she could play her part entirely in the world to which Suvarov had sent her, she was all right; but once her other worlds began to impinge, all the doubts and questions came back to bother and distract her.

It was not until all her housework was done (to salve her conscience for lying to Gerry) and she was lying under the eiderdown with a mug of soup in one hand and a book in the other that she let herself think of Gerry's reactions. Flixe's lips twisted into a bitter little smile as she thought of her elder sister and allowed herself to recognise the momentary sense of power she had felt at Gerry's first question. The satisfaction was quickly banished, but it had been there. For most of their childhood, she had lived in awe of Gerry's cleverness, and to have Gerry playing the supplicant's part for once . . . Flixe stopped herself on that thought and opened the book.

14

Flixe was full of reluctance when she arrived at the Lyons Corner House for her lunch with Gerry. The last thing that Flixe wanted was to discuss Peter Suvarov with Gerry, and she had said too much already about her work, but she cared for her sister too much to refuse whatever reassurance Gerry needed. There was no sign of her in the restaurant and so Flixe found a table for two that was still free and sat down to wait. When the nippy arrived to take her order, she explained that she was 'waiting for a friend' and took out her powder and lipstick. A moment or two later she heard her sister's voice.

'Sorry, Flixe. I couldn't get here any earlier.'

'Trouble?' asked Flixe, folding up the black and gold compact which Jean-Pierre had given her a week or two earlier.

'No, just Peter wanting to go over a report with me. Gosh, Flixe, it is good to be able to talk about the job to you. You can't imagine how often I wanted to when you used to ring me up last year.'

Flixe smiled, but did not reciprocate the confidence.

Gerry, looking a little disappointed, picked up the thread of what she had been saying:

'And I didn't want to explain that I had an appointment with you. It seemed that it would only make things even more tangled if he were involved – if you see what I mean.'

'Absolutely,' said Flixe, picking up the greasy menu and handing it to Gerry. 'What are you going to have? Not that there's all that much choice.'

'Are you all right, Flixe?' asked Gerry, looking searchingly at her sister's pale, beautiful face as she accepted the card.

'Fine. Why not? "Sin" doesn't mark the complexion, you know.' The irony in her sister's voice made Gerry hurry to amplify her question.

'I didn't mean that, honestly. It's just . . . Well, I so hate it when Andrew, you know . . . that I can't bear to think of you going through that with someone who isn't even your husband.' At that Flixe laughed in genuine amusement and people at the tables near them smiled in pleasure: there was so little to amuse anyone at that juncture of the war, when all the news was bad and rationing seemed to bite harder month by month, that anyone's laughter was to be enjoyed.

'Oh, Gerry, you are so funny. I'm sorry Andrew's such a lout. But you know I'm not actually going to bed with Jean-Pierre.' Gerry's face was such a study in shock that Flixe roared with laughter again. Then she said: 'Oh, darling, I'm sorry to shriek, but you did look funny.'

'Well I'm glad I made you laugh, but Flixie, I thought that was what you were telling me yesterday. Wasn't it?'

'Not quite, ducky . . .' began Flixe as the nippy came back, her order book in hand.

'Well, what's it to be?' she said in the bored tones of one who has asked the same question every five minutes for four hours or so.

'Oh, two Welsh rarebits and a pot of tea, please,' said Flixe, then turned to Gerry to add: 'All right with you?'

'Yes, of course – unless you have some bacon?'

'Sorry, dear,' called the nippy over her shoulder as she left them.

Gerry fiddled with the salt and pepper pots for a moment, keeping her eyes lowered. Then she looked full at Flixe once more.

'But mightn't you have to? I mean, given that you presented yourself to him as Peter's . . . well, you know.'

'Mistress?' supplied Flixe, becoming irritated with her elder sister's circumlocutions, and irritated, too, to hear Gerry articulating the questions that she was asking herself more and more often.

'Flixe, hush. People might hear.'

'Oh, Gerry,' she said and then broke off as the waitress reappeared. 'Good, here's the food.'

Each ate with the concentrated enjoyment of what was becoming a rare pleasure. Neither was ever actually hungry, but there was so little variety in the food they could get that anything which tasted as positively as Lyons' Welsh rarebit was to be cherished. Flixe did better, of course, because of the restaurants to which her work took her, where an enormous cover charge got neatly round the government's fiat that no meal was to cost more than five shillings. When the waitress was well clear of their table, Flixe tried to answer her sister's question.

'Gerry, there will undoubtedly come a time when Jean-Pierre propositions me seriously, and then I'll have to do something about it. Until then all we do is flirt, dine, dance and talk. The sort of things that would no doubt make Father decide I was a tart, but quite innocent to anyone else.'

'What do you talk about?' asked Gerry quickly, not feeling up to discussing their father then. It often distressed her that Flixe seemed to hate him so much, and yet she could never quite do anything to interpret the good qualities of each to the other.

'Almost anything. He talks about me, France – the gaieties of Paris, that sort of thing – and paintings and antiques, architecture, books, wine. You see, he knows a lot about everything and tries to educate my tastes. He says that for someone who is one-quarter French I am distressingly ignorant of the most important part of my heritage. You needn't look so surprised; it's all very civilised. He's not some filthy, fumbling bounder. He's a charming, delightful man, with rather Continental ideas about ways to take his pleasure.'

'Oh. You make me feel very provincial.'

Felicity was honest enough to admit to herself that that was partly what she had meant to do, but not enough to say so to her sister, whose shocked disapproval the day before had caught her on the raw. Gerry knew Flixe well enough – and cared enough for her – to see that she had made a mistake and so she quickly changed the subject.

'So, what's happened to your architectural job, Flixe?'

'I still do it. But it's flexible. That's why Peter got me out of the Fanys. But careless talk, Gerry . . .'

'Yes, of course. Oh, there is something I meant to tell you,' she said as she loaded her fork with Welsh rarebit. 'Mother rang me up last night to ask about Christmas. I can't possibly go again, having had last year off, I mean.

230

And Andrew is bound to want to go to his parents if he can get leave. What about you?'

'Go home to Sudbrook House? God forbid! I can't really tell the chaps that I'm off home to Mummy, can I now? It would hardly square with the picture of the character I've been at such pains to create. She'll have to make do with her evacuees and Ming. What's up?'

'I'm not sure. I'm just a bit worried, but I hadn't realised that it showed. Mother said that Ming would be spending a week after Christmas in Sussex, and it sounded as though she thought I would have known about it anyway. But I've hardly heard from her since she told me about staying on to take Higher,' said Gerry slowly.

'I had a letter today. She seemed pretty miserable. With luck Christmas will cheer her up.'

'Oh, well I hope so, but what's this business about Sussex?'

'God knows. Probably she's going to stay with a school friend.'

'Yes, I suppose so. Ah, well, Mother will just have to concentrate on her boys. Isn't it extraordinary how much she seems to like them?' said Gerry with feeling. 'I wonder what Father will think when he comes back.'

'Is he going to?' asked Flixe in horror through her last mouthful of cheese on toast.

'Hadn't you heard?' Gerry answered with all the old stiffness. She tried to relax and talk normally about him. 'Yes, he is coming back, possibly in time for Christmas, possibly not. Depends on what actually happens in North Africa. It seems that he's being promoted and they're bringing him back for some reason. She wants me to entertain him while he's here.'

'That's just what you need now, isn't it? Does she expect you to put him up?'

'No, no – he'll stay at the club, but I'm to receive him as the returning warrior he is. I wonder she hasn't said anything to you.'

'You could hardly expect her to – after all he has always loathed the very sight of me.'

'Oh, nonsense, Flixe. He's just stiff – and bad at talking to females. He doesn't hate me, despite all our rows about Cambridge, and I could never tease him as you always did. You could always make him laugh, however cross he was – and then you never made him as cross as I did about Cambridge,' Gerry said earnestly, really wanting for once to make things easier for Flixe.

'Didn't I just? I put him in a passion of disgust and rage whenever I appeared,' answered Flixe with considerable feeling. She stirred the last of the tea in the pot and then poured them each another cup. 'No, ducky, it's just that I was never scared of him.'

'Lucky you. Anyway, will you give me a hand with him when he comes?'

'Of course, if I can. I'd have thought you'd done your bit in that direction with Andrew. How is he, by the way?' she asked, not really interested in her sister's husband, but glad to turn the subject from their difficult relations with their father.

'Physically OK, I suppose. I mean, obviously having an artificial foot is absolutely ghastly and I do feel truly sorry for him.'

'But?'

'Oh, he just expects me to wait on him,' said Gerry, sounding almost as tired as she felt. 'After a draining day at work I have to queue for food, cook it for him, do his

232

laundry in inadequate supplies of hot water and with – what are we down to now? – eight ounces of soap each week.'

'Poor Gerry. Look, there's the waitress. D'you want more tea?'

'No, I don't think so. It's too filthy. Let's just get the bill. But, you see,' she went on, getting back to the subject that was obviously filling her mind, 'I can't make him understand that my work at RE(1)R is more important than my wifely duties – or frankly than this job they seem to have manufactured for him in Storey's Gate.'

'Fair's fair, Gerry. Just as you can't explain to them what yours is, so he can't.'

'No, you are right.' But in spite of that admission, Gerry had plenty more to say about her difficult husband.

Flixe listened, and really sympathised, but she was surprised that Gerry could take her troubles so seriously. They all seemed rather trivial in the middle of the war. Flixe could imagine that living with Andrew would be tiresome, but Gerry had chosen to marry him after all – it was the price she had to pay for that kind of security and social approval. And surely she could talk to him and explain modern life to him.

'But Gerry,' she felt impelled to say at one moment, 'if it's so ghastly sleeping with him, why not tell him and say you won't any more?'

'Oh I couldn't.'

'Why on earth not? It's obviously doing things to you.'

'He seems so vulnerable – it would hurt him so much,' Gerry said slowly, as though trying to work it all out for herself as she spoke.

'And it's more important to protect him than yourself?' asked Flixe in a noncommittal tone as she remembered

233

poor Johnny Blenkarne.

'Isn't that what we were always taught?'

'There are a great many lessons from our school and governesses and mother and grandfather that we have to unlearn if we are to survive in the real world.'

'I suppose so,' said Gerry, resting her forehead on her left hand. 'Isn't it ridiculous? I'm sure I used to be stronger than this. Lord knows what's happening to me to make me so pathetic. I suppose it's just the war, and rationing and—'

'Gerry, how much of all this is to do with Peter Suvarov?' asked Flixe, interrupting. Gerry flinched, dropped her hand back to the table and looked directly at her sister, blushing.

'I'm not sure. No, no, I'm not trying to pretend anything, Flixe. I just don't know. When I started to work for him I was in seventh heaven: here at last was something important that I could do, I liked them all, Suvarov was so interesting – and, well, challenging. He sort of made me sizzle.'

'And now?' asked Flixe, trying not to wince as she recognised precisely what Gerry meant.

'Well, it all got a bit complicated – he's probably told you.'

'No details.'

'Good,' said Gerry quickly and then as fast tried to cover her pleasure: 'I don't mean that I . . . that you . . . oh, you know, Flixe.'

'Yes, I know. But, Gerry, one thing he hasn't needed to tell me is how much he cares about you.'

'Do you mind?'

'Why should I mind?' Flixe answered aloud, thinking to herself, of course I mind. How could I not? Don't you understand anything?

'Well, please don't say anything to Father if you see him while he's here.'

'Gerry, don't be absurd. I don't propose to tell him anything. I never have. And am I likely to do anything to damage his image of his beloved first-born, who so sensibly married a regular soldier and has always done everything he wanted?'

'Except submit without bitter protest to the no-education-for-females rule.'

They both laughed then, and both felt better for it. But each held new reservations about the other and as they left the restaurant may have toyed with the idea of his finding out about the things she would never actually tell him.

15

Flixe spent Christmas Day idly and for the most part alone. Jean-Pierre had sent round a hamper filled with all kinds of virtually unobtainable delicacies the previous day with a note explaining that he would not be able to see her because of a longstanding commitment. She was surprised to find how much she minded.

A week earlier Anna Kingsley had invited her to dine in Dover Street, explaining that Gerry and Andrew would be there too. Assuming that Jean-Pierre would whisk her off somewhere, Flixe had declined the invitation and was now faced with the choice of dining on her own from his hamper or losing face in front of Anna Kingsley and begging for her invitation to be renewed. The fact that doing so would also involve having to be polite to Andrew made up her mind for her and she decided to stay with her own company.

Now that she was stuck with it, she realised how much she minded being alone. Christmas had never been one of the Alderbrooks' main family celebrations, and if it had been Flixe would probably have hated it, but as she pottered about her flat, trying to think of things to do, she began to feel as though by taking the job Peter had asked her to do she had exiled herself from her family; that in a curious way her loneliness that Christmas was a punishment for all the times when she had subverted the family's guests from their dull conversation into admiration of herself. Doing her best to laugh at herself, Flixe even began to wonder whether her father's attitude to her might not have some justification after all. As her mind reached that pitch of idiocy, her brains reasserted themselves and she explained to herself precisely why she was right to be doing what Peter had asked.

Shortly after eleven in the morning, when she really had got her mind under control again, her front door bell rang and, thinking that there would be a messenger with flowers or more presents from Jean-Pierre, she went to answer it. When she saw Peter Suvarov standing in the hall, her face was lit by a spontaneous smile of welcome.

'May I come in, Flixe?'

'Of course. How lovely! But aren't you going to Etchingham?'

He followed her in to the flat, saying:

'Yes, of course. But I thought I'd pop in to see how you were before I set off. And I thought I'd bring you this.' He held out a flat package wrapped in ordinary brown paper.

Flixe, who had never even thought of buying him anything, blushed as she took it from him.

'Oh, Peter, you shouldn't have,' she said, untying the string.

'I'm afraid it's nothing compared to the kind of presents you get weekly from "that man".'

She laughed, grateful that he was still able to joke about Jean-Pierre, and removed the brown paper to reveal the latest popular novel. When she thanked him, he told her that it was the merest trifle to show how grateful he was that she was tackling such a tricky and disagreeable job so well. Wishing that the present had been more personal and that he had said almost anything else, she turned away for a moment. Then, when she had got her face in order, she turned towards him again.

'Peter, can I offer you a drink? Or a little early lunch? "That man" has sent me an embarrassingly lavish Christmas hamper full of *foie gras* and things. Won't you help me eat some of them?'

He shook his head. 'Flixe, my dear, I really can't. I promised Diana I'd be down at the Dower House for lunch.'

'Oh, of course,' she said with artificial gaiety. 'Well, you'd better not be late then. I'll see you next week.'

'Will you be all right?' he asked with enough gentleness in his voice to reach right through all her defences. Even so, she answered in the same cheerful voice.

'Why not? I've all this to eat and drink and a good book. What more could one want? Except a roaring fire, perhaps.'

He walked towards her and for a moment she thought that he might take her in his arms. She found that she was holding her breath and carefully releasing it. He reached out his right hand and briefly held it to her cheek.

'Take the greatest care of yourself, Flixe,' he said.

'I will, Peter. And you. And thank you for the book. It was very sweet of you to bring it round yourself.'

'How could I resist? Goodbye for now. And Happy Christmas.'

She saw him out and when she had shut the door behind him stood for a moment, leaning her back against it, fighting the sensations he had aroused in her yet again.

238

'Bloody man!' she said aloud at last and walked back into the sitting room. There, she deliberately flung back the lid of Jean-Pierre's hamper, opened one of the half-bottles of Krug and poured herself a glass, warm though the wine was. Even so it tasted wonderful, and when she had finished the bottle, eaten an enormous slice of Strasbourg pie and four Carlsbad plums, she felt better. Then, telling herself that she thoroughly enjoyed being alone after all, and had pined for an evening to herself for months, she took up her book and curled up under her eiderdown for the rest of Christmas Day.

Four days later, Jean-Pierre was back in London and had to be suitably thanked for his hamper and for the gold bracelet he brought with him as what he called her 'real Christmas present'. When she had said all she felt that she ought to have said, he put his arms lightly around her and kissed her.

'Félicitée, you taste delicious,' he murmured when he raised his head. Then he took his hands from her back and began to unbutton the white silk blouse she was wearing. At once, she brought up one of her hands to lay over his.

'Jean-Pierre, my dear, no.'

'But why not? I want it; you want it. Come on, *mignonne*. We have behaved with enormous circumspection for months. I think now is the time . . .'

Pushed to a last-ditch defence, Flixe heard herself saying:

'Well, yes, my dear, except that just this week is not really the time. You see . . . oh, dear, how embarrassing this is.'

'Ah,' he said, doing the buttons up again. 'Why be embarrassed? So, soon then. You will tell me?'

239

Flixe nodded, pleaded a terrible headache as well and eventually got rid of him to go to bed early and lie asking herself all the old questions, which she had always so despised when she came across them in novels or the chatter of her friends. If I don't sleep with him will he disappear after some more willing woman? But if I succumb will he, having had all he wanted, disappear, despising me?

She turned over, burying her face in the pillow, wishing that she could have put the questions to Suvarov. Of course he would not have been able to tell her categorically which course to take, but simply talking to him would have helped her to make up her mind. But Peter Suvarov was the last person she could bear to consult on such a subject. Cherishing his friendship and wishing that it were something more, she had destroyed the ease of communication that she had felt with him at the beginning.

Sleep overtook her as she set herself to remember the best of the times she had spent with him, and she woke the next morning strangely relaxed.

The peaceful mood lasted for about five minutes, when it was shattered by the arrival of her father. Dressed only in her pink-and-green kimono, she opened her front door, let him in and stretched up to kiss his cheek, inhaling the familiar scent of the bay rum mixture he used on his hair and the Sobranie cigarettes he had always smoked. She felt him flinch as she touched him and looked curiously into his face.

'You look years younger than before you went to the desert, Daddy,' she said cheerfully, trying to ignore the cold severity of his expression. 'Oh, yes, and congratulations on the new appointment. Where are they sending you this time?'

'I can't possibly tell you that, Felicity,' he said severely, following her into the flat. 'You ought to know better than to ask.'

'Oh, well, never mind. Can I make you some coffee?'

'No, thank you,' he said. 'I breakfasted some hours ago and what I have to say won't take very long.'

Oh Lord, thought Flixe to herself. This can't be going to be a repetition of the scene with Gerry. I can't take all that again. What has he heard?

'Well, you won't mind if I make myself a cup, will you?' she said aloud, going into the kitchen. She forced herself to make bright conversation as she boiled the kettle and made a small jugful of ersatz coffee. Then she carried her cup into the sitting room and stood, leaning against the chimneypiece, waiting for what he had come to say.

He followed her into the room and stood looking at her with an expression of such disdain that she had to look away.

'Felicity, I want you to tell me—' He broke off, brushed his stiff little moustache first in one direction and then in the other, and then tried again. 'Why aren't you at work?' The question came out as a bark, and Flixe felt that he had already judged and condemned her, just as he always had in the old days.

'My war work takes many forms, Father dear,' she said in a deliberately languorous voice, smoothing her slippery silk kimono down over her thighs.

'So I hear. Good God! How could you do such a thing? I would never have believed that a daughter of mine . . . Have you no feeling for your mother and Gerry at least?'

'Who told you?' she asked, picking a little lump of sticky mascara off her eyelashes with her painted fingernails and rolling it into a ball.

'A man at the War Office. He thought I ought to know that you were going off the rails with a Frenchman so that I could put a stop to it. Good God, Felicity, you might as well be . . . entertaining one of the Germans.'

'Did this busybody know – or tell you – why I was doing it?' she asked, ignoring his characteristic xenophobia.

'No. But they thought I should know. Good God, what father would not? He's virtually an enemy.'

'Of course he's an enemy. Why d'you think I'd be doing it otherwise?' She was going to add, you don't think I'd do it for pleasure, do you? But then she decided that it was not her business to calm him down. Doubtless his beloved Gerry could do that later in the day. And so she just smiled again, the slow, louche smile she had learned for Jean-Pierre.

'I don't understand, Flixe. Flixe, what are you doing?' The use of her nursery name, which he had hardly ever used even when she had been a little child, almost disarmed her, but not quite. There had been too many fights in the past and he had told her what he thought of her once too often.

'They really didn't tell you then. Perhaps they thought you weren't reliable. Well, I know you are, particularly where something like this is concerned. I do it for the good intelligence I collect from it.'

Her father was silent, his freckled face reddening under her eyes and his hands balling into fists at his side. He seemed to be grinding his teeth, and she watched with interest to see what would happen next. After a while he seemed to regain command over his voice and, in a tone of absolute disgust, he said:

'Then he's not the only one? You mean you're a . . . a whore?'

'Oh, really, Father. What a ridiculous word! I don't do it for money . . .' Suddenly it wasn't funny any more, and she wished that she had told him the truth, not tried to bait him as she had. The atmosphere was much too highly charged for her to have analysed there and then what it was she felt, but the hurt of it spurred her on to say:

'What are you looking like that for? You're killing for England, aren't you? Well, I'm fucking for England. And of the two, I'd have said my activity was rather more moral than yours.'

General Alderbrook looked at her as he might have looked at a snake, or a scorpion he had found in his bedroom slippers, and turned to go without another word. As he was pulling the front door of her flat behind him, she found herself saying, 'Daddy,' but he paid no attention.

Left alone again, Flixe discovered that she was shaking and she started to prowl around the flat, trying to walk herself out of her mood. The three men who had come to her flat over the past few days represented such different things, and yet between them they had aroused feelings within her that boiled and seethed, and threatened more than simply her peace of mind.

She was so disturbed by her father's visit, so angry yet needing to justify herself, that she almost wrote him a letter of explanation and apology mixed with accusation. Reason stopped her just in time and instead she telephoned Queen Anne's Gate, on the private number that rang directly on Suvarov's desk. She knew that Gerry had been trained never to answer it even when Suvarov was out and so there was no risk. As it rang, Flixe wondered if he would answer. It was a number to be used in emergency only. She almost put her receiver down, ashamed of the impulse to confide in him, but he did answer. His voice was cold.

'Yes?'

'Peter, it's Flixe. Sorry to use this number.' She waited for some encouraging word, but none came and she went on, trying not to stammer: 'I wonder if I could see you today?'

'Important?'

'Yes. Not . . . not that it's going to affect the war, but important to me.'

'All right, feed the ducks in about twenty minutes. Can you get there?'

'Of course,' she said and put the telephone down. Flinging off the silk kimono, she dressed in an old pair of slacks and a shabby zipped corduroy jacket. A scarf would do instead of a hat, and help to disguise her in case anyone she knew should happen to be walking through Kensington Gardens in the middle of the morning. She let herself out of the flat and walked briskly along the High Street to the park.

As she reached it, she noticed sadly that the flat, diamond-shaped remains of the railings were already rusting into the white stone of the wall's coping and resented the absurd practice of removing all London's ironwork. Unlike the innocent majority who believed everything they were told in newspapers, Flixe knew perfectly well that there had been no point in the sacrifice of the railings. Their scrap value was minimal and the iron they provided could not be used for any of the war industries and must be lying decomposing in some scrap yard. She had heard it said that the move had been designed to bring home to the civilian population the reality of the war. That, of course, had been before the Blitz had so adequately done the job.

Trying to stop herself adding anger on to anger, she walked up towards the palace. As she passed the statue of William IV she decided petulantly that it was typically male – flauntingly arrogant, he looked, and just like the kind of man who . . . She stopped her thought, trying to laugh at herself for her silliness.

It was a relief to walk up the short, steep hill to the Round Pond, and to recognise her chief in the windswept man patrolling the brink, apparently absorbed in watching the few children miserably prodding their recalcitrant boats on the scummy water.

She fell into step beside him and said nothing. After they had walked almost half-way round, he said:

'So, what's happened?'

'Someone at the War Office has told my father that I'm . . . having an affair with a Frenchman,' answered Flixe as calmly as she could.

'Ah,' he said, his voice carrying no overtones of any kind. 'Then the question is whether they did it out of spite, "I thought you ought to know old chap", or a genuine attempt to stymie your work. You were quite right to tell me.'

The relief his detached tone brought her, not to speak of his unemotional reference to her work, helped Flixe towards a more realistic sense of proportion.

'I hadn't really got as far as their motive,' she said, managing to smile at him again. 'I know it's what I ought to have been thinking, but it wasn't. He came to see me just now.'

'And started to behave like a Shakespearean husband who's just discovered he's a cuckold,' suggested Suvarov with such understanding warmth in his dark eyes that she almost hugged him.

'A bit like that,' she agreed, trying to sound lighthearted and not succeeding. She felt his hand on hers.

'Poor Flixe. It is one of the hazards, of course, of a job like yours. But I know you're too rational to crumple under that kind of stupidity.'

'Do you?'

'Flixe, come on. What's happened to the beautiful, gay young warrior who told me – what was it? "It doesn't matter what you do so long as you don't compromise what you believe in." You're not really having doubts, are you?'

She did not answer and walked on beside him, trying to work out what she really did feel. His presence in itself removed a lot of the self-disgust, and his matter-of-fact, if elliptical, acknowledgment of the word her father had used about her helped too.

'Well, never mind for the moment. Since I'm here, you might as well report now as tomorrow,' he said, his dark eyes apparently watching two small boys quarrelling over whose turn it was to adjust the rigging of their sodden yacht.

'All right,' answered Flixe as the boys' nanny separated them, seized the boat and dragged them off towards the Dutch garden. 'There's definitely something going on, but whether it is what we thought or whether it's just some desperate attempt to save one or other of his companies with nefarious import dealings, I'm not so certain.'

'Do you seriously think someone like Jean-Pierre would mess about with black-marketeering?' Suvarov turned away from the small domestic dramas being enacted all round the pond and looked at his agent. She faced him, shook her head and then took a deep breath.

'No, I suppose not. That reminds me: you were right,

246

though, he and Oldridge have met; I got that out of him the other day. But I really don't think Oldridge is involved. He's too wet for one thing, and kept out of the army by TB. He only got out of the sanatorium about a month before the war started.'

They walked on in silence, Flixe trying to make herself tell him something that had been on her mind. After a while he stopped in front of a pair of glossy dark-green mallards fighting over some mould-encrusted bread floating at the edge of the grey water.

'Flixe, what is it? Whatever it is can't be that bad. Tell me.'

She laughed a little at that. 'It's a good thing that I've never tried to lie to you since you can apparently read my mind. I've only not told you because I'm not certain. But I am horribly afraid that you may be right about Anna Kingsley. What put you on to her in the first place?'

'Postal censorship turned up some peculiar letters she's been writing to and getting from France, via Switzerland. There've been too many mentions of a particular town in France that crops up in Jean-Pierre's affairs . . .' He broke off, smiled down at Flixe's concerned face, and then led the way to one of the dark-green benches that ringed the Round Pond.

She sat down, as obedient, she thought, as Ming would have been. He sat down beside her and put a hand on her wrist.

'Miss Kingsley has a lot of friends in high places,' he said. 'Do you think she put one of them on to your father?'

'It is possible. Oh, Peter,' she burst out, using his Christian name for once, 'it's such a filthy business. She's been so good to poor little Ming, and Gerry adores her; could she really do something like that?'

'God knows, but it's possible. And if she was afraid you might get too close to something they wanted to hide, then perhaps the easiest way would be to get your father to intervene.'

'How much does Gerry know of all this?' asked Flixe suddenly.

'Nothing at all. I warned her in a general way about Oldridge when I discovered that they played chess together in the Blitz, but nothing more. Why?'

'She saw our little pantomime last year in Mayfair and I had to tell her it was a put-up job,' said Flixe resolutely looking not at him but at the mallards.

'Did you?' At the peculiar tone of his voice she did look at him and what she saw in his face made her own voice full of asperity.

'Yes, I did. I didn't know precisely what you two are up to, but one look at her face as she was trying to ask me if I was your . . . if we were involved with each other was enough to tell me what her trouble is.'

'Damn. It's a stupid complication. I ought to have had her transferred months ago. It's a pity, rationally speaking, that you did tell her the truth; it could have sorted several problems if she thought . . . No, I'm sorry. It would have been too much to ask.'

'Yes, it bloody would have,' shouted Flixe, losing her temper for the first time since he had recruited her. 'I don't mind what my wretched father thinks, at least I can bear it, but I don't want my sister thinking I'm . . . Never mind.' She looked at him curiously and, thinking that she could see pain in his guarded dark eyes, she said more gently: 'But you would have let her think that, wouldn't you, whatever it did to her ideas about you?'

'I don't know. It's easy to think so, when there's no

248

possibility of it happening now. But I made an ass of myself in that direction once; there's no guarantee I wouldn't have done it again.'

'Peter?' said Flixe, in a small voice.

'Yes,' he said with a wariness that hurt her.

'What is it about Gerry that makes you feel as you do?'

'Flixe, don't. No one can possibly know what she feels in the middle of all this. I like her a lot; she's a terrific help in the office; like you, she's ravishingly pretty. I'm with her for the greater part of every day, we work together – I'd have to be an icicle not to have been a bit sentimental about her.'

'Oh. That's all, is it?' Flixe said, relieved by his oblique compliment, but wanting more.

'Flixe, don't. You, at least, are too sensible. You know too much about the mechanics of these things to make those sort of mistakes. For God's sake, don't.'

Why? Or you might have the inconvenience of feeling 'a bit sentimental' about me too? she asked silently. Aloud she said instead:

'I'm sorry. Look, we've been here twice as long as usual. Surely we ought to part. I'll see if I can't push Anna a bit.'

'All right, but Flixe—' He broke off and then, taking her hand in his, said, 'please be careful of yourself.'

16

Flixe walked away from Suvarov, furious with herself for bringing such an inappropriately personal note into what ought to have been a dispassionate reporting session. And it had done her no good; all she had learned was that he felt 'sentimental' about her sister, and she had made it yet more difficult for herself to ask him what she ought to do about Jean-Pierre's proposition.

Walking past the statue of Physical Energy, she made herself stop to admire yet again the magnificent figure of the rider. Even as a child up in London for a school-holiday treat she had been fascinated with the way the man's toes were stretched out and apart with the muscular effort of keeping his seat on the rearing horse. For a moment she was distracted from her dilemma until something about the rider's eyebrows reminded her of Jean-Pierre's.

Why was it so damnably difficult to cut all one's upbringing out of one's mind? She believed absolutely that it was better to fight any war in the way she was trying to fight than to kill people. Upsetting though it had been, her father's intervention had not shaken that conviction at all. But still she found it difficult to take the last, irrevocable step. Perhaps if she had not begun to like Jean-Pierre it would have been easier, she thought, looking up at the formidable bronze face of the statue.

Impatient suddenly with her wayward emotions, she turned her back on Physical Energy, murmuring to herself, 'The flesh is willing enough, it's the bloody spirit that won't behave,' and strode at a furious pace down towards the Serpentine.

By the time she had walked past the lake with the wind in her face, across Hyde Park, through Robert Adam's great pillared screen and down through Green Park and St James's towards the river, she had tired herself into a kind of peace. She walked on hardly thinking at all until she stood looking across the shuddering traffic to the statue of Boadicea driving her war chariot.

There was one thing to be said, she thought, for the cover job she had been given: at least it was teaching her to look at London as more than a place. In the old days she had hardly noticed that there were statues in it, or buildings that were interesting or beautiful. Like Gerry, she had been given six months in Paris when she left school and was quite accustomed there to see 'sights', but she had never thought to do the same in England. In the old days, before she had had any work to tease her mind into action, she would never have stopped to look at the ancient queen, flying there in dark bronze, magnificent against the angry sky. But now the sight was inspiring.

There was a woman who had not let her sex get in the way of what needed to be done; who had not hesitated to have knives attached to the wheels of her chariot in defiance of any rules of fair play. There was a battle to be won and it had to be won in any way there was by anyone who was qualified to take part. Flixe squared her shoulders, pushed the word her father had used about her down as far as she could, and set off towards Dover Street.

Twenty minutes later she pressed the bell of Anna Kingsley's flat and waited, knowing that she must look quite distraught enough to play the part that had to be played. Anna came to open the front door herself.

'Flixe, my dear child, you look terrible. What is the matter?' she said, sounding as warm and concerned as ever.

'Oh, Anna, I'm in despair. Can I come in and talk to you?'

'Of course, come in. Would you like some luncheon? Strange to say, I have found a teeny piece of smoked salmon at the fishmonger's today. Such a good thing that what my mother always called "the great unwashed" don't like eating fish, particularly when it's smoked! We could share it, and there's a nice bottle of Chablis Jeremy Oldridge gave me the other day.'

Felicity smiled with lips that quivered in almost genuine distress.

'Anna, that sounds lovely.'

'Well come on in and sit down. Make yourself comfortable. Now, what has happened to make you look so tragic — almost exactly like Gerry when she came to London at the beginning of the war?' Anna stopped for a moment and then a look of anxiety so deep that it was almost horror crossed her pale, chiselled face: 'Felicity! Are you pregnant? Have you told Jean-Pierre?'

Flixe took in the implications of Anna's fear as she shook her head. 'I haven't come to have hysterics over you – or ask you for a discreet, reliable doctor who'll do a quiet D and C. No, it's just that my father's in London on leave.'

Anna turned away to assemble a tray full of crockery and cutlery. Then she handed Flixe a bottle and a corkscrew.

'Will you deal with the bottle? I know he is. Your mother asked me to dine him one evening. But why should that make you so upset?'

Flixe turned the corkscrew competently down into the cork and looked up just before she pulled it out.

'Someone – someone who believes that I'm sleeping with Jean-Pierre – has told my respected father that I am little better than a streetwalker.'

Anna's face suddenly lit up, surprising Flixe so much that she put the bottle and corkscrew down on the table, but before she could say anything, Anna forestalled her.

'You mean you're not going to bed with him? Oh, thank goodness, Flixie. But why do you go out with him such a lot? You were at the Ritz with him last night again. Edwin saw you both. Give me that bottle.'

'No, it's all right,' said Flixe, pulling the cork and then pouring a glass of wine for each of them. 'But why does it matter so much to you what I do with Jean-Pierre?'

'Flixe, I know him and I've seen him with many women – and I've seen other men just like him. No, don't look at me like that: I really do know what I'm talking about. The sooner you get yourself away from him the less you're going to suffer.' She sipped her wine and then put down the glass and started to lay the table. 'I wish I knew how to convince you.'

'So it was you,' Flixe said, sad but bitterly angry too.

'I?'

'Who told some man at the War Office to tell my father what you thought I was doing.'

There was a long silence. Then Anna sat down at the table and pushed the plate of smoked salmon towards Flixe's place. Keeping her eyes on Anna's, she sat down but made no move to take any fish. At last Anna said:

'Yes, I suppose I do owe you the truth. It was I. But, Flixe, please don't look like that. I did it to help. I can't bear sitting back to watch you being hurt as . . . as I was once hurt. You and the others are the nearest thing I'll ever have to daughters . . . And I care what happens to you.'

Flixe found it hard to focus on Anna's face and made a supreme effort to keep her mind on the question of Anna's likely motive. After a painful silence, Anna helped herself to some smoked salmon and a slice of brown bread.

'Felicity, please eat. However angry I've made you, you must eat. And give me your glass, you need a refill.'

Flixe obediently handed over the glass, noticing the way the light sparkled on the delicate air-twist stem. Everything Anna Kingsley had owned before the bomb had been lovely to look at, but since her house had been blown to smithereens, Flixe had expected her to be camping with tin mugs and old, cracked, unmatched plates from street stalls such as she had seen in the temporary flats of her other bombed friends. The memory of the bomb and what Anna had suffered forced Flixe to make her voice more gentle.

'Anna,' she said, keeping a careful hold on her emotions, 'I may have been doing you an unjustice.'

'Well don't worry about it now. This is a beastly time for all of us. Here's your wine. Drink up. We don't need to talk about it ever again.'

Everything about Anna seemed to be designed to comfort; if she did not actually invite confidences she had always listened and been ready to offer sympathy or advice as it seemed to be needed. The temptation to confide in her, explain what was really going on and ask her advice on what to do about Jean-Pierre was almost overpowering.

'No, I must get it out,' said Flixe, acting on the impulse. 'You see, I hadn't thought that you might have done it out of concern. I thought you were just making mischief.'

Anna's face stiffened and her green eyes looked hard as malachite for a moment.

'It's extraordinary how much that hurts. But never mind. It's worth it if it will make you send Jean-Pierre away.'

'I can't . . .' began Flixe, but even as she said it and heard the desperation in her voice, she came back to her senses and forced herself back into the part she had to play. She banged the delicate glass down on the highly polished table and said crossly: 'Stop it. I'll accept that you had the best of motives if you say so, but please stop interfering in my life. I can take care of myself.'

'Oh, Flixe, I hope so,' said Anna, covering her eyes with her left hand for a moment. Then she straightened up again, smiled and tried to change the subject. 'What happened to that nice RAF officer you once introduced me to?'

Flixe put down her knife and fork and shrugged. That at least was something she could discuss with Anna.

'Johnny Blenkarne? Yes, poor Johnny. I liked him so much when he was ADC-ing and I was driving. But then . . .' Flixe's delicate features contracted and her lips were compressed into an unforgiving line.

'What happened?' Anna asked, feeling better now that Flixe was talking in the way she always used to talk.

'Oh, he went mushy on me and it became unbearable.'

Anna took another bite of smoked salmon, wondering whether the attraction of Jean-Pierre might be that he could never, ever, be described as 'going mushy over a girl'.

'You mean, I suppose, that he fell in love with you? Just as Gerry says all young men always did.' Flixe looked straight at Anna, her eyes dark with an emotion Anna did not recognise.

'I don't think it was that. Johnny wanted something from me that I couldn't give him. He called it love, but it wasn't.'

'I wonder,' said Anna. All Flixe's defensive instincts rose at the implied criticism, and although she tried not to scowl she knew that Anna had understood her withdrawal.

They finished their little meal talking slightly uncomfortably about other things. After a short silence, Flixe held up the beautiful wine glass with its white twist stem.

'Anna, was there a miracle? Did these survive the bomb or have you had to restock everything?'

'No, the glasses were a present from a friend at Christie's. But the most surprising things did sur— remain unbroken. That vase, for instance.' She pointed to a slimly curved black porcelain jar that stood alone on the white-painted chimney-piece. 'I went back day after day to salvage what I could before the Heavy Rescue men removed the best bits. . . .But it's not only them,' Anna went on, seeing Flixe's expression of shocked sympathy. 'People – thoroughly respectable people – walking past a bombsite and seeing some knick-knack lying on the rubble are quite likely to pick it up.'

'I know,' said Flixe. 'I've felt it myself once or twice:

that idea that things lying about on a heap of derelict timbers and bricks are like hedgerow flowers or leaves in the country – anyone's for the taking. But,' she added, looking round the well-furnished room, 'you seem to have saved quite a lot.'

Anna's face was a study in regret, but her voice betrayed no emotion as she looked around the room.

'Actually most of this belongs to the flat's owner. I took it all over as "furnished rooms", but friends have been very kind and given me many things. But, Flixe, things don't matter at all compared with what happened to—' Anna broke off and it was Flixe who finished the sentence in a hard little voice.

'To Annie. I know. But I still find I can't really talk about her.'

'I'm sorry, Flixe. And I'm sorry too that I've landed you in difficulties with your father. If there is ever anything I can do to help you, will you tell me? Please Flixe. I care what happens to you.'

Longing to believe that Anna was genuine, and her offer honest, Flixe still allowed her burgeoning cynicism to suggest that it was motivated by Anna's need to know if Flixe ever found out anything about Jean-Pierre's business.

'Very well, Anna,' she said politely. 'It's kind of you. But I cannot imagine why I should need help. And thank you very much for the delicious salmon.'

A week later, unable to find any more convincing excuses, Flixe allowed Jean-Pierre into her bed. He had taken her dancing again, and from the way he had held her and moved against her she had known that she would not be able to escape again without blowing her cover irretrievably. There was also an unacknowledged thought in her mind that if her father thought of her as a fallen woman she might as well live down to his expectations of her, and so when Jean-Pierre asked whether he might go home with her, she leaned against him and smiled.

In the taxi back to her flat she found herself worrying about all kinds of practical matters: would Jean-Pierre expect her to undress in front of him? Would she be able to understand what he wanted her to do? Would he want her to do things . . .? Flixe forced herself to stop that train of thought and tried to console herself with the knowledge that a man as sophisticated and clearly experienced as Jean-Pierre would not subject her to the embarrassed and deeply embarrassing fumblings that accompanied her only other foray into the world of passion. A wistful memory came into her mind of Peter's gentleness when he had explained to her what her job might entail. Oh, if only it could have been he who was beside her! For a moment she had an absurd flash of memory of Gerry's wedding to awful Andrew. Gerry, looking somehow misty in the family lace veil, had turned her face to Andrew as the vicar said '. . . and keep ye only unto him as long as ye both shall live?' Oh, Peter, whispered Flixe silently to herself. She shivered.

Jean-Pierre, as though understanding that she was troubled, reached across to stroke her shoulder.

'I too feel as though I can't wait, my darling. But it is not long now; and, as you well know, a little frustration is an excellent intensifier of delight.'

Flixe managed to smile for him with all the gaiety and apparent agreement she could achieve.

Once they were safely in her flat with the door locked, Jean-Pierre took charge so firmly and with so little

258

embarrassment that Flixe began to lose some of her own. By the time she was lying naked beside him on top of the bedclothes and he was running his fingers tinglingly up and down her body she had relaxed enough to smile at him.

'Your skin is like velvet,' he said as his fingers swept down from her breast to the top of her thighs. 'Marvellous.'

Flixe laughed before she could stop herself.

'No, I wasn't being romantic-novelettish,' he said, kissing her lightly. 'I meant it. There's a pile to it. Feel.' He stroked first one way and then the other, but she could feel no difference, and only smiled slowly at the enticing sensations his caresses brought her.

'Won't you undress, too, Jean-Pierre?' she said, stroking his face.

'Not yet. Wait,' he said and began to intensify his caresses, drawing her sensations and his fingers nearer and nearer. At last she felt them slide into her and she gasped.

'That didn't hurt, did it?' Jean-Pierre asked in some surprise.

'Hurt? Good heavens, no,' she replied, and he laughed in triumph. With his free hand he parted her legs and then took his other hand away.

'Don't stop,' she said at once, and once again he laughed, but this with an unwonted tenderness.

'This will be better, *petite*,' he said getting up. As she lay on the bed, every instinct and nerve-ending shrieking at him to finish what he had so tantalisingly begun, he stood in front of her undressing with what seemed like deliberate slowness. At last he came back to the bed and knelt between her feet. He kissed her knees and then the inside of her thighs and then, shockingly, she felt his lips and tongue.

'Jean-Pierre, no,' she said instinctively. He did not raise his head, but his hands slid up her body to grip her shoulders and hold her down against the pillows. After a minute or two she could no longer think. Every faculty seemed to be concentrated on him and on the astonishing response her body was making. When he raised his head at last, all she wanted in the whole world was to feel him inside her and she gave herself up to him in total surrender.

She was consumed by his body and by her own until in one glorious explosion of sensation she rocketed into the very heart of desire.

Afterwards, when he was dressed again and preparing to leave, he held her gently against him and said into her hair:

'That was more than sex, *mignonne*. You were very sweet. I'll telephone you tomorrow. Good night.'

Flixe went back to bed in a daze of pleasure and quite genuine happiness. Some of the things Jean-Pierre had said to her as he made love to her made her wonder whether he really did care for her. It was a dizzying idea. Lying at peace, just before sleep overtook her, she knew that she ought to have softly teased secrets out of him, but with her mind warmed by his words and her body heavy with his pleasure, she had not even wanted to try. With sleep taking in the edges of her mind, she remembered his last words and her own version of them was, 'It was more than conquest; there was real affection there – his for me, perhaps; mine for him, certainly. Not love; not like the love that's Peter's, but something friendly; kind.' She slept.

Over the next eighteen months Flixe gradually became

accustomed to her role as the mistress of a rich and cultivated man. She accepted the endless presents with growing ease, even though she sometimes felt guilty about enjoying them; she dressed in the black-market clothes and silk stockings that he bought her; she ate the delicacies he provided. Sometimes she would feel ashamed as, curled, scented, made-up, and dressed in all her finery, she passed a tired-looking woman making the best of herself and her clothes with all the recommended makeshifts: her legs painted with gravy browning and a line of eyebrow pencil down the back; her hat embellished with some odd flower or feather taken from her children's dressing-up box; and on her face the determined expression of a woman who has to queue for unrationed luxuries to give her family anything to lift their dreary meals.

Flixe found that the only thing to do was to concentrate on the importance of the work she was trying to do and accept the material benefits of it as suitable payment for its distasteful nature. Her distaste dwindled, though, as she learned more about Jean-Pierre, and by the second Christmas of their association, she had come perilously close to falling in love with him. Once or twice as he lay asleep on her shoulder she wondered what she would do if he were to tell her something crucial that would confirm Peter Suvarov's suspicions and perhaps even lead to Jean-Pierre's arrest.

But in fact she found out far more about herself than about him. It was as though in unlocking her body, Jean-Pierre had also removed shutters from the hidden parts of her mind. Much of what she discovered about herself she disliked, but in recognising and acknowledging it she found a kind of freedom. Looking back at

261

the old Felicity Alderbrook, she wondered how the silly creature could have wasted so much time and energy on absurdities: on having more – and more glamorous – partners at every dance than Gerry; forcing every male guest in the house, whatever his age, endowments or attractions, to acknowledge hers; spending hours tending those attractions, as though they were her entire self; looking, she acknowledged at last, for a richer, better-looking, more distinguished husband than Andrew Kyrle to spite her father and his favourite daughter, as though that would satisfy her for ever.

The role Suvarov had designed for her was, paradoxically, the most appropriate anyone could have found. All her mother's teaching and criticism had been designed to help her to make herself agreeable and seductive so that when an appropriately endowed man appeared she would be able to make him want her. The fact that the original plan had been to make the man feed and house her for the rest of her life and Suvarov's version was to make him betray himself and his confrères for the good of her country made little difference. The mechanics were precisely the same.

Ever since her father had shown his disgust so unmistakably, she had been angry about the double standard that her world operated for men and women. Now, she understood that there were other double standards too. Having recognised that, she found herself able to ignore her father's horror and her own shame at last.

Although the revelations of her character made it easier to deal with herself and her feelings, and gave her a curious and unexpected contentment, they were of no use to her job. It was Jean-Pierre's feelings and activities she was supposed to be revealing. Her physical surrender to him taught her that he was a gentle and considerate lover, but that was really all. It was true that as the months passed he spoke more freely to her about his passionate love for France, his detestation of General de Gaulle, and his fear that the increasingly effective actions of the Resistance achieved little except savage reprisals against the civilian population, but she could not feel that that was enough.

She conscientiously passed it all on to Suvarov at their weekly reporting sessions in one or another of London's parks, and received his instructions about new lines of enquiry. She told him of the people – mainly men – that she met in Jean-Pierre's company and the few things he ever said about his work, but she never knew how useful any of it was or how Suvarov's other enquiries were going until one meeting in their favourite park in the middle of June 1943.

It had rained the previous day, but as they met under a statue, the sun was so hot that it brought out the sweet, heavy scents of the roses in the borders that led down to the bombed ruins of the old house. She had not seen Suvarov for a fortnight, because he had been away somewhere the week before, and she was suddenly struck by how weary and spent he looked as he stood waiting for her by the statue. As she came up to him his lined face lit in a smile of rare sweetness and he held out both hands. Flixe took them and smiled back.

'You look so happy these days, Flixe,' he said spontaneously. It was such an unusual beginning to one of their meetings that she took one hand out of his and laid it on his cheek for a moment.

'I wish I could say the same, Peter,' she said gently. 'But

you look ghastly. You're not ill, are you?'

He shook his head, moved out of her grasp, and then said with considerably more frankness than usual:

'No, but there's been a lot on. And we're getting near the end of this particular search, I think. With all of them we seem to reach a tricky time when we finally begin to draw all the strands together to make the pounce – but we've had more successes than failures overall.' Flixe could not help laughing at his mixed metaphor, but his words began to take on an unpleasant significance as she thought about them.

'You mean you're getting the proof about Jean-Pierre after all,' she said carefully. But it was not carefully enough. He stopped walking, turned, gripped her arms, and looked down into her face.

'You haven't fallen for him have you, Flixe?' he said, with a sharpness in his voice that hurt. 'God knows I'm the last person who ought to have ignored that possibility, but it simply never occured to me.'

'Please let me go,' she said, almost frightened by the tightness of his hands. He took them away at once, but did not move away from her. She hesitated, trying to tell him honestly about the feelings that she had not quite acknowledged to herself.

'I don't know. But, Peter, it's quite difficult to remain entirely detached when a charming, intelligent, delightful, generous man . . .' she broke off in some confusion. 'Takes you out to dine at least twice a week for all these months and you have to pretend to all the kinds of emotions that it is most dangerous to have.' Silently she added in her mind, particularly when the man you really do love keeps himself protected behind the barbed-wire fence of his seniority, talks to you about how much he cares for your sister, and debriefs you coldly about the effects of the liaison he himself has set up for you.

'I see,' he said after a while, frowning. She thought he was angry with her and that hurt too. But at last he said: 'I've even more to apologise for than I'd thought. Flixe, if it weren't so important I'd get you out of it now.' When she did not answer, he led her to an old teak bench under one of the immense oak trees and made her sit down.

'Flixe, you do realise exactly what it is that he's doing?' he said at last.

'If we're right and it is him.'

'You've got it quite badly, haven't you? Felicity, could you love a man who is doing his damnedest to wreck all the work that the Fighting French and the Allies are trying to do, who is causing the capture and death of their people and ours, who is trying to arrange to grab France for his rotten conspirators? Who would rather France were utterly ravaged so that there would be nothing and no one in a position to take it over except his organisation? Who doesn't care whether we or the Germans win, because he thinks he'll collect what he wants from whoever the victor is?'

'When you put it like that, no. Of course not. But you see, the Jean-Pierre I know isn't like that. He's a warm, clever, witty, handsome, generous businessman – and he says that he loves me and that makes a difference in itself.'

'Do you believe him?' Flixe was too absorbed in her own feelings to try to read his in his voice or expression.

'Oh God, Suvarov!' she burst out. 'How can I know? How does one ever know? I think that probably he does – some of the time. But what it means I don't know.' She got up from the bench as though she could not bear to sit and listen to his inquisition any longer. After a moment he stood beside her. His voice was gentle but implacable as he carried on.

'Felicity, hasn't it occurred to you that he may be trying to do to you what you are trying to do to him?'

'You mean make me fall for him so that he can find out what you are trying to do and how much you know? Of course I have. If I hadn't, life would be simple.'

They walked on in silence until they had completed almost an entire circuit of the park. Then Suvarov looked at his watch.

'Flixe, I've got to go in a minute. Listen: I've fixed for you to go on a course next week. And as things are it'll be no bad thing for you to be out of his way for a bit, so I think you ought to take some leave as well. You haven't had any for months. Take a fortnight. Get out of London.'

'And go where? On my own. What do you expect me to do for two weeks?' She could hear the angry resentment in her voice and hated it.

'The course is just outside Bristol. Why not go on to your mother's after that? You can ride, walk, rest, see Evelyn ... Even find out from your mother what Miss Kingsley was doing in France for three years after the last war.'

'I've already told you that,' answered Flixe, irritated by what she saw as a diversionary tactic. 'She was having an illicit affair with a married man. If you want his name or any details I suggest you ask Gerry. She and Anna are incredibly thick these days. An antidote to poor bloody Andrew, I suppose.' Hearing her voice sounding more and more like her mother's, she stopped, cursed silently and then looked at him. 'Peter, I'm sorry. With all the rest the last thing you need is my throwing a tantrum. Forgive me?'

He ruffled her fine fair hair with his right hand. 'Of course, best of my searchers. But be careful of yourself please, Flixe.' Then, as though ashamed of the plea, he reverted to a far more official manner than he had used to her in months. 'Now, about the course. Here's your railway warrant; you'll be met at the station and briefed when you get there. OK?'

'Yes. But what shall I be learning, Suvarov?' she asked, also reverting to an artificial formality, as though to create a crust over the emotions she had revealed to him.

'Self-defence,' he answered drily and she could not resist saying:

'How appropriate!'

'That's my Flixe,' he said, laughing. 'Stick to it, sweetheart.'

17

The first person she saw as she walked in through the front door of the requisitioned house somewhere near Bristol was her old suitor Johnny Blenkarne. She was suddenly engulfed in resentment against Peter Suvarov. It was bad enough that he should have discovered this particular aspect of her past, but that he should set out to manipulate her out of her feelings for Jean-Pierre by sending Johnny on the same self-defence course seemed despicable. For one moment she was so angry that she almost turned tail, planning to disobey orders for the first time since she had started to work for Suvarov and go AWOL.

'Flixe! My dear, what luck,' said Johnny, catching sight of her standing in the doorway. 'But what on earth are you doing here? I thought you were out of all this kind of thing?'

'Come on, Johnny, you know better than that. Or have you been sent to try to tease me into indiscretion?' He roared with laughter at that, and, still grinning, came towards her. He leaned down, kissed her cheek, and picked up her bag.

'Let me take this up for you, and then we can go and get a drink. D'you know where they've put you?' Flixe, highly surprised to see him changed from a half-drunk, maudlin lover into this cheerful, casual companion, took her bag back.

'I'm quite capable of carrying this weight, Johnny. I'll take it up and then meet you in the mess. And,' she added with a curious smile hovering about her lips, 'I shall tease you into telling me what's happened to you.'

'That's easy, my dear,' he said in the same happy voice. 'I'm out. Grounded. No more flying. I pranged in the drink – God how I hated their wretched slang – and was pretty ill with pneumonia, exposure and so on and so I'm flying a desk from now on. Calloo, callay, oh frabjous day! I'll tell you all the rest later, old girl. Hurry up. I want to buy you some gin.'

Even Suvarov, Machiavellian pastmaster of the art of manipulation though he might be, could not have wrought such a change in Flying Officer Blenkarne, thought Flixe as she walked upstairs with her luggage. Having unpacked her few clothes, she reported to the CO, was told that reveille would be at six o'clock the following morning, lights-out would be at ten-thirty and that until then she was free to fraternise in the mess as she chose.

Johnny introduced her to the other early arrivals for the course and then took her off to a small table in one corner of the room, carrying their drinks. When they were sitting down, he raised his pink gin and smiled at her deliberately over the top of the glass.

'Here's to you, Flixe. You know you've changed too; but I can't quite work out how or why.'

She smiled, sipped her gin and It and then shrugged.

269

'Yes, Johnny, I've changed. But nothing like to the extent you have. Tell me about it. I mean, last time we met – what? Nearly two years ago – you were . . .' She broke off, unable to think of a polite enough way to describe the pathetic creature in the nightclub. He laughed again and put a heavy hand on her shoulder.

'I know: a drip, a twerp, a weasel. A dead loss, frankly. But, Flixe, I was so jolly frightened. The whole bloody time. I think the only time since I joined the RAF that I wasn't afraid was when my kite was actually shot to bits and I had to bail out. I'd spent all those months expecting it, wincing as flak hit the tailplane, almost feeling my backside roasted as I crashed, imagining every disaster I'd ever heard of, and then there I was, floating peacefully down into the drink, stars overhead, other poor buggers still waiting to get it; nothing I could have done any more. I just hit the water, got rid of the 'chute as instructed, inflated the Mae West, and lay back like the Chinese say you should.'

A smile from Flixe acknowledged his allusion to rape. She raised her glass to him.

'Well, Johnny, here's to you. I think you must have been incredibly brave to go on going up there if you felt like that.'

'You always did know how to make a fellow feel terrific, Flixe,' he said after a while. 'But it's not true: I didn't have any option. I had to go up. But don't I bless that Jerry who shot me down? God, how I do.'

'Oh, Johnny, I'm so glad——' she was beginning, but he interrupted her.

'Never mind me, though, old girl. Tell me about you, and what's taken away that brittleness.'

'Was I brittle, Johnny? I'm sorry for that, too, then.'

Flixe could not, of course, tell him by which route she had arrived at her present state of mind and existence, but they had plenty to talk about without any true confessions from her. She enjoyed herself hugely, removed from not only her responsibilities but also from two men who had been causing her such anguish. By the time they went into dinner, she had already forgiven Suvarov for putting her in touch with Johnny again; but as they drank their fairly disgusting Brown Windsor soup, he told her that he had been ordered on to the course long before she and Suvarov had had their painful discussion in the park and she realised that she had been overestimating his Machiavellian talents, and let herself relax.

Before she and Johnny parted for the night he held out his hand as they stood at the foot of the elegant, curving staircase.

'Friends, Flixe?'

'Friends, Johnny,' she agreed, taking his hand and giving it a squeeze. 'What fun! I came on this course expecting it to be hell, but I think I'm going to enjoy it.'

'I know I am, whatever they have in store for us tomorrow. Good night, angel-eyes.'

And they did enjoy it, both of them. The various instructors allowed them to pair up for any exercises where two were needed to work together, and they collaborated and competed like two prep-school boys vying for a single place in the First XI. Johnny was fitter by far than Flixe, despite his recent illnesses, and could easily outrun her, but when it came to the unarmed combat exercises that were the culmination of the course she did better than he, and far better than either of the other two women on the course.

The instructor for those lessons was an ex-Hong Kong policeman, whose chief purpose was to teach the six pupils how to defend themselves against a murderous attack, launched probably at night, certainly in the middle of a city. Since they were all clearly office workers of one sort or another, they would not be armed and had to learn to kill with their hands, with an umbrella, a hatpin or whatever else they might have about them. They were also taught how to disable an assailant without killing him, and it was on that exercise that Flixe came to grief.

Johnny had been told to stand behind her and grab her by the throat; she was to slide her fingers under his hands, hook his legs from under him and twist sideways so that he was flung to the ground. The instructor, perhaps because he had been irritated to see a woman as delicate and fragile-looking as Flixe flooring a man of six-foot-three, whispered some extra instruction to Johnny and Flixe found herself trying to hook away legs that were not where she had expected them. Surprised, frightened in spite of knowing that her assailant was only Johnny and that they were merely practising, she jammed her elbows backwards, happily missing his groin by a few inches. Nevertheless, he reacted as instinctively as she had and she found herself lying flat on her back on the hard mat on the gym floor, winded and in considerable pain.

In an instant, he was on his knees beside her, his face sheet-white.

'Flixe, have I hurt you? God I'm sorry, darling . . .' He was removed by the horny-handed ex-policeman.

'Out of the way, Flying Officer Blenkarne. Now, Miss Alderbrook, don't try to talk. Concentrate on your breathing: in . . . out . . . in . . . Come on, you can do better than that.'

272

In the end, she managed to get the gasping, painful breathing under control, told the policeman where her back and side hurt, was lifted up, examined and told that she would be all right after an hour or two lying on her bed. As she limped out of the gym, she passed Johnny, still looking horrified and guilty.

'Don't worry, Johnny: it's all part of the game. I'll be all right. And it's my turn to buy the gin tonight.'

His face relaxed slightly and he smiled in gratitude, but later in the mess he told her that he would never have forgiven himself if he had really hurt her.

'It was too horribly like that ghastly. . . .Flixe, I never meant to mention it, but I'm sorry for that too. Desperately sorry.' She touched his lean, brown face, wincing a little as her back muscles protested as she stretched them.

'Don't, Johnny; it was as much my fault as yours. We were just a pair of inexperienced children, hurting each other because we knew no better.'

He covered her hand with his own and smiled. 'You are the most charitable woman. But it was more my fault: I was using you – trying to kill the fear by showing someone that I was . . .'

'Don't, Johnny,' she said again. 'I've learned a lot since then. And I expect you have, too. Let's just write it off to experience and forget it. After all, we're friends now, aren't we?'

'All right, my dear. Thank you,' he said, wondering about what she had learned and from whom, and hoping in some desperation that she had not learned it from the 'dago' he had seen with her in the nightclub. 'How will you go back to work with your back so sore?'

'Oh, that's OK,' she answered cheerfully. 'My chief wangled me some leave. I'm going to stay with mother and

273

her evacuees for a few days.'

They parted, still friends, on the last day of the course, Johnny giving her his address in London and Flixe assuring him yet again that she was not badly hurt and was thoroughly pleased that they had met again, even at the price of an aching back. There could have been no better introduction to a weekend at Sudbrook House, she thought as she sat on the slow cross-country train later that morning, than to have exorcised an unhappiness from the past and made a new – real – friend.

The train steamed into her station two hours later, and she looked along the short platform for her mother. After a few minutes, she was accosted by three urchins.

'You Felicity then?' demanded the biggest of them.

'Yes, I am,' she said, astonished. Then she remembered the evacuees. 'Can it be that my mother has sent you to fetch me?'

''S'right. We brought the cart.'

'Cart?' she repeated, beginning to smile in spite of the impossibility of seeing her mother in the company of such boys.

'Yes, come on. Mustn't be late for luncheon,' cried the head urchin while the other two heaved Flixe's suitcase up into the back of the old governess cart that had been kept under a tarpaulin in the spare stable for as long as she could remember, and offered to help her negotiate the sinking, rickety step. Smothering her amusement that after the physical training she had just been put through she should be offered assistance by a seven-year-old, she found herself wondering snobbishly how long it had taken her mother to teach the urchins to call their midday meal luncheon.

They had harnessed poor old Buttercup between the shafts, and Flixe was interested to see that the leading urchin managed the mare with considerable assurance and a certain deft gentleness. The journey up to the house took nearly twenty minutes and by the time they got there, she had discovered that the driver was Jimmy, the middle-sized boy Sid and the youngest, Dick. She could not wait to see her elegant, resentful mother dealing with them.

As they turned into the short drive, Dick stood up, balancing himself against her bruised thigh, and called out in an ear-splitting shriek:

'We got 'er, Fan.'

Flixe sympathised with Buttercup's sudden stumble and, after making certain that Jimmy managed to steady her, looked in interest for the first sight of her mother. When it came it was in its own way as surprising as the behaviour of the three extraordinary children.

Frances Alderbrook was dressed with all the overtidiness her daughter remembered, but her face had lost its aggrieved lines and her deep-blue eyes were widely opened and lit up by amused affection. When Flixe clambered down from the governess cart her mother came forward and kissed her. Then, keeping one arm around her shoulders, she said proudly:

'Well, what do you think of my boys?'

'Terrific!' said Flixe, unable to think of any more suitable comment. 'How long did it take you to housetrain them?' She wished that she had not sounded so caustic as she saw her mother's expression. To make up for it, she leaned forward to kiss her cheek. 'I'm sorry, Mother. I shouldn't have said that.'

'It's all right, Flixe. I know what you mean. And we

certainly had a few battles at the beginning, but we've come to know how far each side is prepared to go and now we're reasonably peaceable.' She then ruffled little Dick's hair and called out: 'See to Buttercup, will you, Jimmy? Luncheon in fifteen minutes.'

'OK, Fan.'

'Mother, do you really let them call you that?' whispered Flixe, far more naturally.

'I had to if I didn't want them calling me miss or m'um. They couldn't have managed Mrs Alderbrook and anyway it would have become absurd once we knew each other, and "Aunt Fanny" would have been dotty, too.'

'Yes, it does sound as though it should be spoken delicately by a Victorian miss over her embroidery frame.'

'Precisely. Now, sherry while the boys clean up?'

'Lovely.'

'Come on in then and tell me about the war.'

'It seems to have reached even Sudbrook House,' said Flixe, laughing as she followed her mother into the drawing room.

'You could say that. Will you pour us each a glass, Flixe?'

They talked on with a friendliness that Flixe could hardly bring herself to believe in, and even the arrival of the noisy children did not break up the generous atmosphere.

'Mother, you are the last person who I'd have expected to get on so well with a bunch of evacuees like that,' said Flixe after the depressing sausagemeat and potato pie had been consumed and the boys disappeared again into the garden.

'Poor children. They have had the most frightful time,

276

Flixe,' answered her mother, carrying the dirty plates out to the scullery. 'Would you rather wash or dry?'

'Wash, if that's all right with you,' said Flixe, taking up an apron from a hook on the door. 'I can imagine they must have, if they came from the East End. Gerry saw it burning one night when she stood in for Anna Kingsley, and she told me enough about it. I say, are you all right?' she said curiously, aware that her mother had flinched.

'Yes, but that's what happened to their parents.'

'Burned?'

'Yes, mother, father, an uncle and an elder sister,' said Fanny with a break in her voice.

'But why? They always sheltered in the tubes.'

'It was right at the beginning, Flixe, before the . . . when the government was still barring the entrances to the tubes.'

'What?' demanded Flixe, putting the last plate in the rack to drain and letting out the dishwater.

'Yes, they thought that the populace would develop "deep-shelter" mentality unless they were forbidden to use the tubes – and their pathetic houses went up like matchwood. But don't let's talk about it any more; it makes me so angry – and depressed. Let's go and see what's out in the garden; it's such a lovely day.'

'Yes, let's,' answered Flixe, warmly. 'But tell me something: where were these boys in between then and getting to you?'

'Somewhere in Hertfordshire – with a woman who sounds like a fiend,' said Fanny, stopping to pick some lavender spikes. 'I need this to keep the sheets smelling nice. It was ages before they trusted me not to behave like her.'

'But what did she do?'

'I don't know – they still haven't managed to tell me. I expect she was horrified by their lack of cleanliness and some of their habits. They are – no, were – disgusting. But they're such brave boys, Flixe: pitchforked into a life that is completely strange; knowing they've no home, no family to go back to, they keep their spirits up and their wits about them. And what wits! I'd always assumed that that sort were stupid, born ineducable or something, but they're not. They're really bright.'

'They sound like paragons.' It was supposed to be a light, joking comment to help the conversation on, but Flixe could hear bitterness in her voice and hated herself for destroying the happy pride in her mother's face, but it was too late. She waited, not knowing what to say.

Fanny Alderbrook stopped, turned to face her daughter and said gently:

'Don't be jealous, darling. You have so much compared to them.'

They walked on in silence towards the woods. Flixe smarted from that word, jealousy, which had reached right down into some of her worst childhood memories.

'I don't think you've ever called me "darling" before,' she managed to say at last.

'Oh, of course I have,' answered her mother, taken aback. 'I often call you darling.'

'No, I don't think so.' Then the dammed-up words broke through the constraints she had built up over the years: 'Why couldn't you have been kind to us like that? Why did you have to keep it for three strangers who had no rights to it?'

'But, Flixe, what do you mean?' asked Fanny Alderbrook, appalled to see the happiest of her four daughters look and sound so like the perennially

278

difficult Gerry.

'You were always foul to us,' Flixe burst out, quite beyond considerations of tact or even kindness. 'Whatever we did was wrong; anything that was nearly all right just wasn't enough. You spent the whole time criticising us. And everyone else. Whenever we went anywhere, afterwards you would go over and over all the failings of the people we'd seen: their social failings, their dullness, their awful clothes, their voices, their books, their furniture, their taste, their food, their servants, gardens, horses, children. No one was ever good enough for Fanny Alderbrook. I don't think I've ever heard you say anything kind about anyone until those boys.'

'Flixe, that's absurd.' Her mother's voice sounded stricken, but Flixe could not stop now that the sealed wells of childhood misery had been unstopped.

'Any achievement was denigrated, any friend criticised, any aspiration mocked, any wound probed and salted until we screamed in pain.'

'Stop it, Flixe; you're hysterical.'

'No, just slowly coming to understand that one can't hide from it for ever. I've never let myself say those things even to myself. I have spent most of my time blaming Father for most of the miseries of the past. I might have gone on doing it for ever if I hadn't seen what you could have been – if you'd cared for us as you care for those children. He was always bloody to me – and you didn't even try to stop him.' She turned away and began to walk slowly back towards the house. Then, almost as though she were talking to herself, she went on: 'I wonder if it would have been better if we'd been boys. Or were you just getting your revenge on your past by making us as miserable as you had been?'

They were both almost in tears by then, but the last accusation was so extravagant that Mrs Alderbrook pulled herself together. She caught up with Flixe, made her sit down on the stile and herself leaned against the adjacent thick prickly hedge.

'Flixe, you are beside yourself. The war has worn you out and made you see things wildly out of proportion. But try to listen: I care and always did care very much for you all. If I seem kinder to the boys than I did to you, it's because they are so different. I'm not trying to fit them for life; I don't have to watch over them and worry about whether they'll achieve all they have to in order to be safe.'

'Then what are you trying to do for them?' asked Flixe, as though quite uninterested, looking away from the face that was so like her own would be in twenty years.

'To make them happy, of course,' said Mrs Alderbrook.

It was too much. Flixe stood up and said brusquely:

'I'm going to see Evelyn. Don't wait supper for me if I'm not back.'

'Flixe, you can't leave like this. Not after what you've said.'

'I can't stay. I'll be back later. I know you hate the fact that Gerry and I care for Evelyn, but it so happens that without her I'd have said something frightful to you or Father years ago.'

Flixe pushed her hair back away from her forehead and then covered her eyes for a moment, remembering the days in the past when she had gone to Evelyn, flaming with resentment or desperate with half-angry misery. She could feel her mother moving towards her and thought that at that moment she could not bear to be touched, despite having longed for years to have some physical affection from her parents. She took her hands away from her face and stood up straight, facing her mother.

'Evelyn kept me going. And, incidentally, always refused to listen to any criticism of you. She's not like you, you see – she tries to build people up, not destroy the things that help them manage.'

18

When Flixe arrived back at her London flat soon after four on the following Monday, she found a note from Jean-Pierre telling her how much he had missed her and inviting her to dine that evening. After her mother's depressing cooking the prospect of dinner at the Ritz or the Berkeley was enticing, but Flixe knew that she would never repair the ravages of a week's self-defence training and a weekend with her mother and the evacuees in time. Regretfully, she telephoned Jean-Pierre's manservant to leave a message, saying that she would be unable to dine that evening, but would be free the next. Then she wrote to her mother, trying to apologise for what she had said, and to Ming, describing the funnier aspects of the course with as much discretion as she could, and addressed it to the headquarters of the organisation that Ming had joined when she had left school. Her own letters never carried any other address and so although Flixe was certain that Ming was not based there, she had nowhere else to send the letter. Having sealed the envelopes, she scribbled a note to Gerry asking when they could meet, ran out to post all three letters, and returned to unpack and start washing her smalls and pressing the skirts and frocks she had taken away with her.

Later, when she was having a shallow, tepid bath before getting into bed, she caught sight of the enormous bruise on her thigh. The mark had faded a little over the week, but it was still far too distinct to have been explained away to Jean-Pierre. There was little hope that it would have gone even by the following evening: could she tell him that she had walked into a table? Or fallen off her horse? Just as she was running through possible stories, the telephone rang. Cursing mildly, she got out of the bath, wrapped herself in a towel and went to answer it.

'Hello? Flixe?' came the unmistakable voice of her chief.

'Yes, it's me,' she answered ungrammatically. 'How are you, Suvarov?'

'Well enough. But I gather you're a bit damaged,' he said, and she thought that she could hear a laugh at the back of his voice.

'Yes, I was just examining my bruises – a dead giveaway, you know,' she said, laughing aloud.

'Poor you. But, seriously, Flixe, I need to talk to you. Will you feed the ducks tomorrow, one-forty-five?'

'Yes, all right. I'll be there.'

'Good,' he said and rang off.

When they met on the edge of the Round Pond, he looked carefully at her face. A little embarrassed but determined not to be outfaced, she stared back, noticing all over again how beautiful his face was. His eyelashes were thick and black and seemed to give his eyes more definition than anyone else's had, and his nose was perfectly straight, with the nostrils most delicately cut. He seemed to be thinner than the last time she had seen him, and his mouth looked harder.

'You really are all right, then?' he said at last. Feeling suddenly much happier than at any time since she left Johnny Blenkarne at the course, Flixe tucked her hand into her chief's arm.

'Yes. And I think I'll manage to persuade Jean-Pierre that my bruises are the result of coming off Buttercup into the river, when I see him tonight. But never mind that,' she added as she caught a look of impatience in his dark eyes. 'What's so urgent that it couldn't wait until our normal day?'

He squeezed her hand between his arm and side and then released himself, stuffing both hands in the pockets of his uniform trousers.

'Flixe,' he said eventually, and then stopped as though he had forgotten what he wanted to tell her. 'Oh, it's partly that I just wanted to make certain that you were all right. The CO of Naseby House told me about your fall in such graphic detail – not to speak of all the goings-on with your young man that . . .'

'Johnny? Come off it, Peter,' she said, laughing again and wondering for one dizzying moment whether he were jealous of her friendship. ' "Goings-on" indeed. How vulgar! *A propos*, I meant to ask you: did you send me there knowing I'd come across him?'

'To distract you from Jean-Pierre, you mean? It never occurred to me. But I hope you were discreet.'

'Oh, I see,' she said, disappointed that he was only concerned for security after all. 'Yes, I was discreet. Let's sit.'

'No. Too conspicuous in amongst all these children.

284

We'd better move on. Broad Walk?' he suggested, leading the way.

They turned to stroll past the empty bandstand towards the flower-edged Broad Walk. After a while, Flixe broke the silence, which she felt to be tense and unfriendly.

'So what else, Peter?'

'What?' he said, almost as though she had woken him up. 'Oh, well it's just something Gerry let out about Anna Kingsley, and I wondered whether you'd got anything from your mother.'

Flixe stopped, both hands covering her mouth like a child who has been caught out in wrongdoing.

'Oh Lord! D'you know, I'd completely forgotten to ask. We had a bit of a turn-up. I was absolutely bloody to her and we both got rather emotional. I am sorry, Suvarov.'

'Never mind. I expect I can confirm it from other sources,' he said with none of the impatience she had expected. He took both her hands. 'Don't look like that, Flixe. You can't be afraid of me, surely? I'm not going to carpet you.'

'Thanks, Peter. But what did you get out of Gerry?'

'She thinks that Miss Kingsley had a child during the time she was in France and that it was adopted over there. If that's so, it could explain the letters—'

'God yes,' interrupted Flixe. 'Imagine, knowing a child of yours was stuck in France at this juncture. I suppose it must be about my age. No wonder she said . . . and was so set on my giving Jean-Pierre up. Mother must know about it. Damn, I wish I'd asked, and I can't ring or write without it looking too pointed. Peter, I'm sorry.'

Once again he told her not to apologise and they walked on, while he questioned her about the course and her fellow students. Something about him seemed to have changed and Flixe wondered precisely what it was – and why it had happened. She found him far more relaxed and easier to be with than she had at their previous reporting sessions. Quite soon he ceased to ask questions, but did not leave her. Instead they pottered on through the park, talking easily of this and that and nothing much, until at last he looked at his watch.

'Damn, three o'clock. I must go. Flixe, be careful.'

'I shall, Peter. And, after all, now at least I know how to take care of myself.'

He put one of his long, white hands against her cheek in a rare if casual caress and left her at a run.

Walking back towards her flat along the High Street, Flixe passed a hairdresser where she occasionally had her hair set. She went in and asked whether they could fit her in there and then. The receptionist looked bored.

'Certainly, madam,' she said. 'But you will have to bring your own shampoo, towels and pins. Shall we say in half-an-hour's time?'

'Why not?' The last time Flixe had tried them she had had to provide only her own shampoo, and she felt irritated, but not angry enough to struggle with her hair herself.

Two hours later she emerged, glad that she had succumbed to temptation. However hard she tried, she could never achieve quite the smoothness of profession-ally dressed hair. And the colour always seemed better after she had had it washed and dried by someone else. Perhaps it's the rinsing, she murmured to herself as she opened the street door of her block of flats.

The hall porter met her with an immense bunch of late

roses in every colour from palest apricot to deep, rich flame.

'Thank you, Tomkins,' she said, taking it from him and unclipping the florist's envelope as she walked up the stairs. In the flat, she thrust the bouquet into a bucket of water in the kitchen and sat down to read the note. It was in French. Translating it automatically, Flixe read: 'My darling, until this evening. I shall send the car for you at seveny-thirty. J-P.'

How strange, she thought as she looked through her wardrobe for a suitable frock, that he was not coming to collect her as usual. But if he had sent so lavish a selection of flowers, he could not have meant it as an insult. Perhaps he was merely busier than usual.

Shrugging, she chose a dress of parchment-coloured silk that she rarely wore, and laid it out on her bed. It was particularly well cut, but its lack of colour often made her look sallow. She looked carefully at her face in the long glass and decided there was something to be said for her recent activities; for once her skin was glowing with healthy colour. If she pinned two of the coppery roses to the low-cut neck of the dress, she should look all right even for a man as exacting as Jean-Pierre.

She was glad to see in the bath that her bruises were fading suitably, and she returned to the bedroom to dress with a certain pleased anticipation. It felt like months since she had last made up her face with such care or worn a pair of silk stockings. They were quite impossible to buy any longer, but Jean-Pierre had given her five dozen pairs just before their manufacture had been banned and she had kept them for her appointments with him, darning any ladders at once and washing them with extreme care.

The car arrived punctually, and Jean-Pierre's chauffeur handed her into the back seat and laid a light cashmere rug over her knees. It seemed undignified to ask him where they were going and so she merely sat back and waited.

They drew up at last outside a tall, double-fronted house in Duke Street, St James's, and Flixe realised that for the first time since she had met him, Jean-Pierre was inviting her into his own house. With a curiosity matched only by her apprehension, Flixe followed the chauffeur to the door and allowed him to usher her into a dark, narrow hall, whose walls were hung with massive oil paintings in heavy gold frames. There was no time to look at any of them, for a formally dressed manservant took her cloak from her, opened a door on her left and announced her.

'Mademoiselle Alderbrook, monsieur.'

Wondering for the first time how Jean-Pierre managed to keep so many servants, Flixe walked into the room.

'*Mignonne*,' Jean-Pierre said, kissing her hand. 'How I have missed you.'

'And I, you, *mon cher*. But you look well,' answered Flixe, smiling at him in a pleasure that was at least three-quarters genuine. He handed her a tall, flute-shaped glass full of champagne and said caressingly:

'And how do you like my house?'

'Well, I've seen very little of it, so far. But it seems very . . . impressive,' she said looking around her. They were standing in a double drawing-room of sombre magnificence, the walls dark-panelled and hung with more oils and a beautiful and very old tapestry, the parquet floor almost concealed by an immense rug that she assumed must have been made at the Aubusson factory. A small

288

log fire was burning in the black grate beneath an elegant marble chimneypiece. There was an immense looking-glass over it, in a gilt frame almost as elaborate as those of the paintings. The light of innumerable silk-shaded lamps gleamed in its reflection, and a pair of magnificent malachite obelisks flanked the gilded frame. Two sofas covered in dark-green velvet stood on either side of the fireplace, each backed by an elegant mahogany sofa table. Otherwise, there was little furniture except for four superb eighteenth-century pieces, a desk, two commodes and a break-front bookcase, filled with volumes bound in matching dark-green morocco. It was a very masculine room, but luxurious too.

'Impressive,' Flixe repeated. 'Is the furniture French?'

'Yes,' he answered, apparently pleased. 'Most of it came from my grandfather's house in Paris. Come, let me show you around.' He took her hand and led her round the room, describing the origin of each piece of furniture or painting, each small perfect bronze statue. When they had completed the circuit, he asked her if she wanted more champagne. Flixe shook her head, remembering his strictures about women who allowed themselves to become noisy and coarse with too much alcohol, and waited.

He rang the bell and when the servant reappeared told him in French that they wished to dine immediately. Then he held the door open for Flixe and escorted her across the hall to a small dining-room, as superbly furnished as the room she had already seen, and asked her to sit down.

The dinner that the French manservant brought in was of a standard way above even the restaurants and hotels Jean-Pierre regularly patronised and as course succeeded perfect course, each accompanied by the appropriate wine, Flixe began to wonder what on earth was going on. At last, the servant poured coffee for both of them, placed a bottle of Napoleon brandy in front of Jean-Pierre with two glasses and withdrew.

Flixe refused the brandy, and as he sat, slowly swirling the spirit in his glass, she plucked up her courage.

'Jean-Pierre,' she said in a gently teasing voice, 'why do I get the impression that you are going to tell me something?' He looked up, his dark face weirdly lit by the four candles on the round table.

'Tell you, *mignonne*? Why?' She laughed and reached across the table to touch his hand.

'Inviting me to your house for the first time; the champagne, the *foie gras*, the *filet*, the soufflé, all the wines. This is either a celebration or a rather elaborate—' She broke off as her voice faltered on the last word. He did not speak, merely looked across the table at her, his eyes steady and his mouth firm, turning the brandy glass round and round between his hands. 'An elaborate farewell,' she finished.

'One of the things I have always admired in you, my dear Félicitée,' he said at last, putting his brandy glass back on the table, 'is your wits.' At that Flixe lifted her chin, tried to ignore her immediate real response, shook back her gleaming fair curls and laughed.

'Oh, my darling. How is it then that I thought you preferred quite other attributes?' she said.

'No. Your lovely face and seductive body may have enticed me at the beginning, but it is only character that holds a man like me. And you have held me, Félicitée. I don't know quite when or how it happened, but it has happened and now I find that I cannot leave you.' He lifted the glass once more and drank a little of the cognac.

'Then you really are leaving,' said Flixe, sobered once more. 'I think I might need a little brandy after all.'

'Of course, my dear,' he said, pouring some for her. 'Yes, I think I shall have to leave London quite soon, but I don't know exactly when. And it is possible that the need may not arise after all. But . . .'

'But, Jean-Pierre,' said Flixe, not realising that she was interrupting him rudely. 'This is horribly mysterious. What are you talking about?'

'Never mind that. You do not need to know about it – my business affairs. That's all. But I want to ask you: when I send for you, will you come to me?'

Of all the things Flixe had imagined since she had entered his house, this was the very last and she did not know how to respond to it. Part of her wanted to say, of course, Jean-Pierre, wherever you are, whenever you call. Another part answered more caustically, not until I am certain that you are innocent of what Suvarov suspects.

'Well?' Jean-Pierre said at last. 'You look shocked, *mignonne*.'

'No, of course not,' she answered, finding her voice once more. 'But so surprised. I don't understand: are you saying that you will want to marry me?'

'I had not realised that that was a condition, Félicitée, but if you wish it, certainly.' He poured a little more cognac into each glass and then recorked the bottle. 'Ever since I first took you to bed and discovered how inexperienced you were, I have had it in mind that one day we might marry.' He laughed and there was something so tender in the sound that Flixe almost shivered. 'It was a little like deflowering a virgin, *mignonne*. Quite unexpected – and delightful.'

'Of course it's not a condition, *mon cher*,' said Flixe

hurriedly, finding the turn his words had taken both upsetting and a little frightening. 'How could you think that? I just did not understand. And I still don't. But I could not decide now, at this moment. How long will you be here?'

'It is not certain. Drink your cognac and don't worry. It won't be tomorrow anyway. There is still a little time. But . . .' His voice dropped and sounded infinitely more sincere, 'I should hate to leave not knowing whether you will come.' He stood up from the table and came round to stand behind her chair. Flixe felt his hands on her neck, sliding down to her breasts. He kissed her hair.

'*Mignonne*, I have come to love you so much.'

The simplicity of his declaration moved her. How can one ever know, she had asked Suvarov. He had not been able to answer her then and she could still find no confirmation for herself. She leaned back against Jean-Pierre and looked up into his face.

'*Mignonne*?' he said gently when she did not speak.

'I . . . don't know, my dear. It's too sudden and too strange. Where would it be? When would you know? All those questions that because I am a woman I have to ask.'

'And I cannot answer them now – because of the war. One of the smallest, but still painful, tragedies of this war is that no one can speak the truth even to people they love. I hope that one day I shall be able to take you to France. You know that I long to go back and leave all the English side of the businesses to some manager. But until the Germans are thrown out, how can I? I can only ask you to trust me.'

She was silent for a long time. Then at last she made up her mind on a small thing.

'Jean-Pierre, will you take me home now? I must think, and I cannot think while I feel your arms around me.'

'Of course,' he said at once, taking his hands away and moving backwards. Flixe stood up and turned to face him.

'You do understand, don't you?' she asked, thinking how pathetic she must sound.

'I understand. But you are not going to leave me without letting me kiss you, are you?' Flixe shook her blond head. 'Then come here.'

Ming

1943

19

12 March 1941

My dear Mary,

You must never apologise for your letters or
anything you write in them. I am most touched that
you trust me enough to tell me the things you have
and if (as you wrote the week before last) my replies
make life a little easier then I am glad.

You know that I have never had a child, but what
you perhaps don't know is that until I saw you in
that hard, narrow bed at St George's I had never felt
that I lacked anything. At that moment I think I
understood what a father must feel for his daughter;
and it is a sensation I like very much, despite the
great sadness I feel for you in your struggles to live
without Annie. Your last few letters have suggested
that the immediate pain is becoming less sharp, and
if that is so I'm glad. But you are right to hold on to
your memories, and Miss Roseheath is quite wrong,
I'm certain. Annie will always be a part of you and
if you try to pretend that she is not, you will be no
happier now and (I think) less so in the future.

> You talk of a 'strange feeling of anger about Annie', but it's not so strange, Mary, and that too should not be fought . . .

Ming folded up the much-creased, limp sheets of paper and caught sight of the post-script on the last: 'I am so glad, by the way, that you have made such progress in French. M. Julien must be an inspired teacher.' As she slid the folded sheets back into the huge battered brown envelope in which she kept all Peter Suvarov's letters, Ming thought that she understood at last why he had been so pleased with her increasing fluency in French. She stood looking out of her window, across the Etchingham park towards the Dower House. Peter had told her not to decide straight away, and to think very hard before she gave him her answer, but from the moment he had made his suggestion she had known that she would agree.

After Annie's death, Ming had felt almost as though she had just been born at the age of fifteen and a half into a strange new world full of terrors and people speaking a language she hardly understood. The sensation had passed quite soon, of course, but she would never be able to forget the inexpressible comfort brought to her by Peter's first letter. And that first one had been quite impersonal compared with the one she had just read and the others that he had written to her every week since then. Without his letters she sometimes felt that she would never have recovered her health and her wits; even in the last few months when misery swamped her and she wondered whether she would be able to go on living she would get out his letters and find comfort in rereading them.

Because of that she felt that she owed him whatever he

chose to ask.

Turning away from the window, she put the big envelope away and allowed herself to admit just once how terrifying she found his proposition. Suvarov had not tried to minimise the dangers she would face (rather the reverse in fact) and had made no effort to blackmail her into agreeing to go. In fact she could not help feeling that he was thoroughly reluctant to let her go and hoped that she would refuse. After one difficult silence she had asked him why he should have even considered sending someone as unlikely as herself.

'For that very reason,' he had said, looking directly at her with eyes that seemed to express all the affection she had come to rely on in his letters. 'We are going to need a courier who has never had anything to do with any of the secret departments here or anyone who might be suspected for any reason at all. We need someone from a family we know and trust, and you are that as well. And we need someone brave.'

At that Ming had interrupted.

'Peter, don't mock. It isn't kind, and you're the kindest man I know.'

'I'm not mocking, Ming. I mean it. The way you picked yourself up after that bomb and got on with what you had to do when you felt that your life was draining away inside you, showed what stuff you are made of. All you have to do now is to believe it. And in yourself.'

Without looking up at him, she said: 'That was just what it felt like.'

'I know it was,' he had said with all the gentleness she loved in him, and she had looked up then and smiled through the tears that clung to her eyelashes. Somehow it had not mattered any more that he could see them.

Frightened or not, she told herself stoutly, she would have to do what he had so reluctantly asked. He had given her a reason to go on living after Annie's death; he had been her friend and her father, while her own father hardly even knew who she was; he had urged her to stay at school until she was qualified to take a job he could give her. One way and another he had turned the unhappy, terrified schoolgirl into a functioning member of the real world.

Picking up her brush and comb, Ming tidied her hair and went downstairs to the CO's office, where Peter was waiting.

She had always felt that it was the most depressing room in the whole of that enormous house. On the ground floor at the back, overlooking rows of cabbages in the old kitchen garden, it was both large and dark. It had probably been a sitting room for the housekeeper in the days when the house had still been inhabited by Peter's wife, she thought, but the housekeeper's furniture and knick-knacks must have been consigned to the attics. In their place were the typical contents of any office: a big desk, a row of green filing cabinets and ranks of Globe Wernicke bookcases, their glass fronts dusty and scratched. The room was nearly always cold and smelled of damp and cold tobacco smoke. But for once Ming hardly noticed, because Peter was there, sitting in one of the old brown-leather armchairs near the fireplace.

As she crossed the floor towards him he stood up and waited gravely for her to speak. Taking a deep breath, she smiled.

'If you still want me,' she said carefully, 'I'll go to France for you.'

Once she had agreed she started a most rigorous and secret

training schedule: in fitness; in self-defence; in the social and political conditions in France; in escape and evasion techniques; in resisting interrogation; and in colloquial French. For the six months of her training, during which she never once saw Peter, she spoke no English at all, and by the end was reasonably confident of her fluency and comprehension, although she still worried about her accent.

But Peter was reported to be satisfied with her instructors' reports and at last allowed the operation for which she had been trained to go ahead. Her conducting officer took her to Southampton, and the first person she saw there was Peter.

Cold, heavy rain was pouring down out of the sky and so Suvarov suggested that he and Ming wait for the evening tide in one of the disused buildings near the quay. Ming sat on her suitcase and watched him as he prowled around the dusty, empty room. At last he stopped and stared out of the glazed door at the rain.

'Are you certain that you want to go, Ming?' he said. 'You know we only send volunteers. No one would try to stop you if you wanted to change your mind even at this stage.'

'No, I don't want to change my mind,' answered Ming wearily, for he had already asked her that question three times since they had met outside in the rain.

'You should be at the marshes by dawn,' said Suvarov. 'Jean will collect you and see you through the Dordogne, where he will hand you over to the next guide.' He might almost have been talking to someone outside the water-streaked glass panel for all the attention he was paying to Ming. But she felt the strength of his concern despite his turned back and deliberately toneless voice.

'The only thing that might stop Jean getting to you,' he went on quietly, 'would be capture. In case that has happened the boat will be back after dark the following evening. If he doesn't come, all you have to do is lie up until dark, go back to the beach and make the signal. Then you'll be picked up and back here in no time.'

'Yes, Peter,' she said patiently.

'Now, we don't know who your guide to Laville will be yet, but Jean will not leave you until he has safely handed you over.'

'Yes,' agreed Ming, trying to smile. 'You told me.'

Her conducting officer had been over the arrangements time and time again. Once or twice during her training and briefing Ming had thought that if the plans had not been so elaborate, if so many people in France and England had not been involved already, she might have been able to tell him how frightened she was. But months of secret work had gone into the operation; she had been taken out of her dull coding job at Etchingham and specially trained for this one mission. It did not seem possible to back out, and besides, whatever he said, Peter wanted her to go.

At last he turned from his examination of the rain and came towards her. There was very little light in the dusty shed, but she could see that he was smiling at her, although his eyes were full of anxiety. He held out both his hands. She got up off the suitcase.

'Is it time?'

'Yes, Ming,' he said taking her hands. 'You will do splendidly, I know.'

Despite herself, she clung to his hands, but she made herself speak calmly to take the wildness out of his eyes.

'Well I shall do my best anyway.'

'I know you will. I have infinite trust in you, Ming,' he said, holding her hands firmly and trying to will confidence into them both. 'You have great courage and huge resources of character. The imagination that makes you afraid of things is what will keep you safe over there.'

Ming squeezed his hands and then let them go. He kissed her forehead and turned to lead her out of the shed through the pelting rain to the converted fishing boat that was tied up at the old quay, its engines already chugging. Her conducting officer had already checked that she had all her false identity papers and French ration cards, that all her clothes had been stripped of any identifying labels and that she had her cyanide pill just in case she were picked up by the Gestapo and could find no other way of escape. She shook hands with both of the men, took one last look up into Suvarov's face, whispered, 'I love you, Peter,' and went aboard the boat without waiting for his answer.

A young RNVR officer with a thick brown beard swung her suitcase up and yelled at her to get out of the rain into the little cabin. She did as she was told and huddled down by the smelly engine feeling bitterly cold, wet from the short five minutes in the rain, and soon nauseated from the increasing swell and the smell of the engine. She decided to distract herself by running through her instructions.

The boat would drop her at a specified point in the desolate, uninhabited marshes of the area to the south-west of Bordeaux known as Les Landes. All the intelligence reports suggested that there was no German presence there, and there should be no danger. Ming was to wait for the mysterious Jean, a Frenchman, who would escort her through all the posts manned by Germans and the Milice. They would skirt round Bordeaux and he would guide her to the hills above a small town called Laville just above the banks of the Dordogne river. He could not take her into the town because he was not to know her ultimate destination. In this operation, no one was to be trusted with any information that they did not absolutely have to have. In the hills she would be met and taken down into Laville to the bakery, where she would stay for the next three weeks until a message came.

Ming was to pose as a niece of the baker, and so she had had to learn up innumerable facts about him and his family. Among her forged documents were the necessary permissions from her supposed employer in Bordeaux authorising her holiday on the grounds that she had been ill. She was to live and work in the bakery for three weeks, during which a man, an Englishman this time, would come with a message too secret to be trusted to any of the normal channels. Because of its importance – and potential explosiveness – the intelligence had had to wait until Suvarov had found and trained a suitable courier. Ming was then to get herself and the precious message back to another rendezvous with Jean so that he could escort her back to the marshes to pick up the boat once more. Suvarov would be waiting for her at Southampton.

Relayed to herself like that it all sounded simple enough, but there were appalling risks involved at every stage to herself and to everyone who helped her. No one, least of all Suvarov, had ever tried to pretend otherwise. Ming, huddled and cold in her corner of the cabin, prayed that she would not fail and tried not to think how much less frightened she would have been with Annie at her side.

They made the crossing in record time, the bearded officer

told her proudly just before he saw her over the side soon after dawn. Ming smiled her approval and put up her hands to receive the cheap brown suitcase.

'Best of good luck,' whispered the young man, leaning over the gunwale towards her. 'We'll hang around out of sight until tonight, just in case. Otherwise, see you in three weeks.'

Ming nodded and started to wade through the shallow water. The boat reversed slowly away from her, reached deeper water and turned back the way they had come. Ming was alone in the marshes, cold and afraid, but determined not to fail.

In a way, she thought as she waded through the cold water to the beach, this mission was a kind of memorial to Annie. If Ming were to bungle it or behave so stupidly that she were caught, she would be letting Annie down; but if she clung to her memories of Annie's courage and determination then they might strengthen her and help her through.

Ming made her way to the appointed rendezvous and waited for her guide. He was the first person she saw that morning and he identified himself at once with the precise words she had been told to expect. Gathering confidence from this small evidence that the plan was working, Ming smiled and shook his hand.

Short and painfully thin, he looked dangerous, she thought, despite his shabby blue serge clothes.

'Now, we've no time to waste,' he said as soon as the formalities had been completed. 'Give me your luggage. I have a truck not far from here. About two miles.'

Ming wondered whether she could walk two miles without food or some kind of warmth, but she had no option and so she followed him out of the hut and trudged doggedly after him. When they reached the road, she saw an ancient dark-green truck and was relieved to realise that she would be able to sit down at last. Her guide, Jean, threw her suitcase in the back and then gave her a push up into the cab.

He climbed in at the other side and fished under the seat to produce a long package wrapped in what looked like sheets torn from a child's exercise book.

'Here,' he said roughly. 'Eat this. We haven't much.'

Ming tore the squared paper away and found the end of a baguette, split and filled with strips of hard cheese. Watching her tear strips of the stale bread with her hands and stuff them into her mouth, the dark-haired man said, unsmiling:

'You were hungry.'

Ming, her mouth full of bread and cheese, merely nodded.

'OK. Now have you your papers?' She nodded again and when he held out a horny hand, with dirt apparently engrained around the nails, she pulled the papers out of her pocket and handed them to him.

Jean checked each one thoroughly and then grunted, apparently in approval.

'So. Now we go. When we reach a checkpoint, you can pretend to sleep. I will hand over the papers. You look pale enough to be ill, so that is all right.'

Knowing that there was nothing for her to do for some hours, Ming leaned back in the uncomfortable canvas-covered seat and closed her eyes.

She was quite genuinely asleep by the time they reached the first checkpoint and woke only when the German corporal shook her thin shoulder. Her eyes opened on to the grey uniform she had seen only in pictures during her training, and for a second all her faculties were paralysed. Then, as though still half asleep, she turned to Jean and asked in thick, slow French what was happening. The young German answered in French so badly accented that she knew she need no longer be afraid that he would challenge hers.

'I need to see your papers.'

'Jean? Thank you.' She took them from him and handed them to the German, lying back in the canvas seat as though simply too tired to bother about his reaction to them. He examined them meticulously, said something in guttural German, handed them back and then jerked his head sideways, apparently indicating that they were allowed to proceed. Jean let in the clutch, took off the handbrake and the ancient truck crunched its way across the cobbles outside the guard hut.

'You did well there,' said Jean about five miles further on.

'Thank you,' answered Ming. 'We got through anyway.'

'Yes. Now, we can't take the truck beyond Le Bugue, so we leave it here, and cross the river just outside the town. Then I'll take you up into the hills above St Cyprian – it's about twenty-four kilometres – and we wait.'

'For whom?'

'A man. We call him Roland. That's all I know.'

Ming did not try to press him for more information or to make conversation. The less they knew of each other, the safer they would be. Instead of trying to talk, she looked out of the scratched windscreen at the countryside through which they drove.

In her half-ignored fantasies about her mission, she had

imagined this part of France to be strange and wild. Her first sight of Les Landes had come up to every expectation: uninhabited sand dunes and marsh with a few patches of thin, scraggly grass or reeds marking the beige colour of the land. But once they had passed Bordeaux and were driving towards the Dordogne, she might almost have been at home. Fat-looking green fields, bordered with neat hedges, were interrupted only by coppices or streams and the occasional pink-washed barn or farmhouse. The architecture was quite different from the English buildings to which she was accustomed, but not in the way she had expected. All the houses looked so comfortable that she found it hard to tie them up to the stories she had read and heard in England of the privations that were being suffered by the French now that this area too was under German occupation.

Jean stopped the truck after another twenty miles or so and told her that they would have to make the rest of the journey on foot. In almost any other circumstances the walk they took would have been idyllic. The air was soft and quite warm, the sky blue, and the country glorious. They crossed a slow, shallow river outside the town, which he told her was a tributary of the Dordogne, the Vézère, and then followed a steep but well-defined path up through wooded hills on the far side. They passed no one and the only sounds Ming could hear apart from her own laboured breathing on the steeper stretches were the lowing of cattle somewhere near, the soporific buzz of insects, the squelch of her companion's boots crushing nettles and grasses on the muddy path and the occasional far-off drone of aircraft.

Had it not been for a certain intensity in Jean and the silence between them, Ming might almost have imagined

308

herself to be on holiday. But as the day dragged towards evening, and the hill they were crossing seemed to grow longer and steeper with every step they took, the sense of holiday was subsumed into weariness. Ming's feet burned within her necessarily cheap shoes, there was a stitch in her right side, and her head ached from the pounding of blood through the veins in her scalp.

Nearly four hours after they had set off, their path flattened out and for a mile or so there was the relief of walking on the flat. Ming felt her breathing return to nearly normal and the relief of that alone was enough to make her feet and her headache bearable. But then they started to descend and within twenty minutes her knees had begun to wobble. Every few steps she would lean down to hold one or other kneecap to try to stop the juddering within it. The sensation was not a pain; it merely felt as though her knees were about to give way completely. She was ashamed that she, so much better fed and younger than Jean, should be making such heavy weather of the walk while he stalked unfalteringly ahead of her, carrying her suitcase.

At last he turned. By then Ming was walking at least one hundred yards behind him. Hearing him stop tramping ahead, she lifted her head. Through the blur of exhaustion she saw him gesture to his right.

'We stop here.'

'*Dieu soit béni,*' she muttered, and tried to increase her pace to catch up.

When they were sitting side by side, leaning against a thick, mossy rock that stuck out of the earth at just the right height, he pulled a small flask from the pocket of his overalls and offered it to her.

'Cognac.'

Ming shook her head, knowing how little he must have, but he pushed the flask towards her.

'Take some. You need it.'

She obeyed, as she nearly always obeyed people who gave her orders, and felt the spirit's warmth seep through her. Gradually her heart returned to normal and the horrible sweat that had covered her body during the march began to dry as they waited. There was silence between then until a thought struck Ming.

'Jean?'

'Yes.'

'What happens to you tonight? Must you walk all that way back to the truck?'

She saw that he was smiling a little grimly.

'No. With the curfew it would be too dangerous to take the truck out of Le Bugue by the time I'd be back here. I go to a farmhouse we know of near here and return tomorrow.'

'Oh, good,' Ming answered and relaxed against the hardness of the rock.

Together they waited in careful silence, Ming beginning to wonder whether something had gone wrong with their instructions; Jean, what had happened to the mysterious Roland. Jean was just looking at his watch, murmuring, 'But we did not make such good time,' when he heard the sibilant, utterly sinister sound of dogs snuffing through the year's accretion of dead leaves.

Ming heard it too, and the tramp of booted feet that accompanied it. Controlling her instinctive terror, she turned towards Jean, who gripped her wrist hard.

'Roland.'

'Ah good,' she said in a voice that felt artificial. 'Are you certain?'

'No, but it's likely. There's only one man. . . . Listen. The Boches are always more than one. Sit still.'

Ming's training had included sessions on what to do to elude tracking dogs, how to jam a muffled arm down the throat of a charging dog, but nothing on how to sit quite still and without fear as panting dogs came straight for you. Two enormous, dark-brown bloodhounds burst out of the trees, baying.

If it had not been for Jean's hand, cruelly tight on her wrist, Ming thought she might have run. As it was she pulled herself up off the ground into a half-crouch just as the first hound reached the path.

Just as the dogs were about to reach her, a voice from the edge of the trees opposite her halted them and silenced their howls. They sat, eyes fixed on Ming's, panting. A man, dressed in clothes identical to Jean's, followed them. Ming's wrist was released and she straightened up to watch the two men meet in the middle of the path and kiss each other on both stubbly cheeks.

'Roland, here is Mademoiselle Lachine. You have frightened her with those stupid animals of yours.'

The other man, stockier than Jean, grinned up at Ming, still standing by the rock.

'Apologies, m'selle. They're my excuse for roaming the woods – searching for food for my family. The *sales Boches* believe that they're truffle hounds – not so successful, alas, but so long as I give the commandant at least one truffle each month, he is happy for me to keep them.'

'I see,' answered Ming, annoyed to hear her voice shake with reaction. 'I'm glad that you are here.'

'Yes. So now we go. '*Voir* Jean.'

'*A bientôt*,' he replied and then shook Ming's hand formally and brushed away her thanks for his help.

311

20

As they walked behind the truffling dogs, Roland told Ming that it was too dangerous for her to go down into the town that night. A new detachment of Germans had been posted to the large barracks nearby and were milling about Laville in search of relaxation and amusement. They were only in transit and would be gone by noon the following day, and so it had been arranged that Ming would spend the night in a cave not far away. The Germans had been told of its existence soon after they had first come to the town and periodically searched it for escaping airmen or caches of Resistance weapons, but having never found anyone or anything there, appeared to have lost interest.

'I leave you there tonight with food and a light, and tomorrow I or Annette will come for you as early as is safe. OK?'

A little amused at the Americanism, Ming smiled and nodded.

'Yes. That is OK.'

When they reached the cave he pulled aside the shrubs that half concealed its mouth. Bending double, Ming followed him in, stumbling in the sudden darkness. Roland switched on a pocket torch and in that inadequate light they walked, hunched beneath the low, damp roof of the passageway, for some thirty yards. Then he straightened upright and held up the torch for her to see.

They were in a kind of hall that stretched upwards way beyond the reach of the timid light. The walls consisted of tier after tier of stalactites, some as thin as a hedgehog's spines, others looking as thick and muscled as a navvy's forearm. Where the torchlight caught the stone, it gleamed in curious tones of greeny-grey, gold and rust.

Ming looked around her, the strange grandeur of the place banishing every other thought. At her feet was a shallow pool. The constant dripping from three stalactites overhead pushed delicate ripples across its transparent golden surface in an easy rhythm. Roland's voice broke into her silent admiration of the extraordinary place.

'I must go back before the dogs explode. They hate this place.'

Ming looked down at them and noticed for the first time that both were making a thin, high, whining sound that was almost inaudible. She thought of how much better she liked them when they were afraid than when they were hunting.

'Yes, of course.'

'Here is food, and the water in the pool is safe to drink. I leave you the torch, but it won't last too long, so do not use it unless you have to. OK?'

'Yes.'

'And Annette has left you a bedding roll somewhere. It may be damp, but better than nothing, *hein*?'

'Yes, thank you for all your help.'

'We are in this together – to finish the war and get the

Boches out of my country. So, good night. Sleep well.'

Ming just smiled and watched him go. She found the sleeping bag without trouble and unrolled it. The underside was a little damp, but compared to the prospect of sleeping on the hard limestone of the cave's floor, it offered immense comfort.

She drank from the pool, took off her shoes, retrieved a second heavy jersey out of her suitcase, put it on and levered herself into the sleeping bag. Unwrapping the inevitable baguette that Roland had given her, she switched off the precious torch and proceeded to munch her way through the tough bread in the dark.

Sleep overcame her before she had finished more than half of it and when she awoke in pitch blackness she found it still in her left hand. She lay for a moment, letting her mind slot back into gear, before she felt around on the floor at her side for the torch. In its light she saw from her watch that it was only five o'clock. There were at least seven hours to wait before she could possibly be released from the cave and it might be considerably longer.

The sensible thing to do would be to eat a little more, turn over and go back to sleep. Her training officers at Etchingham had endlessly reiterated the importance of ensuring adequate amounts of sleep whenever possible. She did her best and slept for, perhaps, two and a half of the nine hours that she waited. Boredom had banished all the fear from her mind by the time she heard the footsteps, lighter than those of Roland and unaccompanied by any whining or snuffling of his dogs. The steps must belong to Annette, daughter of the baker. Quite soon Ming made out a faint glow from the direction of the entrance passageway, then a distinct circle of light, and a moment later the figure of a young woman.

314

'Marie?' she said.

'Yes,' answered Ming, finding her voice hoarse and rusty as though it were a piece of machinery long disused. 'And you are Annette?'

'Yes. The Germans have gone now. I can take you down to the bakery.' She came to stand close to Ming, who was disentangling herself from the sleeping bag and beginning to roll it up tidily.

'We will leave that here – I can collect it later, and there is no need to alert anyone by carrying suspicious bundles.'

'But what about my suitcase?' asked Ming, glad to be able to ask questions again and to know that she was in capable hands.

'No, that will be all right. Come, I must be back for this afternoon's opening.'

'Of course,' said Ming, displaying the knowledge she had worked so hard to acquire. 'The bakery opens at two-thirty each afternoon except Monday.'

'Well done,' said Annette, with a laugh. 'And today I shall teach you to make bread and brioches with me. Perhaps you will become so proficient that when you are back at home you can take a job in a *Boulangerie française*.'

Of all the things Ming had imagined about her mission to the centre of Nazi-occupied France, nothing had led her to invent such warmth of teasing from a girl no older than Flixe. She clicked the locks on her suitcase, lifted it and smiled at Annette.

'*En avant*,' she said almost gaily.

They reached the main square of the little town without mishap. It was precisely as Ming's briefings had led her to expect: one side was almost completely taken

315

up by the pale-grey stone church; the other three made up of a mixture of pretty old houses and shops, their windows shuttered now and only the swinging signs above the doors displaying their commercial purposes. There was a small café on the left side of the square with a few tables standing under a tattered awning made of red-and-white striped canvas. Shabbily dressed old men were sitting at most of the tables, and as the two girls walked past, one man took his half-smoked cigarette out of his mouth and spat at their feet.

Surprised, but determined not to court danger by showing it, Ming said nothing until they reached the comparative haven of the bakery, just round the corner in one of the streets that led into the square. There, Annette unlocked the door and ushered Ming into the main shop. A counter ran along the centre of the room, bearing a large pair of brass scales. Behind the counter were ranged shelves that held only a fraction of the loaves they could have carried. There was the wonderful warm scent of fermenting yeast from somewhere in the back of the house. Ming opened her mouth to ask about the man in the café, but before she could speak, a quavery, plangent voice called:

'Annette? Is that you? Where have you been? Who is there?'

'Yes, Papa, it is I. And I have Marie Lachine with me. You remember, I told you all about her. She is from Bordeaux.' Annette's voice carried a note of firm reassurance as she called her answers through to the back of the house. Then her voice dropped and she said quietly to Ming: 'He is not well, does not remember anything. But he is all the time afraid, because he does not remember. Come, I will introduce you. Call him Oncle Jean, and say something gentle, won't you?'

Ming nodded, surprised that her briefing had not included this piece of information, and followed Annette through to the family's kitchen. Seated in a rocking chair by the cold stove was a man, not as old as Ming would have expected from the voice; one thing she had been told about him in London was that he was sixty-four or -five. His eyes had the restless, frightened searching of one who knows that his mind is no longer in his own control.

'Papa, here is Marie.'

'Oncle Jean, it is good to see you,' said Ming, in as gentle a voice as she could manage.

'Who are you? Why are you here?' The old man's voice was sharp, but his attention seemed to wander before Ming could even begin to answer.

'I've told you, Papa,' said Annette in the same determinedly cheerful voice that she had used before. 'She is Maman's brother-in-law's niece, Marie Lachine, from Bordeaux. She has come to help me in the bakery for a week or two while we are so busy. Now, I take her upstairs to unpack and then I'll bring you your *déjeuner*.'

The old man sat, with his chin sunk into his chest, mumbling soundlessly, his eyes continuing their restless moving as he sat. Annette's lips tightened as she gestured to Ming to precede her up the stairs. When they reached the small bedroom they were to share, Annette sat down on the bed nearest the window and covered her face with her hands for a moment.

'They didn't tell me about your father: was it the Germans?' asked Ming quietly, her mind full of horrific pictures of some Gestapo brutality.

Annette took her hands away from her eyes and smiled sadly.

'No. He is just getting old; it had started even before

Maman died, the year before the war, but it gets worse.'

'It must make your life so hard,' said Ming, her ready imagination showing her just what Annette would have to do to keep the old man calm.

'Most of the time I can manage,' Annette said. 'I just sometimes feel that it is all too much. He is still so physically strong, you see. Sometimes he helps me with the baking – or in the shop – but usually he just sits like that. And sometimes I get impatient with him and say things that must make him so unhappy.'

'Don't punish yourself,' said Ming, laying one of her hands on Annette's. 'Surely, he can't remember them if he can't even remember the things you tell him.'

'I hope you're right. But we just don't know what he understands or remembers. Never mind. It is so long since I had a friend to talk to, that it all came out. I'm sorry.'

Touched that this brave, burdened girl should look on her as a friend so instantly, Ming tried to distract her.

'Tell me about the man in the square.'

'The one who spat you mean?'

Ming nodded.

'Oh, he's just like all the rest of them, too lazy or scared to help the Resistance, but making himself feel nice and brave by spitting at me.'

'I don't understand,' protested Ming. 'Don't they know that you work for the Resistance – and us?'

'God forbid! I wouldn't trust any of them one inch. No. They see that I am friendly with the Boches, make them special breads, croissants, brioches and so on, and they pretend to think that I am a German whore.'

'But can't you somehow let them know you're not? It's terrible that you have to put up with that as well as everything else,' said Ming, quite horrified.

318

'No. It's good cover. The Germans know that I do not sleep with any of their officers or men, but they think I am well disposed – I have to be to collect information and to hide from them that I supply bread for the Maquis when I can. Don't worry about it, Marie.'

Ming turned away to begin unpacking her meagre luggage, ashamed of her own self-pity and the fears that she had allowed to rule her just after Annie's death.

'I'll go down to Papa. Come when you are ready,' said Annette, sounding cheerfully competent once again.

Over the days that followed, Ming felt that she was living inside some bizarre Surrealist painting. There was everything her training had taught her to fear; there was the terror that she could never suppress when the grey-uniformed Germans stalked and swaggered into the bakery to chat to Annette and give her the scarce ingredients for the delicacies they wanted her to make; there was her horrified pity for Annette and her father, locked together in mutual disunity and hurt; and there was the hostility of the townspeople, which spilled over from Annette on to Ming herself.

Then, in contrast to all that, was the warmth that seemed to grow each day between herself and Annette. Since the bomb had killed Annie, Ming had found herself unable to reach out to anyone. Something in her seemed to have been destroyed by Annie's death. Suvarov had come nearest to breaking it down, and she loved him, but even with him she felt as though there were an invisible wall holding her back. Now, in the strange and terrifying circumstances of her mission for him, she had found a friend. Once, as she lay sleepless in bed thinking about it, she wondered whether she had so instantly trusted and

319

liked Annette because of the similarity between her name and Annie's. But then Ming dismissed the idea as far too simple. There was more to it than that; perhaps the fact that both she and Annette lived almost entirely alone had something to do with their immediate friendship. Each was surrounded by plenty of other people, but they were – or seemed to be – hostile. Ming had lost Annie, in whom she had had absolute trust; Annette had lost her mother.

After a few days, Ming ceased to try to analyse her feelings and simply did whatever she could to lighten the burdens Annette carried. Helping the old man feed himself or keep himself clean were among the tasks she liked least, but she did them until it became clear that her unfamiliar presence fretted him. Then Annette resumed all responsibility for him and Ming did what she could in the bakery itself.

That, too, provided unexpected pleasures, which were sensuous and distracting. There were the warm, comforting scents of yeast and flour and crispy baking bread; the sumptuous sensation of digging her hands into the proving dough to knock it back and knead it into shape; and the tremendous satisfaction of plunging the flat shovels into the bread oven to retrieve a batch of perfect, golden, fragrant baguettes.

Life in the bakery had a rhythm to it, and a simplicity that appealed to Ming. Slowly some of her terrors began to recede as she understood that Annette's cover was apparently impregnable and the German officers held no suspicions of her at all. So far did they trust her that Ming was accepted, too, without a hint of surprise. When she understood that, Ming even began to enjoy her days, assured that she was equal to this part, at least, of her mission. She even began to look forward with a certain strange regret to the day when the message would come.

Annette seemed to enjoy her presence, and that also gave Ming a satisfaction and comfort she had long lacked. They talked whenever it was safe during the day and often for an hour or more as they lay side by side in the two narrow beds upstairs. Ming heard about 'Maman', who had been so greatly beloved and whose death four years earlier had caused the eighteen-year-old Annette her first real anguish. She told, too, of her difficulties with the other children of Laville, who had always spurned and excluded her as though she were some kind of leper.

'But why should they have done that?' asked Ming, one late evening, saddened to hear of yet another burden carried by the tall, dark girl who waited with such lonely courage for the war to end.

'Maman and Papa moved here soon after I was born. They were strangers, and this town is so closed in and parochial that they were never allowed to think of themselves as natives . . . and I suppose the children just wanted to make sure the same thing happened to me.'

'Where did they come from?' asked Ming, unable to comment.

'Somewhere near Switzerland, I think. In the Alps anyway. They inherited some money; I was born; they decided to move away and buy a business. Here we are.'

'Yes, I see. And now you do all the work and look after your father as well, and work for the Allies. It is too much, Annette. You drive yourself too hard.' At that the French girl laughed softly.

'There will be time for talk like that when the war is over. Until then? No! Do you know what is done to people who are caught resisting the Boches? Or who simply refuse to go to forced labour in Germany? Or who are collected as hostages for reprisals after the Allies or the Maquis have destroyed railways or pylons or killed Germans?'

'Yes, a little,' said Ming, closing her eyes. 'Enough, too. But aren't you afraid, Annette?'

'Always,' was the surprising reply. Then, before Ming could ask any questions, Annette went on: 'But angry too. As you would be if you knew. I will tell you the first thing that made me want to help the Resistance.'

Ming lay rigid in the darkness, unable to say weakly that she would prefer not to know, listening to the tale of gratuitous cruelty and horror that Annette told her. When it was over and the waves of shock had subsided, Ming said:

'I would go mad, I think. How can you smile at them as you do?'

There was a slightly scornful note in Annette's voice as she answered that instinctive question.

'You sound like the old men in the café in the square.'

'I'm sorry.'

'No, I am sorry,' said Annette with quick generosity. 'I do understand, and at first I did feel as you do. But, you know, because some of them do such things it does not mean that all are the same. These young men who come here have not done such things.'

'And if they had?'

'I should still smile at them if that were the only way to work against them.' There was silence for a few moments as Ming tried to understand what it must feel like to live for years under such conditions. After a while, Annette said: 'I hope that if I had to I would even become their whore.'

322

'You can't mean that,' said Ming.

'I hope I could do it, if it had to be done,' answered Annette. 'One should do anything, however distasteful, however damaging to oneself, to get rid of people who do to us what the Boches do. The least bad is their telling us what we may read, who we may associate with, what we may eat, say, write, do . . . Perhaps the worst is forcing on the wickedest and weakest of us the same vile cruelty they perpetrate. There are French people who are just as bad as some of them – and English, too, probably. It's not only the Boches, but they have the power to do the things other people just think about.'

All Ming could think of to say was, 'I see.' Annette achieved a small sigh.

'I don't think you do, *chérie*, but don't think about it now. Sleep. Who knows? Perhaps tomorrow the message will come and then you will need all your strength for the journey.'

But it did not come for another eight days, on the penultimate day before Ming had to leave the town, and it came at the worst possible moment. A tall, handsome major who was one of Annette's most faithful customers had just brought her a small packet of butter and some superfine white flour for his weekly batch of croissants, and he was standing, leaning against the wall, out of sight of the door, complimenting her on this and that. The bakery door then opened and a man walked in, dressed as were most of those who came into the town from surrounding farmhouses, but limping and with exhaustion cruelly marking his grey face.

'*Bonjour m'sieur*,' said Ming brightly, and she saw him stiffen infinitesimally as he looked casually around the

323

shop and caught sight of the lounging German officer.

'M'selle,' he said, handing his bread ration card across the counter. Ming wiped her floury hands on her apron, took it, checked it as Annette had taught her, and weighed the correct number of loaves. Then she named the price and began to wrap the bread in thin sheets of tissue paper.

The man was clearly very tense, but Ming put that down to the presence of the German officer, although he had paid no attention at all to this ordinary-looking customer. To Ming's surprise, Annette suddenly interrupted the officer's compliments.

'Herr Major!'

'Yes, Mademoiselle Annette.'

'If that butter is not to spoil, I must put it in the larder. Will you give it to me now?'

He put the wrapped packet in her hand but kept his hands round hers.

'Let me carry it for you to the larder.' Ming expected Annette's usual laughing evasion, but this time she smiled up at him and allowed him to hand her gallantly towards the door that led to the family's quarters.

Shrugging slightly and hoping that Annette's peculiar flirtatiousness would not cause the usual obvious disgust in her shabby French customer, Ming turned back to him, putting out her hand to take his money. Instead he thrust into her outstretched hand a dirty wedge of paper, hissing in English:

'Get it out of sight before he comes back.'

For a second that felt to Ming as though it were half an hour, she could not make herself do anything. The man who was to bring the message was supposed to go through an elaborate routine of question and answer to establish the identities of both of them. If this were really the right man, the presence of the German must have suggested that it would be too dangerous and he had relied on Annette's quick-witted diversion. If he were not the right man, he could only be an *agent provocateur*, trying to trap her into a betrayal that would lead both Annette and herself into the hands of the Gestapo.

'Do as you're told, Marie Lachine,' he said with vicious determination, this time in French. At last able to coordinate her mind and muscles, Ming obeyed and shoved the packet down the front of her dress, where it would be well hidden by the swelling white linen apron she always wore in the bakery.

The man leaned sideways as though to check that there was no sign of the German and whispered again.

'For Christ's sake get it back to Suvarov.'

Not trusting her voice in either language, Ming nodded and tried to show him that she understood and would do as he wished. He turned on his heel and limped towards the door.

'*Moment*,' came a strong German voice from the back of the shop. Ming gripped the splintered edge of the counter to stop herself keeling over, and she saw the thin back under the cheap blue jacket tauten. The man turned. To her astonished admiration, his face was no more than ordinarily cautious.

'Yes?'

'Your bread, m'sieur. If you leave it behind your wife will not be pleased.' The major laughed richly and leaned over towards Ming to seize the loaves. Then he held them out without moving, so that the man had to limp forward and take them. Their hands touched. Ming felt that if the episode did not end soon, she would faint. Annette bustled about tidying the loaves on the shelves and trying to distract them all.

'I haven't seen you in the town before,' said the major. Ming bit a tiny piece of her lower lip between her teeth.

'My wife buys the bread most days. She's sick today,' answered the man casually over his shoulder. The major shrugged and let him go. As the street door shut behind him, the major turned to Annette.

'Have you ever seen him?' She shook her head. 'Or his wife?'

'I don't know. So many come from the farms outside the town. I don't know who he is.' The major turned to Ming, who had managed to unclamp her teeth from her tender lip and her hands from the counter.

'What was the name on the bread card?'

'Dubois, I think. But it was all right, sir. I checked it.'

He leaned over to pat Ming's fair head.

'I know you did, little Marie; Mademoiselle Annette and I both watched you. You were most scrupulous. Nevertheless . . .' He broke off, looked out of the bakery window to where the blue-clad figure was limping across the square towards the church. 'Nevertheless I think I will have a word with our mystery man. *Au revoir, mesdemoiselles.*'

'*A demain, Herr Major,*' answered Annette with a calm teasing note in her voice that filled Ming with admiration.

He strode off across the room, his black boots thudding on the bare wooden floor, and flung open the door with a force that sent the little bell jangling madly. When the door crashed to behind him, Ming turned to Annette.

'No, Marie. Don't say anything, or think it. Just get on with the work. It is the only way,' she said, her lips set

326

and her complexion far paler than Ming had yet seen it. In the face of that; Ming could not ask any of the questions that were burning in her mind, nor shed any of the tensions that were biting at her.

21

The next morning, Annette helped Ming to pack her few belongings and then escorted her to the bus that would take her towards Bordeaux. Making certain that there was no one within earshot, Ming turned to Annette.

'I wish that I didn't have to leave you here.'

Annette leaned down to kiss her on both cheeks.

'Don't be silly. It's vital to get it back; you know that. And your place is there, not here.'

'But will you be all right?' asked Ming, knowing that it was a ludicrous question even as she said it. Annette smiled and shrugged.

'Now, be careful, *petite*,' was all she said.

'And you, Annette. Then after . . . when it's over, we can meet . . .'

'No hostages to fortune, Marie,' said Annette gently, '*Adieu*.'

'*Au revoir*, Annette.'

It was fortunate that the bus appeared just then before either of them could lose control and say any of the things that both knew to be true. Annette kissed Ming again and then turned abruptly away. The last Ming saw of Annette was her walking jauntily back across the square towards the major, waiting at the bakery for his black-market croissants.

Her final instructions had been that Ming was to stay on the bus until it reached St Cyprian. She was then to walk up into the hills behind the town to a specific rendezvous, where Jean would meet her, take her down into Le Bugue and then drive her back to Les Landes. Ming had never asked why she could not have taken the bus on her way to Laville in the first place, although the question had teased the edges of her mind more than once. She was just grateful that she did not have to tackle the whole of that gruelling walk again.

On the bus she chose to sit by the most taciturn-looking elderly peasant she could find. With the vital message stowed beneath her skirt, the last thing she wanted to risk was falling into a conversation in which she might betray herself. The peasant was sitting in the aisle seat and hardly moved to let her past him, but she would not be put off.

It did not occur to her that this mission, with its mixtures of terror and the unexpected affection she had found for and from Annette, had given her something, some kind of confidence in her own judgement. All she could think of was the sight of Annette walking bravely back to her unending task of making up to the German officers and hiding her work for the Resistance. Trying to distract herself, Ming leaned her head against the cool glass of the window, shut her eyes, and concentrated on the moment when Suvarov would receive her on the quay at Southampton.

The dream was interrupted some seven miles from Laville when the jerking progress of the bus was halted with the sound of groaning brakes. Ming opened her eyes and looked around. There was no obvious reason for the dramatic braking. Then the old peasant leaned across her to look out of the window, breathing a fetid mixture of brandy, garlic and tobacco over Ming. She pressed herself back into the seat as he turned his face towards her.

'Another poor bastard taken to pieces by those savages,' he said in a hoarse voice.

Ming could not stop herself peering out of the window in the direction in which he pointed. A German staff car had been halted by the side of the bus. Seated in the back were two men dressed in black leather coats with, between them, the drooping figure of a man. Feeling her insides contracting with horror and pity, Ming found that she could not drag her eyes away. The Gestapo car was too far from her bus for her to distinguish the prisoner's features. She could see the mess that had been made of his face, and the pain he must have suffered, but she could not see whether he was any of the men she had met during her mission. With terrible coldness in her heart she recognised the fact that he might well be the Englishman who had brought her message.

Much later she was to be glad to remember that her first thought was one of pity for the victim, whoever he was; only her second, fear for herself. What if he really were her contact, or even one of the men who had guided her to Laville, and had talked, implicated her, as they beat him? She shivered as though she had been dipped into a bath of icy water, although the inside of the bus was warm. Fear she had often felt during her eighteen years, but never had the object of her terrors been as real, as close, or as terrible as that which now threatened her. She touched the collar of her blouse, into which she had sewn her cyanide pill. Once she had found the thought of the little capsule horrible. Now it was the only thing that gave any comfort.

At last the obstruction, whatever it was, passed and the bus driver let in his brakes. The driver of the staff car pressed his horn arrogantly and the car roared past the bus. Ming began to flog her mind into action: should she leave the bus now and try to find her way on foot in case the poor prisoner had been someone who was able to betray her? Should she dump her papers and trust to luck? No, either of those could be disastrous. All agents were asked to try to hold out for twenty-four hours, during which their colleagues could go to ground, codes could be changed and secret contingency plans put into operation. After twenty-four hours, it was assumed that everything the captured man or woman had known was also known to the Germans. If all went as it should, Ming would be in the middle of the Atlantic, steaming up towards the Channel within fourteen hours; that would make almost thirty-six hours since his arrest.

Into Ming's determinedly impersonal calculations came the memory of Annette. She had no fishing boat waiting to remove her from danger; if Mademoiselle Marie Lachine were unmasked, then nothing could save the woman who had posed as her cousin. That knowledge added a spur to Ming's determination to get the message back to London.

The bus was scheduled to stop four more times before it reached St Cyprian, and at each halt Ming sat with her eyes closed, waiting for the Gestapo's hand on her shoulder. It never came. At last the driver yelled out 'St Cyprian' as he pulled up outside a church. Ming pushed past the old peasant, seized her shabby brown suitcase from the rack over the seats and made her way off the bus.

There was no posse of soldiers waiting for her; the only ones she could see as she walked up the hill away from the little town were a couple sitting at their ease in a café, glasses in hand, talking to each other. The horror of it all suddenly hit her all over again. Here she was in one of the most charming-looking towns she had ever seen, the kind of place she might choose for a holiday, with its lovely old stone houses and beautiful countryside, and there they were: lounging, laughing as they talked of God-knew-what in their hours away from duty that included all the things Annette had described. The memory of the beaten, bloody man in the Gestapo car hurt. The stories of murdered hostages, deported children, young men on the run from forced labour, Jews rounded up and sent away to no-one-knew-what terrible fate, flooded through her mind again and again as she walked through the lush green of the woods towards Jean and his truck.

He was waiting for her when she arrived with blistered feet and aching arms, but he said nothing after one sharp look at her face. She surrendered the suitcase and let him help her up into the cab. Then she sat in silence, staring out of the window to her right as the countryside flashed past, her mind nearly numb. Checkpoints came and went, fear darted into her again each time, but each time they were allowed to pass. The man, if he were the Englishman, must be holding out. Ming found herself hoping with a savagery that was new to her and rather frightening in itself that the message he had brought was truly worth what he might be paying for it.

When they reached the marshes, Jean stopped the van, put an arm over the back of Ming's seat to grab her suitcase and got out on to the road. He opened her door and jerked his head.

'Come on, m'selle. The boat will be there in half an hour. We must get on.'

Ming nodded obediently and followed him. They reached the shore in time and she turned to him to take her case.

'Thank you, Jean. God bless you.'

His mouth twisted into a bitter grimace.

'I don't think God has much to do with life in France nowadays,' he said. There was no answer to that and so Ming smiled tentatively and turned away to make her torchlight signal to the boat she hoped was waiting.

The signal was answered and within ten minutes the two young naval officers were greeting her with exuberant congratulations, a blanket and a mug of Bovril laced with brandy. She accepted all three with a kind of dazed compliance that made the young men glance at each other and leave her alone.

For part of the dreary voyage she slept, but when the weather turned nasty as they were sailing past the Cape of Finisterre, she woke to the horrible urgency of seasickness. It took her a moment to realise what had woken her and that disaster was only seconds away, but she made it to the side before she was actually sick. For a while physical misery took possession of her and she knew and felt nothing except the retching spasms that forced themselves through her.

In one interval she became aware that someone was holding her head and murmuring reassurances. The relief of leaning forward against the strength of that hand brought her back to her senses enough to murmur her thanks, but then she was sick again, and again.

When it was over, and the seas were quietening simultaneously with Ming's insides, the officer wrapped her in the blanket and laid her down to sleep off some of her exhaustion. She lay there, looking up at the stars that looked so sharp against the thick blackness of the sky, and thought of Peter Suvarov.

The fishing boat chugged up to the quay at Southampton nine hours later and Ming disembarked, feeling wrung out emotionally and physically, almost as though she had been put through a mangle by a particularly violent laundress. Having thanked the officers who had brought her back, she lifted her shabby suitcase once more and looked for her chief. Suddenly she needed him badly.

There was a khaki-clad figure standing in the shade at the far end of the quay and Ming set off towards him, wondering why he did not move forward and suppressing her own desire to run at full tilt and fling herself into his arms. Half-way down the quay, she saw that it was not her chief, only her training officer from Etchingham. Walking more and more slowly, she made her way up to him and waited.

'Marie,' he said, using her work name, as he had done from the first moment he was put in charge of her, 'Major Suvarov has been held up in London. He wants you to go straight up there to the flat where you met before, and to give me the packet.'

Ming dumped the suitcase on the ground and fished beneath her clothes for the stained, paper-wrapped bundle. Before she could even hand it over, he had seized it from her hands.

'Oh, well done, Marie,' he said breathlessly.

'You didn't really think I'd come back without it, did

you?' she asked. He looked up and at last smiled at her .

'It was a damned hazardous mission, Marie. You've done well.'

'I'm afraid that the man . . .' she was beginning, when he hushed her with a gesture.

'No, don't tell me anything. Suvarov will debrief you in London. Here's a warrant for the train. There's one leaving in fifteen minutes. I'll drive you to the station if you'll come now.'

'You're not coming, then?' said Ming, making a question of the statement.

'No, I've another of you to come in yet; but we'll meet again, don't worry. Here we are. Hop in.'

He drove her to the station, saw her on to the London train and then shook her hand, repeated his congratulations and left her. Ming sank back against the rough moquette of the seat and tried to understand that she was back in England, her mission accomplished; that the message had been handed over, that she was safe and the episode was over. But despite what her reason tried to make her instinct believe, she knew that while Annette and the unnamed man were still in France risking death and worse it could not be over for her either.

She closed her eyes, deliberately trying to banish all thought of Annette from her mind and feeling like a puppet whose strings have been cut, so that instead of an obediently jerking prancing figure there was only a bundle of painted wooden limbs lying in a useless heap. Almost as though her mental picture had transmitted some message of collapse to her brain, she fell at last into a sleep so deep that even the clatter of the train's arrival at one station after another could not waken her.

The other occupants of the carriage, two respectably

335

dressed middle-aged women, a uniformed soldier and two men in civilian clothes, paid no attention to the exhausted girl until the train stopped at Basingstoke. There the soldier stood up, heaved his kitbag from the luggage rack and made to step past Ming to get out of the compartment. But the train, which had already stopped, jolted once more and he lost his balance, put out a hand against the wall to steady himself and stepped on her feet. Even then she did not wake. One of the women, who was wearing a brown felt hat that looked as though she had converted it from one of her husband's sporting trilbies, half stood and then turned to the other woman.

'Don't you think we ought to do something about the young lady? It can't be natural to sleep like that even when a hulking six-footer has stepped on your toes. Shouldn't we try to wake her?'

Before the other lady could answer, one of the civilian men leaned forward to say quietly:

'Please don't concern yourself, madam. We're keeping an eye on her. She's been on duty a long time and is not very well. She's coming up to London to see a specialist. Her CO asked us to see that she got there in one piece.' He smiled reassuringly as he spoke and since his accent put him somewhere in the higher establishment, the concerned woman in the brown hat blushed with embarrassment at having tried to interfere.

'I do beg your pardon,' she said softly. 'I hadn't realised that you were looking after her. She seemed so alone when she arrived.'

'Not at all,' he answered as quietly. 'How could you know? But please don't be concerned. We shall take good care of her. She's very valuable to us, eh Jimmy?'

The other man nodded and smiled in the same polite

336

way, and the woman was silenced. But she was not quite satisfied and when the train drew into Waterloo, she dropped her open handbag on the floor so that she would have an excuse to fossick around and wait to see what happened to the poor pale girl.

The two men stood up, looked arrogantly down at the stout woman scrabbling on the floor for her lipstick, powder compact, handkerchief and all the other impedimenta that had issued from her bag and exchanged resigned glances. The taller of the two leaned down to shake Ming's shoulder.

'Wake up, my dear,' he said kindly. 'We're here at Waterloo and we've a car waiting.'

Ming opened her dark-blue eyes wide and tried to focus on the man who had spoken to her. She was still half asleep, but part of the sense of what he had said reached her.

'Did Peter send you?' she said, leaning back against the seat and looking up at him. He smiled again.

'That's right. He's anxious about you. Come on up, if you can stand, and we'll get you back to him straight away.'

Ming let him help her up and pull her case off the rack. As she reached the door, one of his hands under her shaky elbow, the other woman finished collecting her possessions and stood up, breathless.

'My dear . . .' she began. Ming turned, her dazed violet-blue eyes looking puzzled. 'Forgive me for troubling you, but are you all right? Can I help at all?'

Ming smiled and a little colour came reassuringly into her pale cheeks.

'Thank you,' she said in a tired voice. 'But these gentlemen will see me . . . home. I'm all right really.'

'Well, if you're sure,' said the woman, embarrassed to have accosted a perfect stranger and tried to interfere in what was obviously an official performance and yet unable to rid her mind of the feeling that something was badly wrong.

'Goodbye, and thank you,' said Ming more firmly and let the two men escort her out of the railway carriage.

LONDON

1943

22

That evening, Flixe was sitting in her flat, trying to get hold of Peter Suvarov. He had not answered the private telephone on his desk at the office all day and she had not dared to risk involving Gerry in what she had to tell him. Flixe had left a discreet message at his club and had dialled the number of his rooms in Pall Mall at half-hourly intervals. She knew that there was no way she could keep Jean-Pierre's declaration secret. Peter had to know about it. But she could not find him.

At half-past seven she was in such a state of confusion, irritation and emotion that she poured herself a strong brandy and soda and sat sipping it by the telephone. When it rang she was so surprised that for a moment or two she did not pick up the receiver. At last she controlled herself.

'Western 0808,' she said.

'Flixe,' came the voice she had wanted all day.

'Peter, thank God, I must talk to you. I've—'

'Not now,' he said icily. 'This is urgent. Have you seen Ming this afternoon?'

So cold was his voice that she did not even stop to

wonder why he was asking and answered simply:

'No. I haven't seen her for months.'

'Damn. Where might she go, Flixe? Try to think: friends? Anyone she might want to see if she were in London?'

Flixe thought for a moment, half-stupefied by his obvious impatience.

'I think . . . there's only Gerry or Anna Kingsley that I know of.'

'Tried them. Oh, God.'

'Peter,' she said sharply, her brain beginning to work again. 'What is the matter? Why are you looking for Ming?'

'I can't explain now, Flixe. She was due at Charles Street four hours ago and she's disappeared.' Then Flixe understood. Somehow Peter had recruited poor, fragile little Ming to work for him. Bitterly angry, she spoke crisply into the telephone.

'There must have been an accident. Ming is too conscientious to go off seeing friends if she had an appointment with her employer. Have you tried the hospitals?'

'Of course. And the police. I must ring off in case they're trying to get through.'

'Peter,' said Flixe urgently, but there was no one at the other end of the telephone. She put her receiver back on its cradle. She was so angry that she could hardly breathe. Gerry might perhaps be thought of as fair game, just as she herself was, but Ming was too delicate, too frightened and far too badly hurt to be exposed to the Suvarov-fascination technique. How could he have done such a thing? How dared he?

Flixe got up off her chair and paced around her

drawing-room, feeling as though her rage were a physical entity that had somehow to be expelled from her. Her teeth were clamped together and she breathed through her nose in vast, deliberate breaths. But it did not help either; it merely left her with an aching head. She gave vent to a howl of frustration, anger and resentment and swore violently, quite forgetting the thinness of the walls of her flat or the possible audience in the other flats.

She expelled the rage in the end, of course; rage was not an emotion she had been bred to feel and all her family's and school's training had been directed at ways to ignore anger or to pretend that it was something else. Exhausted by the effort, feeling as though the top of her head might suddenly detach itself and fly off, she lay down on her bed and buried her face in the pillow.

After five minutes or so she turned over and lay flat on her back, staring up at the ceiling. Her mind felt as vacant and her joints as heavy as they did after Jean-Pierre had made love to her. As the functioning part of her brain understood that, the rest was galvanised by a dreadful thought. The chain of ideas arrived in her mind fully linked: Peter had told her just before he had sent her on the course that he had almost completed his investigation into Jean-Pierre's activities; Jean-Pierre had just told her that he would have to leave London soon; Ming had disappeared on her way to a meeting with Peter.

Flixe's face hardened and her lower lip disappeared between her teeth as she tried to work out whether there was any reason to suppose a connection between the three facts. One second's thought told her that there must be; another's that such a proposition was ludicrous. There was simply no way of knowing without evidence. Instead of fruitless speculation, she forced her mind to consider where Jean-Pierre might have taken Ming if he had indeed abducted her or – since the picture of that elegant, urbane, entertaining, affectionate man doing any such thing was impossible – ordered her to be abducted. A memory of a conversation they had had over dinner one evening came back to her, and she heard again his ironic voice describing the destruction of his company's warehouse in the City. To make conversation she had asked politely whether it was entirely useless and he had said something. Flixe tried to picture the scene again so that she could summon up his precise words. She thought they had been: 'Quite useless for their original purposes, but a few of the offices are still usable and I've lent them to some associates of mine.'

Flixe got off her bed and went towards the telephone. Suvarov would have to know of her suspicions. Whatever she might think or feel about Jean-Pierre, Ming's safety was of paramount importance. 'Thank God,' she said aloud, 'I have the number of the Charles Street flat.' She dialled it, but it rang and rang without being answered. Eventually she put down the receiver. But she could not simply leave her suspicions there, and instead dialled the number of his office.

When the duty officer answered, Flixe asked whether Gerry were still in the building.

'I believe so, madam,' came the polite answer. 'If you'll hold on a moment, I'll put you through.' Flixe was chewing one of the fingers of her left hand in impatience, but soon enough she heard her sister's voice, tense but still polite:

'Mrs Kyrle speaking. Can I help you?'

'Gerry, thank God you're still there. Has Suvarov come back?'

'No. Why? Oh Flixe, have you got some news of Ming?' Gerry's voice had become so eager that Flixe hated to have to disappoint her.

'No. But a faint possibility has occurred to me. I must talk to him,' she said, the desperation in her voice. 'Do you know where he is, Gerry?'

'At the flat, I thought. Charles Street. You know it.'

'Yes, I do. But he's not there. Is there anywhere else?'

'No. I tried his rooms in Pall Mall myself a minute ago. And he'd never go to the club while something like this is on. Oh, Christ, Flixe, what are we going to do?'

It was so unlike Gerry to swear that Flixe was spurred into some kind of decision.

'We'll have to do something ourselves. No . . . we'll need help.' For an agonising minute she could not think who she could possibly ask; and then she remembered how superb her old suitor had turned out to be at Naseby House. 'I'll get Johnny,' she said. 'Stay there, Gerry. If Suvarov rings, tell him what's happened and get a number where we can ring him. If not, don't worry. I'll ring you back in a minute or two.'

She replaced the receiver just as the three minutes were up, and then dialled the number Johnny Blenkarne had given her. His telephone rang for so long that she thought he must be out, but just as she was about to give up he picked it up. She could hear how breathless he was, but she was in too much of a hurry to comment.

'Johnny? Flixe here; something awful may have happened and I need help. Will you . . .?'

'Just tell me what you want me to do,' he said through his panting.

'Have you any transport?' she asked, so grateful that he asked no questions that she did not bother with either explanations or thanks.

'Actually yes, a jeep. And some petrol: about half a tankful. Where are we going?'

'The City. Could you pick me up at the flat?'

'Of course, Flixe. Be with you in ten minutes. Hold on, my dear.'

'Johnny, you're a brick,' she said, feeling tears coming into her eyes. She rang Gerry back and told her to be waiting at Hyde Park Corner in twenty minutes' time. Then she ran into her bedroom and changed into trousers and jersey and exchanged her high-heeled black shoes for a pair of rubber-soled sneakers. A quick look in her pre-war telephone directory gave the address of the only City warehouse belonging to West-Grandison et fils, Importers; it must have been the one about which he had talked. Flixe memorised the address and stuffed a London street map into the capacious pocket of her khaki trousers.

She was downstairs and waiting when Johnny pulled up and she slid into the seat beside him before he had even switched off the engine. As he drove towards Hyde Park Corner, she told him the few facts and her many suspicions, without explaining who Jean-Pierre was, what he meant to her or the conspiracy of which he was suspected. Johnny listened in silence until she had finished.

'Whew! No wonder they sent you on that course, Flixe,' he said at last. 'Are you sure? It all sounds most unlikely.'

'No, I'm not sure at all, Johnny. But don't you see, even if there were one chance in a million that it might be true, since I can't get hold of the boss I have to investigate? And I think it's more likely than that.'

'Yes, of course. And I'm with you all the way even if it is a wild goose chase. Don't fret.'

'Johnny . . .' she was beginning until she caught sight of Gerry standing on the pavement at her left. 'Here's Gerry. Pull up, will you?'

He did as she asked, screeching to a halt, and felt Flixe press closer to him on the front seat to make a room for her sister. He greeted her tersely and then drove off through the darkening streets towards the Tower of London, while Flixe explained what they were going to try to do.

Johnny drove so fast that Gerry was afraid the tyres would not hold and they would skid out of control. But they did not and at last he slowed slightly as he turned north from St Katharine's Dock into a maze of small roads, cratered bomb sites, and weird brick towers that were all that was left of the offices and factories that had once stood there. Astonishingly, in the middle of the devastation were a few buildings, miraculously preserved. Five minutes later they passed the remains of a bombed pub.

'Pull up here, would you, Johnny,' said Flixe, with her finger on the map. He obeyed her as before, and parked neatly by the broken kerb outside the pub. Flixe pushed Gerry out of the jeep and followed her on to the pavement. The old inn sign with its picture of some gentle country scene still hung absurdly outside the burned-out shell of the building, creaking in the wind like the rigging of the *Marie-Celeste*. Gerry shivered involuntarily. Johnny locked the jeep, while Flixe walked round and opened the bonnet. Then she lifted it up and bent forward into the engine for an instant. When she straightened up, Gerry, who was standing behind her, muttered:

'What're you doing?'

'Immobilising the engine, just in case any crooks pass

this way and think it might be handy. Come on, Johnny.'

'Coming. But, look, Flixe. We ought to decide what we're going to do if we do find anything at this place. There's no point charging in with no preparation. Remember Sergeant Plummer's advice?'

Flixe laughed a little at his reference to their course, but recognised the common sense of his intervention.

'OK. Now, from what I can remember of the description of the warehouse, the old main entrance is in one street and the one they actually use now in quite another. So what about this, Johnny? I'll ring the bell at the door they still use and demand Jean-Pierre and be all hysterical and weepy when they say he's not there and generally create, while you approach from the bombed bit and try to get in while I've got at least one of them distracted.'

'OK.'

'And I?' asked Gerry in some asperity.

'It's tricky, Gerry. You haven't had any training in breaking and entering . . . Yes,' she went on, catching sight of her sister's face in the moonlight. 'I have. That's where Johnny and I met up again. Never mind. It's a pity that it's not you who could be realistically searching for Jean-Pierre.'

'How well do the people you think might be here know you?'

'Not at all, I imagine. I've met some of his friends, but . . . why?'

'Because I look pretty much like you, particularly at night, particularly in hysterics.'

'Would you risk it, Gerry?' asked Flixe carefully.

'Yes,' she said with no heroics.

'And if Jean-Pierre himself turns up?'

'That doesn't sound very likely – frankly none of it sounds very likely – but I'll just have to take my chance. He would know the difference I take it?'

Flixe turned to look at her sister and her expression was enough to make Gerry blush and Johnny start suddenly.

'In some ways it's a pity there's such a good moon tonight,' said Flixe, looking up at the dark, starry sky. 'But it'll help us, Johnny, get across the bombed bits.'

'Let me get this straight,' he said. 'You and I approach the functioning bit of this warehouse – we'd better go in from different points at the old entrance – make our way in, beat up anyone who gets in our way and just search everywhere in case they've got Ming. We're going to look pretty silly if there's no sign of her.'

'And probably end up in gaol,' added Gerry quite crisply.

'Just so,' agreed Flixe, adding silently to herself that she would also be throwing away any possibility of happiness with Jean-Pierre if that were the case. 'There'd be the hell of a stink. Oh, God, am I mad to have dragged you both here? There's really nothing to go on. Ming's probably just been held up and is in Charles Street by now. Should we . . .?'

'Don't torment yourself so, Flixe,' said Johnny, suddenly interrupting her. 'We can reconnoitre carefully and find out if there is any evidence that Ming is there. If there is, then we can withdraw, find a telephone, try your boss and if he's still not there get the police.'

'I suppose so,' said Flixe slowly.

'Come on, Flixe,' said Johnny, 'you know that even after Sergeant Plummer's course we are just not equipped to take on a bunch of thugs, who – if you're right about them – are probably armed and certainly violent.'

'It makes sense, Flixe, you must see that,' said Gerry. 'But we'd better start our reconnoitring by finding a telephone box – it would be ghastly if –'

'There was one, a couple of streets back,' said Flixe, her mind slotting into gear once again. 'We'd better check that it's working.'

She reconnected the distributor leads and they got back into the jeep to retreat to where she thought she had seen a red telephone kiosk. Gerry got out, tested the telephone and gave them the thumbs-up. Johnny drove back to the old pub.

'All right,' said Flixe as they parted, 'Gerry, spin out your hysterics as long as you can. We'll need time.'

'I'll do my best.'

'Good,' Flixe said, more in control again. 'Now, according to the map you go down this street, turn first left and then about fifty yards further on, I think, should be a way in, probably with a bell or knocker or something. Give us . . .' she broke off, looked at her watch and then said: 'ten minutes from now and then lean on the bell and do your stuff. We'll meet back at this corner. OK?'

'All right. Good luck.' She caught sight of Flixe's face in the blue light from the full moon and said gently: 'If she is in here, we'll get her out somehow.' She turned away and left them.

'Coming, Johnny?' said Flixe, touching his arm. He nodded and followed her, padding silently on the wet, grimy road. Together they turned the corner and she nodded at the remains of a vast, pompously pedimented entrance. He gripped her hand to show that he understood and sprinted for it.

Flixe followed more slowly, as anguished for Ming as

she knew Gerry was, but desperately worried, too, about what she might discover about Jean-Pierre. She wished that they could have found Suvarov before launching this probably ill-judged rescue attempt. She brushed some hair out of her eyes and her mouth stiffened. Too bad. If some thugs had really kidnapped little Ming, something must be done to get her back. She reached the door and peered round. In the distance she could make out Johnny picking his way across the rubble and around the dangerous pits and craters of the vast warehouse.

The moonlight showed her how the wild flowers had already established themselves amid the wreckage, pale-pink ragged robins and yellow ragwort bending in the damp wind. Rainwater still dripped off the bedraggled flowers into the pools that filled ditches and craters all over the site. The moon was reflected by the rippling water and added to the sinister effect of the patchwork of man-made chaos and reviving nature.

Her distracted mind thought that there must be some lesson somewhere in the story of the flowers' seeding, growing and survival in the bizarrely beautiful ruins of London, but it was not one she could think of at that moment. Taking care where she put her feet, she followed the right-hand wall round towards the dark mass of the still-standing offices. She had expected to see no lights, but had hoped for some indication of activity. She stopped to listen. But the only sound was the faint crunch as Johnny's boots trod on the debris of glass and beams and masonry.

Checking her watch, Flixe realised that she had only two minutes left before Gerry started her diversion and she hurried towards the building. In her haste she tripped over the bent and twisted remains of an iron girder and fell headlong into a small depression that was filled with cold, muddy rainwater.

As the cold seeped through her clothes and the pain in her barked shins intensified, all that Flixe could think about was the noise. She lay still, her face lifted an inch or so above the scummy surface of the improvised pool, listening for any sounds of alert. There was nothing. She gave it at least one more minute and then, as silently as possible, raised herself up.

The wind bit through her wet clothes and she could have cursed herself for being so stupid. But she had wasted enough time already. Gerry must already be involved with someone at the door and Johnny would presumably have found his way into the warehouse by now. Flixe limped forward, taking care now that it was too late, and reached the huddled mass of the office without further mishap.

She felt all round the nearest window she came to, but the boards that secured it were nailed tight. Wincing with cold and frustration and fear for Ming, she moved slowly to her left, pushing at any piece of wood she came to in case it would give. Actually breaking in would defeat her object. At last she came to a pair of iron doors that lay flat on the ground, the kind she had often seen outside pubs for the brewers to use when they delivered beer barrels straight to the cellar. Clenching her teeth at the rusty creaking sound, she hauled up one side of the door and wedged it with a thick, charred piece of timber. Then with infinite care she lowered herself over the edge, feeling around with her rubber-shod feet for a foothold.

Her ankles were grabbed by two strong hands. For a moment she was so afraid that she stopped breathing. Then a familiar voice whispered.

'OK, I've got you. Drop now.'

352

Obediently, she released her grip on the iron edge and dropped into Johnny's arms. She could not afford the luxury of wasting enough time to chastise him for almost killing her with terror. Instead she hissed:

'What have you got?'

'There's someone here anyway.' Then he gestured to a narrow stone staircase to Flixe's right and led the way towards it. Flixe tugged at his sleeve.

'Yes, but where?'

'Almost exactly above us, judging by the noise.'

This time she let him lead her to the stairs and up to the ground floor. As they inched silently along the main corridor, they heard a man with a French accent saying with ill-tempered patience:

'But mademoiselle, I have told you: Monsieur West-Grandison is not here. He never comes to this place nowadays. If it is so urgent that you find him, you must call at his house. If he is such a friend of yours, you must have the address.' Then came Gerry's voice, so pathetically tearful that Flixe almost grinned.

'Of course I have it. Jean-Pierre gave it to me years ago. But there's no answer there, and I must see him. Monsieur, I beg of you. I am in such a terrible situation.'

'I cannot help you, mademoiselle. For the last time: he is not here and we do not expect him.'

'We?' Gerry repeated after him. 'You mean that there is someone else here? A colleague? Perhaps he might know better where I could find Jean-Pierre?'

'A manner of speaking,' came the retort and Flixe could imagine how the man's teeth were clenched as he spat out the words. 'And now if you will forgive me, I am very busy.'

'Oh, please don't shut me out. I have come all this way.

If he isn't here, may I just write him a note? You must have some kind of messenger service. I mean, it is his warehouse, isn't it? Even if it is mostly disused now. He told me it was. I know it is.'

Gerry obviously had him well pinned down and so Flixe and Johnny walked carefully on down the passage towards a faint band of light. As they reached it they could hear Gerry's voice whining on, although they could not make out the actual words she was using. Flixe put her ear to the crack between the door and its frame, where the thin string of light glowed in the darkness.

There was the sound of flesh slapping against flesh and a half-choked short scream that worried her more than a full-blown shriek would have done. She looked up at Johnny. He made a thumbs-up sign and mouthed something at her that she could not understand. Standing back from the door, she leaned towards him. He whispered into her ear:

'Is that Ming?'

'I don't know. But, Johnny, if it is . . .'

'Hold on, Flixe. Whoever it is, we've some justification now in intervening. We must get out and get to that telephone. Come on before Gerry loses her hold on the one at the door. Come on.'

Flixe obeyed and five minutes later she found herself explaining to an apparently limping but resolute Gerry what they had heard.

'Well there's no choice then. We must get the police,' said Gerry and led the way back to the jeep. Flixe's hands were shaking so badly when she tried to telephone that she could hardly jam her pennies in the slot, but she got them there, tried Suvarov's number only to be answered by the endless ringing tone, and then in despair got the operator and said urgently: 'Nine, nine, nine, police, please.'

23

The three amateur conspirators stood at the corner outside the warehouse waiting in a mixture of anxiety and embarrassment for the arrival of the police. The first of the black cars did not stop, despite Flixe's waving arm and yelling, but the second pulled up beside her and an angry-looking man wearing a civilian mackintosh and a dark felt hat wound down his window to call out:

'Was it you who telephoned?'

'Yes. We think our young sister's in there with some . . . some traitors.'

'Oh, spies I suppose,' he said, his voice losing its hard, dramatic edge and his eyebrows climbing almost to the sleek hairline above his low, pale forehead. 'Well, I suppose we'll have to investigate. But I do wish you ladies wouldn't call on hard-pressed emergency services just because you think you've caught a German spy.'

At his tone of patronising patience, Gerry's face hardened, but there was obviously no point in protesting and so she just urged him on and, with Flixe and Johnny, following painfully in the car's wake, smelling the hot, sickening pungency of its exhaust. As they reached the front door they could hear the young uniformed constable thumping on the locked door and calling out in his rich London accent:

'Open up. Police 'ere. Open up.'

There was no answer, and Gerry suppressed her instinct to order them to break the door down. Whether or not Ming was in the building, some victim certainly was, and was probably in danger.

In the chancy light of the half-clouded moon that flashed sometimes off the silver buttons of the dark-blue tunics, Flixe and Gerry could see the young man turn to one of his superiors. The senior officer nodded and three burly young men put their shoulders to the door.

It took four charges, during which Gerry winced for their bruised shoulders, before the wood began to creak and splinter. Then the constable kicked it once, twice, and the door at last caved in. He and his colleagues rushed forward. The Alderbrooks made to follow, but the plain-clothes officer who had first spoken to them grabbed Flixe by the shoulder. His fingers were hard and she flinched, but he did not let go. Gerry was relieved to see that Johnny had not even waited for police permission and had followed the constables into the building.

'Wait,' the policeman began and then stopped as they all heard shouting from inside the building. The officer let Flixe go and she rubbed her shoulder with a cold and shaking hand, while he ran up the steps two at a time. More slowly she followed, now dreading what she might find.

The first sight that met her eyes was Johnny Blenkarne carrying Ming in his arms. Her mind flashed back to Gerry's harrowing description of the Eaton Gate bomb and she climbed the steps to meet him.

'There's no time to wait for an ambulance,' he said before she could speak. 'The police are going to drive her to the nearest hospital.'

'Ming?' she whispered as she looked down into her little sister's face, mottled black in that light and with horribly crusted blood on the thickened, distorted lips that had once looked so delicately pretty.

'So we were right after all. What . . .?' She could not bring herself to say anything else, but he seemed to understand.

'We don't know. It seems to be superficial though no doubt it'll be painful when she comes round. But we must get her checked out by a doctor.'

'Yes, of course.'

'Now, sir,' came an official-sounding voice. 'If you'll just put the young lady on the back seat, we'll get her to hospital.'

Gerry moved forward as though to join the group, but Johnny turned, still carrying Ming in his arms.

'I'll take care of her, Gerry. They'll want to talk to Flixe and you ought to try to get hold of that boss of yours,' he said with such determination that she obeyed.

'All right, but stay with her till we can come,' she said.

'Don't worry, Gerry. I will,' he answered and turned away to lay Ming in the first of the black cars. Gerry watched them drive off and then turned to go into the building with her sister. There was no mistaking the direction they had to follow, for there was a commotion of French and English swearing and expostulation that echoed down the darkened passages and bounced off the stone floors and hard, cream-painted walls.

They followed the noise and turned into the office from which it came, to be confronted by the sight of three men in handcuffs, arguing with the plain-clothes officer. At the sound of their arrival he turned and said:

'I'd like to talk to you two. Come into the passage.'

Outside, standing in the cold of the depressing corridor, Gerry left Flixe to explain what had led them to the warehouse. The policeman listened in gathering disbelief.

'It's a ludicrous story, miss. You must see that.'

'Never mind,' said Gerry crisply. 'If you speak to someone in authority you will discover that my chief has been on to your people all afternoon about my sister. And they may know where he is. But till they find him you will hold these thugs, won't you? You saw what they did to my sister.'

'We saw what had been done to her – we didn't see them do it.'

Gerry opened her mouth to protest but then let Flixe take over again.

'Please try to find Major Suvarov,' said Flixe as calmly as she could. 'We can none of us do anything until you do. We'll stay here and wait for him, if you like.'

She despised herself for not being able to look at the policeman as she spoke, but after a moment, she heard him walk across to the telephone and ask for a number. As he was waiting for the call to be put through Flixe had time to notice the horrible smell that filtered from the room in which Ming had been held. It seemed to be a mixture of bitterly acrid cigarette smoke, alcohol of some kind, sick and blood. She turned to Gerry.

'Let's go and sit on that bench over there. It's foul here.'

'OK,' said Gerry and followed her slowly. There was a hard wooden bench a few feet beyond the doorway and they sat down on that. Flixe got her cigarette case out of her pocket and offered it to Gerry.

They were still sitting there, smoking in silence, when Suvarov arrived three-quarters of an hour later. His British warm was flapping unbuttoned over his khaki uniform, and his face was set. Gerry thought that she had never seen him look so angry. He ignored them both and stood in the doorway into the room. His voice, when he spoke to the inspector, was as hard and sharp as breaking glass.

'I want to talk to you outside.' Then he turned back to the Alderbrooks and Flixe's breath stopped for a moment at the expression on his face. His voice was no warmer or softer when he addressed them.

'Wait here. I'll come back to you.'

They waited in silence until he came back. Then Gerry immediately stubbed out her cigarette and stood up, while Flixe went on smoking where she was.

'I hope you two are proud of yourselves,' he said in a voice colder if possible than that with which he had spoken to the policemen. 'You realise that you may have ruined an operation that has taken months to prepare, cost God-knows-what to your sister, and involved enormous risks to vast numbers of people.'

Gerry was so angry that she could not get out any recognisable words, but Felicity had had two years' self-training in hiding and controlling her emotions.

'Since you had put Ming into appalling danger and then lost her, I don't think it is we who can be said to have ruined the operation.'

He did not speak for a moment; then he said in a slightly milder tone of voice:

'Why did you come rushing in here by yourselves? Why in God's name didn't you tell me about this place?'

360

'I tried,' she said, hoping that she did not sound placatory. 'But you were not in Charles Street, Pall Mall, or your damned office. No one knew where to get you. I couldn't risk waiting, Suvarov.' Then her anger resurfaced and she burst out: 'What the hell gave you the right to play with the health and sanity of a girl as young as Ming? I think you must be mad.'

There was a hideous pause until at last he said with no discernible expression in his voice:

'We are all too angry to speak rationally now and so I think you had better get out while I salvage what I can from this disaster.' Flixe, looking just as angry as he, said bitterly:

'With pleasure. Come on, Gerry.'

'Wait!' he said when they reached the door. 'Where's Jean-Pierre?'

'I don't know. There's no need to look like that. Whatever you think of my delinquencies, *I* don't lie to my own side. I haven't seen him since yesterday evening: and I've been trying to speak to you about that too, all bloody day.' She put a hand under Gerry's elbow and could feel how her sister trembled. Flixe gripped hard, as though she were saying, Pull yourself together, don't show him such weakness. Together they walked out of the building and down the silent streets towards the jeep.

It was only when she had reconnected the distributor leads for the second time that evening and got into the driving seat that Felicity noticed the tears on Gerry's face. Turning on the ignition, she said:

'Don't let him do that to you, Gerry. Whatever we may all have felt for him, he's not worth it. He must have been making us all . . . like him so that he could use us.' She set off, driving north away from the river.

'It wasn't that,' Gerry answered, sniffing and feeling for a handkerchief. 'It's Ming. I should have realised what was going on. I discovered it this evening, but I expect nearly everyone else in the office knew. I should have stopped it. If I hadn't been so absorbed in my stupid difficulties with Andrew, I'd have noticed in time to do something about it.'

'Don't torment yourself. Suvarov's quite clever enough to have made certain that you'd not see what he was doing. Is this the Mile End Road yet?'

'God knows. I've never been here before. Is that where the hospital is?'

'Yes,' said Flixe, peering out of the scratched windows of the jeep. 'I think it must be. There's a huge building down there.' She drove up to the entrance and got out, disconnecting the leads once more. Then she turned and walked up into the hospital.

The first person they saw was Johnny Blenkarne, sitting on a hard chair in the hall, his head lying on his clasped hands. He did not look up until Flixe called his name.

'What have they said, Johnny?'

He brushed his hand over his red-edged eyes and said in a voice she had never heard from him before:

'Nothing yet, except that it is only superficial. Nothing broken and as far as they can see nothing internal.'

'They didn't . . . interfere with her?'

He looked puzzled for a moment as though trying to translate her elliptical phrase into something he could understand and then shook his head.

'No. Nothing like that.'

'Thank God,' said Gerry, sitting down beside him. 'Have you seen her?'

'Not since they put her to bed, Gerry. They won't let me, though they say she's come round.'

'Well, I'll try,' said Flixe, walking towards the reception desk with a decisiveness about her that the other two could only admire.

Half an hour later Felicity had managed to overbear the harassed junior doctor who had been trying to keep her out of the wards in accordance with his superiors' instructions. Then she sat down beside the still figure on the white bed and waited. After a few minutes Ming seemed to sense her presence for she opened her bruised and blackening eyelids.

'Flixe? Is it really over now?'

'Yes, darling. All over. Nothing like that will ever be done to you again . . .' She broke off, wanting to blame Suvarov and shout out her accusations, but fully aware of how little help that would be for Ming.

'Is Peter here?'

'No. Do you want him?'

'I must, Flixe. You see . . .' Flixe was concerned to see a fat tear oozing out of her sister's damaged eye. 'You see . . .' the painful voice broke again. Felicity brushed her fingers over Ming's forehead with a dim recollection of the comfort that a hand on one's head can give, and waited. 'You see, I talked.'

'Oh, Mingie, you mustn't mind about that. We've got those men. They can't do anything with what you told them. They're in police cells right now. Don't think about it.'

'But I must see him. I must tell him. Will you get him for me?'

'I'll try, if you're really sure. But it may take some time. He's got to see that the police do their stuff all right. But listen, baby, Gerry is here outside. D'you want to see her?'

363

The bandaged head nodded slightly on the unbleached pillowcase and Flixe touched her face gently.

'I'll get her now, darling, and then I'll go for Peter. Hold on, Ming.'

She went out of the long silent ward to the hall, far angrier even than she had been when she had first realised that Peter had involved Ming in his plots. At that moment any gentle feelings she had had towards their chief were subsumed in one tremendous flame of fury that he should have taken such risks with Ming. He could have sent anyone – even herself – for the same effect and with far less danger. The child was barely out of school, had seen her twin sister die in the bombed basement of Eaton Gate, knew nothing of the real world and should have been shielded from the war and its terrors, not thrown into one of the most horrible parts of it. Her mind just barely touched on what might have happened if Ming had been picked up by the Gestapo in France and interrogated. The members of the secret divisions dotted around London knew quite a lot by then of what was done to British agents and captured Resistance fighters. How could Suvarov have risked such a thing?

Her face must have shown something of what she was feeling for Gerry instantly said:

'What have the doctors done to her?'

'Nothing that they oughtn't to have. But she wants to see Suvarov. I'm going back now to try to get hold of him. If I take your jeep will you be able to see Gerry home, Johnny?'

'We'll manage. But I think she ought to get that foot seen to while she's here.'

'Why, what's the matter with your foot, Gerry? I saw you limping, but I didn't think it was serious.'

'It's just the big toe. I put it in the way when that Frenchman slammed the door. I think it might be broken – or perhaps just sprained. I'll see if I can't get one of the doctors to look. But, Flixe, I think I'll stay anyway. I don't really want to leave Ming alone here.'

'No. Then I'll see you later. If I can get to a telephone, do you want me to say anything to Andrew?'

'Oh, Lord. I'd quite forgotten him. Yes, would you? Just something to the effect that I've been kept at the office . . . you know the sort of thing.'

'Yes, I know,' said Flixe and her sister wondered a little at the bitterness in her voice.

Flixe drove quickly back to the remains of the warehouse. Suvarov was still there in discussion with the various policemen, and looked round surprised at the sound of her voice.

'What now, Felicity?' he asked.

'Ming wants you. She says that she told them something and you have to know about it.'

His face changed immediately from a mask of cold indifference to one of watchful intelligence. He spoke briefly to the inspector and then told Flixe to take him back to the hospital. She drove in silence until he suddenly asked:

'How deliberate was this, Felicity?'

'Not at all,' she answered coldly, understanding exactly what he had meant by that vague question. 'If it had been, don't you think I'd have been there before they even started on Ming?'

'But you do realise, I hope, that quite apart from the possible waste of her . . . work, you may have thrown away two years or more of your own.'

365

'Are you trying to tell me that the police are going to let those swine go?'

'Use your mind, Flixe,' he said, his voice warming into much more human anger. 'What can they be charged with? GBH, that's all. And I'm not sure a clever lawyer couldn't reasonably persuade a jury that slapping a girl across the face wasn't even that.'

'Surely there's some provision under the Emergency Regulations for you to search the warehouse. There must be evidence of some nefarious activites there if you're only bright enough to spot it when you find it.'

'Did you know she was going over?' he asked, completely ignoring Flixe's interruption.

'Ming? No. How could I? I knew nothing until you telephoned.'

'And what have you told Jean-Pierre since then?'

'This sounds like an interrogation . . .' Flixe began crossly, and Suvarov suddenly said:

'Pull up over there on the left.' When she had obeyed, he seized her by the upper arms and turned her round so that he could look into her face. 'You're bloody right. This is an interrogation. What did you tell Jean-Pierre?'

'Nothing. I haven't spoken to him since yesterday when he informed me that he was probably going away soon and wanted to know whether I would go and live with him if he sent for me. I tried to tell you that, but you wouldn't listen. And there isn't time to go into it now. Ming needs you.'

He gestured for her to drive on and sat in silence until they pulled up outside the hospital. Then, as he was opening the passenger door, he said:

'It sounds horribly as though you do care for Jean-Pierre. How much has that affected what you did this evening?'

'Haven't you understood at all? Whatever treacherous things my subterranean emotions may have been doing, my sisters' well-being – in particular the physical safety of my frightened, vulnerable younger sister – matters more.'

'I hope that's true. No, don't come in. And don't wait. I'll find my own way back.'

'You'll find Gerry and Blenkarne there.'

He said no more and she watched him run up the steps into the hospital.

24

When Flixe woke the next morning, the first thing she did was to telephone the hospital to find out how Ming was. The nurse to whom she spoke was reassuring and told Flixe that her sister would be released later in the day and that with plenty of rest and good food would be well again in no time at all.

Flixe put down the receiver, aware both of relief that Ming's physical hurts were indeed superficial and irritation that the nurse should have thought that physical hurts were the only ones that mattered, and that food and rest could possibly heal the others. She was also aware of the memory of something Gerry had said battering at her. Gerry had felt herself responsible for Ming's predicament, believing that if she had not been so wrapped up in her quarrels with her husband she would have discovered that Suvarov was sending Ming to France. How much more, thought Flixe, was she responsible? If she had not allowed Jean-Pierre to make her fall in love with him, perhaps she would have discovered more about him more quickly and pre-empted Ming's mission, about which she was still woefully ignorant. Or perhaps she would have remembered about his bombed warehouse more quickly, in time to tell Suvarov and get him to stop what had happened to Ming.

Suddenly she knew that she had to make a sharp break with the life she had lived before Ming's abduction and, without thinking very much, she dialled the number of Jean-Pierre's house. The telephone was answered as promptly as usual, but the voice who repeated the telephone number was not that of Jean-Pierre's French manservant. This voice was English, and there was something in its throttled carefulness that suggested officialdom to Flixe. Disguising her own voice by broadening the vowels into a fair imitation of a Gloucestershire accent, she said:

'I'd like to speak to Mr West-Grandison, please.'

'I am afraid that he has been suddenly called away, madam,' came the reply. 'May I know who is requiring him?'

'Never mind,' said Flixe quickly. 'It doesn't matter.'

'Please give me your name, madam.' There was enough urgency in the voice to make Flixe put her own receiver down fast. She no longer had any doubt that she had been speaking to a policeman. The only question that remained was whether Jean-Pierre had left of his own accord or was now languishing in some cell or interrogation room.

She spent the rest of the morning making herself cups of tea and coffee that she hardly drank and wandering about the flat, waiting for the telephone to ring. The only person who did ring, at about eleven-thirty, was the secretary of the architecture committee to enquire why she had not appeared at the office.

'Oh I am sorry, Miss Smith,' Flixe said faintly. 'It's just

that I'm feeling dreadfully unwell. It's too stupid of me not to have called you; I meant to, and then I was . . .'

'I see. Well, Miss Alderbrook, it would be helpful if you could let us know in future when we'll be likely to see you.'

'Yes, of course, Miss Smith. I am sorry. Goodbye.'

At last she gave in and decided that she must see Suvarov. There were too many loose ends, too much she needed to know before she could find any kind of rational serenity ever again. It no longer seemed decent to use the emergency telephone that rang only on his desk and so she dialled the switchboard and asked to speak to Gerry. When she had been put through, she asked Gerry to arrange a meeting.

'All right, Flixe. Hang on a second, will you?' said Gerry. There was a short silence and then she said: 'He says he'll meet you at the "usual place" in an hour.'

'Thank you, Gerry. Are you all right?'

'Yes. Well, bearing up. Andrew and I had another fight.'

'Oh no,' said Flixe, suddenly remembering that she had promised to ring him the previous evening to explain Gerry's absence. 'I never telephoned. Gerry, I am sorry. I can't think what's happened to my mind: it's gone all porridgey.'

'Don't worry. He'd have found something else to hang it on if he had not had that. I must go.'

'Wait a minute. I rang the hospital and they said Ming was coming out today: is she coming to you, or shall I fetch her?'

'Suvarov is whisking her off to Etchingham. Goodbye, Flixe.'

In fact Gerry was not all right at all. The previous evening's events had left her in a turmoil as great as her sister's. After

370

the quarrel with Andrew, Gerry had slept badly and by the time she reached her office she was so tired that her eyes felt rasped and hot, and her every muscle ached as though it had been racked.

Suvarov did not speak when she opened the door, but she knew that he was looking at her. With a certain deliberation she turned her head and looked back, meaning to show him just what she thought of his treatment of her youngest sister. After a while he said:

'Whatever you may be thinking about me, I trust that you will remember the war we are fighting and not allow your personal feelings to get in the way of your work.'

'I shall do my best,' she answered coldly. 'On which subject, have you read the last report from Philippe and Michel?'

'Not yet. Must I?'

'I believe it would be worth your while.'

'Very well.' He returned to the papers he had been studying when she arrived and there was nothing else for Gerry to do but follow his example and sit at her own desk.

For the rest of that morning she tried to work, finding that every tiny noise distracted her as though it had been an explosion. She was more conscious of Suvarov than she had ever been: his breathing, the small clicking noise his buttons made on the edge of his polished desk as he reached across it to pick up something just out of reach, the scrape of his pen, the occasional cough, the rustle of his papers, every noise he made got between Gerry and her concentration. Once she looked across the room at his bent head and wondered how a man like the one he had seemed to be could have done what he had to Ming. And she hated herself for her part in it, asking herself again and again whether if she had not cared for him so much she would have known what he was up to and been able to stop it. She also just let her mind form the question of whether he had deliberately aroused her emotions in order to cloud her judgement.

Mike's original comment came back to her and she began to wonder for the first time whether perhaps Suvarov had not in fact wanted to employ her and, having been forced to take her on by some higher authority, had taken the easiest way of neutralising her. So much of her mind was occupied with its own internal questions that it was a full minute before she realised that he, too, had looked up from his work. She quickly allowed her eyelids to drop as she stood up.

'I have to clarify something with Mike. Is there anything you need taken downstairs?'

'No. Thank you.' It had been months since he had felt the need to thank her for such an ordinary piece of office courtesy.

There was a considerable relief in shutting the door behind her and getting away from those long dark eyes that saw so much more than one wanted to show, and Gerry took her time about walking down the single flight of stairs to the analysts' room. When she could not spin it out any longer, she pushed open the scarred and chipped white door and went in.

The only analyst working at his desk was Mike, but Antoine Eynsham was standing in front of one of the filing cabinets, riffling through a folder of old flimsies. Mike stood up as she came in.

'Oh, don't bother with that,' she said, without really noticing that it was something he never did in normal circumstances.

'What can we do for you today, Gerry?' asked Eynsham, and his New England voice was even softer and more gentle than usual. But Gerry looked at Mike.

'How much did you know?' she asked.

'About what?' At the sight of her face he hurriedly added to his simple question: 'I'm not being disingenuous, Gerry, really. But I am not sure what it is exactly that you're asking.'

'How much did you know about Peter's operation that culminated last night in his agent's ending up in hospital?'

'Not very much. But I knew it was on.'

She looked into his face, and saw that it was as white and strained as it had so often been in the past before his brother had been killed while trying to escape from his prison camp.

'And did you know who the agent was?'

The tightness about his mouth dissolved as she watched and part of her own tension relaxed. If Mike had not known, then there must have been less evidence than she had thought and she had not been quite so criminally careless as she had assumed. He shook his head and then asked his own question.

'Why do you need to know?'

'I just wondered if I was the only one who hadn't been told. What about you, Tony?'

'Yes, I knew,' he said. There was no self-defence in his soft voice.

'But couldn't you have warned me?'

'Of course not. How could I, Gerry?'

She put up a hand to cover her eyes for a moment and he said, slowly and with far less of an accent that she was used to hearing:

'Is she all right?'

'Just.'

'I see. And have you quarrelled with the Chief about it?'

'Not in words. But otherwise, yes.'

'That wasn't fair.' Gerry walked across the stained carpet to look out of the windows across the park. She felt as though she had been drained suddenly of half her anger and it was in an almost meditative tone that she said:

'If you could have seen her face when they'd been at it, you might have taken a different line.'

'She must have been a volunteer. They all are.'

'I know. But don't we all know how he'd have made her offer herself?' After she had said that she regretted the form of words, but it was too late to alter them.

'Would one of you perhaps care to enlighten me?' interrupted Mike. Tony stood silently, waiting for Gerry to begin.

'Peter Suvarov, our esteemed chief, has just sent my eighteen-year-old sister to France for something – what, I still don't know – and at some point on her journey back here she was picked up by some of our target people in this country. They seem to have had a lovely time beating up my poor little Ming before we . . .' Her voice wobbled and she knew that she could not say any more without breaking down.

It was Mike who reached her side first and as he put both arms around Gerry, he jerked his head in dismissal at Eynsham, who after a surprised pause, obeyed and left them in the empty room.

Mike said nothing and did not try to pet or soothe her. He just held her against him, occasionally stroking her fair hair, until she herself straightened up. Then he moved back, taking away his hands.

'Thank you, Mikey. It was what I needed.'

'Gerry . . .' He stopped on her name and just looked at her. Something about the way she seemed to have disintegrated behind her neat exterior gave him a certain courage and he went on. 'Gerry, first of all, how exactly is your sister?'

'Well, when we left the hospital they said that her injuries were in fact quite slight: some bad bruising to her face and one or two small cuts and a nosebleed. That's all. But I am afraid for her. Can't you just imagine the sort of nightmares and terrors that must be biting at her?'

'Yes, I can. And if there is anything at all that I can do to help – you will tell me, won't you?'

'You're a dear, Mike. But the chief seems set on dealing with all the immediate things; he's whisking her off to stay with his wife and sister-in-law this evening. Conscience, I suppose.' The bitterness in her voice surprised Mike, but he tried not to show it.

'Gerry,' he said, 'Why don't you come out for a walk? It's nearly lunchtime.'

She thought for a while, even looked up as though she could see through the ceiling to her chief, and then shrugged.

'D'you know, Mike, I'd love that.'

'Good. Got a coat?'

'Yes, but it's upstairs, with my hat and gas mask.'

'I'll get them for you,' he said, correctly interpreting her expression. 'Go downstairs and wait for me in the hall.'

He joined her breathlessly about seven minutes later and helped her into her old-fashioned woollen coat. Then she slung the canvas gas-mask holder over her shoulder and pulled on an unbecoming but comfortable felt hat and preceded him out of the door and across the road into the park.

375

They walked in silence until they had completed an entire circuit of the lake and then he took hold of her hand and began to talk.

'Gerry, I know that you must be tormented for what your sister has suffered – and may still suffer – but that's not all, is it? Tell me. You know that you can trust me.'

She squeezed his gloved hand with her own.

'Yesterday I'd have said, "Of course I trust you, Mike", but today that's all gone,' she said sadly.

'It shouldn't have.'

'I feel such a fool.' Mike didn't answer, but he did not let go of her either and in the end she answered the question she had wanted him to ask. 'I assumed that I could judge people by the way that they made me feel, which is of course the most stupid, ridiculous, childish, dangerous fallacy in the world.'

'Go on.'

'I despised my husband because he bored and irritated me, and I trusted and liked and wanted Suvarov because . . . And I suppose I trust you and that's why I'm telling you all this because I like you and because you appear to have trusted me.'

'And needed you very much, Gerry. I'm not sure how I'd have coped after I got the news that Simon had been shot, if I'd not had you to talk to. When Simon was killed, I felt that the world was breaking up around me: almost as though anything I stepped on might disintegrate under my feet. No, that's not quite right, but I felt insecure, useless, unhappy – and desperately afraid.' He stopped and turned to face her, speaking quietly but with an intensity that she had not heard from him before. 'You were the only thing in life that I could be certain of.'

'Oh, Mike,' she said inadequately. He saw that she was

not in a fit state to think about anyone else's feelings and so he changed the subject.

'By the way, have I met your husband?'

The abrupt change of tone seemed to bring Gerry up short and jerk her mind into a different gear.

'Not quite. But he saw us once ages ago, in almost these circumstances, and that evening accused me of having an affair with you.' She even laughed a little.

'Pity he wasn't right, isn't it?' It took a little time for the sense of that comment to percolate into Gerry's brain.

'I think I take that as a compliment, Mike,' she said at last. 'And a very sweet one.'

He touched her face briefly, but she was too deeply embroiled in her anxieties to respond. He let his hand drop, started to speak, thought better of it, and then shrugged before saying, almost as though he were joking:

'I might have been tempted to try if you hadn't so obviously belonged to the chief.'

At that she turned quickly away from him and walked rather fast down to the bridge. He ran after her.

'I didn't mean to offend you, Gerry. It just was very clear from almost the first day that he and you were . . . somehow involved. I don't mean that in the crude, physical sense. But it was obvious that there was a tremendous charge between you.'

'Well, we've fused it now, if there ever was.'

'Broken fuses can be mended.'

'Not this one. Look, there's too much work to do for us to be slopping around here telling the darkest secrets of our souls. We ought to eat and then get back.'

'As you choose.' He sounded almost hurt, but Gerry did not have any spare emotion to spend on Mike just then.

*

Two hours later Flixe was sitting on one of the hard green benches at the Round Pond, waiting in increasing anxiety for Suvarov. He came, very late and clearly irritable, and sat down beside her.

'There's a frantic flap on today. I haven't much time. What is it? If you want to tell me what a murderer I am to have sent your sister to France, don't bother. I've had plenty from Gerry, and there's probably more to come.'

Flixe put her elbows on her knees and rested her chin in her hands, feeling that her head was too leaden to support itself.

'No,' she said at last. 'But there are so many things I need to know. What did you send her for?'

'Evidence. You know Jean-Pierre's group was sabotaging our missions over here. We could get no proof from this end. Your information helped, but there was nothing conclusive: you know that. But I've had a man working over there for months – ever since Ming agreed to go to France for me. He got the proof and hung on to it all until she was ready to fetch it. Because we didn't know where they'd infiltrated, we couldn't trust the message to any of the usual channels and I had to choose someone in whom I had absolute faith.'

'How did you know your agent had got it if it was too sensitive to send?' Flixe asked, her professional interest surfacing for a moment.

Suvarov looked at her as though debating whether or not to answer her questions. His face softened slightly and he gave her a reply of a sort.

'We'd agreed to an apparently innocuous message which could be added to his radio operator's normal report – we couldn't have coded the entire report like that because there was far too much of it. But I did use the same method to send back the instruction to sit on the information until Ming was safely trained.'

'And then you let her get kidnapped . . . All wasted and for nothing.'

'No, we got the message. She handed it over at Southampton.'

Flixe's righteous anger began to heat up again and overtake the other, less comfortable, emotions that had been wearing her out all morning.

'And so she had nothing to give them when they were roughing her up. Poor little bitch. You really are a bastard, Suvarov: you make certain that your message is safe, but Ming – flesh, blood and shivering nerve ends – is just left out there with no kind of protection.' She slid her heavy head further down between her arms until her hands were clasping the back of her neck.

'Is that it?' His voice was quite without colour or any kind of emotion. 'Because if so I have to get to the hospital to collect her.'

'Yes, I suppose so,' sighed Flixe, lifting her head and sitting upright once more. 'No, not really. Have you arrested Jean-Pierre or did he get out?'

'I have no power to arrest people. But to answer your question: no, he has not been caught. He got out as you elegantly put it. Somebody tipped him off a little while before we – you – discovered what had happened to Ming.'

This time there was emotion in his voice, such tightly compressed emotion that she turned on the seat to look into his face.

'You can't think it was me,' she said in horror.

He looked at her for a long time, his eyes critical and his lips set.

'No, I don't. For a short time I wondered. But Ming did tell them where she had come from in France. And just after she let it out one of them made a telephone call. It is possible that that was enough to alert him, if as you said he was already planning to go.'

'Thank you,' Flixe said, and then in case he thought that was a sign that she had forgiven him, she added: 'How long will you be keeping Ming incarcerated?'

'Don't, Flixe,' he protested. 'She needs rest, a good doctor, care and peace. She'll get all that with Connie and Diana. And then perhaps you and Gerry could go one weekend soon to stay there with them.'

'Why couldn't you have let me keep my anger?' she said in quiet misery. 'Go on. Go and get her, and give her my love.'

'I will. Goodbye, Flixe.'

An hour after that he was driving slowly through the mess of south-east London with the third Alderbrook sister beside him. Of them all, only Ming did not blame him for what had happened to her. And to her alone he had apologised for it. She sat relaxed in the dark-green leather bucket seat beside him in the Morgan, smoothing her left hand with her right.

'It wasn't your fault, Peter. If I hadn't stopped being afraid it would never have happened.'

'What happened?' Peter asked, not letting his eyes look away from the road ahead. 'I don't mean the sequence of events, but what happened to the fear?'

He heard Ming laugh, a lovely sound that eased some of his bitter regrets.

'Well, Peter, as I expected – and you warned – I was more frightened in France than I ever remember being before; then, when I was back in England and had handed over the message, I let go. For practically the first time in my life I was not afraid of anything: I had done what you asked and so I wasn't afraid of you—'

'Were you ever?' Suvarov asked, interrupting her without apology. There was a pause as though Ming had to work to remember.

'No,' she said at last. 'No, I don't think I was ever afraid of you. But if I had failed, I might have been. For once I was not afraid that I had got on the wrong train; or that I would have lost my ticket and be berated by a furious guard; or that something unspecified, unimagined, but dreadful would happen to me. And because of that, because I had let go of all my fear, I was easy prey.' She broke off and turned her head sideways to look at him. Catching sight of the movement out of the corner of his eye, he risked a quick glance away from the traffic and saw her poor, bruised lips smiling at him. Feeling extraordinarily humbled, he waited for what she was going to say next.

'And so now I understand at last. There's isn't any need to be ashamed of being afraid. And you gave me that, Peter.'

He felt ready to weep. That anyone who had been through what she had in the past weeks should be trying to comfort the man who had sent her to it was astonishing enough, but that someone as young and sensitive as Ming should do it moved him immensely.

'Your sisters can't forgive me for sending you,' he said when he could speak again.

'They don't understand, Peter. Don't let them hurt you.'

25

Flixe spent the next few days alone in a state of introspection and self-doubt quite foreign to her character. She told the secretary of the architecture committee that she would not be able to go in to work for some time and so she had nothing to do but think. At one moment she scribbled a note of apology to Suvarov and posted it before she could change her mind. She wrote several letters to Ming at Etchingham, and even one to her mother trying yet again to atone for the hurt she had caused when she had lashed out during the weekend she had spent at home. But suddenly one Friday evening, she knew that she had to talk to someone in the flesh or she would fret herself into real trouble, but it was hard to know to whom she should go.

Gerry had her own troubles, and in any case Flixe needed someone a little outside the circle of which Suvarov was the centre. Trying to analyse just what it was she did want, she thought of Anna Kingsley. Cleared now of all suspicion, Anna appeared to Flixe in the light in which Gerry had always seen her; a disinterested but affectionate intelligence to whom any appeal could be made. It might be turned down, but it would never be mocked or used against the appellant in any way. The prospect of talking to someone like that made Flixe move decisively at last.

She got up off the low chair and flung off her dressing gown to dress in a jersey and skirt. The sound of the rain against her windows was loud enough to remind her to find her Aquascutum in spite of the turmoil in her mind, and with her umbrella in her hand she let herself out of the flat.

Down in the street the wind seemed to blow all the rain directly into her face however she held the umbrella and so she rolled it up. It cost far more effort to hold it up than its protection was worth. As she was fiddling with the catch to make it hold shut she was aware of a hair-lifting sensation; it felt as though there were someone very close behind her. She strained to hear any betraying sound; but there was nothing to hear except the relentless wet patter of the rain and the occasional distant swishing noise as a vehicle a few streets away drove its nearside wheels through the gutters. Suddenly terrified, she could not think what to do: to look round would seem to invite disaster if there were anyone there, and yet to do nothing would be mad. She finished clipping the umbrella shut and then began to walk forward again, hoping that she had invented the presence she could still sense looming up behind her.

Sickeningly she felt a pair of strong hands gripping her shoulders. There was no mistaking the hands for those of a friend. This was an attack, shattering, and coming with no real warning on a perfectly ordinary wet London night, so near the flat in which she had always felt safe. Fear paralysed all her faculties. A stray thought became recognisable amid the terror: well at least I won't have to agonise over it all any more. Then, as though the very act of thinking had reawakened her, Flixe began to struggle. The man dragged her into an alley behind the block of flats and pressed her up against the wet brick wall, his hands shifting to her throat.

'This will teach you to interfere, *salope*,' he said in a voice whose accent betrayed its nationality as firmly as the obscenity. It galvanised Flixe into action at last. Superimposed on the voice of her attacker was that of the ex-colonial policeman at the requisitioned house near Bristol: 'You've no need of revolvers, or garrottes or suchlike if you've an umbrella in your hands.'

Without even thinking, Flixe stopped trying to hit the man's face. Standing still at last, feeling his hands tighten around her throat, she calmly reversed the umbrella, brought it point upwards between them and before the man could discover what she was doing put both hands on the shaft and with all her strength drove it up under his chin.

Just as her instructor had told her, the brass ferrule, sharpened by years of unintended stropping on the London pavements, pushed through the skin and muscle below the chin, broke through the palate and, entering the brain, killed her aggressor instantly. His hands clenched convulsively round her throat and for a moment dizziness terrified her. But then the big hands relaxed and, still leaning against the wall, Flixe watched the man crumple to his knees and then keel sideways to lie in the wet filth beside three overflowing dustbins.

Too sick and shivery to move for the moment, she tried hard to remember the rest of the lesson, but she could not think what she should do next. She put a wet hand up to her wet face and rubbed her eyes, as though that might help to clear her mind. It did not. All she could think of was her chief. Suvarov would get her out of this mess somehow.

For a reason she did not stop to analyse, Flixe could not bear to go back into her flat and tried to remember where she could find a public telephone. There was one, she was sure, in the Underground station, but she could hardly take her umbrella, bent now and bloody, into such a conspicuous place; nor could she leave it behind. Trying to think, she set off in the direction of the station, looking about her as though the familiar red box might appear in her path.

She found one, of course, right at the end of the dustbin alley and, fumbling her coppers into the slot, dialled the number of Suvarov's Pall Mall flat. He answered at the second ring and she pressed her thumb on to button 'A' so hard that the next day she found the joint bruised.

'Peter,' she said breathlessly. 'Peter.'

'Yes. Flixe?'

It came to her irrelevantly that he was almost the only person apart from their parents who never mistook her voice for Gerry's.

'Peter,' she said again, unable to produce any of the words that had to be said. His voice sharpened:

'Flixe, what is it?' Then as she could not answer, he said, much more gently: 'Where are you? Flixe, you must tell me and I'll come.'

Her teeth were now clattering together as though she were standing naked in a hurricane, but she managed at last to speak:

'Telephone box, Phillimore Walk.' Then she added one word: 'Hurry.'

'Coming. Hold on.' He put the receiver down and all she heard was a buzz. Slowly she put her own down and leaned against the grubby wall of the kiosk, noticing for the first time the revolting, acrid smell of stale urine that filled it. Breathing as shallowly as possible, she stood, holding the umbrella with both hands, its ferrule carefully kept off the ground. There she waited until he came.

He opened the door of the telephone box at last and stood in the poor light looking at her, but he did not speak. She held out the umbrella:

'I used it – as they taught at Naseby House.'

He took it from her, looked at the point and schooled his face with what she could recognise as considerable effort.

'Show me, Flixe.'

Standing aside to let her precede him, he kept his eyes directed at her face. She did not look back at him, but walked a pace or so in front of him along the alley until she reached the three dustbins and her victim.

'There.'

He stood for a moment, looking down at her handi-work. Then he said, without turning round.

'Who is he?'

'Don't know his name, but I've seen him once before. He was Jean-Pierre's manservant.

'OK. You go on up to the flat, Flixe. I'll deal with this.'

'No. Not up there. Not the flat,' she said, gasping, with the first signs of hysteria. Suvarov noted them unsurprised and all he said was:

'OK, then sit on that step. You need to sit down, Flixe.' He bent down on one knee to search the body, flashing his dimmed torch discreetly to examine the identity card and a bundle of papers he retrieved from the inside pocket of the man's jacket. Then he stood up again.

'I must telephone. Coming?'

For answer, Flixe simply stood up and took the hand he held out to her. He gripped it hard, but made no other move or word to comfort her. Together they walked back to the red kiosk and she waited outside, still shivering, until he had finished. She noticed that he had stuffed all the man's papers in his own pocket. When he came out again, he was not smiling.

'That's that. You'd better come to Pall Mall,' he said gravely. 'They'll need to ask some questions, but it'll be simpler if I'm there.'

He led the way to his small green car and opened the passenger door for her. She climbed in and sat down. He shut the door, walked round the car and got in beside her. She waited for him to switch on the ignition, but he did not. With his gloved hands on the wheel he looked sideways at her and said:

'Tell me.'

And so she did: everything that had happened since Jean-Pierre had told her that he would have to leave London; all the things he had said and done then, and what she had answered; all the thoughts she had had, the evasions she had tried, all the excuses, the doubts and the uncertainties; every horrible thought she had had about Suvarov himself. Throughout, he simply listened. When she finally ran out of things to say she waited for comment or criticism or even accusation, but none came. He turned the key in the dashboard and said:

'Let's go.'

He drove fast through the empty, wet streets of Kensington and Knightsbridge, down Constitution Hill, past the Palace and along the Mall, turning up St James's and parking at last outside the white house where he had his rooms. She had never before crossed his threshold and in the emptiness that had followed her confession she found herself wondering about how he had arranged his life.

She had begun to shake again, badly, and there was a threatening nausea in her throat that disgusted her.

'Peter,' she said.

'Yes?' he answered. It was not helpful. Could he not understand that she needed him to tell her that she had not done anything wrong, that she had been trained to kill in case of just such an eventuality, that she had no reason to feel filthy and degraded and bloody? She looked at him, hoping at least to read forgiveness in his dark eyes, but there was only a slightly concerned expression of enquiry. She turned from him and looked instead around the room into which he had brought her.

There was an austerity about it that surprised her. The walls of books she might have expected, but somehow she had envisaged some of the richness of Jean-Pierre's flat. Instead she found a certain comfortable shabbiness, an air of self-containment, as though the room had been designed for its owner alone. There was no display, nothing to suggest that he expected anyone else ever to be there with him.

He told her to put her feet up on the sofa, fetched an eiderdown, presumably from his bedroom, and tucked it round her. Then he went out again and it was nearly ten minutes before he came back with a steaming mug in his hand. He offered it to her and as she smelled the scent of cocoa she almost wept. So, he had understood after all. That someone like Peter Suvarov should trouble to brew a drink like that seemed incongruous; but it was precisely the narcotic that she needed, with all its overtones of nurseries and childhood comfort. She wrapped her hands around the mug's warmth and managed to smile at him.

Peter pulled the swivel chair away from the desk and sat in it beside her.

'Flixe, they will have to ask questions to keep the record straight, but they're in a different class from the ones at the warehouse. They know exactly what has been going on and what is at stake. Nevertheless all I want you to tell them is what happened after you left the flat this evening. Nothing else.'

'You're going to let Jean-Pierre go?'

'No. But a different lot are dealing with the search for him. And it would only complicate the hunt for the police to be involved. They'll come later, when he's found. Can you manage to suppress what's necessary?' She shivered and her face paled noticeably as he talked, but when he had finished, she nodded. Then they waited for nearly thirty minutes until the police arrived.

Watched by two of the three officers, Flixe told them at dictation speed precisely what she had already told Suvarov about what had happened in the alley. The third officer took down what she said while the others listened, never taking their icy eyes off her. Then the most senior of them asked:

'You are certain that his hands were round your neck before you started to struggle?'

'Yes.'

'And you don't think he was simply . . . well, after you for a . . . as a woman?'

'How delicate you are, Inspector,' she said, striving for a tone of detachment to equal his. 'No, I'm certain of that.'

'Thank you. Well, sir,' he added, turning to Suvarov, 'I

389

think we've everything we need. You'll be in your office tomorrow, I take it?'

'Yes. And Miss Alderbrook will be there, too.'

'Thanks. Good night, Miss Alderbrook. Sorry we had to trouble you tonight.'

Flixe nodded her thanks for his apology. Suvarov saw the three men out and then returned. He stood at the end of the sofa and smiled at last.

'Drink, Flixe?'

'No, thank you, Peter.'

'Do you want to get some sleep?'

'Not specially. Why, is there more?'

'It can wait. No, actually, I don't think it can: I have to ask. Are you afraid of what will happen when he's caught?'

'I don't know. I hope not.' She pushed her hair back behind her ears with both hands and screwed up her eyes for a moment. 'Yes, I am. After what he arranged to have done to Ming, I could never bear to see or speak to him again. How could I? But . . . there was once so much . . . Whatever I tell myself about him, I can't quite wipe the memory of it all away. Thank God I don't have to decide any more whether to go to him or send him away.'

He was quiet for so long that she had to look at him again.

'Yes, I'm sorry. That wasn't fair of me. Nor is keeping you up. I'll wake you with breakfast in the morning.' He turned to go.

'Peter—' There was an urgency in her voice that stopped him, but he didn't turn. 'Peter.' Flixe threw back the eiderdown and got off the sofa to walk to his side. She wanted him to take her in his arms, tell her how brave she had been, kiss her, tell her she was forgiven, that he loved her, that the past three years could be forgotten, that she had done everything he had asked of her and would be asked for no more, that she could rest and be herself again.

'Peter.' Her voice sounded petulant and childish in her own ears.

'Felicity, you should sleep,' he said, turning back at last. They were standing very close and she could almost hear the blood beating in his heart. She knew that he must understand what she needed, because he always understood and knew everything. Then she felt his hands on her shoulders and her eyelids closed in relief. Now, everything would be all right. She leaned towards him.

The strength in his hands astonished her as he held her upright. She straightened up and, despising herself, murmured:

'Sorry. It's all been a bit too much for me.'

'I know. But that isn't the way. And this isn't the time, Flixe.' His voice was very kind, but it was not kindness that she wanted from him then.

26

He was as good as his word and she woke the next morning to the clinking of china and the familiar, depressing smell of ersatz coffee. She sat up, pushing the hair and the sleep out of her eyes, mildly embarrassed to be seen in such an uncontrolled state, but grateful for the matter-of-factness of Suvarov's voice and smile.

'I let you sleep as long as I could,' he said. 'But there's not much time for hanging about. We ought to leave in twenty minutes. Can you manage that?'

'Leave?'

'Yes, for the office. I know you've only got trousers with you, but that doesn't matter.'

'So you did mean it. I wondered if it had been a slip of the tongue when you said I'd be there with you. Why?'

'You can hardly go on playing the siren of Kensington now. . . .'

'No. I know. But what'll I do at the office?'

'I was going to add, before you interrupted, that we can use your brains and your experience in the analysts' room. I'll explain to the architecture committee. Hurry up with that breakfast now.'

Flixe was silent. All her life she had sought and aroused admiration for her looks, her vivacity and her ability to charm people out of themselves. Never before had anyone said he wanted her for her brains. She had to cling hard to the memory of Peter's coolness when she had tried to reach him the night before in order to stop herself from blurting out there and then that she loved him and would do or be anything he wanted of her.

'How much do they know about me?' she asked twenty-five minutes later as he led the way across St James's Park.

'I've told them nothing. Eynsham knows that you've been working for me, and Gerry knows whatever you've told her, but that's all. Why? Are you embarrassed?' He looked sideways and was surprised to see that her pale face was suffused with unaccustomed colour.

'Yes, absurd isn't it?' She said, trying to sound amused. 'After the last three years, who'd have thought I could feel as prim as this? Almost like the village spinster. It's a vile sensation.'

'I expect it will pass. Don't think about it. It's probably a natural reaction. Come on. Ah, Bates, here is Miss Alderbrook who'll be working with the analysts. Make out a pass for her, will you?'

'Of course, sir. Morning, miss.'

'Good morning,' answered Flixe and followed her chief up the staircase, whose elegance, she noticed, was hardly diminished by the chipped and dirty paint. They went up two flights and he pushed open a door, saying as he did so:

'Here's our newest recruit – Felicity Alderbrook. Find her a chair, someone, and, Antoine, will you give her a job?'

'Sure, Peter.'

'Can't stop, Flixe, I'm afraid, but you're in good hands. I'll send Gerry down for you later.'

He left and Flixe turned to face the group of men into whose close-knit little world she had just been propelled. There was silence for a moment or two, not accusing, she thought, but certainly critical. It was broken by an exceedingly good-looking RNVR officer with very bright grey-blue eyes and smooth fair hair.

'You have to be Gerry's sister,' he said, smiling and shaking her hand. 'I've never seen two girls so alike in my life.'

'That's right,' she answered, smiling back. 'In the old days we were often mistaken for each other. Where should I sit?'

'I should take the desk to the right of the window. It belonged to one of our traitors.'

'Oh, come on, Mike. Be fair. Michel merely joined the Free French, mademoiselle: hardly a betrayal since we're all on the same side.' Mike laughed easily and sat down again at his desk, picking up a pencil as he spoke.

'Well, near enough the same side, I suppose. We both want the Jerries beaten. But I'll bet he told them every little thing they wanted to know about what goes on here. And I imagine they wanted to know quite a lot.'

'My name is Philippe,' the Frenchman went on smoothly, as though Mike had not interrupted. He held out his hand and Flixe shook it, aware of an instinctive distaste for the sound of his accent.

Sandy, the middle-aged Scottish lawyer, introduced himself and then Eynsham came across the room with a flat manila folder.

'How's your French?' he asked.

'Fairly fluent,' answered Flixe, liking the kindness of

his brown eyes and the gentleness of his New England voice.

'Good. We need these translated and the others are all a bit busy just now.'

'OK. Is there a dictionary I can use if I get stuck?'

'In the bookshelf.' He jerked his head towards a handsome old walnut bureau bookcase to the left of the fireplace.

'Thanks. Oh, where does Gerry work?' Flixe asked as she sat down.

'Upstairs with the boss. We only see her when we're being summoned to the presence, eh, Mike?'

The naval officer grinned, and Flixe was aware of a stinging jealousy of the kind she had not felt for years. It was so sharp that it brought her a frighteningly vivid picture of one Sunday afternoon in her childhood. She must have been about six at the time. Her father had just been posted to somewhere on Salisbury plain and there had been a long celebratory family lunch. Then Major (as he was at the time) Alderbrook retired to his den, telling the two girls that they could bring their sewing and sit there with him. Gerry sat closeted with him until tea time, but Flixe was banished almost at once as too fidgety. She had not thought of the afternoon since and was surprised at the way the memory burned.

Upstairs Suvarov was running through the post with Gerry. When she had handed over the last letter with the various papers he would need in order to answer it, he said:

'Oh, by the way, I've brought your sister in. She'll be working downstairs from now on.'

'Ming? Peter, surely she's not up to that yet. You told me the doctor said she needed plenty of time to recuperate.

'Hang on a minute, Gerry. Ming is still with Diana. I promised that I'd tell you when the doctor says she can come back to London. No, it's Flixe who's here.'

'D'you mean that you've got them all then, all the bastards who did that to Ming?'

'Most of them. And it's got too dangerous to leave Flixe out there any longer. She'll be getting a new flat, too. No, don't ask why. And please don't ask her.'

'I'm not sure that you need to tell me how to behave to my sister,' she said, both offended and annoyed that yet again he should have come between her and Flixe.

'A matter of security, my dear, not inter-family courtesies.'

'Sorry,' she said shortly and went back to her desk to start again on the apparently endless task of collating, rewriting and organising the data from downstairs.

Later, when he asked her to go down to fetch Flixe and Eynsham, Gerry obediently shut her papers in their folders and did as he asked. At the door of the analysts' room she was presented with a picture that made her insides lurch as though she were in a lift that was plummeting out of control down an infinite lift shaft. Flixe was sitting at a desk in the window, with the sun shining directly on and through her fine, pale-gold hair, and Mike was standing behind her leaning one arm on her desk, laughing at her.

Why did Flixe always find it so easy to make friends, Gerry wondered, remembering her first attempts to get on terms with the analysts. Why was Andrew the only person Gerry knew whom Flixe had never even tried to annexe? That, of course, should have been as much of a warning as their mother's constant championship of him.

'Gerry, what's the flap?' came Mike's voice, warm and concerned.

'What? No, there's no flap. Why?'

'You looked absolutely stony; are you all right?'

'Yes; got the sun in my eyes, that's all. Flixe, Suvarov wants you in his office with Antoine. I'll call him if you'll go on up.'

'Come back when you've summoned Tony, won't you, Gerry?' said Mike, smiling at her.

'All right.'

She went over to Eynsham's cubby-hole and told him he was wanted and then walked slowly back to the analysts' room, where Mike was sitting on his own desk, swinging his immaculately polished regulation black shoes.

'Well, do you think my little sister will be any use?' she asked, achieving a laugh with some difficulty.

'She'll add to the gaiety of nations, anyway. We could do with a little feminine charm in this office, couldn't we, Philippe?'

'But of course,' he answered, exaggerating his accent, shrugging his shoulders and pouting in a pantomime of Gallic voluptuousness. Gerry felt a little dizzy. Mike stopped swinging his legs and propelled himself off the desk to stand in front of her. He leaned forward and whispered:

'But she could never take the place of our Mrs Kyrle.'

Gerry felt her face blushing a vivid tomato colour, touched Mike's navy-blue shoulder and said:

'I didn't mean to trail my coat like that, old boy.'

He put one of his hands over hers to hold it on his shoulder for a moment.

'It's only because she's your sister that we let her in, you know,' Mike said in his normal voice.

'What is it about this bloody, endless war that arouses all one's most basic and shaming instincts?' she burst out.

'I don't know,' he said earnestly, 'but if it doesn't stop soon some of my very base instincts are going to get dangerously near the surface.' Then he laughed, and Gerry smiled back at him instinctively. 'Off with you back to your office, Gerry, before we waste all day and get sent to the salt mines.'

Still smiling, she left him, and it was not until she was halfway up the stairs to her office that she began to think about Flixe again, and to wonder whether she might have avoided flirting with Andrew out of loyalty rather than because of any particular antipathy towards him. Gerry wished that she had not let her jealousy lead to such ungenerous thoughts. She cared so much for Flixe that it worried her that she could have been so foul. Seeing Flixe on such pally terms with Mike must have been more upsetting than Gerry had realised.

Hearing her sister's steps at the top of the stairs, Gerry stopped and waited for her. Flixe came down until she stood opposite Gerry. The light was poor on the staircase and for a moment neither could be quite sure what the other was thinking. Then Flixe suddenly leaned forward to fling her arms around Gerry.

'We can work together, can't we, Gerry?' Flixe said into Gerry's shoulder. 'Whatever we both feel about him? And whatever he made us feel about each other?'

Gerry felt as though some inner chamber of her mind had been opened, allowing its cold emptiness to be overtaken by warmth. She leaned against Flixe's strong arms as the chamber was slowly filled.

'Yes, Flixe,' she said at last. 'Let's try.'

A door opened on the floor above them and they pulled away from each other, embarrassed by the emotions they had unleashed. Tony Eynsham walked down the stairs towards them, and Gerry smiled at him.

'I'd better go back to the office now. Shall we have lunch, Flixe?'

'Terrific, Gerry,' she said with assumed heartiness. Then she smiled and went on more calmly. 'Yes, we need to talk.'

In fact, although they were never silent during the hour and a half they spent in a restaurant near the office, neither of them spoke about any of the dangerous emotions she had had about the other. It was as though in that brief moment on the staircase all the past bitterness had been taken away. Their interlocking skins of jealousy might never be forgotten, but they had been peeled away, to reveal two young women, very alike in some ways, utterly different in others, who loved each other. Silently they had acknowledged the hurts they had delivered in the past and the ones they had suffered. It was over.

Gerry walked back to Dover Street that evening feeling tired and somehow scoured, but more peaceful than she could remember. There was no sign of Andrew when she reached the flat and so she lay down on their bed and within five minutes, fully dressed, fell asleep.

When he got in, having dined with some officers of his own regiment on leave in London, he stood looking down at her, wondering what could have happened to lay her out like that. He was ashamed of the scene he had made when she had turned up at the flat the night before with a broken toe and some ridiculously unbelievable story of crises in her office. But ever since he had seen her in St James's Park soon after he got back to London, walking arm in arm with a young naval officer, he had been desperately suspicious of her accounts of what she had

399

been doing. Despite the plausible story she had told him then about the young man's brother's death, Andrew had found it hard to believe her. But he tried.

Wishing that he could find a way to love her that she could accept, wishing passionately that she could love him, he changed into pyjamas and lay down beside her, covering himself with a rug.

He woke, hours later, to find Gerry sliding under the bedclothes, having substituted a nightdress for her coat and skirt.

'Darling,' he murmured, reaching over to kiss her. 'Are you all right?' She turned towards him and, rather to his surprise, kissed him back. It was so long since she had responded physically to him that he reached for her, wanting to make love to her.

Gerry, tired and still feeling churned-up emotionally from her encounter with Flixe, tried to conceal her reluctance, and after a time she conquered it. Later, when he lay quiet beside her, she felt a simple affection for him that was both new and rather comforting.

When she came back into the bedroom after her bath at half-past seven, she took down the blackout and peered out through the grimy windows. Although their basement was as cold as ever, Gerry could see that outside the day was bright and clear, almost breathtaking in its sunny loveliness. As she folded the blackout curtains, she called out spontaneously:

'Andy, it's the most glorious day.'

He was so surprised to hear her speak so naturally – and happily – that he got out of bed, reached for his crutches and manoeuvred his way across the floor to stand behind her. He propped one of the crutches against the wall and put his free arm around her waist, dropping his head on to hers, murmuring:

'Any day when you're happy is glorious to me, my darling.' He knew at once from the stiffening of her muscles beneath the soft crêpe-de-Chine that he had said the wrong thing again, but he held on and tried again: 'I know that was wrong, Gerry, but I don't know why. Can't you tell me?'

His humility and the sensitivity of his question touched her and she tried to match them, forcing herself to lean back against him more softly.

'I think . . .' she began. Then, knowing that if she had gone on to say what she had planned she could have hurt him, she stopped, reminded herself of some of Mike's advice and put her hands on top of Andrew's. 'It's difficult when you put things like that because it sounds as though I am responsible for your pleasure or lack of pleasure,' she said as gently as she could.

'But dearest, you are,' he said, nuzzling her neck and pulling her back even closer to him.

'Don't you see, though? It makes me feel trapped . . .'

She could feel his head lifting away and was sorry that she felt glad at the release.

'No. I don't see. Why should it?' Andrew asked, his voice sounding the familiar note of injured stiffness.

'Please don't be angry,' she said, keeping hold of his hands and edging nearer to what she actually wanted to say. 'It makes me feel that I can't have any feelings of my own, that my pleasure in good weather becomes your property, that I have to share . . .'

'But that's what marriage is about: sharing.' Beginning to get impatient again and wanting to hide it, she removed her hands and pulled away.

'Sometimes I think you wilfully misunderstand what

I'm trying to explain,' she said, keeping her voice as cool as she could. She turned to look at him.

'Gerry, I don't. I'm just trying to understand why you don't want to share your pleasure in something like a beautiful day with me.' The injured tone and whipped-dog expression on his face put the last touches to her anger.

'Oh, stop it. Must we go through this ghastliness every time we talk to each other?' Gerry burst out, her determination to try to make him happy, or at least to stop hurting him, faltering.

'No, of course not. I just want to be allowed to love you. Come to bed again, dearest. Let me.'

Her teeth clenched and she took several deep breaths before saying:

'I don't think that would be a good thing just now, Andrew. And we both have to get to work. Please let me get dressed.'

He stood aside, looking so pathetic in his rumpled pyjamas that she could have hit him. But it was he who spoke:

'Gerry, I try all the time to understand your feelings and help you, but you never seem to think of mine.'

'There's no need to sound injured. I know what your feelings are and I do my best to accommodate them. But I don't share all of them and I can't make myself pretend.' She started to pull on her suspender belt and find her stockings. Then she said quietly: 'And I've never asked you to understand my feelings. I don't want you to understand them; I want you to leave them to me – and let me be free.' On the last word her voice rose despite herself into a kind of wail. She went off into the bathroom with the rest of her clothes and he heard the bolt snap shut.

When she came out again he was half dressed and

buttoning up his shirt. Although he felt at a considerable disadvantage with his bare legs and flapping shirt tails, he said with as much dignity as he could muster.

'I don't know how much more free you can be: you have your job, your own friends. I don't make you tell me where you are or what you're doing all day. You have your own bank account. I don't demand to see your household accounts or cross-examine you about your expenditure. What more could you reasonably ask for?'

She stood in the doorway looking at him. Suddenly she caught the scent of bay rum, just like the mixture her father had always used on his hair, and it put the finishing touch to her defensiveness. Andrew watched her face hardening and felt that his heart would break if she did not smile. She looked just like the sweet, fragilely pretty girl he had fallen in love with and married. He could almost smell the stephanotis she had worn in her soft, fair hair on their wedding day.

'It sounds melodramatic, and selfish, but it's the only way I can explain: when you do this kind of thing I feel like occupied territory. Ask the French — obviously not the starving or the beaten or the deported, but the relatively safe and prosperous, or the ones over here — why they fight and risk so much and die so that their country can be free. Then you might understand.' She left him then and walked miserably to the office. Yet again she had failed him. She tried so hard to be kind, agreeing with something Mike had once said to her — that kindness between human beings was really the only important achievement in life — but time after time she failed.

27

In the next few weeks each of the three surviving Alderbrook sisters fought her own battle: Gerry to find a way to love her husband without sacrificing the identity she had found for herself during the years she had lived without him; Ming to come to terms with the nightmares and memories of France that she could not shake off, and to invent a life for herself that she wanted to live; Flixe to come to terms with the fact that she had killed a man, to forget her past as Suvarov's glamorous whore and Jean-Pierre's treacherous lover, and to learn how to be one of the boys in the analysts' room.

The last was the easiest part of her fight, and she had already had a tiny bit of practice during the Naseby House course in self-defence. By the time Christmas was past she had found a kind of freedom in her new role. Discovering that she was quite as intelligent as any of the men, read French as well as Mike Endlesham even if not as well as Tony Eynsham, and could manage the work she was given without too much difficulty was a revelation, and one that gave her a certain satisfaction. She tried to think as little as possible of Gerry's characteristic position as Suvarov's confidante, working with him in his own room and acting as a kind of immigration control officer to ensure that he was not bothered with unwanted people or information from downstairs.

Flixe did not mind that she hardly saw him, for she still had not quite managed to forgive him for involving Ming in his work or to forgive herself for caring so much for him. Sometimes she thought that he was avoiding her because he found her tiresome; but occasionally she was certain that he understood her state of mind and was trying to give her room to deal with it without distracting or intruding on her.

In the end it was Flixe who precipitated the intrusion. She and Gerry had both been writing to Ming at least once a week. They always shared the letters they got back from her, both finding the woman revealed in the letters quite different from the little sister they thought they knew. One evening in January, Flixe came back from work to find a letter from Ming on her doormat. Reading it with all the admiration to which she was becoming accustomed, Flixe was suddenly determined to make Suvarov let her go to see Ming. However much he wanted to keep them apart, they were sisters and they had the right to talk to each other.

The following morning she got up half an hour earlier than usual and reached the office before Gerry. Having made sure that she would get him to herself, Flixe went into Suvarov's office unannounced. She was brought up short by the sight of him sitting at his desk, his fists balled on either side of the blotter, his lips twisted into a bitter-looking grimace and tears visible on his thin pale cheeks. Flixe stood in the doorway utterly at a loss. Ever since he had first recruited her from the Fanys at the beginning of the real war, she had never known him let his emotions escape from under their very tight restraint.

'Peter, is it anything I can help with?' Flixe asked softly, feeling all the tenderness he had ever aroused in her rushing back.

He looked up as though he had only just become aware of her presence and quickly released his fists, laying his hands elegantly on the blotter.

'No, thank you, Flixe,' he said, making no attempt to wipe away the tearstains. Perhaps, she thought, he does not realise they show.

'Tea, perhaps?' she suggested. 'I could hunt up Madge and get her to make an early brew this morning.'

'Good idea. Do that, will you, Flixe.'

She went out, to reappear in about ten minutes' time, bearing two steaming cups. Handing him one of them, she put hers down on the outer corner of his desk and went to bring her sister's chair up beside it.

'Peter, I don't want to pry, but wouldn't it be better to talk?'

He smiled at that, the irresistibly charming smile of their old innocent friendship in the days before Jean-Pierre, before Ming, before the man in the alley.

'It's all right, Flixe. There's been no tragedy in my life; just my past catching up with me.'

'Your Communist, I mean Russian past?'

'That's right. You've heard about Leningrad I suppose?'

'Yes, I read about it in the paper this morning. Isn't it wonderful? At last they've beaten back the Jerries.' She realised that her note of triumphant delight did not square with what she had seen in his face, and so she went

406

on more quietly: 'But, Peter, why should that make you so sad?'

'Not the lifting of the siege, Flixe. God forbid! But did you know that two million of them have died of starvation since it started? I can't help thinking about it. It was the city where I was born, grew up, lived, loved, fought and nearly died. It's my home. Some of those dead are probably my family, certainly people I knew.'

'I'm so sorry, Peter. I never thought.' Impulsively she leaned across the desk and took his hand. He squeezed hers for a second and smiled at her. Then he let her hand go and drank some of the hot, sweet tea she had brought him.

'Well, as you said, it's all over now, thank God. We'd better get back to work. What are you doing up here, by the way?'

Flixe blushed. After their moment of renewed sympathy, the words she had been planning to use would have been quite out of place. She, too, drank as a way of gaining time to recast her request.

'Come on, my dear, out with it,' he said, laughing. 'What do you want? I've never seen you look so shifty.' Flixe laughed at that.

'Peter, when can I go and see Ming? I don't want to nag you, but it is important to me—' She was about to go on with more persuasions, but he interrupted.

'Don't worry. I was going to suggest it anyway. Diana would love to have you and Gerry for the weekend, and I thought that perhaps you could bring Ming back with you on Sunday.'

'This one coming?'

'Why not? Unless you've got engagements. God knows if Andrew will spare Gerry, but if he is really tiresome, you'll just have to leave her behind.'

407

'No, of course I haven't any engagements,' she said, forgetting the sympathy between them and their recent cheerfulness and wondering how he could have expected her to pick up so soon the life that she had had to drop when she became what he had called 'the siren of Kensington' for him. He looked across the desk at her, noticing her pallor and the marks under her eyes and the way her mouth seemed dragged out of shape by depression or petulance. His own mouth tightened.

'What about that young RAF officer – the knight errant of your dramatic rescue at the warehouse?' Suvarov asked, his voice almost bitter. Flixe looked up surprised at the sound of it.

'Johnny? What about him? I suppose I see a certain amount of him. But there's nothing booked with him for this weekend. And anyway, planning to see Johnny wouldn't be enough to stop me going to get Ming.'

'Sorry, Flixe,' said Suvarov abruptly. 'I can't think what's the matter with me this morning. You'd better get back to work. I'll put the weekend plan to Gerry when she comes in, and you can sort it out with her.'

Wondering what she had done to annoy him, and regretting that their happy moment had disappeared as though it had never happened, Flixe got up, put Gerry's chair back at her desk and walked out of the room. When she got to her own desk, she sat down and stared unseeing out of the window at the park. She did not even see Gerry wave up at her as she crossed the road outside.

So surprised was Gerry to get no response from her sister, whom she could see quite plainly, that she stopped dead, staring upwards. A uniformed park keeper walked over to her to enquire whether anything was the matter. Gerry shook her head and hurried up to her office.

'What's the matter with Flixe?' she asked Suvarov as she hung up her coat and hat.

'Nothing as far as I know,' he answered too casually. 'Why? No, never mind. She was up here earlier, and I passed on to her an invitation from Diana for this weekend. Flixe will go to stay and bring Ming back with her to London on Sunday. Would you like to go too? It would mean going without Andrew: I don't think Diana's up to having strange men in the house. . . . And, in any case, you two both know what Ming was doing . . .' He broke off.

'Yes, yes, I quite understand, Peter,' said Gerry. 'But I'm not sure I can leave him this weekend. Would Diana think me fearfully rude if I said "no"?'

'No, of course not. It's short notice in any case. Is Andrew cutting up rough again about your job?' He hoped that his voice did not betray his surprise. Gerry had appeared to be getting on much better with her husband, and had certainly not mentioned him in the office, as she had always done in the past when she had been having trouble with him.

'No, not exactly. But we had a bit of a do this morning. And if I swan in tonight and say that I'm off for the weekend, it'll look so pointed that he'll think it's deliberate. If you see what I mean.'

'I think so,' he said. 'Don't worry about it. What happened?'

Gerry did not want to tell him and so she simply shrugged and smiled before suggesting that she should go and explain to Flixe that she would have to go to Etchingham alone. Suvarov let Gerry go.

During the rest of the day as she checked the facts in a report of Sandy's on the communications between various Resistance groups in France, Gerry tried but found herself unable to forget what had happened with Andrew that morning, when she had at last found the courage to tell him that they would not be able to have another child and he had cried in her arms.

Flixe went alone to Etchingham, travelling down on a Saturday morning train. The weather was superb: crisp, clear and sunnier than she could remember for months. When her taxi reached the great park at Etchingham, it seemed almost heavenly, despite the leaflessness of the deciduous trees and the lack of all flowers except a few viburnums and camellias. The perfect sweeps of lawn and water, the stark beauty of the naked trees, and the superb darkness of the cedars of Lebanon reflected in the silver-blue of the lake easily made up for the lack of summer's prettiness.

Ming, apparently restored to complete physical health, took her sister on a walk to all her favourite places in the park as soon as lunch was over. Flixe was pleased to see Ming so serene and she was reluctant to test the serenity by asking questions, but in the end she could not resist. They were walking past a tiny ornamental temple on a little knoll above the lake when she said, casually enough:

'Mingie, did you know that Gerry and I were working for Suvarov too?'

Ming, who had been peering into the temple through the cobwebbed windows, turned back to look at Flixe.

'No,' she said, smiling. 'He never told me anything about either of you – or anyone else who worked for him. I suppose, though, that I suspected that Gerry worked for him, because it was she who brought him to see me in the hospital after Annie was killed.'

Flixe was surprised at the ease with which Ming talked of her twin, but before she could ask anything, Ming had managed to open the heavy bronze doors of the temple.

'Look, Flixe, we can get in. Coming?'

'All right. Oh, isn't it pretty!' Flixe said as she followed Ming into the little domed building. It was bitterly cold, but the sunlight picked its way through the cobwebs and lit the blue and gold tessellated floor and the intricate inlaid frieze that ringed the walls below the dome. There was a carved marble bench between two pillars just opposite the double doors Ming had opened.

'Let's sit for a minute, shall we?' she said. Flixe thought that the bench looked hard and uncomfortable, but she felt strongly that this was Ming's day and so she went and sat and disregarded the probability that she would get piles from the coldness of the stone.

'Did you know about me?' asked Ming, curious in her turn.

Flixe shook her blond head, pulling off the fur hat she had been wearing against the cold. 'No; not, that is, until he lost you.'

'Don't sound like that, Flixe,' said Ming, putting a gloved hand on Flixe's arm. 'It was not his fault. It hurt him horribly that you and Gerry were so harsh about it. And honestly, dearest, it wasn't your business to tell him off.'

Flixe, swallowing her astonishment that poor little Ming was taking her to task with such calm determination, said:

'But, Mingie, you're our sister: our younger sister. I think we both felt protective – and furious with him for what he had done.'

'I know. But you don't own me; and you're not

411

responsible for me. And I owe him too much to blame him for what happened.'

'You?' Flixe said, surprised. 'What did he ever do for you to make you owe him?'

Ming turned on the bench to look at her sister, smiling a little sadly.

'His letters – if you like I'll let you read them. They kept me alive, literally, after the bomb. They're the most intelligent, tender, inspiriting things I've ever read; and I re-read them again and again. He has written to me every week since it happened.'

Flixe sat on the marble bench, feeling its coldness seeping up through every part of her, bitterly jealous of her much-loved sister and at the same time desperately grateful to Suvarov for having taken such trouble with her. Flixe had been afraid that he had persuaded Ming to work for him by flirting with her and making her fall in love with him. But never had Flixe imagined that he would have done anything so imaginative – so loving – or become so fundamental a part of Ming's life. Flixe shifted uncomfortably on the hard stone bench.

Ming got up and held out a hand to Flixe, who took it and obediently got up herself, pulling her fur hat back on her head.

'Let's walk,' said Ming. 'It's too cold, really, to sit about.'

'All right,' said Flixe, still trying to find her emotional balance after Ming's revelation. 'Will you tell me what happened in France? Or is it too painful?'

'Not really. Nothing much happened to me, except that I found a friend, I found that although I was frightened I could operate, and a man whose name I still do not know may have been tortured to reveal what he was doing; if he had broken, I should have been taken by the Gestapo. I may owe him everything, and I don't know who he is or what has happened to him.'

Flixe hardly dared to look at Ming as she listened to that extraordinary statement, but when she did she saw that Ming's face, though serious, was calm. The things that Flixe had had to do had seemed hard at the time and she had wasted hours of self-pity and self-accusation on them ever since, but here was Ming, whom she and Gerry had always pitied and worried over, talking with such cool authority about far worse.

'You see,' said Ming in a meditative voice, 'knowing the sorts of things they do to captured agents, I could hardly complain about the little that was done to me, could I?'

'Oh, Mingie,' said Flixe looking across the lake at the dying sun. 'I don't know enough to be able to answer. I should have thought that you could have complained like anything. But if you say not, then you must be right.' Ming suddenly looked at her watch and said in a quite different voice:

'Diana hates it when tea's late; we'd better hurry back.'

'What's she like?' asked Flixe, who had so far only been introduced to Constance Wroughton.

'Terribly beautiful – in an ill sort of way. And full of grace. I suppose before she got ill she must have looked quite like Connie. But you'll see for yourself any minute, Flixe. Do come on.'

Ming led the way into the Dower House through the back door, and the two of them added their muddied gumboots to the rows that stood on the terracotta tiled floor of the passage. Then she urged Flixe up the backstairs to wash quickly and join her in Diana's drawing room.

When they got there, Flixe was surprised to find herself

reluctant to look at Diana Suvarov, as though she were afraid of what she might see. But when she did look, she understood at once why Peter loved his wife so much. Her face bore the marks of pain and illness, but her tired, grey eyes were full of peace and knowledge. Diana must once have been heartstoppingly beautiful with her high forehead and superb bones; now, despite the tragedy of her illness, she would still have compelled attention anywhere. Flixe felt herself strangely moved by the mixture of courage, ruined loveliness and calm in Diana's face.

Flixe was not surprised to see Ming lean over Diana Suvarov's chair and kiss her cheek. When Ming straightened up, she held out a hand to Flixe, smiling at them both.

'Diana, this is my sister, Felicity.' Mrs Suvarov smiled and shook Flixe's hand. Flixe felt its warmth and made herself meet the older woman's eyes.

'Flixe,' said Diana, looking carefully up into the girl's face. 'May I call you that, too?' Flixe, wondering whether it had been Suvarov or Ming who had passed on her nickname, nodded.

'Yes, of course, Mrs Suvarov. It is very good of you to have me to stay.'

'It's a real pleasure for me. I have wanted to know you for a long time now.'

Flixe wondered why, but could not ask.

28

Life in RE(1)R became busier and busier as the spring approached. Everyone knew that the invasion of Europe and the second front were coming at last, although the details continued to be concealed even from the secret departments that were not immediately concerned in the planning.

There were also worrying hints about new super-bombs that the Nazis had been working on for years and had apparently just perfected. In the years since the Blitz Londoners had begun to feel a certain security in their own homes, and at the possibility of a new bombing campaign carried out with unknown but apparently sinisterly effective weapons, those in the know shuddered.

One evening Gerry tried to warn Andrew about what it would be like, but he misread her intentions and thought that she was taunting him again with his old insensitivity to what she had endured at the beginning of the war. On that occasion she protested too much and only made things worse between them, but in spite of such failures, she went on trying to be the kind of wife he wanted, and he, recognising what she was doing, did his best too. They grew slowly happier in each other's company, and for the first time since their marriage he found himself able to let her enjoy her own friends without feeling jealous of any of them.

He had long ago understood that Jeremy Oldridge from the top flat represented no threat at all, and the three of them dined often with Anna Kingsley and Ming, who was now back in London, living in Anna's flat and working peacefully in the postal censorship office. Andrew had never much liked Anna Kingsley, but he recognised that she cared for Gerry, and since Anna's affection could not possibly take anything away from him, he learned not to resent it. And Ming had never aroused in Andrew the mixture of anger and jealousy that Flixe had been able to cause by a word or a look or even by her handwriting on the envelope of a letter to Gerry. Sometimes when Gerry was kept late at work, Andrew would even go up to Anna's flat of his own accord for drinks or chats with the two of them.

Ming, for her part, found him dull and was as surprised as Flixe had always been that Gerry could ever have loved him, but she could recognise unhappiness when she saw it and tried to be kind. So many people had been kind to her – Annette who was still risking everything in France every day, Diana, Anna Kingsley, Peter Suvarov, and her two elder sisters – that she felt she owed kindness to anyone who needed it.

Gradually Andrew began to relax, and as his clutching demands on Gerry grew less urgent, she found it easier and easier to turn to him in affection. By the beginning of June, when the Allied armada had crossed the Channel to fight the Nazis face to face, she even found herself missing

Andrew while he was away on some course outside London, and waiting eagerly for his return.

He reached the flat just as she had finished preparing his favourite rationing dinner of cheese and potato fritters, which she had cooked in the last of the fat.

'Gerry darling, you are kind to make my best supper,' he said as he came up behind her in the little kitchen and kissed her neck. She turned round, smiled and kissed him full on the mouth.

'I'm glad you're pleased. And I thought we might open one of the last of Jeremy's bottles of claret.'

'Why?' Andrew asked, going into the bathroom to dump his briefcase and overcoat. 'Are we celebrating something?'

'Well I thought perhaps we might,' called Gerry, raising her voice and drawing the cork out of the wine bottle. 'What with Overlord, and you and me, and the war looking finally as though it might get won.'

'Oh, Gerry, your language is getting a bit tied up, isn't it? Never mind. It's a good idea. Let's celebrate. D'you want me to lay the table?'

'Please,' she said, loading up a tray for him to carry through to the sitting room. 'How was the course?'

'Pretty dull – at least compared to what's going on in France,' he said, arranging knives and forks on the little round table in the window.

'You must wish that you could have gone with them,' she said gently.

'Yes I do. It seems unfair somehow to have been in at the beginning – a regular – and then have to wait on the sidelines when the amateurs all go over for the victory. A bit like a schoolboy who has worked hard all year and is then dropped from the team just before the match.'

'But there's a long way to go before victory, isn't there?' she asked, knowing the answer perfectly well but happy to let him give her some husbandly information, and a little amused to realise how irritated she would once have been by his characteristic analogy between the war and a cricket match. Since those bad days she had been able to see past the childishness of his way of expressing things, past the inherited and the regimental ways of thinking to the man inside, the man to whom she had first responded, the man she still loved.

'Yes, of course. Jerry isn't going to surrender easily. Still, we're doing all right so far,' said Andrew cheerfully.

'Yes, I suppose so,' she answered and then voiced a quite genuine thought: 'I just wish that we didn't have to bomb French towns and villages – think of all those civilians, who are our allies really, being killed just because they're in the way.'

'What about all the civilians here – and even in places like Cologne?'

'That seems different. At least we and they belonged to belligerent nations,' answered Gerry, absent-mindedly sprinkling salt over her potatoes and cheese.

'Well if the French hadn't given in so easily at the beginning, they would be too. Don't think about it, love. It won't help you get through the time till victory and it won't do them any good.'

She smiled. 'No, you're right there,' she said. 'Eat up while it's hot, Andy.'

When they had finished the wine and washed up the dishes, he took the drying-up cloth out of her hands, hung it on its hook over the sink, and then turned her round to face him.

'Thank you for our celebration,' he said seriously. 'If it

means what I think it means, I'm very happy, darling. Does it?'

'Yes, I think it does. And I'm sorry it took me so long, Andrew.' He kissed her and when he felt her lips move under his, he hugged her tightly in his arms.

'Gerry,' he said, raising his head at last, 'I know that if I hadn't been so thick it would have happened much more quickly.'

'Or I so violent in my growing-up. I just didn't know how to do it any other way. I know that I hurt you often.'

'We both hurt each other. And we'll hurt each other again – it's part of the human condition. But while there are still moments to be had like this, it's worth all the hurt. Come to bed, darling.'

She turned, keeping one arm around his waist, and together they walked into the bedroom.

Two evenings later Flixe was sitting at her desk, trying to ignore her particularly bad period pains so that she could finish the report she was trying to write, when Gerry walked in to say that Suvarov wanted her upstairs. She unfolded her arms from around her stomach and got up from her chair. When she reached his office she said faintly:

'Gerry said that you wanted to see me.'

'Yes,' he agreed, hardly looking at her. 'Sit down, will you?'

She obeyed and waited in silence as he seemed to struggle with his thoughts. It was so unlike him not to be able to say whatever was in his mind that at last she prompted him.

'Is it something you want to tell me, Peter?'

'Yes,' he said again, this time more firmly. But he

paused again before he could go on. 'It's Jean-Pierre. He's dead. You know that they've been hunting him since last autumn? Well, he was cornered last night, and he shot himself.'

Because she did not speak, he had to look up at her. Her delicately-featured face was completely white and her mouth looked like a thin, bitter old woman's.

'Felicity. It was better that way. He must have done it because he knew what he would face.'

'Yes, I know,' she said. 'But think how lonely he must have been.' Suvarov winced, but she was too deep into her own feelings to notice.

'Think of the things he did, my dear.'

'I know, and I've hated him because of Ming. But I loved him once, and I can't forget that completely.' She was gripping her abdomen again.

'I think I ought to get you home, Felicity,' he said just as an extraordinary whistling sound wailed overhead. They both looked at each other in surprise, but before either could speak, there was the sound of an immense explosion somewhere to the north of them.

'Oh, God, not again,' Flixe said, getting up from her chair. 'Haven't we had enough?'

Suvarov swung round on his swivel chair and looked out of the window, but there was nothing to see.

'It didn't sound like an ordinary bomb: it must have been one of the new rocket-powered ones. Still, it was miles away. Come on, I've got a car outside; I'll drive you back to Kensington.'

Flixe shook her head.

'No, but thank you, Peter. I promised to go and have supper with Ming and Anna Kingsley this evening. I'll just walk across the park with Gerry when she's ready to go.'

'Are you sure, Flixe? Shouldn't you go and lie down or something?'

'Why? Just because the man I tricked into caring for me so that we could get information from him has shot himself? Why should that make me need to be driven home?' She hated the bitter, sarcastic sound of her voice, but it came out before she could stop it. Peter Suvarov dropped his face into his hands and did not try to answer. Ashamed of herself, Flixe backed out of his office and went to look for her sister.

Gerry looked at her face and quickly said:

'You look ghastly, Flixe. What did he want? Surely he didn't upset you?'

'What? No, of course not. If I look washed out it's because I've got frightful curse pains,' said Flixe, not wanting to have to talk about Jean-Pierre. She wanted to tell someone about what had happened, but not Gerry.

They walked back across the park and then Gerry insisted on fetching Flixe some A-K tablets from her flat before they went up to see Ming. When she opened the door to them the first thing she said was:

'Gerry, Andrew rang Anna earlier on today to say that he had to go out to some kind of meeting this afternoon and so he's likely to be back late. Anna says, would you like to have dinner with us and Flixe?'

'How gorgeous! Anna's cooking is always such a treat. You're looking well, Mingie,' said Gerry, following her sister in through the front door. 'Flixe, why don't you come and put your feet up in the drawing-room?'

'I'm all right, Gerry. Don't fuss. I'm going to have a word with Anna. She in the kitchen, Ming?'

'Yes, that's right. Did you hear that awful bomb?'

'Yes,' answered Gerry as they went to pour themselves

drinks. 'We'd better have the news on later in case they tell us anything.'

Flixe left them chatting and walked slowly down the passage to the kitchen, where Anna was standing as usual surrounded by delectable scents of food and wine. Even rationing did not seem to reduce her to the state of bored panic with which most women seemed to face the prospect of making adequate meals from the dingy, dreary materials available.

'Well, Flixe?' she said, looking up from her pestle and mortar.

'Not really. Jean-Pierre's dead.'

Anna put down the green-covered pestle, got up from the table and came to stand in front of Flixe. She did not touch her, but there was a look of such sympathy in her face that Flixe's chin puckered like a child's and tears fell from her eyes. Anna said nothing, but she held out a clean drying-up cloth, which Flixe used to mop her face.

'Thanks, Anna. I had to tell someone. Don't pass it on to the girls, will you? They don't know enough about it all.'

'All right. Sit here for a minute. Would you like a drop of cooking brandy?'

Flixe smiled shakily.

'That would be wonderful, Anna.' She accepted a medicine glass half-filled, and sipped.

'I'm not sure that I know enough about it either, Flixe,' Anna said after a quiet interval. 'I know that you haven't seen him since last year. And I can't help thinking that there was more to it all than there seemed to be. Not that I'm trying to force your confidence.'

'I know, Anna,' answered Flixe, putting down the glass. 'And there was more, but nothing I can tell you. Anyway, not yet.'

422

'Oh, this wretched war.'

'That's right, Anna. But it is going to end soon. And some things have come right, haven't they?' said Flixe, trying once more to count her blessings as a way of coping with the hurts.

'Ming, you mean,' said Anna, an extraordinarily sweet smile washing across her face. 'Isn't it wonderful? All that grace and goodness in a child of her age, who's been through so much. And Gerry, too, is better.'

'Yes,' agreed Flixe. 'Somehow, she seems to have found something to love in that husband of hers. I just hope she's not deceiving herself. I'm sorry, Anna, that sounds bitchy.'

'A bit . . . Never mind: if you can't be bitchy about your sister to someone who cares for you both, who could you be bitchy about?' Flixe smiled at Anna, opened her mouth as though she was going to say something and then shut it again quickly. Anna looked carefully at her.

'Flixe, when you want to talk, I'm here. When you can, I mean.'

'Thanks, Anna,' Flixe said, looking hard at the row of copper pans hanging on the wall to her left. Then she looked back at Anna, standing so elegant and self-contained in front of her cooker. 'There is one thing I want to ask, if I may?'

'Ask away, Flixe.'

'How did you do it, Anna? How did you learn to forget and reconstruct yourself so that it didn't hurt any more? How did you learn to live without other people?'

Anna put the wooden spoon down on the table, lowered the heat under her pans and came to sit opposite Flixe, taking one of her hands in a light clasp.

'Flixe,' she said very gently. 'Don't try to do what I did.

It's not worth it. I did it, and it took this war to teach me how mad I'd been.'

'But you were content, Anna,' protested Flixe, trying to remove her hand from under Anna's.

'Yes, that's true,' Anna said, letting Flixe's hand go. 'But dead, really. It is better to let yourself care about people and risk being hurt than that. Oh Lord, something's burning.' Anna got up from the table and whisked a pan off the cooker. 'I must cope with this. Will you tell the others that we can eat in about five minutes?'

Flixe obeyed, bitterly disappointed to have been denied her one possibility of escape. Well, she said to herself as she walked out of the kitchen towards her sisters, Anna learned how to insulate herself; I can do it too. Whatever she says, it must be better than this. When she reached the drawing room her sisters were listening to the news for information about the bomb. When it came it was the usual discreetly inadequate announcement that there had been a bomb leading to 'some loss of life and damage to private property'. Flixe got up and walked over to the wireless and switched it off just as Anna appeared with a tray full of dishes and plates.

They ate the simple, delicious food and drank the wine Anna provided and then Flixe, pleading tiredness, left them to go back to her own flat. She thought no more about the bomb until she met Gerry again the following day in the office. Gerry's face was even paler than usual and before Flixe could ask what the trouble was, Gerry had told her.

'Andrew didn't come home last night. The War Office doesn't know where he is. That meeting was in Harrow.'

'Harrow?' repeated Flixe, stupidly. 'I don't understand.'

'That's where the bomb was.' Flixe sat down in her chair, unable to produce the usual consolatory sentences about being sure Andrew would be all right. She simply looked at Gerry with pity in her eyes.

The confirmation came in the end, of course. Someone at the War Office telephoned Gerry at work to tell her that Andrew had been caught by a collapsing wall on his way back from the meeting, and had been killed instantly with four other people. When Gerry put down the telephone, she could not feel anything at all, and just sat staring at the wall beside Suvarov's desk. After a while her stillness registered with him and he looked up from his work.

'Bad news, Gerry?'

'Yes,' she said, still staring at the wall. 'Andrew's been killed.'

'Oh, my dear, I am sorry,' he said, getting up from his desk. He waited, but she neither spoke nor looked at him. He did not know what to do or say. After a painful moment she said, 'Oh, Peter,' but he was not sure what she wanted from him. Moving slowly, as though with terrible reluctance, he laid one of his hands on her bowed head and very gently stroked her hair, touching her tense hands as he did so. Then he slid his hands down to her face and carefully lifted her head so that he could look at her.

'Gerry, he is dead. It is over. You've done so much to try to make him happy. You have to let yourself off now.'

'How?'

'I don't know. We each have to work that out for ourselves. I can't stay, my dear, but shall I find Flixe for you?'

Gerry shook her head. 'No, but would you tell her for

me? And if Mike's there, could I . . . do you think I could have him for a minute?'

'Yes, of course,' answered Suvarov, covering his surprise.

Gerry cried a little as he shut the door, and when Mike came up a few minutes later, her face looked childishly grubby under its tearstains. That did not worry him at all; it seemed normal. What put the fear of God into him was the expression in her eyes. They looked so dark as to be almost black and there was a brooding intensity in them he had never seen before.

'Gerry, dearest Gerry, Peter told me. I'm so sorry.'

'Oh, Mike,' said Gerry, bursting at last into a storm of real tears. 'I tried so hard. And now he's dead.'

'I know you tried,' said Mike, cradling her body in his arms. 'I know you did, Gerry. But he's free now, darling. Nothing can hurt him any more.' She withdrew a little and he immediately released her.

'You're so good, Mike,' Gerry said, but there was no spark in her voice, no confiding smile or gentle hand. He pushed away all the thoughts he had cherished for the long, weary years of the war and walked across the room to sit on the edge of Suvarov's desk.

'You were very good to me, Gerry, when I was at the bottom of the pit,' he said in an easy, warm voice. 'And you seemed to know about it even then.'

'How did you get out?' The bitter unhappiness in her voice made his teeth ache as though he had just swallowed a mouthful of icy water.

'Don't worry about it now, Gerry,' he said, crossing the room and briefly touching her bright hair. 'Just know that you will get out, that there is a ladder.'

'I just wish that I hadn't spent so long hating him. And

426

making him so unhappy.'

'Go easy on yourself, my dear,' said Mike, trying to ignore all the needs that were shrieking in his brain. 'He made you unhappy, too. Don't make it all worse by trying to hate yourself.'

29

Suvarov insisted that Gerry took some compassionate leave for and after Andrew's funeral, and by the evening of the following Friday she was safely ensconced in the drawing room of Evelyn Adamson's house, pretending to listen to the news with her. All the stone-mullioned windows stood open, for it had been a boiling day and the evening breeze was still warm and spiced with the scents of wallflowers and night-scented stocks, which grew just outside the house. Gerry heard the deep, authoritative voice of the man reading the news, just as she heard the twittering of the last few starlings, the lowing of the neighbouring farmers' cows and all the other sounds of a Cotswold summer's night, but she could not take in the sense of what he said. Her mind was almost entirely occupied with the past thirty-six hours.

She had travelled to Andrew's old home on the same train as his coffin. His parents must have known as well as she that the elaborate oak box with its expensive brass handles and name plate probably contained most of someone else's body – or indeed bits and pieces of many people's – and Gerry could not understand why they did not share her distaste for the whole sinister masquerade of the funeral. But they did not. When she reached the house, mercifully driven in a car different from the hearse that carried the coffin, she found the hall piled high with flowers and wreaths, and Andrew's mother dressed in full, old-fashioned mourning.

Old Mrs Kyrle had taken Gerry's right hand in both of hers and pressed it, gazing into her eyes and murmuring:

'This terrible war. My poor boy.'

Instinctively recoiling from the saccharine voice, Gerry knew that her mother-in-law was sincere, genuinely heart-broken, but she did not know what to say to try to comfort her. The mixture of regrets, powerlessness and distaste brought tears welling into her dark-blue eyes. It was the best thing that could have happened. Mrs Kyrle released Gerry's hand, put an arm around her shoulders and led her into the drawing room, saying:

'Poor child. I understand. But you must try to be brave. I always knew that you loved him; even when he was so troubled I told him that it would all come right. And it did, didn't it, Gerry? It's the only comfort I have that everything was all right again between you two before he was taken. He was so lucky to have had you, Gerry dear.'

Gerry suddenly shivered at the memory of those inaccurate words, and Evelyn, who was sitting beside her with some khaki knitting in her hands, said:

'You must be tired.'

'I am rather. Sorry to be such poor company, Evelyn.'

'Don't be silly. This is not the moment to try to be the life and soul of the party. But if you want to talk I hope you will. I mean, don't try to be a British heroine with an upper lip like board.'

'No, I promise. When I can talk about it without

429

bursting into tears, I'll start.'

'I don't mind tears either. I've poured out a goodly share myself.'

'Where's Bob?' asked Gerry suddenly, as though only just becoming aware that he was not in the house.

'He's over there.'

'France? Oh, Evelyn, I'm so sorry: here I am again, so sunk in my own mind that I didn't . . . Will you forgive me?'

'Of course, and there isn't any need to be so anxious. He's not in the front line. He's just an adviser.'

'Is he working for Peter, too?'

'I imagine so. I've never asked and neither of them has told me.'

'It took me a long time to understand how far Peter's tentacles stretched, how powerful he is, how many lives he . . .' She broke off, the infuriating tears starting into her eyes.

'Try not to hate him, Gerry.'

'Oh I don't hate him, Evelyn. I've no right to.' She laughed unhappily. Evelyn came to the end of the stocking she was knitting and started to cast off.

'Gerry,' she said, apparently concentrating on what she was doing, 'how much did Peter have to do with your difficulties with poor Andrew?'

'Everything,' she said without thinking, and then, 'No, nothing. Oh, Evelyn, I don't know. No. It had started before: that was why I came here the day I first met Peter. Do you remember? Andrew had forbidden me to join the WRNS.'

'What were the grounds? I've forgotten,' she asked, folding up the completed stocking and beginning to cast on the stitches for its pair.

'He didn't say then, but later I discovered. At that juncture regulars like Andrew believed that the women's services were hotbeds of immorality, and that if I joined up I should be coarsened and made unfit to be the wife of a man like him. Besides, he thought my duty was to be at his side and if I couldn't be that because of my health and the state of the Mediterranean then I jolly well shouldn't be at anyone else's side instead. Absurd.' She got up from the sofa and went to stand at one of the open windows, breathing in draughts of the warm, scented air.

'And pathetic,' said Evelyn from behind Gerry. 'He must have been very uncertain of himself to have behaved like that.'

'I don't think so, honestly, Evelyn,' answered Gerry, still addressing the dark garden. 'He just hadn't thought. He'd lived all his adult life in a world where the lives, friends, activities, dress, status and everything else of women depended on the rank of the men to whom they were married. To him women did not really have any existence apart from their husbands . . . decent women, I mean.' She laughed sadly and came back to where Evelyn was sitting. 'You see he knew absolutely nothing about real life. And since I was only just beginning to learn about it myself, I couldn't help. I could only fight him, until I realised what I was doing to him.'

'Did he know about Peter?'

'No. He thought I was having a liaison with someone. Which I wasn't. I mean, whatever you think about Peter and me, it wasn't that. There had been one occasion, but that wasn't . . . It didn't mean anything.' Gerry was embarrassed, but she and Evelyn seemed to have reached a pitch of communication where it was possible to hint at anything, even if not actually to put it all into words.

431

'So it really wasn't Peter's fault then?'

'No. I can't blame him for showing me things – life, myself, misery, great happiness, what it means really to care about people – all sorts of things of which I was as ignorant as Andrew. No, it wasn't his fault.' She sat down, but, restless, picked the completed stocking out of Evelyn's knitting basket and unfolded it as though to examine it for quality. Then she refolded it, stood up, sat down again and at last said: 'But I do hate the way he uses people.'

Evelyn stopped knitting. 'So do I, Gerry,' she said. 'The only consolation I've found for myself – and I pass it on to you for whatever it may be worth – is that he doesn't do it without knowing what he's doing.'

'What do you mean?'

'Well,' said Evelyn carefully. 'He was here one weekend last autumn in a dreadful state about something. He was closeted most of the time with Bob, but he did come for a walk with me. We were standing on the hill looking down at your mother's house when he said: "Eve, did you ever do something you hated because you knew you had to?"'

'And what did you say?' Gerry asked. Hearing a note of genuine interest in the voice that had been dull and heavy with pain all day, Evelyn decided to tell the truth.

'That I had never faced anything like what he was obviously facing then, but that long ago I had had to do something the possible consequences of which might have been dreadful.'

'But they weren't?'

'That's just what he said, in just that tone. No, as it turned out, it was the right thing to have done, but I didn't know that then,' said Evelyn.

'Evelyn, I don't want to pry, but would you tell me about it?' Gerry said, watching Evelyn's long fingers so expertly manipulating the dull-looking wool around the needles.

'It's quite simple – but for your ears only. Bob and I brought Peter out from Russia during the civil war after the revolution, although he was in fact a prisoner of the British army. He was very ill and about to be abandoned to the White Russians in Archangel when your troops left. He would probably have been shot or sent to one of their murderous work camps on the islands in the bay up there; I think they reckoned to get about two years' work out of their prisoners before they died. We took him away and smuggled him back here.'

'I'd heard in the office that he had been a Communist, but no one seems to know that story. When did he stop being one?'

'I don't know exactly. Something happened to Peter in Moscow when he was alone – after the rest of the family had fled up north – and his "conversion" may have happened as early as that. Certainly he started to work for the government here very soon after he recovered his health, and presumably that is an indication of his political allegiance.'

'Have you never asked him?' Gerry said, astonished.

'No. We don't talk about any of it. Almost the only time he has spoken to me seriously about Russia is when he came to tell me that an uncle of his had been shot there.' Evelyn's voice faltered as she spoke, and Gerry hesitated to ask anything else. But after a while Evelyn picked up the thread of her story again.

'I don't know how he had heard about it, but he knew how much I cared for his uncle and so he told me. Nikolai

Alexandrovitch Suvarov, shot for anti-Soviet activity, which turned out to have been trying to organise some kind of food distribution among the peasants who were starving in the villages around his home.'

'When?'

'What? Oh, about five years before the war. A long time ago now. And he would have been quite an old man then.'

'Tell me about him,' said Gerry warmly, trying to help Evelyn as she had always helped everyone who came to her.

'I haven't spoken about him for years, but there aren't many days when he isn't somewhere in my thoughts. He was a wonderful man, Gerry, with all Peter's sensitivity to other people and that tremendous power of attraction, but with more solidity of character and ... well, I suppose the only way of putting it is to say that he was much more careful of people than Peter is. No; that's not really it You could just say that he was kind, much kinder than Peter.'

'Sometimes he can be very kind,' said Gerry in a far gentler voice than she had used before. 'He was wonderful to Ming at the beginning.'

'I know,' said Evelyn, smiling at her, 'and sometimes he looks and sounds so like Nikki that it almost breaks my heart. But there is something hard and twisted in Peter that would have been quite foreign to Nikki.'

'Twisted?' repeated Gerry, looking puzzled. 'Why?'

'I've never been able to discover,' said Evelyn sadly. 'Bob, who really knew him better than anyone else in the old days, thinks that Peter may have suffered some terrible disillusion – betrayal even – in 1918. He was so young then – and frightfully idealistic about the

434

revolution. Something made him leave the relative safety of Moscow for the actual fighting in the civil war. Bob even thinks it's possible that Peter wanted to be killed, perhaps because he couldn't bear what was being done to Russia by the Bolsheviks. I don't know.'

'Could it have had something to do with his brother? They were twins, weren't they?' At Gerry's questions, Evelyn flinched.

'I have sometimes wondered,' she said. 'His brother was a "White", you see; it is just possible that he was caught and perhaps shot. Perhaps Peter even had to order it.' Evelyn covered her eyes for a moment. Then she took her hand away from her face and straightened her shoulders. 'But, as I say, we've never spoken about what happened to him after we all left for Archangel and he stayed behind. Whatever it was, it seems to have damaged something in him, some fundamental kindness, and made him do these awful things to people.'

'What . . . what kind of things?' asked Gerry, wanting to know and yet afraid of what she might hear.

'Oh, what I was trying to warn you about at the beginning. He makes people love him and then when they have broken open their shells for him, trusted him, let him see and know and touch all their loneliness, he forgets about them, and they are left on their own in the cold with all their protection smashed. It's not pretty – or defensible.'

'But why does he do it? He said once to Ming that having lost a twin she would be lonely all her life and I took that to mean that that was what had happened to him. He was so kind to her. Why should he hurt people like that if he knows what it feels like?'

'I don't know, Gerry, but it may be that he is so

frightened of what people could do to him if he trusted them that when he starts to get close to anyone he drops them before they can hurt him. He was trying to stop it, I could see, before the war. Now I see so little of him and he is so hedged about by secrets that it's difficult to tell. The one saving grace is that he has always loved Diana and does not desert her.'

'But he is protected from closeness to her by her illness,' said Gerry, suddenly becoming aware of a thought that must have been simmering for some time.

'They're right about you, Gerry.'

'Who?'

'Bob and Peter. They say that you have great insight.' They sat in silence until Gerry eventually said that she was so tired she wanted to go to bed. Then Evelyn kissed her and they parted.

Gerry left Evelyn's beautiful, peace-drenched house when her fortnight's leave was up, and returned to the office, calmer than when she had left, but so sad that Mike nearly despaired for her. Flixe watched them together, noticing how much Mike cared for Gerry and unhappy for him that Gerry seemed not to have noticed. One afternoon Flixe tried to broach the subject with Mike, who made her promise never to say anything to Gerry.

'All right,' said Flixe, pacifically. 'But it would make her so much happier to know. Won't you tell her?'

'As soon as I can. But there hasn't been the right moment yet,' said Mike, with an expression of such longing in his grey-blue eyes that Flixe could hardly bear it. Envy made her voice sharper than it ought to have been.

'Don't worry about her so much,' Flixe said, patting his arm. 'She's really quite tough underneath it all.'

436

'I do worry,' he said simply and walked out of the room, leaving Flixe staring after him.

When Gerry came back to the office, she hardly seemed to notice the constraint that Flixe felt, just as she did not appear to understand, let alone share, the extravagant delight that the others felt when General de Gaulle took control of Paris on 25 August 1944. The threat of Communist revolution that had seemed so menacing disappeared overnight. As Jean-Pierre had once told Flixe, there had been Communists in every branch of the Resistance, in positions of potential power throughout France, and many of them and their watchers had assumed that victory over the Germans in France would be the signal for them to seize power.

But it did not happen; the threat ceased to exist; and de Gaulle set about re-establishing peace in France. For the first two months something like anarchy reigned. Communications and transport facilities had been devastated by a combination of the German occupation, sabotage, the Allied invasion and the vital efforts of the Resistance in support of that invasion. There was terrible scarcity of food and fuel. But above all there was a legacy of four years' frustrated hate that had been forcing its way to the surface in unofficial trials of collaborators, informers and torturers even before the liberation of France. Uncounted tribunals ended in humiliation, punishment, torture, or execution, and it became horribly clear that not all the victims of such executions were guilty of any crime. In the anarchic state of virtual civil war there were private scores being settled.

One morning in early September, Flixe arrived at the office before any of the other analysts. It had become the usual practice for the first analyst to arrive to pick up anything that had been left overnight in the work tray and do whatever was necessary, passing it on to one of the others only if some special knowledge were needed.

Flixe took off her coat and hat and then went to collect the first bunch of papers in the tray. It consisted of several sheets of flimsy paper covered in close typing, which needed translating from the French. Pinned to one corner was a note from someone in one of the other secret departments saying:

'Wasn't she one of yours?'

Puzzled, Flixe began her translation. It was not until she reached the fourth paragraph that she realised that the subject of the paper was the Annette of whom Ming had told her in such glowing detail at Etchingham. With growing horror, Flixe read that a group of men in Laville had seized on the excuse of the liberation and the hunt for collaborators with the Germans to settle their old scores with Annette. She had been accused of collaboration, black-marketeering, sleeping with Germans and a long string of other offences. After a ludicrously sham trial, held without any kind of pretence of legality, she had been convicted. As Flixe began to translate the account of the various things that had been done to Annette, from rape to having her head shaved, she was tempted to give up and make one of the men take over. Then it seemed to her that in some way she owed it to Ming and Annette to do it herself.

Thirty-five minutes later Sandy arrived and said something to Flixe. Although the sense of his remark did not penetrate her consciousness, she was aware that someone had spoken and she looked up, saying:

'What? Did you want me?'

Sandy took in the whiteness of her cheeks and the way

438

her eyes seemed to have swollen and darkened and shook his head.

'I only said good morning. Are you all right, Felicity?'

'Yes, I suppose so. Did you know what they were doing in France? To women they accuse of collaboration, I mean.'

'Ah. Yes, I've some idea. What have you got there?'

'A report for the chief about one of these unofficial trials.'

'Would you rather I dealt with it?' Sandy asked, not entirely sure what was upsetting her most.

'No. I'd better get on with it. Thanks though.' She bent her head again and re-read the last paragraph she had written to make certain that she had not mistranslated it.

Desperately trying to understand, to be fair, to the men who could have done such unspeakable things to a woman who was in fact innocent of any crime, Flixe wondered what would have happened if England had been occupied, if she had lived in the kind of terror the French Resisters had had to survive for four years, if she had seen her friends carted off to some Gestapo torture chamber. At last, realising that those were not questions that could possibly be answered, she gave up even thinking and turned herself into a kind of translating machine. Then when she had finished she took her translation and the original report over to Sandy.

'Could you do the evaluations, Sandy? It's too much for me. I'm fairly certain the translation's right, but I'm not up to sorting out how likely it is to be accurate — or even weigh up the significance if it is.'

'Fine. Don't you worry, Felicity. There's plenty more in the tray. You can do my next one instead.' He handed her another bunch of flimsies in exchange for her own and

439

made no comment on the material she had given him, for which she was enormously grateful.

But, however hard she tried to concentrate on other work throughout the next few days, the thought of Annette kept returning to her. Even if she had been guilty of consorting with Germans, would that have justified what had been done to her? She might have been coerced into it through fear of physical brutality to herself or – worse – her family. What if she had done it to protect someone else, save someone from death or deportation? And then came the worst thought of all, which became less and less easy to escape, had the things of which Annette had been accused been so very different from what Flixe herself had done? True, she had only slept with Jean-Pierre at Suvarov's request. But it had not been any good. Gerry's reaction, she was certain, would have been an unpleasant experience, and it had brought in its train black-market food, nylon stockings, orchids, unjustifiable luxury.

At times she knew that she was being irrational and longed to be able to talk to someone about it. She even thought of trying to explain herself to Gerry, but that wouldn't have been any good. Gerry's reaction, she was certain, would have been an immediate and generous protest that there could be no connection between what her sister had done and what had happened in France. And it would not have been fair to burden Gerry with anything else while she was battling with her feelings about Andrew.

Then there came an idea, which made Flixe feel cold. Annette, whom she felt that she almost knew, must have been precisely the age of Anna Kingsley's daughter, who had been given for adoption in France. With the memory of Ming's description of Annette's tall thin figure and dark hair, with the similarity of Christian names, with Annette's apparent predilection for the English and alienation from the people of Laville, Flixe became more and more convinced. She had already been tempted to tell Ming about Annette's ordeal, but stopped herself because there was nothing Ming could do to take it away and the knowledge of it could only make her miserable. Now she was still more tempted to talk to Anna Kingsley. But obviously she could not do that either. The more she thought about it all, the more worried and unhappy she became.

In the end Mike Endlesham took a hand and told Peter Suvarov that there was something seriously wrong with Felicity Alderbrook.

'She looks like a ghost. Anyone would think it was she who had been widowed. She's never shown any kind of feeling like it. I think she needs help.' Suvarov looked at his young subordinate, vaguely wondering what had happened to change him from the neurotic, ill-looking fanatic of the early days of RE(1)R into someone who could worry so much about the condition of one of his colleagues.

'Ah, Mike, thanks for alerting me,' he said, smiling. 'I'd better see her this evening in case it's anything to do with her work. Look, I'll send Gerry home at five-thirty sharp. Will you tell Flixe I want to see her at quarter to six?'

'OK, Peter,' said Mike, turning to go. 'But look, I've got a better idea. Why don't I take Gerry out somewhere? She'll only get suspicious if you make her leave early and I don't think she should have anything extra to worry about just now.'

Suvarov looked thoughtfully at Mike for a moment, his long dark eyes narrowing slightly. Mike began to blush.

'All right, Mike. Off you go now. But be a little careful of her, won't you? I don't imagine that she's ready . . .' He broke off. To his surprise, Mike grinned.

'Don't worry. I know what I'm doing – for once.'

30

As they had agreed, Mike climbed the stairs to the third floor at precisely twenty-five minutes past five. He put his tousled head round the door and said:

'I say, Gerry, I've finished that blessed report at last. Will you come and celebrate?'

She looked round, first at Mike and then, more doubtfully, at Suvarov, before saying:

'Oh, Mike, I'd love to, but it's a bit early. I can't really go quite yet. Could you bear to wait for your celebration, for an hour or so?'

Suvarov, who had clasped both hands behind his neck and was performing some complicated-looking manoeuvre to ease his back and neck muscles, said:

'Gerry, why not go? There's nothing on your desk that couldn't actually wait until tomorrow morning, and if your conscience won't let you skive for an hour or so, you could always come in early then.'

'Well, all right. Thanks, Peter. Mike, I'll be with you in a minute.'

'Good girl. I'll take your hat and coat and wait for you down in the hall.'

He gave her no time to protest, but seized her outdoor clothes from the curly rack to the left of the door and almost pranced out of the room. His cheerfulness made her feel a bit tired and she wondered whether it would not be more peaceful to stay at her desk. But she could not disappoint Mike; he had been angelic to her when she had been having such trouble being kind to Andrew and, during the last few months since Andrew's death, Mike had always been there when she needed to talk to someone. If he wanted a celebration now, it was the least she could do to let him have one. She said good night to Suvarov and followed Mike down the staircase, missing her sister by a bare ten minutes.

He took Gerry across the park to the Ritz. When they were settled in an inconspicuous corner table and he had ordered their drinks, Gerry said with almost her old mischievous smile:

'Champagne cocktails! Well, this certainly is a celebration.'

'Only partly, Gerry.'

Suddenly very still, she sat looking down at her hands and Andrew's ring on her left hand.

'Gerry, please look at me,' he said in a voice she barely recognised. There was an indescribable expression on his familiar face, but when he smiled, Gerry found her lips curving in return.

'That's my girl,' he said, taking her left hand in his. 'Gerry, I haven't made a catastrophic mistake, have I? I've begun to be nearly certain that you felt it a bit too.'

She was just opening her lips to answer him when the waiter came back with the glasses. They waited until he had arranged them and gone, and then Gerry took a deep breath.

'Mike . . .' At almost the same instant, he said:

'I'm not wrong, am I?'

'No, you're not wrong, my dear.'

At that he picked up her hand and held it against his cheek.

'Thank God, darling.'

'But, Mike. It's too soon . . .'

'I know. I promise I won't ask anything you don't want to have to say yet, but I had to be sure. I've . . . Oh, Gerry, I've waited such a long time.'

'Have you, Mike?' she asked, a blush warming up her cheeks again and a much more natural smile curling her mouth.

'Yes, what is it, nearly three and a half years, I suppose.'

'And all that time I was being such a clot. I'm so sorry. I just didn't see it until recently.'

'I know.' There was such a wealth of warm, tolerant love in his voice that she found some courage.

'There's something else you ought to know, though,' she said in a determined voice, taking her hand out of his.

'No, darling, I don't think so.'

'Yes, Mike. I want to tell you. It's about Suvarov. You know, of course, that I spent months and months embroiled in a stupid girlish fantasy about him . . .' She stopped, released her hand from his. Then she took a deep breath and said quite steadily: 'But it wasn't all fantasy.'

'I know that, Gerry. Even Sandy could see that the chief was head over heels about you. For ages it made me despair. What had I got to offer compared to a dashing, beautiful Russian hero like that?'

She laughed a little and then murmured, 'I'm not sure it

would be good for you if I told you how much.' Then she sobered again, took a sip of the champagne cocktail and went on: 'But that wasn't what I meant, even if it's true, and I'm not sure that it is. Once, early in '41, he and I . . .'

She could not say more because Mike had laid one of his hands across her lips.

'You don't need to tell me anything, Gerry. I'm not about to demand retrospective fidelity from you. How could I? I just want to be able to say how much I care about you and to know that you care a bit, too. That's all . . . for now anyway.'

All the tension suddenly went out of her body and he watched her lean against the hard gilt chairback completely relaxed. He picked up his glass.

'To my best beloved.' She raised hers and echoed his Kiplingesque toast, feeling as though she were a mariner who alone had come through tempests, calms, mutinies, sickness and terror, and was at last in sight of a safe landfall.

They talked then, voraciously, telling each other all kinds of things and asking question after question, secure for the moment in their unassailable trust in each other. He ordered more champagne cocktails and then took her to the grill for dinner, before escorting her across Piccadilly to her flat.

At the top of the basement steps he took her face between his hands, studied it for a long time in the starlight and then kissed her. As he raised his head, he said breathlessly:

'Oh, I have waited for that.' Gerry smiled up at him, but her eyes were worried.

'But, Mikey, I couldn't . . . I mean I must wait a bit more before . . . I'm sorry.'

'Don't be,' he said, leaning forward to kiss her cheek. 'I don't mind waiting now that I know. Good night, beloved.'

'Good night.'

He waited while she climbed down the precipitous stairs and unlocked her door and then he left, to walk through London, feeling weightless in his extreme elation and never even sparing a thought for anyone or anything except Gerry and what he felt for her.

Meanwhile, Flixe was sitting in front of her chief, waiting for him to explain why he had summoned her. When at last he spoke, he surprised her.

'I feel very guilty, Flixe,' he said.

'But why?' asked Flixe, smiling a little for the first time in days.

'Because it took Mike Endlesham to tell me what I ought to have seen from one look at your face. My dear, what's happened to you?'

She put an elbow on his desk, and rested her head in her hands. Then, not looking up, she started to try to tell him.

'It's not anything that's happened to me. I'm just in a turmoil. That's not helpful, I know.'

'Flixe, look at me,' he said. She obeyed, and as she looked at his face she remembered how easy it had once been to talk to him about everything.

'Peter,' she began, taking a deep breath. 'Did Sandy send up that report about the woman in Laville?'

'Yes. Is that it? I'm not surprised it upset you; it's a horrible story, but it is one that's being repeated all over France, I gather. It's not just because she worked for us.' Flixe shook her head.

'That's not the aspect that was worrying me. But she is the woman who took care of Ming, isn't she? Don't be angry with Ming for telling me. It was when I went to Etchingham.'

'I'm not angry,' he said. 'Yes, it is she. And we're doing our best to get her over here. It's been tricky, but I can tell you now that she will be in London in a month or so.' He stared carefully at Flixe and then said: 'I can't help feeling that there's more, though, Flixe. Can't you tell me?'

'There is a bit,' she said carefully. 'But the question I wanted to ask you is, could she be the daughter of Anna Kingsley's that you told me about?'

'No, dearest Flixe,' he said very gently, almost as though he had understood the other things that she could not say. 'That's one thing you don't have to worry about. Miss Kingsley's child has been safe in Switzerland for eighteen months or so.'

'She got her out then?'

'Yes. And it was when we found out about the Swiss escape that we understood what all the letters had been about and were able to clear her off the list of suspects.'

'Thank God,' said Flixe and burst into tears. He let her cry for a couple of minutes and then offered her his handkerchief. When she was wiping the tears out of her eyes, he swivelled his chair round so that he was looking out of the window and she could collect herself in some privacy.

'There is one thing I'd like to say to you, Flixe,' he said.

'Yes?'

'Any parallels you may have been drawing between what you did for us here and what certain Frenchwomen are being punished for are illusory. The cases are quite different, and if you are drawing any such parallel, I want you to stop at once.'

It took Flixe a moment to find her voice, for she had forgotten that he had always known everything she was thinking. Then, folding up his wet handkerchief and pushing it up the sleeve of her jersey, she said:

'Easier said than done.'

'I know. But you must try. Because there is no comparison. Will you promise to try?'

'All right, Peter,' she said, her voice threatening to break on his name. He swung his chair back and, looking at her once again, said:

'Good.'

She worked at it, throughout the autumn and winter, and eventually found a certain easing of her mind. But even so, she felt divided from both her sisters by the difference in what they had had to do and what she herself had done for the war. In sad envy she watched Gerry and Mike Endlesham finding more and more delight in one another's company every week, and Ming apparently letting Johnny Blenkarne fall in love with her. He could usually be found in Anna Kingsley's flat in the evenings, dining with them or collecting Ming to take her out dancing.

Flixe herself could not have loved either man, and she was genuinely pleased for her sisters, but still she felt cut off from what she saw as their innocence. It was an innocence that allowed each of them to confide endlessly in her, unaware of most of the things she was thinking. Gerry was bothered by the disloyalty of falling in love so soon after her husband had been killed and Flixe tried to keep the asperity out of her voice when she put her view that since Andrew was dead it would not matter to him one way or the other.

Gerry, who was sitting on the floor in Flixe's flat in front of the hissing gas fire, twisting her rings round and round on her finger, looked pleased.

'I suppose you're right. And I can't run my life for ever wondering whether I'm upsetting his mother.'

'No, of course not,' said Flixe, pouring a cup of tea for each of them.

'D'you think I'm doing the right thing?' asked Gerry, accepting a cup.

'In being in love with Mike Endlesham?'

'No,' said Gerry, smiling into the red and blue flames of the small fire. 'I couldn't have helped that. But in saying I'll marry him?'

Flixe sat down on the floor beside her sister and hugged her, saying, 'Gerry, I didn't know it had come to that; it's wonderful news. You'll do so much better with Mike.'

'Yes, I think so,' she answered happily. 'But, tell me, Flixe. Why do you think so?'

Flixe, recognising that Gerry longed to talk and hear about Mike's qualities, did her best.

'Because he's much more intelligent than Andrew was; because he loves you for what and who you are; not as material to be shaped to fit his mould of the ideal wife; because you have chosen him yourself, without reference to our parents; because he sees further than Andrew ever could in a million years.'

'Yes,' said Gerry, sighing. Then she laughed. 'Oh, Flixie, I know. I'm being childish. But it's extraordinary to feel so happy after everything that's happened. All those mistakes and unnecessary agonising. And all the time there was Mike and I simply didn't see him.'

'How did you learn to see?' asked Flixe, still trying generously to give Gerry her opportunity to talk.

'It just sort of happened without my noticing. I mean, one day I was down in the analysts' room collecting some stuff and he just looked up from his work and grinned at me and then I realised what I'd actually been feeling for ages. And luckily he turned out to have been feeling it too.'

'I'm so glad,' said Flixe. Then she added in a careful tone: 'What does Suvarov say?'

'Nothing,' answered Gerry looking startled. 'I didn't know that he knew anything about it.' At that piece of naïvety, Flixe allowed herself to laugh.

'Oh, Gerry, you are a clot. Not only do you and Mike have beacons flaming in your eyes that would tell anyone what was happening to you, but Suvarov could see through six brick walls to what was being hidden. Anyway, he and Mike seemed to be talking about it downstairs when I left the office this evening. Never mind; he'll talk to you about it in the end.' Flixe could feel the ice in her mind hardening at the prospect. Ever since Andrew's death she had tried not to let herself think that with Gerry free at last, Suvarov might allow himself to love her. Now with the added spur of Mike's obvious devotion, perhaps Suvarov might not be able to resist. Flixe took a deep breath.

'Now,' she said decisively, 'shall I take you out to dinner to celebrate?'

'All right, Flixie. Thank you.'

The following morning, Gerry waited in some anxiety for the arrival of their chief. He came about ten minutes after she had sat down at her desk. Standing in the doorway, holding a tiny bunch of red roses, he smiled.

'Congratulations, Gerry,' he said. She stood up and

waited while he brought the flowers to her. Then he kissed her hand, and when she smiled her thanks, he patted her cheek.

'Gerry, I'm so happy for you and young Mike. It's the best thing I've heard for months.'

'You know that nothing's to be announced till next June.'

'Yes, Mike said. And perhaps this bloody war will be over by then.'

'Wouldn't that be wonderful? But d'you think it's possible?'

'Possible, yes. Certainly in Europe. I was bothered after the Arnhem fiasco, but things are looking better now. God knows what's happening in the East, though,' said Suvarov, taking off his overcoat and walking across to his desk.

'It's been almost like two completely separate wars, hasn't it?'

Gerry contributed, wondering why he had so quickly changed the subject. Ashamed though she might be to admit it, she was infinitely more interested in Mike and herself than in the war. 'One knows almost nothing of what's happening there – except those ghastly stories about the railway and the camps.'

'I know. One way and another I'd say this really has been what they call a just war.' Suvarov unlocked the middle drawer of his desk and started to read his confidential papers.

'Monte Cassino?' Gerry asked, aware that he wanted to work, but herself too emotional to settle down so soon. 'Saturation bombing of civilian targets?'

Peter looked across at her, half-irritated, half-amused that his anxious, intelligent assistant should be behaving so like a seventeen-year-old. Gerry sat and blushed in silence. After a while he found an answer of a sort.

'There have been mistakes and cruelties on this side, hideous ones. But I still think that the balance is with us this time.'

Gerry was to think of that conversation often as news came back from the Allies' slow and bloody advance into the heart of the Nazis' world, especially in the spring when the first reports appeared after the liberation of Hitler's concentration camps. Then moral scruples about what the Allies had done to ensure victory came to seem irrelevant in the horror that was revealed.

Ming came down to Gerry's basement flat on the evening after the first report had appeared in *The Times* and asked if she could have a drink. Gerry had had a heavy day and her head was aching so badly that she longed for bed, but Ming so rarely asked for anything that Gerry could not refuse such a simple request.

'Of course, Mingie. Come in. I'm afraid I've only got gin and It. Is that all right?'

'Yes, of course. It's not actually the drink I'm after. . . .But if you'd rather have wine yourself, there's masses of Anna's upstairs. She's out this evening, but I know she wouldn't mind if we had some. Shall I get it?'

'Only if you want it. Gin and It's fine for me. Sit down, Ming, and tell me what's bothering you.'

Her sister looked rather surprised and then shook her head.

'Nothing special. I've just been reading that article about the camp. D'you think it's true?' Gerry sat down on the lumpy sofa, smoothing Anna's old-rose silk shawl behind her, not at all sure what to say. The camps were a subject about which she could hardly bear to think, let alone talk. At last, Ming sat back in the wing chair.

'I don't see how it couldn't be, do you?' said Gerry. 'I mean we knew that there were camps, and why should anyone make up something so . . . Oh, Ming, all the words one could use seem so debased. I mean, we all talk about an unspeakable meal, or a terrible book. What can one say about something like Belsen?'

'I know. It's not going to be possible ever to see the world – or people, or oneself – in the same way again. It makes what's happened to all of us seem so . . . minute in comparison.'

Gerry was silent for some time, wanting to encourage Ming to talk out all the things that she must have been thinking ever since her twin had been killed, but not at all sure how to prompt her, or whether in such a context she should even try. At last she said:

'Mingie, what has happened to you since your fifteenth birthday is not "minute", however many much worse things have happened to other people.'

'Perhaps not. But it makes me ashamed of the things I've been thinking.'

'Such as?' asked Gerry, but Ming shook her head, unable to say that ever since she had been rescued from the warehouse, she had felt desperately, achingly guilty that she was safe and well and surrounded by people who loved her whenever she thought of Annette and the unknown man who had brought the message to her in France. Now there were all these discoveries of inhuman torture on an immense scale, and she felt even worse: self-centred and self-indulgent.

Every day as she sat at her dull work in the postal censorship office, Ming wished that she could find out

454

what had happened to Annette and the nameless Englishman, but Peter had told her nothing and there was no one else she could ask. Johnny, sweetly protective of her though he was, could know nothing and she had found herself unable to talk to him about either of them.

'Ming, have you had any food today?' asked Gerry suddenly. Ming shook her head again. 'Then you must have some now. I'm afraid it'll be wretched powdered scrambled egg, unless you'd like to go out.'

'Oh, no, Gerry. Thank you. But I couldn't ... Not today.'

'All right, I'll do some eggs. Put on the fire if you're cold – if there's any gas that is. I won't be long.'

She went into the tiny kitchen and started laboriously stirring the two tablespoons of greyish egg powder into the requisite four tablespoonfuls of water, pressing the lumps against the side of the bowl as the magazines said you should. She was just melting the last of her margarine ration into a saucepan when she heard a knock at the door.

'Ming, could you go? If I leave it now it'll be ruined and there's nothing else.'

'Of course....Hello, Mike. Gerry's in the kitchen making scrambled egg. Come in.'

'Not if I'm disturbing you,' called Mike.

'Not at all, Mike. Come on in and let Ming give you a drink.'

'Thank you. By the way I've brought some sardines. Would they help the egg?'

'Wonderful!' exclaimed Gerry leaning around the doorway, with the pan in her hands. 'Will you open them while I divide this nauseating-looking mess?'

As they sat round the cherrywood table eating their

depressing food, it struck Gerry that Mike's ability to get on with her sisters was remarkable. He had somehow fitted himself into their lives without trying to smash through the walls and tunnels of character that connected and divided them. It was as though he felt no need to establish a place for himself, and so their lives had been able to absorb him and give him a space in their very centre. They existed, and he existed, and all of them could allow the others just to be.

In her sudden delight at the thought she laughed. The other two, who had been talking about bathing off the south coast again when the war was over, looked up.

'What's so funny?' asked Ming, and her voice sounded infinitely lighter and more relaxed than when she and Gerry had been talking earlier.

'Oh, I was just thinking of something. Wouldn't it be nice if Flixe were here too?'

'Lovely,' agreed Mike. 'But there'll be lots of times when peace comes when we can be together, eh, Ming?'

'Yes . . . yes I suppose there will,' she answered with a curious kind of significance, which Gerry could not altogether understand. 'I say, Gerry, when are you going to take Mike home? Mother ought to meet him soon.'

'I know. It is partly that we're so busy . . .'

'Now, come on, Gerry. Why not take him soon? It'll be so much easier while she's happy with the evacuees. When the war's over and Father comes home again, don't you think it might all revert?'

Remembering the timidity of Ming's dealings with their mother in the summer holidays after France had fallen, and the way she had often tried to temper her elder sisters' complaints about their parents, Gerry was amazed, both at Ming's perception and the freedom with which she had expressed it. Suppressing her shock, she smiled.

'I think you're probably right, Mingie. It's just that Mother liked Andrew so much . . . It was the only time she approved of me, when he and I got engaged I mean . . .'

'You sound almost as though you're frightened of her,' said Mike. 'Surely not?'

'Not precisely. Though I see now that I was for years and the rage was just hiding it from me. No, it's . . .' She stopped, looked at him, blushed a little and then took his hand in both of hers. 'It's just that this is the best thing that's ever happened to me and I don't want her spoiling it.'

He leaned forward to kiss her. Then he said: 'Nothing could, Gerry.' Then, with a sensitivity that made Gerry's heart rejoice, he turned to her sister to say teasingly: 'I apologise for that exhibition of appalling sentimentality, Ming.'

'Don't,' she said, smiling at him in delight. 'It's lovely to see Gerry so happy again.'

31

During the next week or so it became very clear that the Nazis must surrender soon. They had been defeated on all fronts. Monty had crossed the Rhine on 23 March, and the Russians were racing for Berlin. Then at the end of April, when they had encircled the city, came the news of Hitler's suicide in the bunker, followed on 7 May by the formal surrender of the German High Command.

The first news of the surrender was announced on German radio and picked up by the BBC and broadcast at lunchtime. The only person at RE(1)R who was listening in at the time was Jenkins, the janitor. Madge, who would have been there at any other time, was brewing up a huge pot of thick brown tea for the analysts who had had to work through lunch. She had just turned on the tap of the urn and was watching the steaming, boiling water gush down on to the tea leaves when Jenkins burst into the cubby-hole, yelling:

'We've done it! We've done it! They've just given in.'

Madge started at his first shout and rounded on him for making her splash boiling water on her hand. She was still grumbling as he tried to organise his triumphant mind enough to explain. At last he said:

'Madge, my only love, we have won the war. The fighting is over. The Jerries have surrendered.'

'Well, I never,' she answered. 'At last. You'd have thought they could have done it all on the same day, wouldn't you? I mean. Think of that there general giving in to Monty. I thought it was all over then.' She heaved the heavy, two-handled brown enamel pot up on to the stained shelf where she kept the cups and saucers and then turned back to Jenkins. 'You better run up to tell the boys. They don't have no wireless up there. They oughter know.'

'Right. And then we'll celebrate, eh, Madge?'

'Get along with you,' she said to him, wiggling her shoulders coyly and ducking her chin into her chest.

He patted her ample backside and hurried off up the stairs, two and three at a time. At the top he met Lieutenant Endlesham and poured out his news in breathless excitement. Mike gave Jenkins's shoulder a tremendous buffet.

'Great news, old boy! Thanks for coming up with it.'

'Aren't you going to tell the others, sir?'

'Of course. Oh, you want to see the excitement, do you? Well, you've earned it for bringing the news. OK. Come on.' He strode to the door of the analysts' room and flung it back. 'Listen to Jenkins, chaps – and chappess – he's a bit of news for you. I'm off to break it to the chief.'

'And the lovely Mrs Kyrle, no doubt,' called Eynsham caustically. But Mike only laughed, said, 'You just wait for it, Tony,' and waltzed out again. He had sobered up by the time he reached Suvarov's office and he gave the announcement quite quietly. But his face was alight with pleasure and affection as he turned to Gerry, to say:

'So now we can get on with our lives.' She stretched out her left hand instinctively and he gripped it. Together they faced Suvarov, who was sitting in his swivel chair with his head thrown back and his hands loosely relaxed on the blotter. After a minute or so he straightened his head and smiled, not the smile of the man who had once made love to Gerry in that very room, not even the comforting smile of the exhausted and tense chief of RE(1)R; it was the smile of a small boy who has just pulled off some splendid coup in a conker fight or marble match. The other two grinned back.

'Well, thank God for that. Not that it's much surprise after the Luneberg surrender, but even so . . .'

'Oh, Peter,' said Gerry, 'after six years nearly . . .'

'Of course the problems in Europe will be only just starting now. And the Japanese haven't surrendered yet.'

'No, but they will, surely, as soon as they've found a face-saving way to do it.'

'What problems, Peter?' asked Gerry, rather upset and not thinking at all. He laughed.

'I seem to remember explaining to you once exactly how many wars were being fought out in Europe alone. Only the one against National Socialism is over today. The rest will carry on, in less obvious ways perhaps, but carry on they will.' He caught himself up as he saw the stricken look in her eyes and the tension with which she clutched Mike's hand. Peter's face softened and he smiled again. 'But your life won't be affected, Gerry. You and Mike are all set to walk hand in hand into the sunset. You two will be all right.'

The red telephone on his desk shrilled before either of them could answer. He listened, answered shortly and then replaced the receiver.

'Well, I'm summoned. See you both later.'

He went out, leaving them to look at each other. In

spite of his chief's depressing forecast, Mike could not keep down the exultation that was beating through his mind. Without speaking, he pulled Gerry out of her chair and put both arms around her in an enormous hug. She let her head go down on his shoulder and together they stood in a shaft of dusty sunlight from the window over Suvarov's desk.

Before they left that evening, they invited Flixe to join them in a celebration dinner at the Ritz with Anna Kingsley and Ming and Johnny, but Flixe shook her head.

'No. Thank you, though. I think this is one evening you two ought to have to yourselves. Have fun.' She watched them go, wishing she had someone to celebrate with, thinking for the first time in weeks of Jean-Pierre, wondering whether Suvarov would come back to the office after his meeting, and trying to feel the kind of pleasure at victory she ought to feel. A hand came down on her shoulder and she looked up quickly.

'Antoine! What can I do for you?'

'Sandy and I quite see why you didn't want to be gooseberry to the two young lovers, but we wondered if you'd come and dine with us two old men?'

There was the faintest moment of hesitation and Sandy filled it by saying:

'We tried to get the chief too, but he thought he'd have to dine with our original master at the club.'

Flixe smiled gratefully and accepted their invitation. They took her to a tiny restaurant in Soho, where they fed her on various delicacies of unknown origin but delectable taste, and insisted on standing her champagne. Flixe enjoyed herself and tried to show them her enjoyment, but there were other feelings mixed in with

461

her pleasure: sadness that Peter was not with them; humiliation that they had known that she had been hoping to spend the evening with them; envy of Gerry, not for Mike himself but for being settled; and above all a horrible feeling that with her war now over most of her character and talents were redundant.

That feeling persisted as the two middle-aged analysts escorted her home through streets that were packed with laughing, singing, dancing, cheering people, past houses decked with Union Jacks and occasionally the red hammer-and-sickle flag of the Soviet Union. And she woke with it at the front of her mind the following morning.

Looking out of the window at about half-past seven she was even further disheartened to see that a thin cold rain was dripping down from a grey and miserable sky. She turned over in bed and buried her face in the pillow, trying to force herself back to sleep. Today was a national holiday; even if she could not feel flooded with rejoicing, she might at least get a decent night's sleep, she thought crossly.

An hour later, she gave up the struggle and got out of bed. Self-pity was the most useless waste of energy, she told herself. The war was over; she was only twenty-six years old; there must be a million things she would be able to do with her life. Anna Kingsley would help her to learn how to put her past behind her and forget Peter Suvarov. Gerry and Ming, even if they did both marry their young men, were still her sisters and would be a part of her life.

None of her bracing thoughts helped at all. Wrapping herself in her old grey school dressing gown, she pushed her untidy hair behind her ears and went to the kitchen to make a cup of coffee. Then she took it back to bed and thought about pretending to be ill. At least that would stop her having to go out and join the revellers in the world outside her little flat.

At nine-fifteen the telephone rang and she leaned across the empty half of the double bed to pick up the receiver. Her elder sister's voice came vibrantly down the wire.

'At last. I've been trying to get through for forty minutes. Flixie, we're all going to St Paul's. Will you come too?'

'St Paul's, why? Who?' said Flixe, unable to cope with such evident exuberance.

'It seems such a symbol, having survived I mean. And Mike wants to go to one of the thanksgiving services they're having. Ming's coming too, and Anna, and it would be lovely if you did. . . .'

'Oh, Gerry, I'm sorry. I'm still in bed. I'd hold you all up so much. And I've . . . I'm not at my best just now. You go. We could meet later.'

'All right, ducky. Have fun. 'Bye.'

'Goodbye,' answered Flixe and put the receiver back, glad that they were taking Ming. Then she thought she had better get dressed.

Just as she was pulling up her utterly unglamorous but practical lisle stockings, the door bell rang. Thanking heaven that at least she was not still in her dressing gown, Flixe went to open it.

In the doorway stood Suvarov, dressed in an old dark-grey civilian suit. He looked tired, and his skin had a yellow tinge to it, but he smiled as he said:

'May I come in, Flixe?'

'Of course,' she said, stepping backwards and wishing to goodness she had washed her hair, or at least brushed it. 'I'm sorry I'm such a mess.' He shook his head, as though to contradict her, and followed her into the small sitting room.

'Would you like coffee, or sherry or something?'

'Not just yet, Flixe. I want to talk to you.'

'Oh?' she said inadequately.

'Yes,' he went on more firmly. 'I've wanted to wait until I could face you as I am – not as your senior officer, and all that.'

This time she could not even manage to say oh, and just sat down on the sofa. He came and sat at the other end of it.

'Flixe, I went down to Etchingham a few weeks ago to see Diana.'

'Yes, I know.'

'I went to ask her . . . to explain to her that I had fallen in love, and to ask her whether I could tell you.'

'Peter,' said Flixe, at last finding her voice. 'That wasn't fair. She's so ill.'

'I know, Flixe. But she said to me years ago that I wasn't her prisoner, that she wanted me to be free to love her and that to do so meant that I had to be free of her. I'm not certain if you'll understand this, but I want to tell you. I do love her; I always shall. I admire her and care for her and enjoy her company. But the illness – and the fact that she is far happier living at Etchingham with Connie than she ever could be with me and my clumsier care – means that we cannot have a marriage. And she told me all those years ago that if I ever fell in love with someone with whom I could have a marriage then I was to tell her.

'Well, I did. And she gave us her blessing. So, Flixe, such as I am, I'm yours – if you'll have me.'

464

He sat, half-turned towards her, not making any move to touch her. She looked into his face, trying to see what he really meant, searching the long, dark eyes that had always been able to hide what he was really thinking.

'Will you, Flixe?' he said, still not moving towards her. It would have been so much easier if he had seized her passionately so that there would have been no need for words. But part of her brain recognised that there had to be words and so with an enormous effort, of the kind that a dreamer feels trying to wake herself out of a nightmare, she said:

'Peter, how much has this to do with Gerry?' For a moment he was completely at a loss, his face relaxing out of the tensions that had held it, but puzzled and a little worried.

'Gerry? Nothing. What could it have to do with her?'

'Well, now that she is marrying Mike. I mean . . .' She looked up at the ceiling so that she did not have to see the wise, all-searching eyes directed at her face. 'I mean, I couldn't bear it if you were asking me because you couldn't have her.'

At that he did move, and seize hold of her and kiss her with such urgency that she hardly had time to think before sensation engulfed her. After a few breathless, terrifyingly exhilarating moments, he released her, but only to hold her face between his long, cool hands and say quietly:

'So, my very dear Felicity, will you have me?'

'Yes, Peter, I will.'

Much later, as they were sitting with his head on her shoulder and her head on his, he attempted to answer her question.

'Flixe, shall I try to explain about Gerry? I behaved so badly – so stupidly – that . . . Oh, darling, I was such a fool, but I never thought that you didn't understand.'

She lifted her head for a moment and took one of his thin hands in hers.

'Tell me now.'

'She's so like you, you know.'

'Yes, I know. But you of all people could hardly have mistaken us.'

He laughed at that with a sound infinitely warm and infinitely reassuring.

'That wasn't what I was going to say; nor that I wondered whether she might not do me instead.' Flixe laughed back at him, thawing every moment out of the frozen unhappiness into which she had woken that morning. 'She looks like you, sometimes she sounds as though it's you speaking; you share gestures, phrases, expressions. And yet, you are completely different.

'As she probably told you, there was a moment, way back at the beginning of the war, when she and I were lovers.'

'She never quite told me, but I gathered as much.'

'Of course I shouldn't have done it. There's no excuse. But she's lovely, we'd had a weekend at Evelyn's that somehow stirred up everything I'd ever felt about you – I couldn't have you; I'd sent you to do difficult, dangerous, "unsuitable" work; I felt as though I used everybody and gave no one anything. And there was Gerry, looking at me with those eyes of yours, but filled with what looked like love—'

'Peter,' Flixe interrupted, 'you don't have to tell me anything about it. I only wanted to be sure that it wasn't her you wanted – that I wasn't second best.'

'That's what I was trying to explain. But I got side-tracked. Gerry's lovely and I care about her, but she is not you. I could no more have made love to you in amongst all that than I could have . . . could have killed you. It was when I understood that, even when we met that day for your report at the Round Pond when you said . . . asked . . . do you remember?'

'Yes, I remember.'

'It was then that I understood that with you I was different. Something in you forces me to be honest and to want more than the simple pleasure I've found so easily with other people.'

'Ah, Peter,' she said, every ancient wound healing under his hands.

'And then when I thought you were really in love with Jean-Pierre . . . No, it's all right,' he said as he felt her tense. 'We won't talk about any of it unless you want to. But I've never hated anyone in my life as much as I hated him. My God, if I hadn't known before, I'd have known all right then.'

'What would you have known?' she asked, longing for a reassurance she no longer needed. He sat up as though he understood and, facing her once again, with her hands in his, he said formally:

'That unless I could spend the rest of my life with you I didn't want it. That I loved you and that if you did not love me then nothing would be worth anything to me. That without you I should be lonely until I died. That with you, the word loneliness would have no meaning.'

Felicity moved her hands within his clasp and smiled at him. There was something in her dark amethyst eyes that he had never seen before. It made him want to kneel at her feet and beg her for the absolution that he knew she would

467

give him. Her lips parted.

'We've come home at last, haven't we, Peter?'

Don't miss the second exciting novel from Daphne Wright in *The Threaded Dances* series:

NEVER SUCH INNOCENCE

Set in post World War II London and Venice, this compelling new novel is to be published in hardcover by Michael Joseph in August 1991 and in paperback by Sphere Books in the summer of 1992.

1

_____

'Isn't it wonderful?' yelled Mark over the heads of the crowd between them. In all the din, Julia could not hear what he said, but she could see his face and read his lips. Pushing her way towards him through the packed, sweating, embracing bodies of her fellow-Londoners, she shouted back:

'At least it's over. We did it. Thank God.'

Someone's Union Jack slapped her face in a sudden breeze and someone else trod heavily on her right foot as a new sound began to float across the great circle in front of the palace.

'What's that tune?' asked Mark more quietly as she reached him at last.

'I don't know,' said Julia, listening to the sound of a jazz band thumping up from the Mall. 'It's familiar, though.'

'It's _High Society_, you poor, middle-aged miseries,' said Mark's son, Richard, leaning on his stick and laughing at them. He looked younger by years than he had since he had been repatriated from France the previous year. 'I've just been told the trumpeter's

Humphrey Lyttelton.'

Not wanting to add to his picture of a 'middle-aged misery', neither Julia nor Mark asked any more questions. Another heavy foot mashed down on Julia's as an excited group of hatless girls and half-drunk men in uniform danced past, and her patience gave out.

'Let's get on,' she said to the others. 'It's all very wonderful, but it's damned uncomfortable. Oh, good, here's George. I thought we'd lost you in all this. I'm heading off. Are you coming?'

'Rather. It's all a bit much, isn't it? I can't think what they're all hanging around here for. The royals aren't likely to appear again,' said George Wilson, gesturing to the red-draped balcony in the centre of the palace's smooth, grey-stone façade. 'I'll push a way, Julia, if you stick close behind. Mark and Richard can look after each other.'

George Wilson, tall, thin and asthmatic, headed off into the dense, shifting crowd and Julia followed, wishing that she could share the ecstasy she saw on the faces all around her. She felt detached from the crowd and rather unreal, as though an important part of herself had been mislaid somewhere early in the war and she had only just noticed the lack.

'Come on darling, give us a kiss.'

A large navvy pushed his red face towards her as she fought her way through towards Green Park. When she gave him her famous cold stare, he made a rude face and yelled after her:

'Nothing to be sour about any more, ducks. Haven't they told you? We won the war. Hitler's dead!'

'I know,' said Julia under her breath. 'And thank God for it.'

A space opened up in front of her and she saw a vast mass of flames crackling and spitting on the grass. Above them, through the new leaves that were shrivelling and turning brown in the heat, she could see searchlights sweeping and meeting across the darkening blue of the twilit sky. Fireworks exploded somewhere close by, splattering the sky with coloured fragments that looked like the hundreds-and-thousands she had sprinkled on her bread and butter as a child.

For a moment Julia forgot her troubles and her dislike of crowds and let herself share the triumph. A pair of golden fountains shot upwards, spread and began to fall, their sparks fading and dying. In the light of the fire she saw faces that looked happy as well as mindlessly excited; a young woman with a toddler in her arms watched the fireworks with an expression of such abandoned relief that Julia could feel it too. A major in uniform who was standing close behind her put a hand on her shoulder and she dropped her head slightly to stroke his hand with her cheek. They were happy; the war was truly over for them; they were beginning again.

The stick of a rocket plunged back to earth with the kind of whining whistle all Londoners had come to dread, and Julia tried to cling to the faith that had kept her going for so long.

'Think of the good things,' she apostrophised herself, 'Look for the good things.'

That was an exercise that she had practised increasingly often as the war dragged on and on, and it had helped her to keep up the appearance of stoic calm for which she was well known among her colleagues. There were plenty of good things to look at in the crowds around the leaping, spitting fire and Julia gradually fought down the memories of the Blitz and the V1s, which the fire and the lights and the explosions had brought so vividly to mind.

She felt an arm across her shoulders and looked round expecting another Bacchanalian reveller. All she saw was Mark's familiar, worn face, full of concern.

'All right, Julia?' he asked. 'You look pale.'

She nodded and then explained about the fire and the bangs and the searchlights, and the avid excitement on some of the faces in the crowd. There had always been some who had looked like that at any 'incident' in the Blitz, people who had loved the drama of watching bodies being carried up out of the rubble and apparently found it easy to ignore the agony.

Think of the good things.

'Don't they look happy?' she said to Mark, gesturing towards a couple embracing under a tree as completely abandoned to each other as though they were in their own bedroom.

'Perhaps, but I think it's a bit much, carrying on like that in public,' he said severely. Julia managed to laugh at his dry voice.

'Well at least they don't look as though they're trying to remember the bombs,' she said.

'I don't suppose any of us who were here will ever forget, do you?' said Mark, remembering the night the Temple was bombed. He and Julia had arrived for work the following morning to find half their chambers blown apart, their carefully hoarded library burned and the remains of confidential trial documents blowing in the street.

'Quicker than those poor devils in Cologne and Dresden, I expect,' answered Julia, thinking of the horrific newsreel films she had seen. Then she remembered those other newsreel films of what had been revealed when the Nazis' concentration camps were opened, and she shuddered. She sometimes thought that the sick horror she had felt then would never leave her. Mark squeezed her shoulder and then removed his arm.

'Don't think about any of it,' he said firmly. 'Tonight it's over. Tonight it's reasonable to forget and to celebrate. The courts are closed. The bells have rung; the lights are up. Tonight we ought just to let rip like the rest of them. What did the old man say in Whitehall? Someone told me . . . Richard, wasn't it you?'

'Something about giving ourselves a short period of celebration. I can't remember exactly. Father, we're going to be late if we don't get a move on, and you know what Mother's like,' he said.

Mark looked at Julia in the dusk and gave her a small, unhappy smile that seemed to hold an apology for his wife and a plea for Julia to understand her, and perhaps a hint of nostalgia too. Then he turned back to his only-surviving son.

'Yes, I know. You go on ahead. George and Julia and I will follow on in our middle-aged way,' he said.

'Speak for yourself,' said Julia, falling into a teasing voice as though determined to join in the celebration. 'I don't admit to middle age, myself.'

Mark laughed and they walked up the hill towards Piccadilly in deliberate cheerfulness.

Sylvia Heathwood was indeed waiting for them in the restaurant Mark had chosen for their celebration. They found her tapping her foot in irritation as she sipped a cocktail. They had agreed not to dress, but Sylvia was wearing a beautifully draped silk frock in her favourite lavender colour with an immense diamond brooch on the left shoulder. As always, Julia was amazed by the other woman's immaculate clothes and hair, and by her apparently inexhaustible supply of silk stockings and cosmetics. It was as though for Sylvia the war with all its terrors and readjustments and shortages had never happened.

Julia herself eked out her own miserable supply of stockings and lipstick for as long as she could by going unpainted to court every day and wearing thick, ugly lisle stockings for all but the very best occasions. Her own dark-grey utility suit and well-washed pre-war blouse looked decidedly shabby beside Sylvia's elegance.

'How sweet you look, Julia dear,' said Sylvia, holding out a scented, creamed hand for Julia to shake. 'But Mark must be working you far too hard,' she went on. 'You look exhausted – and far too thin. And he really ought to give you time off to get your hair properly done. It's too bad of you, darling,' she said, turning to her husband and displaying her ownership of him with a minatory pat.

'It isn't Mark, Mrs Heathwood,' said Julia, wryly noticing Sylvia's need to place her as an unalluring, ill-dressed bluestocking, 'but my clerk who insists on giving me too many cases and works me far too hard. As for being too thin, thank God for it! At least the war's meant that there's been no need for banting. I always tended to put on weight in the old days.' She laughed, but Sylvia ignored her, turning her impeccably dressed silvery-blonde head towards her son and waiting to be kissed.

Richard obliged and then called a waitress over to order drinks for them all. In the confusion Mark whispered to Julia:

'Sorry about all that.'

'It couldn't matter less, Mark,' she said. 'She feels at a

476

disadvantage — understandably — and is trying to turn the tables. It's not important.'

'A son is such a comfort, Julia,' Sylvia called across the little group as she noticed Julia and Mark talking quietly with their heads close together. Julia felt Mark flinch beside her.

'Richard's a dear,' she said with as much sincerity as tact. 'You're very lucky.' Richard grinned at her and raised his glass in a silent toast.

'Well, here's to peace,' said Mark suddenly, raising his own glass.

They all echoed his toast and then George made one of his own: 'And to absent friends,' he said quietly, looking at Julia. She saw his expression and smiled shakily in gratitude for his remembering. To control her sudden childish urge to cry, she took a large gulp of her cocktail and almost choked as the spirit burned her throat. She hoped passionately that somewhere, anywhere, Anthony might benefit from the toast.

'Shall we go in?' said Sylvia, getting up to lead the way into the high, pink-and-gold dining room. Julia followed obediently. She was only twelve years younger than Sylvia Heathwood, but whenever they were together Sylvia behaved as though she were a great lady and Julia a cross between a poor relation and a skivvy. Having had plenty of practice in dealing with her mother's disdain for her appearance, Julia usually managed to ignore both the patronage and the sneers, and almost always allowed Sylvia her petty triumphs. The only things she had that Julia envied in the least were the presence of her husband, safe and well in London, and her son.

'Won't it be wonderful to have new clothes again?' Sylvia said as she was shaking out her napkin and laying it on her silken lap. 'And proper shoes and hats.'

'And hot baths,' said George Wilson, entering gamely into the spirit of her conversation. 'What about you, Julia? What things – material things – have you missed most?'

'Since 1939?' she said to give herself time to think of anything other than Anthony. 'Um, fresh butter, I think. Lots and lots of melting butter on crisp, hot crumpets for tea after a long, cold, winter's walk.' In fact, almost more than any food she longed for inexhaustible supplies of sanitary towels and lavatory paper, which had at various times during the past five years been almost impossible to buy in adequate quantities. She turned to Mark Heathwood. 'What about you, Mark?'

'Petrol – the freedom to get in a car and go anywhere that takes my fancy,' said Mark with a grin that transformed his thin, serious face, which looked so much older than his forty-eight years, into an almost boyish mask.

'But darling,' protested his wife in her most irritating drawl, 'you never – ever – went anywhere of your own free will. Don't you remember, Richard? I always used to have to drag Daddy off to Cassis in the summer or Scotland for the shooting. All he ever wanted to do was work and sweat out the summers in chambers even out of term time.' She directed a venomous look at Julia as she spoke, although before the war Julia had been far too junior a member of chambers to have had much influence on Mark Heathwood KC.

'Holidays!' she exclaimed to deflect Sylvia's attention. 'Just think: we'll be able to go abroad again. . . .'

'Yes, and swim in the sea without risking bumping up against a mine,' said Richard cheerfully. He had been horrified by the change in his mother when he had been invalided home the year before, but he had become accustomed to her new character by then and was quite used to jollying her along and ignoring her attempts to provoke arguments. 'No more barbed wire on the cliffs either – or mines on the beaches.'

'Back to innocence, perhaps,' said George more seriously. 'Ah, food. Thank you.' He looked down at the plate a waitress had put in front of him and then raised his eyes again. 'What I look forward to most is proper meals again. None of this "if you have bread with your soup, you can't have pudding" nonsense. Game and burgundy on a winter's evening after Julia's crumpets . . .'

'Caviare and vodka,' said Richard with a beatific expression on his face. Julia rather doubted whether he had eaten much caviare before the war, which had, after all, broken out when he was seventeen.

'Vulgar!' said his mother, lifting up her knife and fork.

Through all the lighthearted discussion that followed of what they planned to do in the new world of peace and plenty, Julia thought of her husband. Until she knew where he was she could not bring herself to make any plans at all, even the most trivial. It was only when the conversation turned to what each of them most dreaded about life after the war that she came to life again and joined in their frivolity.

'That all the things I've missed so far because of it, and longed for, will turn out to be dull after all,' was Richard's contribution, which raised a laugh from his elders.

George, who had been exempted from conscription because of his weak heart and his asthma, said seriously:

'That we'll mess things up. There's such a chance now to put right everything that was wrong before the war, let alone during it, but can we do it?'

'I doubt it,' said Mark. 'Not everything.'

'Here or internationally?' asked Julia, interested.

'Both, I suppose,' answered George, having drunk a spoonful of his depressing-looking soup, 'but I really meant here: employment, housing, education and so forth. But what about you, Mark? What do you most dread?'

'Much the same as you, I suppose,' he said, carefully not looking at his wife. 'Finding that nothing has really changed despite the horror and the sacrifices. Julia?'

Knowing that what she most dreaded was not a suitable matter for conversation on such a night, she buried it again and smiled disarmingly at her two colleagues.

'All the men coming back from the war and competing for briefs. I can see it now: that wretchedly misogynist clerk of mine will give me nothing but contracts and arbitrations and written opinions; I'll never see the inside of a court again; my wig will fall to pieces through lack of use; and my sharply honed advocacy skills will be blunted by time and boredom; and I'll be forced into premature retirement and will have to learn to cook.'

Everyone except Sylvia laughed at Julia's mock-tragic tone. Mark looked as though he was about to speak, but George started first.

'Even Bill Tomkins is too sensible to let his well-known views on girl barristers make him waste the talents of one of the best juniors of either sex,' he said.

Julia was touched and her face took on a gentleness it rarely wore in the company of any of her fellow barristers.

'Thank you for that, George,' she said seriously.

*

480

Two weeks later Mark walked into her room in chambers and asked her if she had a minute to spare. Laying aside the brief on which she was working and closing her copy of Archbold, Julia leaned back in her revolving chair and waited for what he had to say. When it came it surprised her.

'I've been asked to go to Nuremberg for the UN trials,' he said abruptly, 'and I'll need an assistant. Would you come if I asked you? We'd probably have to leave in July or August.'

'I can't, Mark,' she said, without even thinking about the pros and cons of his proposition.

'Why not?' he asked, his head on one side as he examined her face. 'Surely you're not one of these people who don't believe that the Nazi leaders must be tried?'

'Good Lord no!' she said, 'and I should think it would be a fascinating job . . . if rather horrible. It's good of you to think of taking me with you. I'm flattered.'

'But you won't come,' said Mark, ignoring her politeness and answering the tone of her voice. 'You're not really worried about your career at the bar when the men come back, are you? George was right on VE night: you of all people have no need to worry.'

Julia smiled at that and shook her head, although it was a real concern to her.

'Then what?' asked Mark.

'Mark, how could I leave London?' she said. 'Now at last there's a real possibility of getting news of Anthony. If I were to go away and he came back home, what would he feel? What would you feel if you were in his position?'

Mark sat straighter in his chair and grasped the lapels of his jacket as though they were the edges of his gown. His face settled into the familiar persuasive seriousness

481

with which he always addressed juries on difficult points in a case. Julia looked out of the window at the plane trees in the middle of the square. Their leaves were heavy with dust. She did not want to hear what she knew he was about to say, but she could not stop him. All she could do was detach herself by looking away from him as he said it.

'Julia, you mustn't pin your hopes on his coming back. If there was any chance that he was still alive I'd urge you to stay; you know that. It's not for my own selfishness that I want you to come away – although it would make life there much . . . never mind that now – but because I just don't want you to be living here on your own, waiting for news that's never going to come.'

At that piece of pessimistic common sense Julia's normally well-controlled temper snapped. She stopped looking patiently at the plane trees and faced him across her desk.

'There is no more reason to suppose him dead than there is to believe that he is alive,' she said as coldly as she had ever spoken to Mark. He winced and so she tried to moderate her voice as she went on: 'You should know that. It's our job to weigh up evidence. Anthony is missing. There is nothing to prove any more or less. He escaped from the camp when Italy surrendered to us in 1943. He's probably been in hiding somewhere, unable even to get to Switzerland ever since. You know what it's been like in Italy since they changed sides. . . .Remember that piece I showed you from *The Times* last year about the British, American and Australian ex-prisoners who have been running partisan groups in the mountains?'

'I don't know what it's been like in Italy and nor do you,' said Mark. 'Julia, God forbid that I should make you unhappier than you already must be: I just cannot bear the thought of your being strung out on unrealistic hope for years to come. You have to get on with your life. It's two years since Anthony escaped from that camp. Don't you think that if he had either been recaptured or successfully evaded capture for so long you would have heard by now?'

'Not necessarily,' answered Julia stubbornly. She got out of her chair and walked across the room to the long mahogany bookshelves that lined the wall opposite her desk. Squinting sideways at the dull gilt titles of the books, she went on: 'You and I have meant a lot to each other in the last couple of years, and I'll never forget what you've done for me or cease to thank you for it. I'll always care about you more than anyone except . . . but I can't let you take my last hopes away.' She looked away from the books and addressed the back of Mark's greying head. 'They're all I have now.'

'Oh my dear,' he said, sighing. He turned in his chair so that he could look at her and balanced himself with his hands on the chair back. Julia stood with her back against the bookshelves and watched his face. The misery in it dispelled some of her residual anger.

'Mark, you seem to think that I'm clinging to a forlorn hope. It isn't like that. Now that the war is over, there is a real chance of news. Until now there have been all sorts of reasons why I might not have heard anything. I'm not mad enough to spend the rest of my life waiting for him,' she said. 'Don't forget that it's been only two years – the law doesn't allow a presumption of death after so short a time. Why should I?'

Something about the way she lifted her chin as she made her declaration touched Mark Heathwood and he could not protest any more. He had admired Julia Gillingham ever since she had come to his chambers as a shy but determined pupil ten years earlier, and he had watched her coming to terms with the intensely masculine and competitive world she had entered and gradually beating back its prejudices against her.

Somewhere on her journey to her present security in that world Mark had fallen in love with her: not with her face, which was no more than pleasantly attractive with its good bones and warm brown eyes, nor with her charm, which she rarely exercised. At times he had asked himself almost despairingly what he could possibly see in her to arouse such depths of feeling in himself. In the end he had decided that it was her gallantry, the courage with which she met difficulty and tedium and the horrible moral choices that their job threw up from time to time.

But there was more to it than that. Despite Julia's determined avoidance of sentimentality, there was a tremendous fund of warmth in her, and it was on that he had drawn so heavily during the excruciating misery he had suffered when his elder son had been killed in Crete. Without Julia's unfailing if rarely expressed sympathy, he sometimes thought he would not have been able to go on. Sylvia had dealt with their tragedy by pretending that it had never happened and that she had never had another son but Richard.

There had been times in the months after the telegram when Mark had watched his wife endlessly prinking before her looking-glass and wanted to throttle her. He could not even remember what it had been about her that made him believe himself in love with her twenty-five years earlier. His hands clenched on the back of his chair.

'Mark?' Julia's cool voice broke into his thoughts. His

eyes focused and he relaxed his grip on the back of the chair, untwisted his back and stood up.

'Sorry,' he said abruptly. 'I was dreaming.'

Julia's pale face broke into a smile of such affectionate sympathy that he almost lost control of himself and told her again that he loved her, that if her husband could be proved to have died, he would divorce Sylvia and beg Julia to marry him. But they had fought that battle long ago and had agreed to ignore the temptation that each represented for the other.

'What were we talking about?' he said, feeling exhausted almost beyond bearing by the struggle to keep going, to forget his anguish for his dead son and his anxiety for Richard, crippled at twenty-one; to ignore his frustrated love for the sensible, rational, kind, intelligent woman in front of him, and his growing loathing for the beautiful, unintelligent one that he had married so long ago.

'You were trying to persuade me again that Anthony is dead,' Julia said drily. 'Please don't.'

He shook his head.

'No, it was Nuremberg. Are you really sure, Julia? It would do your career no harm at all. It's the most important trial I can imagine happening in my lifetime or yours . . .'

'I can't leave London,' she said again, walking back towards her laden desk. 'Not until I know what has happened and . . .' Her voice almost broke and she took a deep breath before ending the sentence: 'whether he is alive or dead.'

A RULING PASSION

Judith Michael

THREE LIVES. THREE CAREERS. BOUND TOGETHER IN A DANGEROUS DANCE OF LOVE, INTRIGUE, REVENGE AND MURDER . . .

VALERIE STERLING was born in the lap of luxury. Beautiful, rich and pampered, she possessed all of life's winning cards – until fate dealt her a loser. Broke and alone, she is left to make it on her own. And so emerges her talent as an investigative reporter – and a rekindled passion for an old flame . . .

NICHOLAS FIELDING'S only big mistake was his marriage. Now divorced, he is the wealthy owner of a successful cable TV network. The future's looking good – until the past returns, wielding a two-edged sword . . .

SYBILLE MORGAN was born hungry – for money, power and fame. She didn't get where she is today by being nice, and she isn't going to start now. Especially when she's so close to smashing her lifelong enemy into tiny little pieces . . .

0 7221 0570 3
GENERAL FICITON